THEIR EYES LOCKED

Without warning, Wilson lifted his carbine, firing with a deafening roar into Lieutenant Westhoff's face, the ball catching his upturned chin, pitching him backward from his horse. From the hole under his chin, blood dripped into the dirt.

Hopping on one foot and the other, Inman circled the body of Westhoff.

"You kilt' him dead," he cried. "They'll hang us sure now."

Pumping the empty cartridge jacket out, Wilson dropped the carbine back into the saddle holster.

"Ain't no one taking my stripes," he said, pulling out his pocketknife and tossing it to Inman. "Take his scalp."

Stunned, Inman's chin dropped.

"I can't take a white man's scalp," he said. "It ain't right."

"Take his scalp and dust out those tracks. Ain't no one to ever know but what the Cheyenne took him, riding across the country by hisself like that."

Hands trembling, Inman obeyed.

BOOK YOUR PLACE ON OUR WEBSITE AND MAKE THE READING CONNECTION!

We've created a customized website just for our very special readers, where you can get the inside scoop on everything that's going on with Zebra, Pinnacle and Kensington books.

When you come online, you'll have the exciting opportunity to:

- View covers of upcoming books
- Read sample chapters
- Learn about our future publishing schedule (listed by publication month *and author*)
- Find out when your favorite authors will be visiting a city near you
- Search for and order backlist books from our online catalog
- Check out author bios and background information
- Send e-mail to your favorite authors
- Meet the Kensington staff online
- Join us in weekly chats with authors, readers and other guests
- Get writing guidelines
- AND MUCH MORE!

**Visit our website at
http://www.pinnaclebooks.com**

REQUIEM AT DAWN

Sheldon Russell

PINNACLE BOOKS
Kensington Publishing Corp.
http://www.pinnaclebooks.com

PINNACLE BOOKS are published by

Kensington Publishing Corp.
850 Third Avenue
New York, NY 10022

First Pinnacle Printing: April, 2000
10 9 8 7 6 5 4 3 2 1

Printed in the United States of America

To my wife, Nancy,
my life, my center

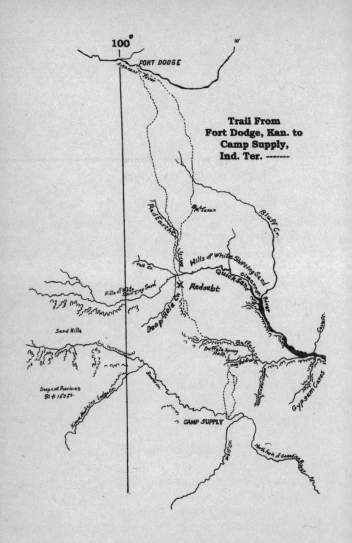

100°   30′

FORT DODGE

Arkansas River

**Trail From
Fort Dodge, Kan. to
Camp Supply,
Ind. Ter.** -------

Red Earth Cr.

Mt Jesus

Bluff Cr.

Salt Cr.

Hills of White Shifting Sand

Cimarron River

Quicksand

Hills of White Shifting Sand

✕ Redoubt

Deep Hole Cr.

Sand Hills

Buffalo Spring Hole

Buffalo Cr.

Cr.

Dog Cr.

Canyon

Deepcut Ravines
80 & 150 ft.

River

Gypsum Caves

Upper Medicine Lodge

Buff Cr.

✦ CAMP SUPPLY

North Fork of Canadian River

One

A hard-earned career as surgeon in the Army failed to prepare Dr. McReynolds for what now lay quivering before him in the tent.

"What is it, soldier?" he asked, leaning into the dim light.

Madness stared back at him; anguish, pain, fear. Sliding against the tent wall, Private Withom gulped for air, eyes rolling white, sweat beading across his forehead as he searched for McReynolds's voice. Behind those eyes, something loathsome and ignoble scrambled his brains with a stick, and it was there like death under the dim light of the lantern. With deliberate care, the private formed his words, issuing primitive and contorted sounds that caused the hair to move on McReynolds's neck.

This time McReynolds directed his question to the soldier's bunkmate.

"What's your name, Lance Corporal?"

"Roston, sir."

"What's happening here, Roston?"

"Don't rightly know, sir. He's been acting peculiar, complaining of headache and not eating. Turned down roasted buffalo tongue like it was hardtack and then he quit talking altogether, sir, and Private Withom ain't never quit talking, 'less threatened with a rifle butt. That's when I knew something gone crazy, sir."

"That's it?"

Turning over his hands, he studied them as if the answers were inscribed there on his palms.

"Yes, sir," he said. "Peculiarity has always been Withom's way. Hard to tell which side is normal, if you know what I mean. Course, there was that skunk thing a few weeks back."

"Skunk thing?" McReynolds asked, exasperated. Getting information from soldiers was like striking water from a rock. "What skunk thing, Corporal?"

"After we arrived from Fort Dodge, we was chopping trees and clearing brush for this here cantonment. It was so hot you could cook a cow pie on a rock, and Private Withom kept talking about home and women and cool mountain breezes. That's when Private Rafford threatened to open him up and hang his guts on the tent pole if he didn't shut up, begging your pardon, sir."

"And?"

"Withom stomped out mad and pitched his bed up there in the sagebrush. I told him some Cheyenne Dog Soldier might take his scalp if he went too far from camp, and when that scream came out of the black night, I nearly died of fright, thinking what I said had come true."

Sanity seeped back into Withom's eyes for a moment, and he pointed a trembling finger at the back of his head. Even in the yellow light, McReynolds could see the swelling, a lump the size of an apple protruding at the base of Withom's neck. At its center, puncture wounds, feverish, ulcerated holes, drained reddish liquid onto the collar of his shirt.

"Go on," McReynolds said.

"Weren't nothing but a skunk," Roston said, "that

latched onto his neck for all it was worth, and Withom yelling like he was on fire."

"Was the skunk normal-acting?"

"Kind of scrappy, like it was afraid of nothing. I tried to shoo it away, but it just hung on like it didn't care a bit. Maybe it was a Cheyenne skunk, 'cause it just hung on growling something fierce. Finally I got hold its tail and yanked for all I was worth, flinging it into the brush."

Standing, Roston walked to the tent flap and looked out across the compound.

"That's when I commenced to running from the stink and then I commenced to pukin', and soon enough everyone was running and pukin' and threatening to shoot Withom. I ain't got the stink out of my nose yet."

Moaning, Withom shook his head in weak confirmation of the story. Trying to raise his hand, it flopped out of control in his lap, and the monster in his head scrambled his brain again and peeked back from the dark recesses of his eyes.

Turning, McReynolds took in the lay of the place, a standard Sibley tent that looked for the world like a Commanche lodge, a camp chair made of sticks and rawhide, a mess chest, field cot, two changes of clothes, and one pair of boots per man. Given their conditions, enlisted men were an amiable lot, if not prone to fighting and sudden desertion.

"Go get the hospital steward," he said. "Tell him to bring a canteen of water and a length of rope."

"Sir?"

"You heard me, and be quick about it, Corporal. Then I want you and the others to move out of here until further notice. Do I make myself clear?"

"Yes, sir."

"And Corporal?"

"Yes, sir?"

"Let me see your hands."

"Sir?"

"Let me see them. Have you any open wounds? Did you have any when you grabbed hold of that fool skunk?"

Holding out his hands, the corporal looked puzzled.

"Not that I recall, sir. Just blisters from all that chopping."

After a careful examination, McReynolds slapped him on the back.

"Go on now and do what I told you."

Drool wet the front of Private Withom's shirt as he leaned into the lamplight, watching it with intense fascination. The faint, metallic smell of skunk was still in his clothing, and McReynolds knew that the soldier before him was doomed to an unspeakable end. His death would be the first since their arrival, but from McReynolds's experience, and there was more of it than he cared to remember, it would not be the last.

The Seventh Cavalry out of Fort Gibson had been ordered to the confluence of Wolf and Beaver creeks to establish a supply camp. For a month now they had chopped and hauled and worked from dusk to dawn, but what was to be Fort Supply was still little more than sagebrush, weary soldiers, and August heat clinging to the far reaches of Indian Territory, a place of river sand, of zinging locusts, of loneliness as bitter as the hot winds.

The orders had been simple enough, to build a camp at the western edge of Indian Territory, to establish a trail to Fort Dodge, where supplies would arrive from the north.

With a steady supply of food and horse forage available within the Indian Territory, short forays could then be sent out during the winter months to punish those Indians who had committed depredations, or who had refused to obey the treaties. The reasoning was that since Indians rarely provided forage for their horses in the winter, their own military capabilities would be reduced during the winter months, a time reserved for rest in the warmer valleys to the south. If kept on the move, the Indians would have no recourse but to accept the reservation provided for them in Indian Territory by the Medicine Lodge Treaty. This then was to be Fort Supply's sole purpose, first to punish, then to contain, then to feed.

The assignment was simple, or so Washington thought, but simple it was not. No one in Washington understood the strength of the Indians' resolve, nor the depths of their despair, nor understood that the Army had all it could do to feed and protect itself, much less take care of others.

Out there beyond the hills awaited half the Indian nation, Cheyenne Dog Soldiers, Arapahos, Kiowa, all driven to the wall by the land-hungry foreigners whose malignant growth doubled every month at the border less than a hundred miles away. No one in Washington understood, but the soldiers did, because on a still night the Indian drum beat in the distance, its voice crying of fear, of hatred, of bitter resentment. The sound throbbed hour after hour like an open wound, riding in on the night and settling among them as they slept on the hot sand. At the darkest hours the beat pierced their hearts, and in the blackness their souls rose up and winged away.

This young dying soldier before him was but a child the last time McReynolds had been in this country. Many years had passed since the Seventh Cavalry was trapped by winter not far from here, living like prairie dogs in their holes, the cold nights like razors a few feet above. He remembered the fear, the vulnerability, the empty gnawing of hunger and helplessness.

Only one other man still remained who'd endured that terrible winter—besides himself, there was his hospital steward, Sergeant Number, an upstart private back then, known for his fierce independence. At constant odds with the command, his rank had risen and fallen with the seasons. At one point, Number had even held the honorary rank of regimental color sergeant for bravery and skill in battle but lost it a week later for getting drunk and burning down the privy behind the enlisted men's barracks. Said that a hand cold as death came right up that hole, grabbed him by the balls, and pulled him down into the depths of hell. Said he'd burned it to the ground, not only to save himself but any other poor soul called upon to visit the privy in the dead of night.

In a rage, the commander tore both Number's sleeves off trying to strip him of his rank. But this McReynolds knew, and so did the commander, that drunk or sober, Number was worth ten men, that his loyalty to the Army and to McReynolds in particular was beyond reproach. By summer's end Number sported sergeant stripes once again, but now void of the dot of color that signified bravery.

For McReynolds, that lost winter was as clear as yesterday, but the fear was not as keen now, the years dulling its blade, rounding its edges into a less frightening instrument, but even still he remembered how it was. Out there Nurse Mary Cromley had stayed behind with a tribe of Osage to nurse them through the pox. Word never came of her fate, except on that single day a few months later when Corporal Adam Renfro stood at the dark edges of the Cross Timbers. "Left her early spring, sir," he'd said, "delivering papooses and saving souls." But that had been many years ago now. Their love had been short but real, and he missed her still.

And of course there had been Twobirds, the Kiowa girl, whose love and memory he carried with him even today. They had lost Renfro in the cave of silver, or so they'd thought, and their coming together was a natural and honorable thing. Neither would've betrayed Renfro had they known he was still alive, not for anything. It had been in Renfro's way for it to remain unsaid. It was in his way to understand the pain they'd shared and the silence that was needed.

Both loves, McReynolds lost as they came, but over and over he'd fashioned their faces in his mind, until the faces were the faces of strangers, and the emptiness was a wall of ice between him and the world. There'd been other women, but always beyond the wall of ice, and it had made him a cold and confined man.

The leaders in Withom's neck corded like rope under the skin, and his head jerked back as he shuddered against the molten poison racing through his veins. To die of rabies was to die at Satan's hand, and this poor soul was now in his fiery grip.

A scream erupted from Withom, rising from his feverish and contorted throat, a pitiful cry of anguish, of despair, of hopelessness, and McReynolds retreated to that place inside where all doctors retreat when reality is too much to bear, to that place inside that is silent and safe and clean. Make decisions, consider the alternatives, let science reign in its cool objectivity, or the crushing futility and cruelty of life will smear you into the earth.

Stepping into the tent, Number assessed the situation.

"Here's the rope, sir, and the canteen of water. You going to hang him or drown him?"

"Sergeant Number, I've asked you not to speak that way in front of the patients."

"Sorry, sir," he said, looking Withom over. "Guess my bedside manner could use a little work."

"Like the Sahara could use a little rain," McReynolds said.

Smiling, Number shrugged and pushed up his sleeves.

Considering the fact that Number was illiterate, he'd picked up a fair amount of medical information over the years as hospital steward and was an invaluable assistant to McReynolds. But his dress was disheveled, and his manner was as unsophisticated as the first day McReynolds met him many years ago. The one thing that McReynolds knew was that beneath that exterior lay the heart of a giant and the loyalty of a son, and for those reasons his manner and dress were of no serious matter.

"Cut that rope in half and bind his hands and feet."

"Sir?"

"Do it, Sergeant."

"Yes, sir," Number said, opening his knife and halving the rope.

"Bind them tight, Sergeant Number."

Finishing the job, Number stepped back among the men who had gathered at the door of the tent.

"Guess he can't run away and join the Cheyenne now, sir, if that's what was worrying you."

Shaking his head, McReynolds picked up the canteen and waited for Withom to come around. Holding it high, he poured a trickle of the water against the light of the lantern and let it fall onto the trampled earth floor of the tent. At first Withom failed to locate the sound, his eyes ungoverned orbs roaming about the room, but little by little his consciousness separated the sound from the demons plundering his brain. Fear concentrated his energy. Lightning ripped through sinew and bone as he lunged against his restraints, a mad terrifying struggle against the water that rose to his chin, over his mouth, down his nose in a suffocating rush. Drowning, he gasped for air, choked on the smothering liquid that filled his lungs and spilled into the cavity of his body.

Leaping against the ropes in terror and revulsion, his back arched upward in convulsion from the lack of oxygen and the imminence of death. Urine spread across his front, a sweet and sickly smell, and the sand clung to his cheeks and forehead as he scrubbed his face into the hard-packed earth.

"Particular about his drink, ain't he, sir?" Number said.

Choosing to ignore Number's remark, McReynolds leaned over and comforted the soldier. Humor was Number's armor against pain, and he'd seen plenty of it over the years. Perhaps he'd earned the right to deal with it the best way he could.

"Hydrophobia," McReynolds said. "Rabies, like I thought."

"How'd he get it, sir? Did the Cheyenne give it to him?"

Reaching for his pocketknife, McReynolds cut loose the restraining ropes.

"Skunk would be my guess, Sergeant. Rabies is passed through saliva into an open wound. Symptoms don't occur for thirty to fifty days depending on the location of the bite. This poor soul was bitten on the neck, which accelerated the process."

Stuffing his hands in his pockets, Number looked at the quivering soldier on the floor.

"Is there much chance, Dr. McReynolds?"

Picking up his black bag, McReynolds shook his head.

"There isn't anything in this bag or in God's kingdom that can turn this around. Soon the agitation will increase, then paralysis, then death."

"What we going to do, sir?"

Turning, McReynolds took a last look at the soldier who lay exhausted on the floor, his head thrown back, his face scarlet, his jaw jutting to the side at a contorted angle.

"Tell Lance Corporal Roston to report to me, and then pray for this man's death. It's life that's his enemy now."

Two

Lighting his pipe, McReynolds watched the sunset from the door of his tent. Orange swatches of paint tipped the silvery clouds that floated across the horizon like majestic clippers. Rays shot skyward through every breach announcing the end of the day in a grand finale of light, and from across the compound, the desperate screams of Private Withom fell unheard at the feet of God.

"Sir," Lance Corporal Roston said from behind him, "you wanted to see me?"

Tapping the coal from his pipe on the heel of his boot, McReynolds turned to face his duty.

"That's right, Corporal. How is Private Withom doing?"

"I ain't never seen nothing like it, sir. It's a pity and a shame to watch, him kicking and gasping like a fish out of water. Ain't there something to be done?"

"I've got Sergeant Number seeing that he doesn't hurt himself or others, but beyond that, he's in the hands of a higher authority, I'm afraid."

"Maybe it's a Cheyenne curse, you know, coming down on us like a cold rain from those drums beating night after night."

"It's not a curse, Corporal," he said, tucking his pipe

into his shirt pocket. "It's a disease called rabies, and it came from that skunk."

"If my horse was in such a trial, I'd put a bullet in his brain and call it done," he said, shaking his head.

Reaching for his camp chair, McReynolds sat down. Sometimes a weariness swept through him like a dark storm and washed away his resolve.

"It's not an option for doctors, Corporal, and believe me there's been many occasion I wished that it were."

"You wanted to see me, sir?"

For the first time McReynolds looked into his face, young, as he knew, innocent still of the world's barbarity, a mother's child gone west on an adventure.

A piteous cry rose from across the compound, laden with pain and despair, and the corporal looked at his feet and buried his hands in his pockets.

"It's about that skunk," McReynolds said. "Full of disease when it bit the private, leaving its corruption behind. Do you understand?"

"Yes, sir," he said.

Standing, McReynolds put his hand on the corporal's shoulder.

"What I'm trying to say is that you are in some danger of the same."

"Oh, no, sir. That skunk didn't bite me. I just flung it away by the tail."

"And you may be right, Corporal. There probably is no problem, but you had blisters on your hands. If the saliva got into the blisters, the disease might have been transferred."

"But I feel fine, sir, and Private Withom's down."

"That's true enough, Corporal"—he patted him on the shoulder—"and like I say, there is but a small chance of contagion. Of course, what we must remember is that the location of contact dictates the timing of the symptoms, and Withom had a direct bite into the bloodstream, close to the head besides."

Holding out his hands, Roston looked them over in the fading light.

"So it might be there already," he said. "Just growing and growing till it brings me down like poor Withom?"

Sitting down in his chair, McReynolds didn't look him in the eyes, because he knew the terror that must be there.

"The chances are remote, Corporal, but I thought you should know."

Even as the last light dropped away on the horizon, the cries of Withom faded, and it was the silence that bore in on them.

After a long while, Roston spoke.

"How will I know, sir?"

Taking his pipe from his shirt, McReynolds packed it with tobacco and then struck a match, letting it dip and flare in the darkness. Roston stepped back.

"Excitement, agitation, sensitivity to light, later a fear of water. You'll know."

At what point Roston left, McReynolds was not certain, but when he turned, he was gone into the liquid black of the night.

Three

Morning broke hot as McReynolds listened to Number report on the night's affairs. Mosquitoes from the river swarmed at their ears, and the smell of sage wafted in on the southwesterly breeze.

"He's dead then?" McReynolds asked.

"Yes, sir, three o'clock this morning. Didn't see no need in shaking you out. Like you said, there was little to be done, 'cept pray for a quick end." Looking away, he rubbed at his face. "But that was not in the making."

"Where's the body?" McReynolds asked.

"Wrapped and stored in his tent, best we could. With this heat, he better be planted quick, or the Cheyenne will be riding in thinking we got a buffalo kill."

"Go get some sleep, Sergeant. I'll make the arrangements."

"Yes, sir," he said, turning to leave. "Oh, by the way, sir, we had a visitor about dawn."

"A visitor?"

"Yes, sir, Corporal Roston, bearing arms and looking for an end to his bunkmate. Said no man should be left to suffer like that, and he was there to do what God nor medicine couldn't."

Swatting at the mosquitoes, McReynolds tucked in his shirt and began pulling on his boots.

"Where is he now, Sergeant?"

"Cooling down in a set of chains, lest he bring down the wrath of God on us all."

"Let him go."

"Sir?"

Strapping on his revolver, McReynolds snubbed up the belt. After all these years, he'd never had occasion to use it, but soldiers viewed his job as woman's work at best. The revolver gave him credibility.

"There's little harm he can do now. Withom's dead, isn't he?"

Peeking from under the brim of his hat against the morning sun, Number nodded.

"Stiff as a carp, sir, and not giving a damn about the comings and goings of his fellow man. I'll see it's done."

After sick call, McReynolds made arrangements for Withom's burial ceremony. The Army's relationship with death was an odd one. In complete disregard for a man's life, it would ride him into the bleakest circumstance or starve him on hardtack and thin soup. But when at last they'd killed him, there was no ceremony too elaborate or honor too generous to bestow.

Finding that the first sergeant was gone, having taken three men out to shoot a deer that had bogged down at the river crossing, McReynolds left.

"Between 'em," the clerk had said with a grin, "ought to kill him. Can't run, can't fight, can't call for help, can he?"

In need of coffee, McReynolds walked the narrow path to the cook tent down by the river.

Things were comfortable with General Sully gone, having left a week earlier for Fort Dodge to organize a supply train, the first of many needed to provide food for the new reservation a few miles east of the fort.

The fort itself was built too close to the river, as they always were. Human nature being what it was, soldiers didn't favor carrying water, even if it meant drowning in the first flood that came along. A sudden downpour had already floated the garbage wagon three miles downstream. To make matters worse, the camp dog was tied to the seat spring. The garden, too, had been decimated by a foot of river silt.

Pouring himself a cup of coffee, McReynolds watched Cookey stoke the fire.

"Morning, Cookey," he said, sipping at the edge of the cup.

"It's a grand day, isn't it, sir, what with the sun shining and the wind down?"

"It is indeed," McReynolds said.

Wiping the smoke from his eyes, Cookey bent the kinks out of his back, arms, and legs, folding out like struts on a camp chair.

"Yes, sir, a fine day, and I hear soon enough the laundresses will be coming."

"That a fact," McReynolds replied, smiling. Army laundresses were known for a variety of unofficial services. "Guess your duds getting pretty stiff by now?"

"Night and day, nearly," Cookey quipped, grinning and displaying a set of crooked teeth.

Blind-proud of the hardest and most thankless job in the regiment, Cookey was an eternal optimist and insufferable egotist, but without those qualities, a man wouldn't last a week as field cook in the Army. The camp stove was little more than a ditch with a makeshift chimney at one end. A few iron utensils hung on a green pole suspended between the yokes of upright limbs. Beans, bacon, flour, and rice comprised the staples in the wooden larder. Beyond that, there were few amenities, coffee, desiccated vegetables, and an occasional pound of honey stolen from the local bees. Meat was little more than what was killed by the soldiers themselves and usually in a condition best left unexamined.

Of course there was always the bread, eighteen ounces per man per day. It was what sustained them, saved them from madness, saved them from the choking banality of their existence, and from killing the annoying Cookey with one of his own frying pans. No one baked better bread than Cookey, and for that reason alone his life was spared.

"Good coffee," McReynolds said.

"Yes, sir, thank you, sir. It's a rare thing, good coffee. Not everyone can do it, you know? Takes a touch, you know?" Wiping the ash from the front of his shirt, he leaned toward McReynolds with concentration. "It's in the roasting, slow and gentle, with a pinch of sugar to keep the beans from burning and clean water strained through a horse blanket, and a brisk fire." Walking about the camp, he hooked his thumbs in his belt. "Yes, sir, a touch, and here's the secret. Not everybody in this outfit I'd tell this to, sir. When all's done right, then a dash of cold water to settle the grounds and strained a final time." Lifting his arms, he spoke, and his voice rose in excitement. "It's in the touch, you know? One final strain and right there before you is the single finest cup of coffee ever made. Not everyone can do that, sir, if I say so myself."

"Well," McReynolds said, tossing the remaining coffee into the fire, "it's fine coffee alright."

Kneeling down on one knee, Cookey pushed back his hat.

"If you don't mind my asking, sir, about that fearsome sound last night. It was the Cheyenne, wasn't it, skinning one of our own? You can tell me. I've seen the worst of the worst and fear nothing but bad cooking and bad women."

"Rabies, Cookey. Withom, I'm afraid. Died about three this morning."

"Oh, Lord Jesus," he said, his eyes growing wide. "It ain't contagious, is it?"

"Not unless a rabid skunk has been sleeping in your bunk."

"No, sir," he paused, "not a rabid one. Course, I've seen worse. Saw a man back into a lard-rendering pot one time, wasn't nothing left but head and hands." Looking off into the horizon, he reflected on the scene. "Didn't scream or close his eyes, and when they tried to lift him out, he just crumbled away into dust."

The encampment was quiet as McReynolds made his way to the southernmost edge of the clearing to find the work detail. With Sully gone, only a skeleton work crew had remained behind to construct quarters for the officers and their wives, most of whom were to arrive at any time. Even without signs of Indian unrest, being so shorthanded made McReynolds uneasy.

The cantonment site had been picked for its strategic location and for its ample supply of water. Building materials such as gypsum, clay, and even some limestone were available within the area, as well, but hardly a single tree of appropriate size for lumber grew within a hundred-mile radius. Without the lowly cottonwood that clung to the muddy riverbanks, the landscape would have been adorned by little more than the tenacious sagebrush.

There was the Cross Timbers, of course, that forbidding hardwood forest that cut across the territory, that place where he had bid farewell to Corporal Adam Renfro and Twobirds so many years ago, but that was as distant and unreachable now as the years themselves.

Often he'd thought of them, wondered of the lives they must have lived, Adam, a white man, a deserter living among the Kiowa. In all those years McReynolds had never spoken of Adam Renfro's return from the cave of silver, or of his desertion, but rarely a day passed that he hadn't thought of them both and of that desperate year spent together under the tyrannical command of Lieutenant Reginald Sheets. But it was a hard and ruthless land at best, and with the disappearance of the buffalo, their chances of survival had diminished. The few remaining pockets of game were difficult to find and required an inordinate expenditure of energy, causing even the young, strong warriors to fall despondent.

When McReynolds found the work detail, they were stripped to their waists, digging pits into the soft sand, throwing it high over their backs and into the pathway beyond. Watching from the shade was the regiment engineer, Captain Roscoe Wallace, his sleeves rolled up, his shirt wet with perspiration.

"Captain." McReynolds touched the brim of his hat.

"Major McReynolds," he said, "hope you're not here to recruit the few remaining men I have left."

Finding a comfortable rock, McReynolds sat down to watch the men at work.

"Seeing as how the hospital at this point is a tent and a pair of bullet forceps, I'm not much in need of man power at the moment. How does the construction go, Captain?"

Putting his hands on his waist, the captain studied the beginnings of the officers' housing.

"Considering the fact that there's not a tree within a hundred miles, that the scorpions are as big as saddlebags, and that I've got thirty men instead of two hundred, I'd say it's going just fine. Now, that's not to mention the fact that I didn't sleep a wink all night 'cause of listening to a man screaming hisself to death. I got four men sicker than lords from drinking a bottle of horse liniment, and my laundry's stacked to my chin. No, sir, everything's just fine, I'd say."

"The news travels fast," McReynolds said.

"It's the only thing around here that does," Wallace said, wiping the sweat from his forehead with the sleeve of his shirt. "If I don't get these quarters done, Sully's going to tack my hide to the flagpole, and that's not to mention what the officers' wives are going to do when they see they've got buffalo wallows for a home."

"Glad you're having a bright day, Captain. How you building these things anyway?"

Motioning for him to follow, the captain made his way down the path.

"Here," he said, "a pit four and a half foot deep, and then cottonwood poles planted side by side and daubed with river mud. Over the top will be two feet of earth. It's called picket construction," he said, taking a chew from his pocket and loading his cheek. "That's another word for shit construction, and the first hard rain's likely to wash the whole goddamn thing to Mexico." A stream of tobacco juice nailed an unfortunate scorpion that scurried across his boot. "And after that, some plaster made up of this here gypsum, the same stuff that turns your bowels into a drizzling storm, is mixed up with straw and buffalo pies. With luck the whole mess sets up before it begins to stink, and maybe by the time winter hits, providing I ain't dead from consumption, or skunk bit, and providing a Cheyenne don't hang my balls off his saddle, then everything will be just fine, won't it."

Rubbing at his temples, McReynolds nursed an impending headache. Sometimes he was convinced that the U.S. Cavalry recruited from an insane asylum.

"Got to go," he said, waving off the engineer's tirade. "There's a burial detail that has to be arranged. Thanks, Wallace, you're an inspiration."

Flashing a tobacco-stained grin, Wallace turned to his work.

"Anytime, Doc," he laughed, "anytime."

Cutting across the clearing, McReynolds headed toward the stable, which was little more than a ditch cut into a bank and covered with mud and straw. But it provided some shade during the heat of the day and a safe haven at night against the ever horse-hungry Cheyenne. Being a city man by birth, McReynolds had never taken to animals, never understood them, not until Adam Renfro that is, who had taught him the warmth and quivering life of a horse's chin, the strength of its massive chest, the simple wisdom and tenacity of the mule. Now he came here often before taking on the duties of the day, to collect his thoughts, to find his own center.

A hot wind swept down the valley and swirled the dirt into his eyes as he climbed the stable fence to scratch the ears of the horses that lined up below. A saddle hung from the rafter and twisted in the shadows from the wind. But his heart sank as boot toes turned into the light that bled from the doorway.

Climbing over the fence, McReynolds stepped into the shade of the stable and looked up into the light-riddled roof, into the bruised and swollen face still shocked from the unforgiving rope, into the irreverent swarm of blowflies buzzing from its nostrils, and he knew why.

Last night they both had known, he supposed, in that single ominous moment, in the flare of his match, in the haunted eyes of Lance Corporal Roston.

Four

As far as Little Dog could see, skinned and swollen buffalo carcasses were strewn to the horizon like naked giants upon the blood-soaked sand. Flies churned in the sea of flesh, and the sweet smell of death hung in the morning air. Turkey buzzards rose in a black flurry from their grizzly work as he and Crooked Leg approached. Like black-winged spirits, the buzzards lifted into the warm currents one after another and with silent dignity circled high above. To wait was their burden and their certainty, because on the plains, death was claimed by no other.

"It is over," Little Dog said.

Stepping between the carcasses, Crooked Leg shook his head.

"Too many to count," he said.

For three days they had followed the tracks of the herd, and for three days they had thought of nothing else but the meat they would soon take home.

Pointing to the wagon ruts, Little Dog lifted his bow into the air with anger.

"It is the white hunter with his wagon. See how heavy with hides, how deep the ruts. Soon the buzzards will circle his camp from the smell, and we will kill him."

Making his way back, Crooked Leg slipped in the

frothy blood, his hand sinking into the carcass of a cow as he tried to catch himself. At her side lay her calf, still alive, too small for the buffalo hunters to waste a bullet. Without a word, Crooked Leg cut its throat.

"And now the buzzards will circle me," he said, shaking his hand.

As a boy Crooked Leg had wandered away from camp, fallen into a ravine and crushed his ankle, which had grown back as a solid piece of bone. Ever since, he'd walked on the side of his foot, resulting in an unusual and distinct gait. But when mounted on a warhorse, there was none more swift or lethal, and his bravery as a Cheyenne Dog Soldier was legendary. On a single occasion, Crooked Leg had killed three Osage warriors and a squaw, all the while with an arrow embedded in the small of his back. The scar was still there yet for all to see and admire.

They hunted often together. Crooked Leg, being older and more experienced, had taught Little Dog much. Over the past few years, their friendship had deepened, and there was nothing Little Dog enjoyed more than hunting with his ole friend.

Looking at the obscenity about him, Little Dog's heart ached. Even on this summer day, the feel of autumn was in the air. Soon the ground would be white, the bitter winds lapping at their teepees. Without the buffalo, their chances for survival were slim.

"They cannot be far," he said. "If we ride on, we can find them before night and then kill them in the morning while they sleep."

Scrubbing the blood from his hands with clean sand, Crooked Leg shook his head.

"It will bring the soldiers to our camp, and many will die."

Mounting his horse, Little Dog leaned forward and let the sun warm his back.

"Already my son's stomach swells from his mother's milk," he said, "which is thin as water, and the Cheyenne Dog Soldier grubs in the earth for roots like the opossum." Pulling back the reins, Little Dog hooked his heels into the flanks of his horse, letting him dance. "They kill us now," he said, "more certain than in battle. Soon I will not be able to look into my peoples' eyes or know that I am still a Cheyenne Dog Soldier. Soon the buzzards will pick the bones of our children.

"There," he pointed his bow to the north, "no more than a week's ride, the white man waits. This is how they kill us because without the buffalo there can be no Cheyenne."

Working his way to his horse, Crooked Leg did not speak, but the weariness was there in his face. With deftness belying his age, he swung onto his mount. High above, the buzzards descended, knowing their wait had ended.

"We kill them in the morning," he said.

The evening cooled as they rode in silence under the blue light of the moon. So deep were the wagon ruts that the tracking was easy even in the night. But the darkness of their hearts could not be lit by the moon. To fight with honor and skill was beyond question. This they had always done. No people were braver, or more skilled in war than the Cheyenne, each warrior praying to die young and brave, to deny the contempt of old age in a single glorious moment. Many nights they'd ridden under this same moon, the enemies' scalp locks still warm with body heat against their legs, the stolen horses thundering behind, the exaltation, the sweetness and pride of victory. Many nights they'd ridden back to camp, the beat of the drums, the tittering girls, the adoring eyes of young warriors.

But this night, this battle would be different, because to kill the white man was sooner or later to be killed by him, to know a faceless death from his spitting rifle, to die despised like the skinned and rotting buffalo he left behind. For each white killed there would be crushing and certain retaliation against them all. In this night there was only the end of hope.

When the smell of the hunters' campfire reached them, they tied their horses, creeping forward in the darkness until they looked down on the twinkling light of their fire. Beyond the trees, coyotes yipped at the scent of the rotting buffalo hides.

An hour passed before dawn broke, pockets of fog nestling in the crevices and crannies below them. Touching Little Dog's shoulder, Crooked Leg pointed to the guard, his head drooped in sleep, and then to the hunter standing at the edge of camp relieving himself, and then to the others still wrapped in their blankets about the fire.

Stringing his bow, Little Dog tested its strength and voice with his own practiced knowledge of distance and speed. With a well-placed arrow, a man could be killed without a sound.

Stepping back, Crooked Leg offered the first shot, knowing full-well that Little Dog's skill was unsurpassed, that if they were to survive, they must first even the odds before the others awakened. Working his way down the hill, Little Dog positioned himself so that the light fell across the shoulders of the sentry. With intense concentration he analyzed the shot, the distance, the wind, the overhanging limbs that dipped where the trees opened onto the camp.

When at last confident, he strung the arrow, releasing it at the end of a singular sweep of the eye on an irrevocable and deadly path. The arrow struck below the sentry's left shoulder blade, penetrating his heart, spilling him forward onto the ground without a sound.

With a half turn, Little Dog strung a second arrow to bring down the hunter at the edge of the camp. In an unwavering trajectory it sped through the base of the hunter's neck, sending him clawing at the shaft now lodged in his windpipe.

By this time Crooked Leg had moved into the open, placing an arrow at close range into the top of the skull of one of the sleeping men.

The hunter nearest the fire scrambled from his bed, fear-struck, breaking into a dead run toward the clump of cottonwoods a hundred yards to the east. Whirling about, Little Dog shot from his waist, the arrow traveling too low, an oblique path into the kidneys of the escaping hunter. Even as the second arrow entered his chest, his scream fractured the morning dawn like broken shards of glass.

Shocked, the other hunters sat upright, sleep in their eyes like wistful boys awakened for breakfast. Smoke curled from their fire in a silent reptilian track through the morning sky.

Time was short, Little Dog knew this, since white men slept with their weapons. Blazing carbines would soon enough end their lives. Throwing his bow to the ground, he unsheathed his knife, looking to his side for Crooked Leg, knowing he would be there. With tomahawk drawn, Crooked Leg nodded, the timing, the consent, the killing moment, and in this moment they turned to their enemies.

Little Dog attacked first, his knife at the hunter's throat, yanking his prey's head back by the hair, the rolling eyes, the shinning gold of his teeth, the fiery red of his ash-covered beard. Leaning in, Little Dog set the knife, bringing it about with the weight of his shoulder, the telling rush, the gamey smell, the falling away.

At his side, Crooked Leg brought about a rounding swing of his tomahawk, burying it deep into the temple of a bewildered hunter, but even as Crooked Leg recovered, a rifle report thundered across the camp.

Springing forward, Little Dog plunged his knife under the shooter's uplifted arm, air rushing from his fatal wound, rifle clattering to his side, and an eerie silence fell across the camp. Next to the fire, Crooked Leg rocked in pain.

"Where are you wounded?" Little Dog asked, kneeling.

Taking his knife, Crooked Leg split his leggings, showing Little Dog where the bullet had entered his leg.

Pressing his fingers about the wound, Little Dog shook his head.

"The bone has been damaged," he said. "It will heal in time, but now we must change your name to Crooked *Legs,* I think."

From under the pain, Crooked Leg smiled and looked away.

By the time the sun broke over the top of the cottonwoods, Little Dog had moved the wagons into the center of the camp, taken scalp locks, carried wood from the grove, stacked the bodies and hides on top, and set the whole thing ablaze in a roaring fire.

As they rode home, the black smoke darkened the sky behind. In his pain, Crooked Leg had grown silent, but words mattered little now.

Not the honor of their coup, nor the scalps tied to their saddles, nor the string of horses at their backs was sufficient glory for the price they knew would be paid.

Five

Most military surgeons were in charge of the post journal, being among the few literate men on camp. Usually McReynolds didn't mind taking a moment to collect and organize his thoughts. It was not a task that he found painful, except on days when he had to re-count the death of two fine boys. At least he didn't have to write the letters home, a job reserved for the commander.

"Sir," Sergeant Number said at the door, "the scout says General Sully's five miles out with a wagon train coming in. Most of the men are working on officers' quarters. You want me to call formation?"

Closing the journal, McReynolds followed Number into the morning light.

"Best be on it, Sergeant. You know how the General likes his warm receptions, especially after being with Sheridan for a week."

"Yes, sir," Number said, "kisses and hugs for our returning commander. Hope he brought the laun-dresses. Getting far behind on my washing, you know."

"Be on your way," he countered, smiling, "and alert Cookey and Captain Wallace. We don't want to put the General in a bad mood, do we?"

There were times when Sully could be stormy, as was the case with most commanders he'd served under, but for the most part he was an even-tempered and intelligent leader. It was true that he was conservative, avoiding conflict whenever possible. Personally, McReynolds found him to be both judicious and effective.

Rumor had it that General Sheridan thought Sully too quick to compromise, too quick to avoid a fight, and that he was thinking of bringing in Custer to get things moving. It would be a blow to Sully's ego, of that McReynolds was certain.

By noon, the first dust of the supply train rose in a red cloud on the horizon and was then followed by the distant braying of mules and the lowing of oxen as they clattered across the prairie like a giant slithering snake. Within the hour, fifty army wagons rolled into camp, swamping the small compound.

Dismounting, Sully viewed the troops with obvious pleasure as they marched by. He was a small man, keen black eyes, a well-trimmed and perky beard that grayed at the corners of his mouth. After the brief ceremony, McReynolds approached.

"Welcome home, sir. How was the trip?"

"Thank you, Major. It was difficult but successful as you can see. The weather held, but the trail is poorly marked still. Course, there was a nasty turn, about thirty miles back, buffalo hunters' camp. Wasn't much left between the fire and the vultures." Pulling at his beard, he leafed through his memory. "Cheyenne Dog Soldiers by the look of it. Poor fellows didn't have a chance."

Turning about, General Sully searched over the faces of the men.

"Where is Captain Wallace?"

"Bringing in a load of gypsum, sir."

"And are the supply depots ready?"

"Yes, sir, I believe they are, open-sided still but sufficient to keep out the heavy weather."

"Well, that will have to do, I suppose, and my quarters?"

"Complete," McReynolds answered with a nod, "as best they could, sir."

"Tell Cookey to prepare a special meal from the supply wagons for the men tonight and to set dinner for five in my quarters at around six. I've brought a new officer and his wife from Fort Dodge. Perhaps you and Captain Wallace would join us for dinner?"

"I'd like that very much, sir. It's been some time since I dined with fair company." Looking about at the teeming activity, McReynolds hesitated. "I hate to bring this up now, sir, but we lost a couple of men, rabid skunk as it turns out."

Handing the reins of his mount over to McReynolds, Sully shook his head.

"Damn shame. Saw a man die from it once. Fill me in on the details later. I'm worn to a snubbin' from Sheridan's exuberance and the backbone of this horse. Tell the quartermaster to get those supplies secured as soon as possible, will you?"

"Yes, sir," McReynolds said.

That afternoon McReynolds found Quartermaster Shoats supervising the unloading of the wagons at the southernmost supply depot. Legions of sweating soldiers carried sacks of flour and cornmeal into the makeshift shelters.

Hooking a foot on the wagon wheel, McReynolds watched.

"Enough food here to feed an army," he said to Shoats.

"Yes, sir," Shoats said, "liked to wore the prairie out getting her here."

Rearing back, he hooked his thumbs under his sus-

penders. Like most quartermasters McReynolds knew,
Shoats considered himself exceedingly important because of his control over all things good. Like most
quartermasters, he was selective in his application of
the rules and in his dispensing of favors.

"Twenty-five thousand pounds of grain," he continued, "two thousand pounds of salt, a hundred pounds
of tobacco, cheese, boots, forty gallons of whiskey, and
a wagon load of the heartiest laundresses this side of
the Mississippi. Yes, sir," he said, "and that's just the
start. General Sully tells me that before it's done, there
will be eight hundred thousand pounds of grain right
here at this camp and enough beef to feed one pound
per man per week to every Indian between here and
Kansas. It's the job of this here quartermaster in particular to have on hand fifty days' subsistence for a
thousand men at any given moment. At this very hour
there's over thirteen hundred Arapaho gathering up
not twenty miles from here for their rations. Course,
the Dog Soldiers ain't, too busy skinning buffalo hunters and stealing horses." Tucking in his chin, he
viewed the long line of wagons with pride. "Guess
there ain't never been a quartermaster dealing with
more than I am on this day, nor likely to in the future."

A wagon moved from across camp, pulling under a
cottonwood for shade, a dozen ladies climbing out of
the back, chirping and gurgling like a covey of quail.

"And that would be the laundresses?" McReynolds
asked.

Smiling, the quartermaster looked them over.

"Yes, sir, it is, and a fine hardworking lot they are.
Soon enough every man in camp will have new
scrubbed pants. Ain't nothing improves a soldier's disposition or calms his soul more than a clean set of
clothes. Cuts down on the scrapping, fighting, and

general disorder. Gives a man pride in hisself. Wouldn't you agree, sir?"

Squinting against the sun, McReynolds looked at Quartermaster Shoats.

"Well, Cookey believes it, but then I can't see much change in his disposition, clean clothes or dirty."

With a roaring laugh, Shoats snapped his suspenders.

"Well, by God, you got a point there, sir. Takes more than a laundress to clean up some souls."

Leaving Shoats to his important business, McReynolds sought out Cookey, finding him laboring over a steaming kettle.

"Morning, sir," Cookey said, "a fine day, ain't it?"

"Appears so," McReynolds said, pouring himself a cup of coffee. "Just saw a wagon load of laundresses."

Stirring the pot, Cookey smiled and then tossed the wooden spoon into the wash pan.

"Yes, sir, and one with burning red hair and a laugh like rolling thunder."

Ducking his head to escape the smoke, McReynolds smiled.

"Redheads do better laundry, Cookey?"

"Can't say I'd know, sir, not as of today at least."

"Quartermaster Sergeant Shoats has a theory that clean laundry changes a man's disposition."

"Sharpens it, sir, what with time and opportunity."

Cleaning his cup out in the pan of water, McReynolds started to leave.

"Oh, by the way, forgot why I came. General Sully says fix a special meal for the men out of the new supplies and see there's a table for five set in his quarters."

"There's some corned beef to be had, mostly good," Cookey said, "except one barrel turned rank, Cheyenne probably."

"You need help, just recruit some of those boys sleeping down there in the stables and then make yourself some time for laundry, hear?"

"Yes, sir." He grinned, popping a salute.

Finding Captain Wallace was not so easy, and by the time McReynolds located him unloading gypsum on top of a hill just north of the camp, the day had turned hot and sultry. White gypsum clung to the captain's eyebrows and mustache. In spite of the heat, his men shoveled with purpose, the fine powder gathering on the sweat of their backs, to do otherwise was to risk the captain's wrath.

"Morning, Captain," McReynolds said, "the General missed you at formation."

With deadly accuracy, Wallace spit tobacco juice into the white dust.

"Well, that's just fine, ain't it. Here I am in charge of building this blame cantonment with little more than my own bare hands, and now I'm supposed to show up in dress uniform to kiss Sully's ass, just 'cause he's spent a couple weeks drinking and whoring in Dodge. I suppose he's sore, too, 'cause he don't have a window in his quarters so's he can look out and watch the rest of us sweat like Arkansas mules."

Taking out his handkerchief, McReynolds dusted off the toe of his boot. It drove Wallace crazy.

"Says he wants you to come to dinner tonight," McReynolds said, "to meet the new lieutenant and his wife."

"What's the matter, Doctor, get your shiny boots all mucked up out here in the dirt? Why didn't you just send some private out to tell me I was to come in and have tea and crumpets with the General?"

"No, no," McReynolds said, "I'm sure the General knows that your work is more important than his dinner party, so I'll just tell him that Captain Wallace is too busy. I'm certain he'll understand."

Taking off his hat, Wallace slapped the side of his leg, and gypsum powder exploded into the air.

"Well, ain't that just fine," he said. "I've got enlisted barracks, a blacksmith shop, and a guardhouse waiting to be built, and God knows we'll need one of those soon enough, and now I'm threatened by a sawbones, whose sole job is to carry a little black bag around and to show off the shine of his boots. Seems to me that if the General wanted his ass kissed, he'd prefer the more genteel lips of an Army surgeon."

Taking out his handkerchief, McReynolds dusted off the other boot.

"Oh, he does, but if it were my ass needed kissing, I'd fancy the crude, if not overworked, lips of an Army engineer." Before Wallace could answer, McReynolds tipped his hat. "See you at dinner, Captain."

The afternoon passed quickly since there was a fair number of scrapes and blisters to attend to from the trail ride. Even at that, McReynolds found himself thinking about the evening, looking forward to it even. Time fell heavy on the frontier, with little to do but listen to the rough banter of tough and simple men. At Fort Gibson he had access to the post library, limited to be sure, but new titles came along from the continuous flow of humanity through the fort gates. Here on the edge of the territory there was naught but the blackness of night and the pressing memories of things past to keep one occupied.

Evening arrived in a burst of color as the sun dropped into the dust of the western sky. When McReynolds knocked on the plank door of the General's quarters, a young private, cleaned and spiffed, ushered him into the makeshift cabin where the General and Captain Wallace were having a whiskey.

Emptying his glass, the General pointed to a chair.

"Here, Doctor, have a seat while the private fixes you a drink."

"Thank you, sir," McReynolds said, "a whiskey would be nice.

"And I'll have another"—Sully handed his glass to the private—"and what about you, Captain Wallace?"

"Yes, sir, I think I will. Fine whiskey it is, sir."

No sooner had the drinks arrived when the private ushered in the lieutenant and his wife. Standing for introductions, McReynolds came face-to-face with a most striking woman, eyes the color of turquoise smiling back at him as he tried to regain his composure.

"And this is Mrs. Sarah Roland," General Sully said somewhere in the background. "Meet Doctor Joseph McReynolds."

Reaching for his hand, she smiled, and let her fingers drop cool into his own.

"A doctor, how interesting," she said, her voice rolling like a pure and resonant stream.

"My pleasure," he said, chancing another look.

Even after the rigors of the trip from Fort Dodge, she was as fresh as the morning light, skin the color of pearl, hair as yellow as the chinaberry that hung from the trees; tall, too, nearly as tall as he, slender like a filly but with breasts laden and full. The smell of her sachet stirred memories long since lost.

"And this is Lieutenant David Roland," Sully said, "just arrived from Pennsylvania."

"Welcome to Fort Supply, Lieutenant," McReynolds said, shaking his hand. "We're glad you brought this lovely creature with you to brighten up the place."

"Had no choice," Roland said. "Sarah was determined to come, even against my better judgment. I don't think the Territory is a good place for a woman, but my Sarah has a mind of her own."

"And whose mind would you prefer I have, David?" She smiled.

"You see," he laughed, "a mind of her own."

"And over here," Sully said, "is our engineer, Captain Wallace."

"How are you?" Lieutenant Roland shook Wallace's hand.

"Just fine," Wallace said, "considering."

Moving closer, Sarah looked Wallace over.

"So you're the one who's building our quarters?"

"Yes ma'am," he mumbled, "such as they are, but you have to understand it's the best we could do with what we had."

"I haven't seen them yet, but I'm certain they will be fine, Captain Wallace. You look like a resourceful man to me."

"Oh, he is." McReynolds smiled. "Resourceful and uncomplaining."

Dinner was excellent, with corned beef, mercifully free of buckshot, boiled rice, and lamb's-quarter greens picked from the bank of the Beaver River. And of course there was an ample serving of Cookey's sourdough bread heaped with fresh butter and a side dish of apricot preserve.

Although the cabin was crowded, it was dry and above ground, having been built from wagon sideboards and canvas tarps.

Undaunted by the seasoned men about him, Lieutenant Roland related stories teeming with bravado and half-truths while Sarah picked delicately at her food, embarrassed by his impertinence. All through dinner McReynolds watched her, the grace, the quiet beauty, the proud way she held her head in spite of her husband's ineptness.

When dinner was over, General Sully passed a box of cigars around the table. First Roland smelled his cigar, then rolled it between his fingers as he listened to it with his ear.

"My father sends me the best cigars," he said, "hand-rolled Cubans. You can always tell the difference."

"Difficult to get Cubans on the frontier," Sully said. "You'll forgive us, Mrs. Roland, if we talk business."

"Of course, General. I do hope I'm not in the way."

"No, no, you could never be in the way." Turning to McReynolds, he pointed his cigar. "Now, about this rabies thing?"

Lighting his cigar, McReynolds let the rich smoke languish at his nostrils.

"Private Withom first, sir, a severe bite on the neck, directly into the bloodstream. There was little chance. And when the Roston boy developed symptoms, he hanged himself down at the stables."

"Oh, my," Sarah said, "how pitiful."

"Rabies is a god-awful way to die," the General said. "Guess Roston wasn't keen on doing the same." Taking a thoughtful drink from his glass, he pursed his lips. "Can't say I blame him. You give 'em a good send-off, Doctor?"

"Full-dress ceremony, sir, complete with riderless horses, and then I dispensed their belongings amongst the men."

"By damn." He shook his head. "Excuse me, ma'am, but a cavalry burial ceremony is just the grandest thing. When my time comes, hope someone sees fit to ride my carcass around the parade ground a few times."

"I'm certain of that, General," Sarah said with a smile, "a man of your distinction."

In the dim glow of the candlelight, McReynolds could see that the General was pleased. Here was a woman who knew her way around an ego.

"Why, thank you, ma'am. Now, Major McReynolds, have you taken precautions against future problems with these rabid skunks?"

"I've talked to the men, sir, but as you know, they're sleeping on the ground. You should exercise great caution, ma'am," McReynolds said, turning to Sarah, "to avoid skunks, squirrels, or any such animal during the deadly heat of summer, especially if they are agitated or uncommonly fearless."

"Any rabid skunk comes into my view will meet with an uncommon death," Lieutenant Roland said, clutching his fist.

"Thank you, Doctor," she said, ignoring her husband. "I'll exercise caution until the heat passes."

Another round of drinks was poured. So low was the canvas roof of the General's quarters that the top of the private's head brushed against the cottonwood support when he stood upright.

"Sergeant Shoats tells me that more supplies will have to be brought in," McReynolds said, filling the silence.

"That's just it, isn't it," Sully said. "Orders are to have reserves sufficient to feed the Arapaho, Kiowa, and the Cheyenne, if we ever get them all rounded up. And then we have Satanta raising hell on the southern route, whiskey ranches are already popping up like toadstools, and half of Kansas is squatting on the wrong side of the border. Dodge City has it that Slippery Jack Gallagher and Frenchy have started up a gang and plan to earn a living off the trail and that the Santa Fe railroad has run out of new track money. Now, we could take care of just about any one of those problems one at a time, but put them all together and I'm a little less confident."

Leaning over on his elbows, Sully looked hard across the table.

"Sheridan promises relief by providing contract mule teams for the bringing in of monthly supplies. If he does what he says, and that's not always been so, the troops will be freed up for riding escort, fighting bandits, Indians, or squatters, take your choice, and that's not counting a half-dozen cattle companies creeping across the southern border and a hundred or so buffalo hunters dead set on killing everything with four legs."

Leaning back, he took a long pull on his cigar.

"If these Indian depredations continue, we'll have to build redoubts on the Dodge Supply Trail, or we are going to lose this skirmish. The Cimarron crossing at Deep Hole Creek seems a likely start, but I don't know if it can be defended. It needs checking out, but that's where the Indians like to lay in wait until the wagons are hub-deep in the muck."

"What are redoubts, General?" Sarah asked.

Tapping the ashes from his cigar into the palm of his hand, Sully looked at Wallace.

"Let's ask our expert here, Captain Wallace."

"Defensive earthworks, ma'am, a miniature fortification complete with howitzers, an officer, and twenty or so men, pens for the horses, a milk cow if you're lucky, and a supply shack to keep things dry. There're separate quarters for the officer and a parapet for defense. Redoubts are just fine for reconnaissance or for patrolling a trail, but their small size makes them vulnerable to being overrun by a large force."

"How exciting," she said, placing her hand over her mouth.

"Yes ma'am," he said, "it can be plumb exhilarating, when it ain't deadly dull."

"I'd like that duty myself," Lieutenant Roland said. "Give me a chance to kill some of those Cheyenne."

"You ever been in a redoubt, Doctor McReynolds?" Sarah asked.

Looking over at McReynolds, Captain Wallace's eyes crinkled with mischief.

"Course he ain't, ma'am. As a rule, doctors don't go to redoubts, 'cause perchance they'd scuff up their shiny boots or get their fingernails dirty or miss their afternoon naps."

"Or be maimed or killed from an ill-constructed fortress built by an engineer who thinks sticks and mud are just fine," McReynolds said, winking at Sarah.

Holding up his hand, General Sully laughed.

"Alright now, gentlemen, I'm sure we'd like to hear the end of this debate, but we've not had the luxury of a bed for a while, so another time. Perhaps we should retire. I suspect Mrs. Roland could use a good night's rest."

"Indeed," she said. "It's been a wonderful evening, but I'm very tired."

Standing, McReynolds shook hands with the lieutenant and then offered his hand to Sarah.

"Good night," she said, "I do hope a truce is forthcoming between you and Captain Wallace."

"We will work on the captain's manners." He smiled.

As he made his way back to his tent, McReynolds could feel the distant drums like a worrisome and erratic pulse, but above him the sky erupted with stars, a wondrous cascade of dazzling lights that dwarfed his own weariness and dimension. Already the moldy smell of fall was in the air, and soon enough these stars would cut through the bitter nights like broken glass. But even these thoughts failed to dampen his spirit.

In the darkest morning hours as the sky deepened beyond reach, and the Indian drums fell silent, McReynolds lay awake under the warmth of his blanket. Sea-green eyes watched him from the darkness, and the wall of ice within him melted and moved the smallest measure.

Now he understood why he'd reached for her hand, why he'd reached for it twice in a single night.

Six

The children laughed and pointed in amazement from their encampment beside the trail as Brothers Jacob and Alexander rattled by in their wagon. Waving, Brother Jacob forced a smile. Even though the rule of St. Benedict was clear in its instruction to love children gladly, he'd always found them irritating. But, he supposed, seeing two Benedictine monks plodding across the southwestern plains of Kansas in a wagon was an odd sight even for children.

Many hours he'd prostrated himself before the door of the oratory in repentance for his fiery temperament, but with only marginal results. In spite of it all, the noise and thoughtlessness of children annoyed him beyond repair. Sometimes he wondered if monastic life for him was but an escape from universal crudeness and the wet noses of children.

Of course there had been many such startled looks since he and Brother Alexander had left the abbey back in Atchison. It wasn't all that often that monks traveled beyond the walls of the monastery, so they were, no doubt, a curious pair in their tunics and cowls. Most people didn't know that the French padres were among the first whites to settle Kansas, back even to Marquette, but then most didn't care, either, as he recalled.

"Giddap," he said, snapping the reins against Shorty's rump. Even though Shorty was by far the strongest horse in the team, his lack of enthusiasm for pulling was renowned, and it was a constant struggle to keep him up with Cody, a horse much smaller but infinitely more determined.

"Do you think we will make Fort Coffee tonight?" Brother Alexander asked.

"I think not," Brother Jacob said. "Already the sun drops, and soon it will be dark. Perhaps tomorrow."

"Then another night on the prairie?" he asked, adjusting his position against the heat of the setting sun.

"Yes," he said, electing not to acknowledge the uneasiness in Brother Alexander's voice. "Keep an eye out for water and wood. We will make camp early."

"I thought perhaps we would be in the fort tonight."

"Come on, Shorty," he said, clucking his tongue. "No," he continued, "but the sky is clear, the day warm, and a balmy night is in the making. The horses need rest even more than us. By noon tomorrow we should be there."

Pulling at his beard, Brother Alexander checked the sky.

"Being away is more difficult than I thought," he said, "such emptiness and space. I feel as if I might slip over the edge of the world."

Brother Jacob, too, missed the custody of the monastery, its stone walls standing like sentries against the vulgarity beyond, its structure and fraternity like a secure and warm bed on a cold winter night, but sometimes one had no choice but to deal with the reality of the world. Nodding, he again popped the reins against Shorty's rump, sending dust spiraling into the air.

"Soon enough we'll have a new monastery," he said, more to himself than to Brother Alexander, "like an island of peace in the storm-tossed ocean. Lost souls will see its beacon and know that here is a refuge of serenity and beauty."

This was their charge, to go forth and establish a monastic farm, to prepare the way for others to follow. It was, they'd been told, the final step in taming the savage heart of Indian Territory. What Brother Jacob knew, but had not repeated, was closer to the truth, that the abbey was in financial distress, that the monastic farm was a last-ditch effort to save the order from extinction. It had been his misfortune to overhear the conversation and his burden to keep it from the others.

"I hope you are right," Brother Alexander said, "for this a fearful place, such distances and such heat." The sun lit the gray in his beard. "I wonder if Brother Henri has gotten the supplies on the train as planned?"

"I'm sure he will come soon. In any case we should have enough food until he arrives. There is still the bread."

"Perhaps we should have brought supplies instead of the altar," Brother Alexander said. "Perhaps the altar should have come later."

Though they had been together many years, had grown old together in their prayers and on their knees, there were times Brother Alexander's apprehension was like a rock in Brother Jacob's shoe.

"Without the altar, there would be no monastic farm," he said, keeping his voice conciliatory. "It is the altar that makes the difference. Above all is the liturgy of the church. Everything else God will provide."

In the silence that followed, Brother Alexander dozed, his head bobbing against the rhythm of the wagon. Within the hour, Brother Jacob spotted a narrow stream and pulled the wagon over. Water, red as blood, pooled in a shallow, and whiskered crawdads peeked back from their mud castles with bulbous eyes.

There was no wood, no buffalo chips, no fuel of any sort. A cold camp was always burdensome, but on the frontier it was both dangerous and frightening. Already the trail faded under the lengthening shadows of dusk, so, good or bad, this would be their camp tonight.

After hobbling the horses, they finished their chores and chewed on the bread Brother Huber had prepared for them at the monastery. As the blackness of night fell, they sought solace in vespers before crawling under their blankets.

"The horses are hungry," Brother Alexander said from the darkness, "but there is little for them to eat. The grass is brown and filled with burrs, and the night proves to be colder than we thought."

"Remember," Brother Jacob said, shivering under his thin blanket, "to have the vision of death before your eyes daily."

Turning on his side, Brother Alexander whispered, "But never before has it had such meaning."

Smiling, Brother Jacob pulled the blanket up to cover his ears, which stung from the cold. To sleep so near was disturbing. The monastery rule was to sleep apart and fully dressed, lest there be call to prayers, and with a candle burning throughout the night to ward away evil thoughts. But what to worry, in such a place and in such cold there was little room left for evil thoughts.

Dawn broke under a heavy frost as Brother Jacob and Brother Alexander stood over the hobbles strewn across the camp.

"Gone," Brother Jacob said, rubbing the cold from

his fingers. "See, the hobbles were too loose, and they've stepped out of them."

"It's my fault," Brother Alexander said. "I didn't want to hurt their ankles. Now they've fled, and we're killed from my stupidity."

"Nonsense," Brother Jacob comforted him. "First we will eat and then we will track them. How far could they be with Shorty in the lead?"

"Track them?" Brother Alexander moaned. "What do monks know of tracking? Now we'll starve or be killed by the Indians. It's my fault. I should have never left the monastery."

Patting his broad shoulders, Brother Jacob smiled.

"How hard can it be? See, there are the tracks clear as day. We'll take the ropes and follow them. They're looking for forage, and when they find it, they will stop and then we will rope them. God has many ways of testing our faith."

"And found it lacking." Brother Alexander shook his head in despair.

Taking a loaf of the bread from the box, Brother Jacob said a prayer before tearing it in half.

"Remember," he said, "when you came to the monastery to become a monk?"

"I do," Brother Alexander said, "like it was yesterday."

"And what happened?" he asked, chewing on the stale bread.

"I knocked at the door to plead my case."

"And?"

"No one answered."

"So what did you do then?"

Brushing the crumbs from his beard, Brother Alexander reflected.

"I went away and came back the next day."

"And what happened?"

"No one answered, so I went away and came back the next day. For seven days no one answered, but I kept coming back."

"Yes," Brother Jacob said, "and why did you return so many times without an answer?"

"Because I wanted it more than anything in the world."

Standing, Brother Jacob dusted his hands together and proclaimed in a resolute voice, "And so it was given and so shall this be. He is testing our resolve, and we will not be found lacking."

But tracking was not as easy as Brother Jacob had predicted. Sometimes the tracks were clear, or partially clear, or sometimes disappearing altogether under the ceaseless prairie sands. Only providence and blind determination moved them on.

Just as they were about to despair, Brother Alexander squatted at a manure pile steaming from a rock outcrop. With intense concentration he analyzed his discovery.

"Is it horse?" he finally asked.

Poking it with a stick, Brother Jacob shrugged.

"Could be," he said.

"Maybe it's cougar," Brother Alexander said.

"I hope never to see a cougar this big," Brother Jacob said, lifting his brows.

"Is it Shorty's?"

Shrugging, Brother Jacob kicked the balls into disarray with the toe of his shoe.

"It's not a subject I've studied, Brother Alexander, but it strikes me that horse manure is more generic than biographical."

With feelings bruised, Brother Alexander fell in behind as they made yet one more circle to see if they could pick up the tracks.

By noon, the sun hung suspended in the blue sky,

a molten and fervent globe, and the sweat dripped from their noses as they studied the earth for signs of Shorty and Cody. The red and tepid water stained the corners of their mouths as they drank from the canteen. Devil claws hitched rides on the tails of their tunics, and sticktights gathered in their socks. Horseflies sucked blood from their veins while their lips dried into leather under the relentless southwesterly wind. By late afternoon, they were no closer to finding the horses than when they had struck out that morning.

Like lonely ghosts they trudged across the prairie, tunics encrusted with salt, eyes caked with sand, faith eroding under the corrosive prairie heat. Once they thought they saw Shorty's back disappearing into a break, but it was only the tail of a hard-bitten coyote making a meal of a dried buffalo hoof.

"I could never be a hermit," Brother Alexander said.

"Being a cenobite is difficult enough," Brother Jacob agreed. "The hermits are a chosen few."

Stopping for a moment, Brother Alexander wiped the perspiration from his brow.

"Such torment," he said, "to live alone. When the abbot ostracized me for showing pride, I thought I might die from loneliness. How could the hermit choose to live in loneliness?"

"God said, 'In much speaking, thou shalt not escape sin.' It is the rule of Benedict that the brothers should have no idle or coarse words and that there should be no laughter. Who follows that rule better than the hermit?"

For some time they walked in silence, searching the barren ground for the slightest sign of Shorty and Cody. It occurred to Brother Jacob that being a hermit would not be so bad since they had little opportunity to suffer children gladly.

Stopping, Brother Alexander looked at him, concern on his face.

"The yoke of the rule is sometimes heavy, Brother Jacob. Have you ever doubted?"

"We've all had doubts, Brother Alexander."

"Yes," he said, stopping to check a mark in the sand, "but the rule was written by St. Benedict himself and is our calling."

"Yes," Brother Jacob agreed, dismissing the track in the sand as only the trail of a windswept weed, "to follow it, for it was written by St. Benedict and has in it the power to shape a single mind from the minds of many and a single spirit from the spirits of many."

Several seconds passed as Brother Alexander pondered Brother Jacob's words.

"But they say his signature could not be found on the rules."

"Burned in a great fire and so is gone forever."

Shaking the canteen to check the level of the water, Brother Alexander sighed.

"I wish God would have given us the signature."

"But then our need for faith would be less. To believe without the signature is more holy, don't you agree?"

When he looked up, Brother Alexander was pointing at his feet.

"Look," he said, "more droppings, and they are fresh like the others."

"You are right," Brother Jacob said, examining the green balls.

"And they are the same shape," Brother Alexander proclaimed with confidence, "and have the same smell. I think they belong to Shorty. See how they are scattered as if he continued to graze as they dropped? This is Shorty's temperament, don't you agree?"

"That would be like Shorty, I suppose."

"And there," he said, dropping to his knees, "the tracks, we have found the tracks."

And so they were, deep and clear in the soft soil like a sign from Heaven, and they followed them for two hours as fast as they could walk. There were two sets, Brother Jacob could see them now, one larger, one smaller, and his confidence grew that just ahead somewhere were Shorty and Cody waiting to be captured.

But as the sun dropped lower and weariness ached in their trail-worn bodies, they had not caught a single glimpse of the horses. Despair swept them as their shadows lengthened in the oblique light of sunset, and night closed like a coffin lid over their heads. The sun's heat bled into the thinning sky, and the smallest hint of breath fogged from their nostrils.

Wordless and despondent they topped the knoll. Below, like a specter under the ivory moon, Shorty and Cody stood with their heads in the wagon, black crows at a garbage pail. Collapsing on their knees, Brother Alexander and Brother Jacob watched as Shorty lifted the last loaf from the bread box, shaking it with his great yellow teeth.

That night neither said a word as they climbed under their blankets with empty stomachs to face the bitter cold. Hobbled at the wagon, Shorty and Cody stood, ropes marshaled about their necks. But in Shorty's eyes was contentment, crumbs of sourdough clinging to his chin whiskers.

Sleep came in spite of the deepening cold, and soon Brother Alexander snored beneath his blanket. But as the stars brightened against the inky blackness of the sky, Brother Jacob stirred, pulling his knees up for warmth, and he dreamed of his childhood dog, his heart aching, of her warm muzzle wet against him, of her black eyes watching, of her cold and tattered body beyond his reach. Somewhere, coyotes bayed, and the night's stillness pealed like church bells to mourn her death.

Listening beyond the night silence, it came again but like a woman's cry. Standing, he wrapped his blanket about his shoulders and walked to the edge of camp, where the light of the fire flickered at the rim of darkness. Again it came, sad and mournful from beyond the light, and chills sped down his back.

"Brother Alexander," he said, his voice shaking.

"What? What?" Brother Alexander threw back the blanket, his white hair askew, his face confused and frightened. "The horses have fled?" he asked. "They are gone again?"

"No, someone is out there," Brother Jacob whispered. "Listen."

And the voice cried of pain.

"Holy Mother of God," Brother Alexander said, "we must go help."

Tucked under the rock outcropping, she lay curled like a fawn, her hair caked with dirt, her face drawn from want of water. Even in the darkness, Brother Jacob could see that she was not young, but there was beauty still in her face and strength in her hand.

"You must be angels," she said, "or saints sent by God."

Kneeling, he lifted her head, and she moaned.

"We are but lowly monks who are lost in the prairie."

"My leg is broken," she said.

Even in the darkness, he could see the odd angle of her leg, like a twig snapped in a storm.

"Why are you here in this desolate place?" he asked, patting her hand in comfort.

"I am Mary Cromley, nurse among the Osage. I fell from my horse a week ago and could no longer ride. They left me at the side of the trail."

"Such savagery," Brother Alexander said.

Adjusting herself to see him, she groaned with pain. "My time had come, that's all."

"You wait," Brother Jacob said, "and we will bring a litter. You wait, and don't fear our return."

Squeezing his hand, she smiled.

"I stopped fearing long ago."

Back at the wagon, Brother Jacob rigged a litter from his blanket and tied the canteen about his waist. From the darkness, Shorty snorted at the intrusion as Brother Alexander cut lengths of rope from his hobble.

Double-checking the equipment, he paused and looked up into the heavens.

"What will we do now?" he prayed. "What will we do now?"

Seven

During the night, a mist rolled down the valley silencing summer in its coolness, and the morning air smelled of leaves, wood smoke, and sugar-cured bacon. When McReynolds arrived for breakfast, Cookey was busy baking bread on his new Shiras oven.

"Morning, Cookey," he said, "new oven, huh?"

"Yes, sir, came in on the supply train, for baking the bread and none better this side of Fort Gibson."

"Perky this morning, are we?"

"Oh, yes, sir," he grinned, ladling out a helping of fried beans and topping it with a thick slice of sourdough. "Care for a slab of yellow onion, sir, or some bubble and squeak made up from the leftovers of the General's dinner party?"

"Beans will do, Cookey. Maybe a little butter there for the bread."

"Yes, sir," he said, drizzling a dipper of melted butter from the can that warmed next to the fire.

It was simple fare but good, and McReynolds washed it down with another cup of the stout coffee. Lighting his pipe, he watched as Cookey worked at the bread.

"That was mighty fine, Cookey. Guess having clean clothes peaks a man's performance."

"It's all in the washing, sir, and never knew a woman better at the scrub board than that redhead."

"It's mighty fine eating, and the bread was excellent. Guess you got the touch, alright."

Rolling up his sleeves, Cookey gave him a serious look.

"Course I wouldn't tell everybody, sir, but you being such a fine doctor and a friend, I guess I could share the secret." Sitting down on the camp stool next to McReynolds, Cookey gave it deep thought before beginning. "It's all in the ferment, see. First you boil a peck or so of potatoes with their jackets on and mash 'em up good with some flour, and it's got to be done up with the hands. Folks who know less about bread might use a spoon or paddle, but it's in the hands where the goodness comes. Bread is a live and growing thing and wants the human touch. Add about six pails of water and six quarts of fine yeast, and put her in a sugar barrel big enough where she can grow and squirm in the darkness. That's the secret, sir, the human touch and a doze in the dark. Course a little red dirt and ashes blowed in keeps it from binding the bowels, not that I mean to intrude over into doctoring or nothing."

"Well, I'm glad to hear it, Cookey, 'cause if you could practice medicine like you bake bread, I'd be out of work. Now I'm off to check those new medical supplies before sick call. Next time you see that redhead, get some of her soap and use it in the dishwater around here. They tell me it goes a long ways in cutting down on the trots."

"That a fact." He shook his head. "You can depend on me, sir, for helping out my fellow man and the medical profession whenever the call comes."

On his way to the supply wagons, McReynolds passed the new officers' quarters. Soldiers unloaded household goods into the end hut while Sarah Roland looked on from the shade of a tree. Taking the opportunity, he watched her as she directed the activities. One of the soldiers backed out of the wagon and went sprawling at her feet. Clapping her hands together, she laughed, her hair the color of July wheat falling about her face, her voice bubbling with humor and intelligence. Grinning, the young soldier brushed himself off and climbed back into the wagon.

Moving on before she saw him, McReynolds found the empty supply wagons lined up two deep across the compound, with only a few remaining to be emptied. Under the tarp of the first wagon, he located his medical supplies, powders, bandages, alcohol, splints of all orders, forceps—three different sizes, a luxury on the frontier—and a complete new set of scalpels. Just as he was turning to leave, General Sully rode up, looking for the world like a small boy atop his big bay horse.

"Morning, General." McReynolds saluted.

"Morning, Doctor. Finding everything in order, are you?"

"Yes, sir, especially these new instruments. Mine were about worn to no good, sir."

Climbing off his horse, Sully propped his foot up on the wagon wheel and examined the supplies.

"I've sent that new lieutenant north to scout the redoubt location," he said. "The more I think on it, the more I'm convinced that the supply trail is too long, and we're too shorthanded to ever manage it from here."

"If confidence will do the job, then the lieutenant shouldn't have any problems, sir."

Laughing, Sully pushed back his hat.

"Confidence, you call it, do you? Well, by God, you doctors aren't nothing if not diplomatic. Arrogance is what I call it, pure and simple, and lack of experience. He's apt to get more experience than he bargained for on that trail. But I need that redoubt, and I don't have a choice. If a fire breaks out in more than one place, we're in serious trouble around here."

Pulling down the wagon tarp, McReynolds studied the horizon.

"Seems unlikely the Indians would attack a redoubt, since there isn't that much to steal, and they must know how swift and severe the retaliation would be."

"That's the way I see it, Major, and with runners we could be alerted to trouble within a day or two at most." Looking about, he lowered his voice. "Another thing, something I didn't bring up last night, but seems Sheridan is bringing Custer in for the winter campaign and leaving me in charge of the supply route."

"Sorry to hear that, sir."

"No, no," he answered, holding up his hand. "It's not our place to question Sheridan's decisions, and keeping these supplies going is an important job. I'm prepared to do it to the best of my ability, by God, and assume Sheridan had his reasons, but that's not what worries me."

"What's that, sir?"

"To put it straight, Custer is a braggart and son of a bitch and likely to stir up trouble where there is none, and that's the one thing we don't need around here."

"If I can be of help, General?"

Sticking his hands in his pockets, Sully looked into the sun, and it lit the crevices and crannies of his face. He was older than he looked.

"I appreciate that, Major. The fact is, I'm real short-handed in the officer area, and I've got to get back to Dodge to arrange a shipping contract. So, in short, I might be asking for some help now and then."

"Yes, sir, anything I can do."

"Like this afternoon for instance. The Army's bought two hundred head of prime Texas longhorns from a cattle company on the southern border, and they should arrive sometime today. We've got a party of Cheyenne coming in from the north. It's our intention that one meets the other, you see, and comes to understand that in the absence of the buffalo, there's the Texas longhorn steak, and once tasted, by God, they'll go forth and convert the heathen. Sugar works better than vinegar, least that's what my ma and the Bible always say. Do you think you could round up some help and see that accomplished so I can get on my way?"

"Yes, sir. Are there vouchers or records need kept?"

"The beef is paid for free and clear with no obligation or recompense. Those Cheyenne sons of bitches need to understand just how generous the U.S. Army can be. What with all the beef they can eat, they ain't got a reason to go hunting buffalo, now have they?"

Climbing back on his horse, Sully tipped his hat and rode off, leaving McReynolds to ponder his assignment. More than once he'd found himself performing the duties of a cavalry officer, soldier first, surgeon second. That's the way it was.

Before seeking out Captain Wallace, he located Sergeant Number and asked him to take sick call, then made his way down to the new guardhouse site, where the engineers were busy assembling the floor. Four pairs of feet stuck out from under the structure.

"No, no," Wallace said from underneath, "here, let me hold it, and you drive the nail. Now, don't hit my thumb."

Stooping over, McReynolds peered under the floor and said, "That you, Captain Wallace?"

"God almighty!" he yelled. "He hit my thumb!" Scrambling out from under the floor joists, Wallace held his wounded thumb in front of him like a cobra in a basket. Dirt clung to his uniform, and sweat dripped from the end of his nose.

"Here, let me take a look," McReynolds said.

"Look at what! It's gone, see, smashed flatter than a cornmeal flapjack. Where is that soldier so I can kill him?"

"Took off, Captain, and can't say I blame him."

Taking hold of his arm, McReynolds examined the bruised thumb.

" 'Don't hit my thumb,' I said. Last thing I said was, 'Don't hit my thumb.' " Dancing a little from one foot to another, he looked at his smashed appendage and then at McReynolds. "It was you that distracted him," he said, "poking around like a dog sniffing tails."

"You're going to live, Captain Wallace, unfortunately; but your thumb is no longer opposable, and I'm certain that was the last distinguishing feature between you and those mules out there."

Pushing back the mop of hair that had fallen over his eyes, Wallace shook his head.

"Ain't that just fine. Here I got a guardhouse to build, walls to put up, and a well to dig, and so this is the day the corporal removes my thumb with a framing hammer. To top it off, the Army surgeon here looks on with his pipe in his mouth and a grin on his face." Shaking his hand, he examined the nail, which was already turning the color of a fall turnip. "What you doing down here anyway? Don't you have enough pain and misery with rabid skunks and carbuncles to keep you happy?"

Taking out his pocketknife, McReynolds wiped the blade on his trousers.

"Let me see that again."

"What you going to do, cut it off at the joint and throw it in the campfire?"

Locking Captain Wallace's arm under his own, he

trimmed away the damaged flesh of the thumb, lifting up the corner of the fingernail to allow it to drain.

"God almighty!" Wallace hollered. "Why don't you just twist it off and feed it to the coyotees?"

"There," McReynolds said, folding up his knife, "you wash that with hot water and soap, and have Sergeant Number bandage it. See if you can't keep it out of your mouth for a few days."

Tucking his hands under his armpits, Captain Wallace walked the length of the guardhouse and back again.

"So what is it you want, Doctor, or are you just whiling away a little time before dinner?"

"General Sully says a herd of longhorns is arriving today for allocation to some Cheyenne. He wants us to see that it's accomplished in an orderly manner while he's away to Fort Dodge."

"Well, ain't that just fine. Fort Dodge is it, for a little drinking and whoring, I suppose, while the rest of us build a fort out of red dirt and sweat, I suppose. Would have thought with all the ass kissing he got last night, the General wouldn't have been in such a rush to leave."

"Still," McReynolds said, "ass kissing's got to be shared up and down the chain of command. Course if you can't help out, I'm sure he'll understand."

Reaching into his hip pocket, McReynolds retrieved his handkerchief and dusted off the toes of his boots.

"Oh, course, course," Wallace said, "especially since I got nothing better to do but build a whole fort on the edge of nowhere with nothing but straw and blowing dust. Why, I'd be charmed to take care of the General's business and the doctor's business, too, or any other sons of bitches' business that comes along, and ain't I sorry you got a little blood there on your shiny boots and all. I hope it ain't spoiled your day altogether."

"No, no," McReynolds replied, smiling, "it came off nicely, thank you. See you later, Captain."

While walking back to the medical tent, he noticed the wagon was gone from the Roland cabin and on impulse cut back in that direction. As luck would have it, Sarah was in the front yard examining the contents of a camp bureau, a modest piece of Army furniture with broken mirror and odd number of pulls.

"Morning," he said, "beautiful day, isn't it?"

Smiling, she lifted a red silk blouse from the bureau and said, "Moved in at last and that makes it a fine day."

The white delicacy of her hands lay against the red silk blouse like a masterpiece rendered in oil. Green eyes, emeralds refracting the sun's rays, looked up at him, and her smile deepened. From behind her, rose the coarse-cut cottonwood logs, crooked and untrue, an ax-hewed, mud-daubed profanity, a shanty built by a child on a hot summer day, and he was ashamed for her to be there.

"You got the end house," he said. "This is good because it will provide you more privacy."

Standing, she held the red blouse to her breasts and touched her lip with her finger.

"Shhh," she said, "you mustn't say, or someone with higher rank will take it from me."

The sun moved behind the grove of cottonwoods just as a breeze swept their tops. Light scattered and danced on her face, the full but delicate cut of her mouth, its graceful form, its color like the faint pink of an autumn rose, and he averted his eyes so that she wouldn't see.

"The General tells me he has sent your husband to scout a redoubt site?"

"True." She stood, draping the silk blouse over her arm, and the scent of her sachet caught on the breeze. "And so soon, but the soldiers have been more than helpful."

"Yes," he said, "I suspect so. Well, if there's anything I can do?"

"They're to take this old thing away and bring me another, but there is one thing."

"Just name it, Sarah. May I call you that?"

"Please do. It is my name, you know?"

"And mine's Joseph."

Closing the bureau drawer, she thought for a moment before answering. "I think I'll just call you 'Major,' if you don't mind."

"As you wish," he said. In the distance he could see the first signs of dust, probably the longhorns. Might be the Cheyenne, but they would be coming in from the north, unless they were lost, of course, but he'd yet to come across a lost Cheyenne, young or old. "What is it I could do for you?"

"Well, I hate to ask," she said, brushing at the front of her dress, "but there are no other women here yet, except the laundresses, and since my husband is away, I have no one to talk to. Perhaps if you could just come by once in a while, when you are not busy, for a chat or a cup of tea. I don't want to take you away from your work or anything, but I do get so lonely. There are only so many letters one can write home."

"I would be delighted," he said, and his heart leapt. Even though he knew that this was wrong, that this was something he should not do, he also knew that there was nothing in God's kingdom that could stop him. "Good day to you," he said, tipping his hat as the sun emerged from behind the cottonwood grove and lit her face for a last glance.

By three o'clock the cloud of dust turned into two

hundred head of Texas longhorns, bellowing and churning ahead of a half-dozen of the toughest bunch of men McReynolds had ever seen. Circling under the watchful eyes of the drovers, the cattle shook their great horns and mounted each other's backs. Most of the so-called steers were bulls, their great balls swinging like pendulums between their legs. Twisting their enormous horns, they bulged their eyes and snorted blasts of liquid from their flared nostrils. There were no calves, even though many of the cows labored with strutted utters, because on the trail, calves were shot the moment they were born.

Dust boiled from under the longhorns' hooves as they ebbed and flowed within the confines of their keep. An occasional bull would paw, kicking the dust high into the air, causing black flies to lift in a swarming cloud above the backs of the herd. Would take a hungry man indeed, McReynolds thought, to eat the likes of these trail-worn critters.

The boss approached, his sweat-stained hat pulled down against the sun, his shirt encrusted from perspiration and countless meals of jerk and beans.

"You the General?" he asked.

"No," McReynolds said, "but I'm representing the General."

"Here they are," he said, tugging on the brim of his hat. "Guess we'll be on our way now."

"Wait a minute. Wait a minute," McReynolds said. "You're just going to walk off and leave them here?"

Scratching at his chin, the trail boss looked over the herd.

"That's right," he said. "The deal was to deliver them, and there they are, unless you think I shied you too many head. Did eat one or two but picked up a few strays along the way, so figure it turned out about even. Course, if you think I'm a thief, I reckon you could count 'em."

"Count 'em?" he said, looking at Captain Wallace, who was too busy examining the bandage on his thumb to give him any help. "How can you count something that never stops moving?"

Grinning, the trail boss mounted his horse.

"Easy," he said over his shoulder as he rode away, "just count their legs and divide by four."

Before the drovers had reached the river, a dozen of the longhorns broke and headed due west in a slow gallop to Mexico.

"Holy day," Captain Wallace said, "they're breaking up and going every which direction."

"Well, go after them," McReynolds said, "before the others follow."

It was late afternoon by the time Wallace and a handful of men returned with the strays. In the meantime, keeping the main herd in tow had taken every man in the garrison, and a wagon of oats out of the mule barn, for bait. Even then, the longhorns straggled about the camp like relatives come home for Christmas, poking here and there, satisfying their bovine curiosity. An old roan bull with horns as twisted as mountain juniper lifted the skirt of an unsuspecting laundress as she leaned over a washtub and checked her disposition with his wet nose. Bolting at her terrified screams, he threw his head high and curled up his lip.

By midafternoon they'd rounded up the last stray, posted men on horseback to keep the longhorns contained, and collapsed under the shade of a tree for a well-deserved rest.

"How's the thumb?" McReynolds asked Wallace, who leaned against the tree trunk with his eyes closed.

Holding the bandaged thumb up, Wallace examined the frayed wrapping.

"Oh, just fine," he said, "given it's been smashed with a framing hammer, sawed off with a dull pocket-knife, and then pounded against a saddle horn for three hours. It's just fine, I'd say."

Closing his eyes again, he said no more and soon snored under his hat. Scanning the horizon, McReynolds looked for the Cheyenne. If they didn't show, what was he to do with two hundred head of half-starved longhorns?

Then he saw them, maybe as many as fifty stretched along the northern horizon, lances held at their sides, feathers blowing in the wind. Only the warriors had come, and in their finest regalia.

"Hey, Captain," he said, "we've got visitors."

Rubbing at his eyes, Wallace stood and searched the horizon.

"Well, there they are, come to town for a free meal. Hope they can speak English, because my Cheyenne could use a little work."

"Your English could use a little work," McReynolds said, "but these boys are hungry, and you don't need words for that."

Within minutes the Cheyenne warriors arrived at the edge of camp, their mounts dancing, their colors flashing against the late sun. A squad of armed soldiers stood behind McReynolds just in case. Determined to pull this off right, McReynolds had sent for one of the scouts to interpret. Captain Wallace stood at McReynolds's side, and for this he was grateful.

The warrior with the headdress dismounted and approached, lance at the ready, an enormous bear-claw necklace hanging from his neck. Holding up his hand, he spoke with deliberate care, his words falling like well-placed stones.

Turning, the scout relayed the speech to McReynolds.

"He says to tell the General that he has come for the longhorns and that he will trade horses for them on another day."

"Tell him," McReynolds said, "that I am not the General but have the authority to turn over the longhorns. Tell him that there is to be no payment, that the longhorns are his free and clear, and that if they decide to join the reservation, they will be provided like this forever."

Lifting himself in his saddle, the chief looked back at his warriors and then at the herd of longhorns, which had at last settled down. A grin spread across his face, exposing an absent tooth, and with a chilling war whoop, he held his lance in the air.

"God almighty," Wallace yelled, "he's going to attack."

Before either of them could move, the warriors rode past at full gallop toward the herd of longhorns, which watched with alarm.

"What the hell!" McReynolds said, his heart leaping in his chest.

Even as he spoke, the Indians strung their bows, racing headlong into the herd of terrified longhorns. The chief let go an arrow, sending it speeding into the heart of the old roan bull. Stunned, it fell to its knees, collapsing in a heap into the red dust. All mayhem broke loose as the warriors followed suit, whooping and screaming with lances and arrows flying in all directions. The bewildered longhorns scrambled, trying to escape the bedlam, but when one would find an opening, a warrior would race after it, shooting a well-placed arrow into its vital organs. Within minutes the camp was awash in blood and littered with the carcasses of two hundred longhorn cattle, give or take the one or two the drovers had poached along the way.

With great flourish the chief hoisted his lance over his head while his warriors whooped and hollered and rode in circles about him. Leaning over, he said something to the scout before riding off in a cloud of dust.

Dazed, McReynolds looked at Wallace and then at the carnage stretching across camp. Dead longhorns with arrows sticking out of them lay scattered as far east as the riverbank. Beyond, he could see the last of the Indian party as it topped the ridge and rode out of sight.

"It's going to take a heap of ass smooching to get out of this one," Wallace said, shaking his head.

Picking his way through the dead longhorns, McReynolds worked his way over to where the scout stood.

"What did he say?" he asked, still thunderstruck by the event that had unfolded before him.

With considerable reflection, the scout rubbed at the scar on his cheek as he translated the words into English.

"He said to thank the General because it had been many moons since his warriors had hunted with such success, and that when the buffalo returned, he would tie some by the legs so that the General could come to his camp and shoot them, that he would find them much better to eat. For now, his people were hungry and must go hunt the buffalo before winter fell."

As the sun dropped and the damp cool evening settled into the valley, McReynolds and Wallace made their way back to camp.

"What you going to do?" Wallace finally asked.

Shrugging his shoulders, McReynolds stopped and filled his pipe with tobacco. In the distance he could see the lamplight in Sarah Roland's window.

Striking a match, he touched the tobacco and watched it glow red in the darkness.

"Sometimes you can't do anything about life, Captain, except go along. Go tell Cookey we're having steaks for dinner tonight, all around."

Eight

When Fort Coffee broke into view, Brother Jacob let out an uncharacteristic whoop and snapped the reins against Shorty's rump. It was apparent why it was called Fort Coffee, the walls being nothing more than coffee bags filled with dirt, but visions of food danced in front of them as they rode through the gate of the tiny fortress, and they were glad enough to be there.

For three days they'd crept across the prairie, easing through gullies and across buffalo wallows with deliberate and painstaking care. For three days they'd listened to the Osage nurse moan, and for every moan, Brother Alexander himself moaned. At night they prayed for her recovery and listened to their bellies growl above the din of coyotes—God's Dogs, she called them—crying for their souls.

Only once had the brothers checked her wound, glancing quickly at the whiteness of her thigh. The break was serious, shattered bone protruding through a purple bruise just above her knee. Without food or water there was little to do but keep her covered and as warm as possible. At times her talk was incoherent, her brow fevered, murmuring of times lost, of her mother, of a man called Joseph.

"Will you look at that," the guard at the gate said. "And who might you be?"

"We're Brothers Jacob and Alexander from the Benedictine Order," Brother Jacob said. "We've a hurt woman in the back in dire need of medical attention. Could you help us?"

"Well," he drawled, pulling at the crotch of his pants, "if you can call it help. We ain't got but a horse doctor, and he ain't saved a horse since we got here."

"Her leg's broke," Brother Jacob said, climbing down from the wagon and opening up the back, "splintered, you see, and we've had nothing to eat for several days."

Lying on a blanket under the altar, Nurse Cromley lifted her head to look at them. Dust clung in her hair from the wheels of the wagon, and her eyes were weary with pain. The guard looked at her thigh too long.

"I'm a nurse," she said, "and know how to set a leg. Go get your commander."

"They're escorting an ox train," he said, "and ain't likely to get back this century."

Rising on an elbow, she leveled a look at the guard.

"Then go get the horse doctor and be smart about it."

"Yes, ma'am," he said.

There was something in her voice that caused him to move, and soon he was back with the horse doctor, an enormous man, smelling of liniment and whiskey. With ease he lifted her from the wagon and carried her to the commander's dugout, laying her on top of the table. Dark blood seeped from her wound onto the table, and flies gathered to feast.

"You're very strong," she said.

"Yes, ma'am," he said, looking at his hands, callused hard from work in the stables. "I always been strong, I guess. Time was I could lift a full-grown mule till its feet dangled."

Turning on her side, she groaned with pain.

"You ever set a leg before, soldier?"

"No, ma'am," he said, tugging at the leather belt that encircled his girth. "You be a horse, I'd shot you where you fell."

"Yes," she said, "and there have been times these last few days I wished someone would have. Now, here's what we're going to do. I want you to collect two wagon slats and cut them leg-length and then tear a bedsheet into strips for binding. You got any rubbing alcohol?"

"No, ma'am."

"Lamp kerosene?"

"Got some horse liniment for stoved-up animals," he said.

"Well, that's me, I guess, and get some food in those monks. I'm sick and tired of listening to their bellies."

"Yes, ma'am," he said, ducking under the door.

Lying back to wait, she allowed herself to rest. It had been many years since she'd been on an Army post, fifteen now, maybe more, and a great deal had happened in those years. She'd known such pride as the first female nurse at Fort Gibson, such eagerness and naivete, and of course there was Joseph McReynolds, his enormous capacity as a doctor, his courage, but what she remembered most was that night in each other's arms, that passionate night as the storm raged outside his cabin. Sometimes in dark and lonely hours, curled beneath the warmth of buffalo hides, she dreamed of him still, when the snows stacked outside her teepee or when the melancholy fall rains murmured against the stretched hides. Times like those she thought of him and wondered of her decision to stay with the Osage. Had it been the right one, her youth spent, but then youth was always spent, she supposed, one way or the other. Because of her, others had lived, and this was a legacy worth having.

The horse doctor cast a large shadow as he stood at

the end of the table with the wagon slats in hand. White strips of sheet hung about his huge neck, and the smell of whiskey was stronger than before. A bottle of liniment sat on the chair, and the brothers stood behind him like a pair of black crows.

"Like you said, ma'am. So now what do we do?"

"First show the good brothers out. One person screaming around here will be enough, thank you."

The brothers disappeared out the door, closing it behind them.

"Put pillows under my back so that I can watch, and do what I tell you." Settling herself in, she gripped the edges of the table. "Now this is going to hurt like sin, and I'm going to yell like a charging Cheyenne 'cause there's nothing between me and that broken bone down there. It's your job to keep pulling until you can't see that bone anymore. Do you understand?"

"Yes, ma'am," he said, "but what am I supposed to do with these wagon slats?"

"Once straight, put that ham you call a hand around my leg and hold it together while I set those slats and get them secured for splints."

Casting an uncertain glance at the door, he nodded.

"I ain't never touched a woman's leg before."

"Now, look, I don't want to go through this twice. Once we start, we go until it's finished. If you quit on me, I'll hunt you down and kill you."

"Yes, ma'am," he said.

Taking a deep breath, she waited for the pain to wash over her like a blue hot light, her scream rising, leaving, returning again, a murderous stranger at the door, stomach quivering, bile rising in her throat, the choking stink of whiskey and liniment.

"Alright, ma'am," he said.

Blinking the pain from her eyes, she lifted herself on shaking arms. His massive hands held her leg straight. Blood, thick and dark as molasses, dripped from between his colossal fingers.

With what strength she had left, she tied off the slats.

"Now," she took a deep breath, "wrap the whole splint with the remaining strips. Make them tight enough that they won't slip but not so tight that my foot drops off from gangrene."

"Yessum," he said, and she could see that his hand was trembling.

"And when that's finished, put a blanket over me and let me rest. I've got nothing left to give."

As he pulled the blanket over her, she reached for his hand and held it to her cheek.

"You're a good man and probably a good horse doctor, but I hope you and me never have to go through this again."

"Yes, ma'am," he grinned, "me too, ma'am."

Within a week Nurse Cromley was up and around with the help of a walking crutch carved out of a bois' de arc branch by Brother Alexander. In two weeks she had gained nearly all of her strength back, but her attempts to dissuade the brothers from their folly was futile.

By the end of the third week Brother Henri arrived with his wagon of building supplies, door frames, two glass windows, and a variety of hand tools. An unfortunate circumstance in Dodge City had nearly landed him in jail, when he was rounded up with a bunch of ruffians who were prowling the streets. Although shaken, he had managed to convince the judge that Benedictine monks were not in the habit of stealing money from citizens. In the meantime, he'd received word to return to the Order as soon as the supplies were delivered.

It took all of Nurse Cromley's persuasive powers, and

a small dose of feminine wiles, to convince the young sergeant that his worn-out wagon was fair exchange for a broken-down mule used for hauling waste to a nearby trench, but convince him she did, and soon Brother Henri rode out of Fort Coffee on the mule. In his bedroll was enough food to reach Fort Dodge.

Sitting with hands folded, Bother Jacob listened to her story.

"I am not a sister, as you can see, but I've dedicated myself to His glory, and I could be of great assistance to you."

"But we are a monastery, and no outsiders are permitted, especially a woman," he said, lowering his head.

"I know," she said, "but only for temporary, until I can get back to the Osage, until then. In the meantime I can sleep in the wagon, and I can be of medical service to those who come to you. I've also learned much about living on the prairie, and believe me, you're going to need all the help you can get."

"Let her come," Brother Alexander said, "for Christ Himself has said, 'I was sick, and ye visited Me; and what ye did to one of these, My least brethern, ye did to Me.' We can not leave her here among the soldiers, especially since she has not yet healed from her wound."

Within the week, she and the brothers clattered out of the gate of Fort Coffee with a month's supply of beans, flour, and sugar in search of their new life.

For a week they rattled across the prairie in quest of the perfect spot. On a bright morning, Brother Jacob stood atop the knoll and turned in a slow circle.

"This is it, Brother Alexander," he said. "Look how far you can see, the grass like rolling waves on an ocean." Bending over, he placed his hand in the clear stream of water. "So cold it makes my hand ache, a spring from the heart of the earth, and yonder see the layers of limestone for building blocks."

"And nothing between us and the north wind but emptiness," Brother Alexander said. "We will need shelter very soon."

"No protection for a hundred miles," Nurse Cromley said as she climbed from the wagon, hooking her crutch under her arm. "What happens when the Cheyenne ride in or whiskey ranchers looking for easy pickings? What happens then?"

"God will provide," Brother Jacob said without hesitation. "And also I heard a rumor at Fort Coffee that there is to be a redoubt built at the Cimarron crossing at Deep Hole Creek. If we have trouble, that would be only a few day's ride. So, this is to be His place, and we will call it Monte Cassino, after Saint Benedict's sanctuary."

"No," Brother Alexander said, "but, *Bueffel Au Monte Cassino,* a grove for buffaloes. It is only fitting."

"And so it shall be," Brother Jacob said, laying his hand on Brother Alexander's shoulder in a rare display of affection. "But first we must pray."

As they prayed, Nurse Cromley listened, and memories from her youth rushed back, the hours in prayer, the spiritual resolve, the obsession. How distant all that now, how far she'd strayed from that singular goal. Perhaps the circle was complete.

Preparing the meal fell to Nurse Cromley, and the gathering of dried buffalo chips to Brother Alexander. While beans and biscuits were meager enough fare, a find of wild onions growing along the streambed promised a tasty meal. Meanwhile, Brother Jacob unloaded the wagon to make way for a bed until shelter could be built. The horses were hobbled and turned out to graze.

When at last they were finished, they gathered

around the fire and said prayer. As they ate their beans the vast blackness stretched out behind them, and their little fire flickered atop the knoll.

That night as they slept, the winds swept down from the north, snapping the wagon tarp like bullwhips. Sand pelted the wagon bed, and tumbleweeds gathered in the wheels. In the darkness the dying embers of the campfire winked like red eyes. Beyond the black expanse, coyotes lifted their voices in fevered chase, their soprano choral pitched and ardent as they smelled the hot breath of their prey. Leaning against the wagon bed, Nurse Cromley rubbed at her leg between the bandages and knew that it was not the coyotes, nor the Cheyenne, nor the whiskey ranchers who were to fear, but the growing pain beneath her bandages.

For three days they dug like badgers into the ridge of the knoll as they prepared their dugout. Try as she may, Nurse Cromley could not convince the brothers to exchange their robes for shirts, so like great sweating beasts, they shoveled and toiled under the sun. Even though still weak, Nurse Cromley would make her way to the stream every couple hours where she soaked rags in the cold water for the brothers to put around their necks.

"Thank you," Brother Alexander said, squeezing the water over his head. "How are you doing, Nurse Cromley?"

"Making it," she said, "but better when there is a roof over our heads. The winters here can be severe, and we must have shelter, or we will perish."

"Tomorrow I go for the ridge pole, a big cottonwood down at the head of the spring, and then we'll cover the roof with a thick layer of clay and grass to shed the water, a chimney, windows, even a door. Monte Cassino will be born."

Sitting on the trunk, Nurse Cromley stretched her leg out in front of her. The pain had stopped the last few days. Even the roughness of the slats had ceased to cut and itch beneath the wrappings.

"And another thing," she said, "the beans and flour will sustain us, but sooner or later we must have other food."

"But it is too late in the season for a garden, perhaps turnips, even too late for corn, I think."

"We need a milk cow," she said, "and then we'll have fresh milk, butter for our biscuits, cheese from time to time."

"But where would we get a cow?"

"We passed a squatter a few days back, remember, a couple miles from the fork of the Arkansas. They had a small herd of cattle. We should have gotten one then, but my mind was not clear. Perhaps Brother Alexander could go back, try for a trade. Take one of the horses and a rope. Maybe they would be interested in some flour or beans."

Scratching at his bald pate, Brother Alexander looked at the retreating prairie.

"But I know nothing of cows, Nurse Cromley. How will I pick?"

"Just tell the man you want a milker and then cut a good trade. In the meantime, Brother Jacob and I will build a corral with stone from the quarry."

"I don't know," he said, shaking his big head.

"You will do fine. Now, come on and I'll prepare food for your journey. Believe me, when the snow flies, you will be glad of the milk cow."

As the sun climbed high into the blue sky, Brother Jacob and Nurse Cromley watched as Brother Alexander rode away. At the edge of the knoll, he turned and waved goodbye.

For two days they waited for his return as they carried the flat slabs of limestone to build the fence. By the third day, they watched the horizon as the afternoon wore on. When at last Brother Alexander topped the hill to the south, they both shouted with relief.

Pulling at the reins of his weary horse, Brother Alexander made his way toward them. Secured to the saddle horn with a rope was the most ill-begotten critter that Nurse Cromley had ever seen. Looking more like a buck deer than a cow, she dug her front feet into the earth, knees locked, eyes bulging in protest. Slobbers glistened from her mouth in the sunlight. Every two or three steps, her tongue extruded from her mouth like a great blue sausage, followed by a most pitiful bellowing, an inexplicable honking rising higher and higher until disappearing beyond the range of human discernment.

"Where have you been?" Brother Jacob asked.

Wiping the sweat from his brow, Brother Alexander looked to the heavens.

"I have dragged and coaxed and pleaded with this creature for three days. I have plowed the prairie with her hooves and listened to her incessant bugling until I thought I would go mad. Once, she broke loose and ran for the river. It was only luck and God's will that I managed to get hold of the rope. Look," he said, turning in a circle, "where she dragged me down a dry gulch on my back. I will lie prostrate before the door of the oratory until I'm an old man for the thoughts I've had."

"I hope you made a good bargain," Nurse Cromley said, looking at the shriveled teats of the cow. "She doesn't look to me like there's a cup of milk in her."

"Oh, yes," he said, examining the hole in his tunic, "a bargain. I had two sacks of flour and a sack of beans left to bring home, but during the night, this hateful creature ate them and trampled what was left into the ground." Walking in a circle about the cow, Brother Alexander studied her. "And then one night as I was sitting at my fire, the heavens opened, and the northern star shined like a brilliant eye in the blackness, a singular and indisputable sign it was, and then I knew."

"Knew what?" Brother Jacob asked, leaning forward.

"That she is the Anti-christ incarnate," he said, "this hateful creature."

At that moment the cow's tongue extended like a blue serpent, flicking first in one nostril and then in the other, her eyes protruding from her lumpy skull. With tail twisted above her back, she bawled, spewing green across Brother Alexander's shoes. "See," he wailed, "to test my faith, and were I not a humble servant . . ."

"Now, now," Nurse Cromley soothed him, "you are just weary from your journey. We'll call her 'Blue Tongue,' and put her in the corral. Tomorrow we will milk her. I'll make gravy for your biscuits. Won't that be nice?"

But Brother Alexander could not be consoled, slumping away to rest in the wagon while Brother Jacob and Nurse Cromley corralled the cow.

Twenty minutes later, Blue Tongue's front feet hung over the top of the stones as she lunged again and again against the fence, her bellow echoing across the plains like Satan's howl, sending chills down Brother Jacob's spine.

That night under a crystalline sky, the cold deepened, and the moon, big as a wagon wheel, hung suspended above them. Banking the fire, they went to bed, trying hard not to notice the peculiar noises from behind the stone wall, and the steam rising from Blue Tongue's nostrils into the cold night air.

Each morning Brothers Jacob and Alexander would

walk to the corral as if going to the gallows, and each day they returned empty-handed.

"She stood on my foot," Brother Alexander explained, "and the harder I pushed, the harder she leaned until my toe is but a squashed and miserable stump."

"And I was backed into the corner for an hour, afraid to move or call out, for fear she would gore me to death," Brother Jacob said.

"Yesterday she smacked me in the face with a tail full of burrs and then made a mess in the milk bucket while I was rubbing my eyes."

Working the biscuit dough with her fingers, Nurse Cromley shook her head.

"Aren't you a fine pair, letting ole Blue Tongue get the best of you. Do you want gravy for your biscuits or not?"

"Her bag is like an apple, and her teats are the size of pencils," Brother Alexander said, looking at her with sad eyes and rubbing his bald head. "Perhaps we should give her to someone who needs her more."

Placing the biscuits in a frying pan, she snuggled it into the coals and looked up at them.

"I'm ashamed of the both of you. Now who can you think of that needs that milk more than we do? If I didn't have my leg broke, I'd go milk that cow myself."

Making her way to the wagon, she cut off a length of rope and tossed it to Brother Alexander.

"One of you distract her while the other ties her back legs together. A cow can't kick with both feet at once. When you're finished, I'll make us some white gravy for our biscuits with lots of black pepper, and I've been saving back some coffee I got at the fort. Now you two go milk that cow, you hear?"

Standing at the gate, they peered in at Blue Tongue, who had backed into the corner, head down, nose blowing puffs of dirt into the air. Pawing the ground, she shook her head, her horns gleaming in the morning sun.

"We'll roll this barrel in to stand behind," Brother Alexander said. "You distract her, and I'll tie her legs."

With an anxious look, Brother Jacob opened the gate, rolling the barrel in first, stepping behind it like a man facing a firing squad.

The ground shook as Blue Tongue charged. In that moment Brother Jacob remembered how he'd watched the torrential floodwaters race beneath a trembling wooden bridge when he was a boy. Now he closed his eyes and prayed, his heart standing still as Blue Tongue lifted the barrel onto her horns, smashing it against the wall behind her.

When he opened his eyes again, Brother Alexander lay on the ground, his robe covered with red dirt, his hair matted with cow manure, a broad grin on his face.

Perplexed, Blue Tongue promenaded about the corral, petite ballerina steps, her tongue lolling from her mouth like disgorged viscera, her back legs secured together with Nurse Cromley's rope.

"We got her now." Brother Alexander clapped his hands together. "We got ole Blue Tongue right where we want her now. You get hold of her tail while I milk her," he said, "and it's white gravy and biscuits tonight."

Positioning himself behind Blue Tongue, Brother Jacob grabbed her tail, winding the hair about his hand. By digging both heels into the dirt, he slowed her to a stop. Holding the bucket under her, Brother Alexander squeezed her teat until a thin blue dewdrop formed on its end.

Like a gathering storm, Blue Tongue glared at her robed interloper, at the one who dared touch the forbidden fruit. With a diabolic howl, she dropped to her front knees, burying her head into the dirt, and with the precision and velocity of a jack mule, kicked Brother Jacob square in the chest with both back feet.

With wistful blinks of the eyes, Brother Jacob tried to refocus on the blue sky above and wondered if he would ever breathe again, and wondered if a monk could eat white gravy with two holes in his chest. After some moments, he rose from the ground like a spirit from the grave and walked straight to the gate, pushing it open with his foot. With the same deliberation, he walked over to Blue Tongue, pulled off her ropes, and watched as she sprinted out the gate.

Turning to Brother Alexander, he wiped the hoof prints from off his chest.

"I think Blue Tongue has escaped," he said.

"Yes," Brother Alexander said as the trail of dust settled in the still air. "Even Christ cast evil from the temple."

And so that night they ate dry biscuits and beans in silence. Attempts to initiate conversation with Nurse Cromley failed. Convinced that she was angry beyond repair, they scrubbed their dishes with sand and retreated to bed.

For the longest time Nurse Cromley watched the fire, the warmth against her face. It had not been ole Blue Tongue or the lack of milk that had caused her to fall silent, but the recurring memory of times past.

Nine

The ground was still warm from yesterday's sun as Owl Talker dug out the floor of the teepee with her hands. Even though leaves plummeted from the grove of oaks like huge snowflakes, the morning light fell in a warm sprinkle about her. Winter camps were her favorite because several months would pass before they would move again. Here there was plenty of wood and water, and with luck the buffalo would come to stay in the sheltered valleys as was their custom. Even Little Dog's spirits were high when he and Crooked Leg left for the morning hunt, and she knew that he, too, was happy for the winter rest. Here she would have time to walk in the trees, to gather acorns and roots, to work on her quilling. Already the menstrual hut had been built and lodge skins hung as the camp took form. This was her life, where she ruled, where she belonged. Here Heammawhio, the wise one above, would watch over them and provide through the winter.

With practiced skill she dropped the heated rocks into the buffalo paunch and waited for the water to boil. Today they would have buffalo liver sprinkled with gall, and boiled tongue, a great delicacy, and tonight they would make love on the warm buffalo robes as the baby slept. Many years had passed since Little

Dog had removed her protective string, and for many years their marriage had been a happy one. Never did she worry that he might throw her away and shame her in front of the others. Even though her sister joined them when her husband was killed, she made demands only a few times a month on Little Dog. Of course, Little Dog provided meat and protection when necessary, but his hunting skills were great, and only rarely did they hunger.

After the meal was finished, she combed her black hair with a dried buffalo tongue and braided the strands that hung over her shoulders. After that, she painted red stripes across them, one for each of Little Dog's coup. It was with pride she painted the stripes because all knew that within the Dog Soldier band no one counted more coup than Little Dog. When the meal had been secured in the parfleche, she loaded the baby on her stomach, wrapping him securely against her breasts, and made her way to the spring. Each day the water must be renewed because overnight its life fled away, and no one should drink dead water.

When Little Dog and Crooked Leg had not returned by late afternoon, she walked to the mound that rose on the prairie like a woman's breast and studied the horizon for signs. She should not worry, this she knew, for Little Dog was a brave warrior, fearless like the sandhill crane, willing to fight anything to death, and his medicine in the Dog Soldier Clan was strong. Winter was not the time for war, and no enemies came even to steal the horses. Still, she could not help but worry and promised to the spirit Maiyun a strip of skin from her arm if Little Dog were returned safely to her teepee.

At sundown she built the fire higher and listened for the sound of Little Dog's horse as the sky blackened, and the cold night fell silent about her. Walking

Horse stopped at her fire to talk, but she ignored him by working at her quilling. When Walking Horse was a member of the Fox Soldier Clan, he had killed another Fox Soldier over a woman and was driven from the clan. For three years now he had ridden with the Dog Soldiers but was never allowed to hunt because he smelled of death and decay, and the buffalo would always run away.

Walking Horse left her fire and went to his teepee on the edge of camp. This was good because Little Dog's patience with Walking Horse was short since he was of great trouble and of little use to the band.

While working at her quills, she studied the fire and listened. Perhaps Little Dog had dropped his bow and was waiting for someone to pick it up. No member of the Dog Soldiers was permitted to recover anything that was dropped, it was the way, or perhaps they had killed many buffalo and were cutting the meat or were building a travois to bring it to camp.

And then she heard the sound of his horse, snorting through his nose as he often did, and Crooked Leg's horse answering in turn, and she stood to tend the coals. Dismounting, Little Dog and Crooked Leg squatted at the fire and warmed their hands. There was no meat and no travois and no signs of battle, but she did not ask because she did not wish to shame them or to cause any sort of bad luck to befall them. She prepared beans, and strong juniper tea to soothe them, and sliced the liver and gall, and gave them buffalo tongue to warm in the fire. All this time she did not speak or give sign that she had been worried, for to worry was to doubt the medicine of her husband, and this she would never do. It was after some time that Little Dog and Crooked Leg began their story.

"We were tracking fox," Little Dog said, pointing to the south. "Since we had taken the dogs to worry the buffalo, and since there were no buffalo, we thought to use the dogs to trail the fox. Fresh tracks were hit just where the river bends, and we followed them upstream with the dogs trailing as fast as they could run."

Drawing the bend of the river in the sand with his finger, Crooked Leg shook his head in agreement.

"And then the dogs ran back to stand between our legs and whine," he said, looking into the coals of the fire. "That's when I felt the *mistai,* the ghost, touch my arm, and I knew that the dogs had smelled him, and that's why the dogs stood shaking between our legs."

Slicing off a piece of tongue, Little Dog chewed as he retraced their steps in his mind.

"We drove the dogs from us, but they would not hunt anymore," he said, "and so we tied our horses in a chinaberry grove and followed the trail on foot. Sometimes we sang loudly, and sometimes we blew on our bird whistles to keep the *mistai* away, but then the fox heard and ran faster to escape our arrows." He paused as he sipped his tea. "Soon there was no fox, only a strange track as large as a bear's but with split hoof like the buffalo or the white man's cow."

Owl Talker did not speak but only listened as she cleaned the baby with leaves and dusted his bottom with a puffball.

Wiping the grease from his hands on his leggings, Little Dog continued.

"Just as we entered the valley where the sun rests on the mesa and the cottonwoods stretch along the stream, an evil sound filled the valley, and our shadows fled in fear."

Standing, Crooked Leg looked into the fire, and the light flickered in his black eyes.

"My horse bolted," he said, "and threw me on my back, opening again the wound on my leg, but then I said, 'It is nothing, only a slight fall.' To cry out in pain or speak otherwise would have caused the *mistai* to take me away."

Stepping up behind them, Owl Talker offered the chokecherry pemmican that she had saved for a snowy day because she could see that a powerful spirit had been in their presence to so affect the bravest warriors of the Dog Soldier Clan.

Munching on the sweet, Little Dog unstrung his bow and hung it on the ridge pole, sitting back down at the fire.

"I think we must renew the arrows now, or our luck will be as cold as the winter."

Even though Owl Talker ached to hear the finish of the story, she picked up the baby and offered her breast to him as she waited.

Some time passed before Little Dog began again, and a north wind rippled across the tops of the oaks sending gray and gold leaves about them in a flurry.

"Just as the shadows of the trees stretched across the valley," he said, "and the sun's light tuned gold, it came out of the break in a dead run." Falling silent again, he stirred the fire with a piece of firewood. Sparks rode the column of smoke into the still night air. "In my manhood I have hunted much, the cougar, the bear, even the rutting buffalo bull, but never have I known such fierceness."

Rubbing at his ankle, Crooked Leg stood and walked to the edge of the light, looking out into the darkness.

"And the howl," he said, "like a hundred wolves on a snowy night and the eyes, like glowing coals in a fire. Its teats were no bigger than a baby's fingers. When it bellowed, its great blue tongue hung from its mouth into the dirt."

"I shot two arrows straight to its heart," Little Dog

said, "the ones with the eagle feathers taken from my father's bonnet, but the arrows did not stop it."

Turning, Crooked Leg walked back to the fire, his limp worse than before, his face drawn with fatigue.

"Had it not been for the cottonwood tree that Little Dog and I climbed we would not be here at this fire now," he said. "For three hours the great blue tongue kept us in the tree. And each time it left, we tried to climb from the tree, but then it would charge from the woods again, butting the tree with its ugly head."

"And the leaves and twigs from the highest branches fell," Little Dog said, "and clouds of steam came from its nose as it pawed dirt high over its back. For many generations our people will be telling the story of the battle with the blue-tongue spirit.

"And our horses were scattered into the hills," he continued, "and the dogs ran yelping into the prairie. Finally it came no more, but each step we took, we waited for it to charge once again from behind a rock or out of a break and kill us." Brushing the pemmican from his hands, Little Dog stood. "I think it is because of Walking Horse and his smell of death. The blue beast smelled him on the wind and was called then from the underworld."

Nodding in agreement, Crooked Leg picked up his bow and the blanket from his horse that he sat on.

"Tomorrow," he said, "we will talk again and decide when to renew the arrows and decide if Walking Horse must be banned from the Dog Soldiers."

That night Owl Talker lay against her husband, the steady beat of his heart against her arm. They did not talk more nor make love because there were too many evil spirits about and too much bad luck in their camp. When the clear night deepened and frost glistened on their lodge and a small curl of smoke twisted upward from the dying fire, Owl Talker rose and went out.

With a knife she sliced a strip of skin from her forearm and lay it in the fire as she promised she would do if Little Dog were brought home safely, and then she took another to ward off the *mistai* that might have followed them home and put her child in danger, for it was always the children who were most in danger from evil spirits. Wrapping her arm, she crawled under the buffalo robe, taking care not to awaken Little Dog, and slept against the rise and fall of his breast.

When Owl Talker awoke, the morning sun shined through the skins of the lodge, and the dank smell of camp smoke hung in the morning air. She listened for the birds, but the camp was silent and still. Perhaps the night cold or the death smell of Walking Horse had driven them away. Removing herself from the bed, so as not to awaken Little Dog or the baby, she stepped into the morning sun and lifted her arms above her as she stretched away the night's sleep.

Checking Walking Horse's camp, as she always did, because sometimes he watched her from across his fire, her eyes widened. As usual Walking Horse sat against his lodge, but this time his hands lay open at his side, his intestines spilling across his lap. Steam rose from them in the morning cold.

There was no cry or sound from Owl Talker as the rifle ball tore through her temple, and she fell into the ashes of the campfire.

Startled from his sleep, Little Dog leapt from his bed, reached for his bow, the few remaining arrows from yesterday's hunt, and in his nakedness opened the teepee flap to face the enemy. From every direction soldiers fired, the volleys ravaging the morning stillness. Warriors rushed from their tents, and the women covered their sleepy children with their bodies, but all about they fell, like the oak leaves fell, never to rise again.

Dropping to his knees at the body of Owl Talker, Little Dog strung his bow, but the rifle ball snapped his head, and the grit of his shattered teeth filled his mouth. From behind, his son's cry focused his strength, and he reached for the bow now lying across Owl Talker's back. When the black boot of the soldier crushed his hand, Owl Talker's entombed breath rattled from her lungs. With his free hand Little Dog pulled his knife, blood spilling from the grisly wound in his face, and brought it full bore into the extended leg of the soldier. It was not the scream of pain nor the sweetness of death, but the gray smell of gunpowder that followed Little Dog into the black abyss.

As sunset came, the birds returned, and their songs filled the oak grove. For a brief time they pecked and played like happy children among the oak leaves and the swollen corpses of the Dog Soldier Clan. As darkness fell, a cold drizzle commenced, dampening the leaves and quenching the smoldering ashes of Owl Talker's fire. At her side lay Little Dog, his body naked and blood-streaked, and next to him, the baby, like a crumpled and discarded doll.

As the night hushed, a chilling fog drifted over the forsaken camp, and the coyotes came, moving with caution as they tugged at the bodies, yipping, growling, flashing their grudging white teeth.

With exacting slowness, Little Dog's arm edged through the leaves to touch the fingers of Owl Talker's hand, to pull his son's cold body into his bosom.

Ten

When Adam Renfro saw Chimney Rock, memories swept over him. Pulling his horse to a stop, he held his hand over his eyes and gazed at the towering pinnacle. Creed, his son, hung onto his waist as he looked up at the rock in amazement. Fifteen fast years had passed since the last time Adam stood here, and in those fifteen years he'd lived a rich and full life with his beloved Twobirds. But all things change, they say, and a month ago his life had changed forever.

After he'd deserted the expedition to join Twobirds, they'd lived with her people, the Kiowa. But acceptance was not the same as tolerance, and for a while they'd survived on the edge of camp and the edge of life. When Creed was born, the decision to live apart from the tribe was made. It was not an easy decision because to live alone in the wilderness was a dangerous prospect at best. Without the tribe, the slightest problem could turn to disaster, the absence of an extra hand, or a loaned robe, or shelter on a cold winter night.

But live it they had, surrounded by the vast beauty and dangers of the prairie. When the droughts came, they carried water by hand from muddy holes, and when the floods raged, they clung to each other for comfort and solace. When the food was scarce, they shared the morsels between them and at night warmed each other's bodies against the biting cold. She was his comforter, his lover, his companion for life, and never once in all those years did he regret leaving his people to be at her side.

Now she was gone, dead from the cholera that rode into their camp one night masked as a farmer with a wagon load of children. Twobirds insisted on feeding them, sharing her robes, her water. It cost her her life, and things were forever changed.

Had it not been for Creed, Adam would have joined her that day, would have climbed onto her death scaffold to lay at her side, to wait for the vultures, but he'd made a promise, to return Creed to the white world. "It must be," she'd said, "if he is to live." The onslaught of the white man was no stranger to Twobirds, and she, better than anyone, knew the end of her world was near.

"See how it reaches into the sky," Adam said.

"It makes me dizzy," Creed said, "and the clouds are moving so fast."

"I slept here one stormy night many years ago and thought to blow away. And in that direction, a few days' ride, my ole molly mule gave up her life. That was long ago, but I remember it."

"But when will we stop? Are we to come to my mother's people soon?"

Turning, Adam looked at him, his black hair falling over his brown eyes. There would be no delaying Creed for long because, like his mother, his sense for truth was strong.

"I haven't told you everything, Creed. I didn't want to worry you so soon after your mother's death."

"What is it?" he asked, studying Adam's face.

"We'll make camp and talk tonight. Perhaps it will be drier than the last time I slept here."

"But what is it that you haven't told me?"

"Tonight, after supper, I'll explain. In the meanwhile you locate some wood or buffalo chips while I unpack the gear. Hurry before dark and watch for rattlers. They gather in the rocks when the weather turns."

Unpacking was a small matter, since much of what they'd owned, Adam had left behind. It was to be a new way of life. "Promise me," she'd said, clutching his hand, and so he'd promised, because there was nothing he would not promise her.

Riding from the camp that day, he'd turned for a last look, the buffalo-hide tent, the robes on which they'd loved and slept, the cooking utensils filling already with the ever-drifting sand. It was only the beaded satchel he kept, and the memory, Twobirds lying on the scaffold, her hair fluttering in the prairie winds.

Building their fire small, Adam and Creed nestled in one of the crannies that washed away at the base of Chimney Rock. Here they ate in silence as the fiery sun plunged below the horizon.

"This is the pemmican Mother made from the buffalo you killed last summer," Creed said. "Do you remember how she laughed when she saw its size?"

"Yes," he said, "a rabbit she called it, with the horns of a buffalo."

"Yes," Creed laughed, "a rabbit."

Holding a blanket next to the fire, Adam warmed it before handing it to Creed.

"You and me have set many a camp together," he said.

Poking the fire with a stick, Creed did not answer. The firelight flickered in the blackness of his eyes.

From the beginning, Adam knew that this boy was special, unusual in mind and in courage. What devastation for him to lose his mother, what ruin and grief to lose a mother like Twobirds.

"We are not going back to my mother's people, are we?" Creed asked.

Rolling out the blanket, Adam lay on his back and studied the sky above. The northern star winked beyond the orange light of sunset, and a lone coyote mourned from the ridge.

"No," Adam said.

"But where will we go?" he asked.

Sitting up, Adam looked into the face of his son.

"You must have wondered why I came to be here so far from my people?"

"Mother said because of too many fences and too few friends."

Smiling, he leaned back on an elbow and studied the fire.

"Your mother was a wise woman, but it was her beauty and spirit I could not resist. No man could. But there are those who think that I should not have left. Do you understand?"

Crossing his legs, Creed leaned forward, putting his chin in his hands.

"You mean, your people would do you harm?"

"I would be punished for having left. There are those who did not approve."

"Of being with my mother?"

"Of leaving the Army," he said, "for no one could disapprove of your mother."

After thinking a while, Creed nodded his head, his chin still in his hand.

"Would they kill you or ban you from your tribe?"

Reaching into his saddlebag, Adam retrieved Two-birds's beaded satchel.

"No, they would not kill me, but they might take

me away from you. Here," he said, handing the satchel
to Creed, "she wanted you to have this."

Taking the satchel, Creed studied the fine beadwork
and the frayed leather tongs.

"What are we to do?"

"If we meet my people, they must not know who I
am. Many years have passed, and few would ever recognize me. There is little chance of any problem."

"But what would I say if someone asks?"

Looking up at Chimney Rock climbing into the
blackness, Adam pondered.

"Tell them I was a mule skinner, and that is all you
know."

"That's all?"

"Yes," Adam said. "Now it is time for you to sleep,
and tomorrow I will know better how to answer your
questions."

In the night, the cold deepened. Behind the ash of
the campfire, the last ember faded into gray, and
across the empty prairie, Twobirds lay shrouded and
still atop the scaffold.

The next day the ride was hard but fast as they
pushed northward. Without travois or tent the miles
passed, and soon they approached the edge of a canyon. Falling silent, Adam looked at the abyss, a jagged
red slash cutting across the prairie like an open wound.
Twisting down the canyon wall was the faint trace of
a foot path. Sensing his uncertainty, Creed waited.

"We're going down," Adam said. "We'll hobble the
horse here because the trail is too steep."

Sliding from the back of the horse, Creed dropped
to the ground. While Adam tied off the hobble, Creed
found a bush and checked the weeping sores that had
been rubbed raw inside his legs. For miles they had
pained him, but he did not complain. Complaints were

of children and of women. What he did now was of men, and he would do it well.

The trail steepened within feet of the rim, plunging into the precarious craggy rock that loosened from the canyon wall. Below, the stream twisted like a silver thread through the red earth, the green cedar erupting wherever a foothold presented itself. The dank smell of rotted leaves rode the currents of air and rustled the dried yuccas. Overhead, buzzards banked in the cobalt sky, unflagging sentinels of death.

Stopping to rest, Adam wedged the heel of his boot against a rock, leaning against the warmth of the canyon wall. Covering his eyes from the sun, he watched the buzzards circle overhead.

"You know," he said, "my people bury their dead in caskets of iron, but the Indian joins the world again as soon as possible. It's a wonderful thing."

"I was just thinking," Creed said.

"I know," he said, "and it's okay to think about these things and to talk about them, too."

"Do you think we will ever see her again?" he asked.

Some time passed before Adam spoke.

"To be a man is to know only the question," he said.

As they made their way down, Adam soon departed the main trail, following a narrow path into a stand of cattails. The smell of mud hung in the air, the black ooze sucking at the soles of his shoes. Long-since browned from the fall frost, the cattails whispered in the breeze. Cutting handfuls of the tails for torches, Adam wrapped them into tight bundles and stacked them on the ground.

The spring bog had changed little in fifteen years— water bugs floating on its silvery surface; dragonflies hovering, darting, coupling in air; tracks of coon, opossum, bobcat, come to probe the dark waters under the protection of night. How many trips from the cave had he made that winter to prepare the torches, how long and lonely the hours.

When finished, they gathered wood for a small fire to heat their food. Eating in silence, Adam watched his son, knowing that it was time, that now he must speak the truth.

"Below," he said, slicing off a piece of jerked meat and handing it to Creed, "there is an opening into a cave."

Chewing on the meat, Creed studied his father's face.

"We are going there?"

"It was a place of your mother's people, a place where Spanish silver specie was hidden by them. While on expedition many years ago, my lieutenant forced your mother to bring us here so that he might steal the silver for himself." Slicing off another piece of meat, he stuck his knife in the ground. "But it was not to be. I was shot and left for dead when he discovered the Kiowa had put the silver at the bottom of a deep spring."

"What did you do?" Creed asked.

"Had it not been for this bog," he said, "and the creatures it brought, I would have perished soon enough." Slicing off another piece of meat, he put it into his mouth and chewed slowly as he thought. "When I regained my strength, I went back to the cave and brought down the ceiling. I have not been back since."

Walking to the edge of the bog, Adam looked down at the depths of the canyon.

"The spring is the same that flows through the cave below. Think of the mighty work it has done, Creed."

Knowing there was more to be told, Creed waited.

"There is something I've never told anyone," Adam

continued, "not even your mother." Turning, he looked at Creed. "It was not to hide from her, but to keep her from harm." Squatting at the fire, he warmed his hands. "Before I brought the ceiling down, I recovered the silver. Time after time I dove into the waters, warming my frozen fingers over the torch before diving again so that I could hold the bags of silver. When there was but one torch left, I would leave the cave and come here to make more and to rest. At night I would wait for the coon and the opossum and take them as they drank, and when I was rested, I would return to dive again until there was no more silver."

Sitting up, Creed crossed his legs and leaned forward on his elbows. There were wet spots on his trouser legs where the blisters had drained.

"The silver is here?" he asked.

"Buried and marked with a hackberry stick, the same stick I left as a message to your mother, to let her know that the lieutenant had missed his mark, and that I was still alive. Later, I buried the silver in that same spot, near the entrance of the cave. Then I brought the ceiling down so that no others could get to the spring. I thought never to take it for myself, Creed. But now that she's gone, there is nothing left for us, for you, but the silver."

"Do you think it's still there?"

"Only one way to know," Adam said, helping him up, "and tonight we'll put some grease on those blisters."

So changed was the entrance of the cave that at first Adam didn't recognize it. But by backtracking, he reoriented himself, realizing that the entrance had been closed by a rock slide and recut by water higher up on the ridge.

"Here," he said, looking into the hole. "See where the sunlight falls on the floor of the cave."

Leaning over the edge, Creed looked in, the cool

air rising against his face like a spirit's touch, the acid smell of bat droppings burning his nostrils.

First, Adam lowered Creed by his arms into the darkness and silence of the cave, dropping a lit torch in next to him. With the torch Creed found a way down the rock slide that extended some feet from the entrance. Soon Adam was at his side.

From the ceiling, bats squirmed under the torchlight, their ears swiveling in protest at the intrusion. With bony fingers, they clutched their breasts, lifted their heads, bared their needled teeth.

Lighting another torch, they walked the perimeter, making their way back to where the sunlight fell on the floor.

"It's changed so," Adam said. "It was but a forked stick."

"Look," Creed said, holding his torch high. "Where the light falls from the opening, a tree has grown."

"Twisted and stunted from such poor light," Adam said, "but determined to live, I reckon." Touching the rough bark with his fingers, he knew. "It's a hackberry, sure enough, living down here on its own."

"What does it mean?" Creed asked.

"Took life and grew in this patch of light. One chance in a million that spot of sun would've brought that marker to life and kept her going all this time. Stick that torch in the ground, boy, and let's find out if the gods are with us."

Sweat dripped from their noses in the still air of the cave as they dug with their hands. Surface dirt had washed in from the hole above, building up over the years, but it was soft and free of rock.

"It's not here," Creed said from above. "Someone has stolen it, or perhaps this is not the right place."

"We will dig farther," Adam said, wiping the sweat from his brow.

Breathing labored and heavy in the dankness, they fell to work once more. Soon water gathered at the bottom, seeping cold and wet into their shoes, its bitter cold coming back to Adam, its reluctant treasure, its black depths. The loneliness and loss of this place was frozen forever in his memory, as was the yellow dot of the torch shimmering in the black waters above.

"What is it, Father?" Creed asked.

"Hand me the torch?" Adam said.

"Is it the silver?"

Without answering, Adam lifted the first bag from its mooring, placing it at Creed's feet. Mold-encrusted coins the color of jade spilled from the rotted bag. Taking his knife, Adam scraped a silver streak across its surface.

"Now we must hurry before dark sets in," he said.

By the time the moon's light eased into the canyon, the silver was secured in new bags made from one of their blankets and carried back to camp. Warming their feet at the fire, they drank hot sage tea and watched the moon as it rose into the sky.

"Tonight, I guess, we share a blanket," Adam said.

It was not to be said but being near his father comforted Creed, filled the emptiness that was within him.

Warming jerked meat on a stick, Adam handed a piece to Creed and then took a piece for himself. Beyond in the bog, an owl hooted, and a cold wind swept down the canyon. Winter waited not far beyond the horizon.

"What are you going to do with the silver?" Creed asked. "It seems of little use to me."

"I ain't never been much," Adam said, looking deep into the fire, "and without your mother, I ain't likely to, far as that goes. A man like me never was set to go a single direction and without that, the distance traveled in a life is short."

Waiting, Creed looked at the fire, the bags of silver, the beaded satchel his father had given him.

"It is not so," he said.

"But there is one thing I do know and that's mules. I know how they think and when they think. I know most of all, what they think. Your mother always said the only difference between me and a mule was that a mule had a plan." Rising, he walked to the edge of the canyon and watched the moonlight sparkle on the river below. "What I'm getting at is this, Creed. Rumor has it that the Army's looking to contract supply trains, to haul goods down from Fort Dodge to the Territory. Seems to me this is something we could do. With this silver we can buy wagons, mules, and gear, go into business for ourselves. This silver would set us up, but I wouldn't do it without your say-so." Reaching up, he broke off a twig and tucked it in the corner of his mouth. "You think on it a while and let me know?"

As the moon dropped below the canyon wall, and the night darkened, Creed lay awake. Overhead, the bats returned to the cave, blind and silent specters sweeping down the canyon. A fog spilled from the canyon rim filling its depth. These things Creed feared not, for they were of his world. But the white man's world was a strange and perilous place that twisted in his stomach even at its thought.

"Father," he said.

"Yes," Adam said, for he did not sleep.

"I am not afraid."

Turning on his side, he looked at Creed in the dying light of the fire.

"Then," he said, "I, too, am not afraid."

Eleven

Frost glistened in the trees like silver down, black ribbons of smoke rising from the new barracks across the way, as Dr. McReynolds lay aside the journal article. He'd elected to stay in his tent until the new hospital was finished because it gave him privacy and an opportunity to keep up on his reading. Staying current with the latest advances in medicine was not easy, so far from the cities. Sometimes the medical journals would not arrive for several months, only to be dumped at his door in great quantities, dated and in disrepair from their journey. Often entire pages were missing where the soldiers tore them out for kindling or for less dignified functions.

There were times he despaired with medicine, its endless emetics, bloodletting, blister packs, and tonics. What couldn't be poisoned was amputated, and what couldn't be amputated was left to the ravages of nature. Anything that produced any change at all, good or bad, was deemed effective, leading to the use of the most potent and harsh chemicals for the mildest of ailments. A simple numerical count of survival rate had convinced him of the fallacy of such thinking.

But then, often the brightest medical students were skimmed off by the clergy, the law, or letters, leaving a bizarre assortment of leftovers for the practice of medicine. There was much on the horizon, though, a thing called "theory-building." Medical societies had been organized in the east, and there was continued talk of developing medical institutions for the sole purpose of training doctors. Heroic therapy, too, had gained respectability among many. Even here at the far reaches of civilization, McReynolds sensed a new age in medicine, and it all made him wish he were much younger. As soon as his new hospital was finished, he was determined to try some of these tech niques at the first opportunity.

Lighting his pipe, he watched the awakening of the camp, the soldiers with hair tousled and suspenders hanging as they made their way to the privies. In the air was the decided feel of weather, and with it an unexplained excitement.

Setting aside his journal, he relit his pipe, pressing the palm of his hand over the bowl, coaxing it to life with long and deliberate draws. From across the compound, Sergeant Number stepped out of the door, stretching his arms above his head. With bold strides he made for McReynolds's tent. How often they'd repeated this scene over the years, Number reporting on the sick-call list, him responding with orders for the day. There was seldom mention of the terrible fire that scarred Number forever, nor discussion of McReynolds's role in saving his life, but there was a loyalty and understanding between them that went beyond words.

"Morning, sir," Number said, stepping into McReynolds's tent.

"Morning, Sergeant. How's sick call?"

"About double, sir, what with the smell of winter in the air. Guess the bunk and a hot fire's more tempting than usual. Think a little liquor slipped through on that last supply train, too, sir."

Knocking his pipe clean in the palm of his hand, McReynolds smiled.

"Suppose you could handle sick call yourself this morning, Sergeant? Thought I might go check out the new hospital building."

"Yes, sir. I'll give 'em all a dose of jalap and let 'em spend the day in the privy. Tomorrow they'll be glad enough to go back to work." As he was leaving, Number stopped and turned around, the morning sun falling across his shoulders. "I've been wondering, sir, about that new lieutenant's wife. No one's seen hide nor hair of her since he left."

"I'll stop by on my way back," McReynolds said.

"Oh, I near forgot. Sergeant Major Berman says there was a dispatch delivered from General Sully to you this morning."

"Thanks, Sergeant."

"Yes, sir," he said, smiling. "I'll catch up with you after sick call, sir." As McReynolds watched him stroll across the compound, he wondered if his feelings about Sarah had been apparent to the others. For two weeks now, he'd avoided her cabin, taking the path by the new blockhouse instead. Perhaps that in itself was transparent, but then it would be like Number to sense his feelings before anyone else.

To become involved with another man's wife violated McReynolds's sense of honor; it was not something he'd condoned, not even as a young man when his blood was hot and his judgment weak. It had not been that way with Twobirds, nor with any woman in his life.

It was ridiculous, anyway, to have such thoughts about Sarah, her being married, the difference in their ages. Still, the feelings could not be denied altogether, manifest even in his struggle to keep them at bay. But what if she *were* sick, or hurt? Wouldn't it be unethical to deny her help simply because of his own confused feelings?

The smell of fresh-cut wood filled the air as McReynolds leaned against the wall of the blockhouse. Tilting his hat to shadow the page from the bright sun, he read the dispatch.

Major Joseph McReynolds, Surgeon
Camp Supply, Indian Territory

Dear Major McReynolds:

Have received word of the cattle incident with the Cheyenne. It is through their own ignorance that their bellies will go empty as I try to make arrangements for more cattle.

Lieutenant David Roland has located a redoubt site near the Cimarron crossing at Deep Hole Creek and is camped there awaiting my orders. It is my determination that construction on that site begin as soon as possible. It is my hope that through this action, I can reduce the encroachment of cattle companies and the flow of illegal liquor.

I am having great difficulty contracting mule trains for the supply route, since the Santa Fe Trail is more lucrative and safer than the Dodge-Supply Trail through Indian Territory. All able-bodied men and mules between here and St. Louis have been pressed into service.

Because of the delay, I've advised Captain Winfield in the post quartermasters' office that he is to assume command of Camp Supply until my return. Now I must also ask you to assume the responsibility for leading a detachment to the proposed redoubt site with provisions and support troops for construction. We will need Captain Wallace's assistance, a cook, a blacksmith, and enough carpenters to make short work of the project.

Have the ordnance sergeant provide you with the necessary munitions for an adequate defense of the redoubt.

Since Lieutenant Roland will be placed in permanent command of the redoubt, separate quarters will be provided for him. His wife may join him there at her convenience, with the understanding that the facilities are isolated and primitive, and there will be almost certainly no female companionship.

The judicious use of troops is essential, as you must know, since Camp Supply must not be left vulnerable, particularly with the uncertainty of General Custer's winter campaign. It is difficult to predict what such a policy of intimidation will have on Indian depredations. The thrust of the campaign, however, has moved south into the Washita area, and it is my conclusion that there is little reason to fear hostilities as far north as the redoubt site. We therefore should make haste, taking full advantage of the opportunity to complete our defenses.

Report back to Camp Supply upon completion of the assignment and Godspeed.

General Alfred Sully

The walls of the hospital were nearly complete, and the outline of the roof was visible. Hanging by an arm, Captain Wallace leaned out to drive in a nail.

"Morning, Captain," McReynolds said.

"Morning, Doctor. Out for your constitution, are you?"

Sitting down on the porch, McReynolds took the dispatch from his pocket and waved it at Wallace. It was the sort of gesture, the sort of kidding, that was possible only because of their mutual respect.

"Better be careful how you talk to me, Captain. Seems I'm about to be your new commander, and it's been some time since those privies were moved and new holes dug."

"Commander of what?" he looked down, a nail dangling from the corner of his mouth.

"Sully wants that redoubt built, and guess who gets to go along?"

"Well, ain't that just fine and dandy," Wallace said. "Here we are sitting on the edge of Hell with nothing but Cheyenne and grasshoppers for a hundred miles, and the Army sees fit to put a sawbones in charge of getting us kilt'. What's the matter, ain't there no arms left to saw off, or bowels to poison, or asses to smooch?"

"Now, now, Captain, we both know that even in the Army, cream eventually rises to the top."

"And who's to build this here camp in the meantime? The guardhouse ain't finished; the powder monkey's house still needs a roof, and you can see what's left of this here hospital building."

Taking his handkerchief from his pocket, McReynolds dusted off the toes of his boots and watched Wallace's face turn red.

"Couldn't you tidy it up a bit around here, Captain? Seems an awful shambles to me."

"Why, yes, sir, Commander," he said, climbing down. "Next time we'll have you a stone path to walk on and maybe some flowers planted along the way, maybe an umbrella, too, so's the sun won't strike your milk-white skin."

"No, no, I wouldn't want to put you out, but a cleared path at least would be nice for the ranking officer. Well, I got to go now and see things arranged. I figure week's end ought to be enough time to get organized."

Looking down on the river that twisted below, McReynolds paused.

"Ever notice how Army engineers always build next to a river where diseases abide and floodwaters flow?"

"Well, sir," Wallace said, "that's 'cause the Army don't build forts except in the wilderness, and seeing as how there ain't no dug wells when they arrive, or no clay pipes leading to their tents, or no know-it-all doctor to give them advice, they just do the best they can with what they got, I guess."

"I guess you must be right, Captain. Glad you're coming along in any case."

"Yes, sir." Wallace smiled, snapping a halfhearted salute. "By the way," he said, pointing in the direction of the married officers' quarters, "that pretty little girl ain't been out of her cabin for a week. Maybe she's in there pining, or skunk bit, or scalped by the Cheyenne. Ain't no place for a young thing like her to be left all alone, and them laundresses won't give her the time of day, either."

"Thanks, Captain. I'll give her a check on the way back."

Looking the hospital over one last time, he headed down the path. The amount of building that had taken place in such a short time was impressive. How the Army managed to get people of Wallace's skills, drag them to the ends of the Earth, pay them a small fraction of what they were worth, and hang onto them for twenty years, never ceased to amaze him.

At the last moment, he decided to cut back toward the new mess. It was early yet, and he was not anxious to start rumors by arriving at Sarah's at such an early hour. Besides, what every good soldier knew, was that there's no greater misery on the trail than a bad cook and no greater comfort than a good one. With a little luck maybe he could land a good one.

"Morning, Cookey."

Up to his elbows in onions, Cookey smiled.

"Morning, sir," he said, wiping at his eyes with his sleeve.

"What we fixing today?" McReynolds asked, looking into the pot that steamed on the stove behind Cookey.

"Well, sir, started off as beef soup, seeing as how we had a surplus of beef. Turns out all the beef's turned bad, Cheyenne probably, so's then I decided to make pea soup, but the ordnance sergeant said he'd fire off a keg of black powder up my bum, begging your pardon, sir, if he ever smelled pea soup again so long as he lived. Far as I know, he ain't been kilt', 'less the Cheyenne took him in the night. So, that leaves bean soup; so, that's what it is, bean soup."

"Bean soup, is it?"

"Yes, sir, it is—spiced with red pepper, onions, and a dash of vinegar, mashed with a stick, and served with a slab of fatback. Of course, now all the laundresses are mad. Say they're tired of fatback and beans and men farting all over the camp like mules on green oats. Betsey Greer says her husband died from eating beans, exploded in his bed in the middle of the night. Says that if we'd feed beans to the Cheyenne instead of beef, that soon enough Cheyenne would be exploding all over the prairie like popcorn in a hot skillet, and that would be the end of depredations and scalpings."

"You believe that, Cookey?"

"No, sir, 'cause you'd still have the Kiowa, the Arapaho, whiskey ranchers, squatters, horse thieves and deserters, that ain't to mention politicians, preachers, and buffalo hunters. There just ain't enough beans or time left on Earth to explode all the misery waltzing up and down this trail. Still, I don't like making the laundresses sore 'cause then my clothes don't get washed like they ought."

"Might have to do your own laundry for a while, I guess?"

"Yes, sir," he said, smiling, "but it ain't the same as having it done for you, if you know what I mean, sir."

"Listen, Cookey, you got someone could take over for you here?"

"How's that, sir?"

"Someone who could supervise the kitchen here while you were away for a month or so?"

Laying down his knife, he rinsed off his hands, and then dried them on the apron around his waist.

"Why, yes, sir, there's any number could step up and take over. Where am I going, sir?"

"We're taking a detachment to build a redoubt at the Cimarron crossing at Deep Hole Creek. Shouldn't be over twenty-five or thirty men to cook for. Think you could have supplies in order by the end of the week?"

"Yes, sir," he said. "I about had all this indoor cooking I can stand anyway. I'll need a wagon fitted out."

"Good," McReynolds said, "and leave those peas behind, will you, Cookey? I never could tell the difference between split-pea soup and a cow pie myself."

As he was leaving the mess, Sergeant Number called him from across the compound.

"Horses run the garbage wagon under a tree, sir. Got two men down, one with his teeth stumped out and the other with his arm broke. Both are screaming like Cheyenne on the warpath and smelling like buffalo kill. Maybe you could come."

By the time McReynolds finished extracting stumps, setting bones, and cleaning off the stench of Army garbage, the sun had dropped into the western sky. Its morning warmth was now but a distant and cold light.

As he made his way to Sarah's cabin, the wind shifted to the north, a cold and icy gale that set him

to shivering. The horizon had darkened to the color
of gunpowder, orange columns streaking skyward from
behind its dark center. Soldiers scurried across the
camp to the warmth of their fires, while leaves swirled
in eddies at the edges of the path. When her cabin
came into view, his stomach tightened like a surgeon's
stitch, and he took a deep breath to relax.

As he knocked on the door, rain started to fall, first
a light mist and then crystalline drops that drummed
on his hat. Knocking again, he listened for movement
from inside. Spiders poked their heads from the cracks
and crannies of the soddy to watch him. Wallace had
been right, this was no place for her, not a home, not
fit for a stable.

"Hello," he said, but there was no response, the soft
splat of raindrops and the smell of settling dust.
"Hello," he said again, trying the door with his hand.
It gave, opening a crack, light falling across the floor.
"Mrs. Roland, it's Dr. McReynolds, are you here?" As
his eyes adjusted, he could see that someone lay under
the disheveled covers. "Sarah," he said again, louder
this time.

"Who is it?" she said, her voice weak, uncertain.

"Dr. McReynolds. May I come in? It has started to
rain."

"Oh," she said, "I'm not feeling well."

The rain deepened, and McReynolds turned up his
collar against the cold wind. The sky darkened overhead, churning like gray smoke, the distant rumble of
thunder trembling under his feet. Rain swept across
the compound, and he held his hat to keep it from
lifting into the wind.

"I'm getting very wet," he said, "and I *am* a doctor.
Perhaps we should have a look."

"Very well," she said in a soft voice.

After lighting the lamp, he looked about the room,

a cold place smelling of damp earth. A bowl of sugar sat on the table, a caravan of ants moving down its side. From the corners of the room, crickets watched the flame of his lantern with licorice eyes.

"You've no fire," he said.

"Sometimes I am cold but then again so hot," she said.

"Well, first the fire," he said.

By the time fire lapped at the edges of the fireplace, Sarah slept again. Sitting on the bed next to her, he felt her forehead. In the light he could see the redness of her lips against her pale skin.

"Sarah," he said.

"I'm not a strong person always," she said, her voice trailing.

"How long has this been going on?" he asked, pushing her hair back from her face.

"Not so long," she said.

Holding the lantern close, he checked the glands in her neck, the skin on the inside of her arms. It was not scarlatina as he had suspected. With such white skin the rash would be at once apparent.

Outside, the rain fell in torrents, small trickles racing here and there down the inside of the soddy walls.

"Have you had the sweats?" he asked.

"I think," she said, laying her hand against her cheek, "and each time is worse."

Turning her hand over, he touched her palm, his fingers lingering against her warmth. To deny her simple request for company had been wrong, and then to find her this way now.

Soon she began to shake, her body racked with chills, sapping her of energy. He covered her with blankets and fed the fire until it blazed hot against his face. When at last the chills subsided, she fell into a deep but troubled sleep. When her fever pitched again, it rose at an alarming rate. With a damp cloth he bathed her face, her neck, the beat of her heart tripping in the white softness of her throat.

Opening the door of the soddy, he watched the rain, furious sweeps whipping down the path. From across the compound the yellow lantern lights winked on and off through the cottonwoods as they bowed against the winds. Lighting his pipe, he watched as the sky fumed and boiled, growing ever darker with moisture-laden clouds. From behind, Sarah mumbled from a feverish dream.

Slipping on his coat and hat, he knocked the coal from his pipe and looked out across the river. It was probably malaria, and why not, living in this sty on the bank of a river. What he knew was that with each cycle, her body would weaken, until consumption set in. At some point her heart would simply give out. Something had to be done, and soon. Of this much he was certain: There would be no doses of calomel. That lesson he'd learned the hard way in the epidemic at Fort Gibson. Cinchona bark was now the more favored therapy, but the doses of the bitter powder were massive, resulting often in cruel and dangerous convulsions. Its effectiveness was unpredictable in any event, sometimes reducing a fever dramatically, sometimes not at all.

Stepping into the rain, he pulled his collar up and his hat down over his eyes. Not too long ago he'd received a bottle of concentrated alkaloid of cinchona bark from the Surgeon General of the 1st Division, Ohio Militia, recommending its use. But such recommendations were often based on little more than wild speculation or even superstitions. What choice was there? What did he have to lose, except the most important thing in his life?

Even the familiar path was difficult to follow in the

blinding rain, falling now with a relentless roar. Red water boiled down the sides of the path, white foam gathering at each rock or turn in direction. Through the trees, he could see the river, sliding high and powerful in its banks.

His tent was barely visible in the deluge, its top laden with water, the rain drumming against the saturated canvas. Once inside, he lit the lamp and searched for the bottle. Finding it pushed to the back of the shelf, he held it to the light of the lantern: "Quinine, for the reduction of fevers related to marshmiasm and organic decompositions."

Removing his hat, he shook off the water and then placed it back on his head. Dropping the bottle of quinine into his pocket, he blew out the lamp.

The trail back was even more precarious, the incline slick as grease, the piercing rain stinging his face as it whipped across the path. Even in the impending darkness, he could see the river, its serpentine movement, its swollen belly spilling across the lowlands beyond.

"Sarah?" he said at the door, trying not to startle her. "I'm back."

But she lay still, consumed by her fever, and did not respond. Going to the bed, he pushed back her hair and lay his hand on her forehead, her lips parting, her eyes searching, her breathing labored. Lifting her head, he cradled her in his arm, her body hotter even than the fire at his back. "I want you to take this for me," he said, touching the bottle to her lips. "It is bitter, but I think it might help with the fever. Can you do that for me?"

"I think so," she whispered. "I'll try."

Taking his hand, she drank, strangling as the astringent liquid filled her throat.

"Once more," he said, "and then you can rest."

Within moments, she slept, her hair tangled across

her shoulders. Easing himself down, so as not to awaken her, he lay at her side, the rain sweeping against the cabin door, and he dozed.

When he awakened, the rain had deepened, an impermeable roar between them and the world, and he rose to stoke the fire, a red glow now under the bed of gray ash.

Touching Sarah's cheek, he found her fever stabilized, her breathing less labored. In the dim light he retrieved his stethoscope from his bag and warmed it against the fire before hooking it about his neck.

"Sarah," he said, "I need to check your heart. I've warmed the stethoscope."

But she did not answer, her sleep sound and deep. With deliberate care he unbuttoned her cotton nightshirt, aware of the rise and fall of her breasts in the darkness. He listened through the stethoscope, the measured and determined beat of her heart filling him with hope.

The second time he awoke, the wind had grown sullen, rain falling, heavy and rushing, into the valley.

Rising, he stoked the fire, holding his hands to the flame. Above him on the mantel, her books were stacked. A porcelain doll with legs sewn from the American flag leaned against them and watched him with painted eyes. Even though the room was sparse, it was ordered and neat, clothes folded, shoes placed at the foot of her bed. Stirring, Sarah called out a name, but it was not his name, so he did not answer.

Taking down a book, he read, and dozed, and read again. When next he woke, the rain, too, had stopped, and the world was silent. The cold morning light seeped through the cracks of the door, falling across the foot of Sarah's bed. The dankness had returned with the dying of the fire, and he rose to stoke it, her book falling from his lap onto the floor.

"Who is it?" she asked, rising on an elbow.

"It's Dr. McReynolds."

"Dr. McReynolds," she said, looking up at him through the strands of hair that had fallen across her eyes. "What are you doing here?"

Going to her side, he held his hand against her forehead.

"You've been sick, Sarah," he said.

"I'm afraid I don't remember much."

"You were delusional with fever and chills. I spent the night with your books there, so I could monitor your condition."

"All I remember is wanting to sleep, like being pulled into a dark tunnel."

"Malaria," he said, holding up the bottle of quinine. "For once the Army knew what it was talking about, a specific medicine for a specific illness."

Buttoning the buttons on her nightshirt, she tilted her head, the way little girls do when they sense their own beauty.

"I hope my condition was not too unpleasant?"

"No," he said, "not at all."

"Well, I'm starved," she said, "and look the fire is dead. You've burned all my wood, and my coal oil, too, by the looks of it."

Putting on his hat, McReynolds walked to the door. Legions of thorny black crickets vaulted ahead of his boots, snapping and popping like water in hot grease. Dozens clung to his pants legs, antenna swiveling in indecision as they readied for their next leap. Pinching one by its sawtooth legs, McReynolds plucked it off. It scrubbed against his fingers with astonishing strength.

"I'll get you some wood and be on my way," he said, "and I'll have Sergeant Number drop by later today to see how you're doing."

Without looking back, he reached for the door, because to look back now would acknowledge what had been imagined, to turn thus on an irrevocable course.

First it was sound, like the hushed and powerful slide of an anaconda, the throaty gurgling of a pot before it boils, the dying bump of thunder on the distant horizon. He propped his hand on the doorjamb and stared in disbelief at the expanse of water that churned down the valley. Trees torn from the earth, sped down its center like deserted ships, their roots rising from the water like the hands of drowning giants. A crow watched him with indifference as it raced past on its perch at the top. Water lapped at the slab of cottonwood that passed for Sarah's threshold, and crickets lined its length as if to greet relatives long lost somewhere from upriver. The dark smell of mud and manure hung in the air.

The other officers' quarters were collapsed, their melted structures no more than crawdad mounds in the back-swill of muddy water. The river spilled from its banks, separating them from the compound proper. From across its expanse, he could see the soldiers waving. Taking off his hat, he returned their signal. Dropping the cricket into the water, he watched it ride away on the current.

"The world would have me stay, it seems," he said, turning to Sarah.

Light refracting from the rushing waters of the river behind him fell across her eyes, the exact hue of verdigris he'd once seen formed on an ancient and enigmatic bronze.

Twelve

Loosening the hobble, Renfro lifted Buck's knee to free his leg. Buck nibbled at his collar and blew puffs of hot air through his nostrils against his neck.

"Morning there, ole friend," Renfro said, rubbing behind his ears and under his wiry chin. "Ready for a walk?" Buck shook his head, letting it roll down his body like a wet dog and commenced to pulling sprigs of buffalo grass from between the soapy mounds of gypsum. Slipping the halter over the horse's nose, Renfro brought it up in a seamless motion over the top of Buck's ears. "Well, guess I can't blame you," he said, catching up the rope. "Let's go shake out the boy and have ourselves some breakfast."

Still asleep, Creed was curled beneath the blanket with only his hands exposed, Twobirds's hands, Renfro thought, fingers as long and wispy as spring lilacs but with a sure and useful strength. For all the love he had for this boy, those hands could never be his.

Swiping his hat back and forth, Renfro nursed the fire to life, and wood smoke filled the morning.

Last night as they'd made their last trip from the cave, they'd jumped a covey of quail, snuggled like brown petals under the shelter of a clump of grass. Blinded by the torch, they were easy pickings, and he'd uncorked their heads, tossing their dancing bodies into the grass to bleed out. Weary from the night's dig, he'd left them there for morning. With luck, maybe they'd escaped the watchful coyote.

Luck held, and he found the quail where he'd left them, their beaded eyes staring at him from the pile of silent heads. After shucking the feathers, he trimmed out the small, succulent breasts with his knife. It was a good knife, honed from a wagon spring he'd found and tempered in the fire, not as big as the bowie he'd seen bullwhackers carry, but well-balanced and keen.

Ammunition being hard to get, he'd come to rely on the trap and knife for much of his hunting. Years with the Indians had taught him a considerable amount about survival, and he was a fair hand with the bow, too, though the long and tiresome death wait was never something he'd taken to.

Laying the breasts on a piece of wood, he counted them, eight in all, a good feed on any day. The tiny drumsticks were delicious, too, but no bigger than a man's thumb and not worth the effort to clean. "For Mr. Coyote," he said, tossing the remains into the pile of bloody feathers and slipping the knife back into his boot.

By the time Creed stirred, the quail crackled in a pan of grease, and a curl of steam rose from the center of the corn pone. Cooking was not something Renfro had done a lot of but enough to get by. He cooled the pan, wiped the grease clean with his fingers, and stored it in the parfleche. While Creed languished under the cover, Renfro saddled Buck and tied the bags of silver across the back of the saddle. Opening one of the bags, he lifted a handful of the coins, letting them fall back in a slide, their weight, their pappy sound, their acidic smell on the edge of his tongue.

For the first time, he wondered how much there was. The silver had always been there, buried deep in the

earth, deep in his consciousness, too, he supposed, but
it was a question he'd never asked until this moment.
Of this he was certain: There was enough for his pur-
poses, and then some.

"Morning," Creed said, scratching at his mussed hair.
"Ready for some fried quail and corn pone?"

Nodding his head, he smiled and slipped on his shoes.

Sitting around the fire, they ate, sucking the grease
from their fingers and washing down the corn pone
with hot cups of sage tea. Overhead in the branches,
crows complained with angry voices of their wait.

Within the hour, they were on their way; Buck moving
at a steady and deliberate pace, a strong and good horse,
given to Adam on his wedding day by Twobirds's clan.
Creed rode in silence. Behind them, mist rose from the
distant canyon against the warmth of the morning sun.
Somewhere beneath them the cave twisted deep and
dark into the far reaches of the earth, and Adam knew
that he would never return to this place.

Ahead, the land rose in a gentle swell, the red clay
turning to sand where grasses of all natures grew in community—some tall and fine, some coarse with puffed
tops swinging like flags in the wind, some short and
nappy with brown curls hugging the earth and dropping
seeds so tiny they could not be seen with the naked eye.

From a distance, a wave crested in the grass, rolling
down the hill ahead of the wind, sweeping past with
an invisible touch and whisper, and with it Renfro's
spirit sped, riding the crest in its loneliness to the
death tree beyond. There was within him a profound
emptiness, a burned and blackened core, a weariness
that drew more from him than he could replenish. But
the promise had been made, and the boy would not
know his despair.

At noon they stopped, squatting like prairie dogs in
the grass, and ate the last of the quail. A jack popped

up, freezing in its tracks at so unexpected an encounter, and Creed gave chase. The jack's big ears sprung at odd angles as if broken, and its black eyes bulged like agate marbles. When Creed returned, his arms were covered with sand, and sticktights clung to his britches like empty ticks.

"If he would've run in a straight line, I would've caught him," Creed said, trying to regain his breath.

"The sentiment of many a skinny coyote," Renfro observed, smiling.

Sitting down, Creed crossed his legs and settled his chin in his hand. After some time, he spoke.

"Where do we go from here?"

The question was unbounded, and in it, all the fear and uncertainty that made up their lives.

"North to Dodge, sooner or later," Adam said, wiping the grease from his fingers on the legs of his trousers, "but first we're going to see if we can't flesh out an outfit for freighting. We're going to need mules, oxen, too, if you ain't in a hurry, wagons, and men to drive them. Winter's setting in fast," he said, pointing to the north, "and lots of them trains that are bound for Santa Fe will be shutting down and grazing out their mules to wait for weather and nerve. I figure by the time we get there, they'll be thinking of home and dreading the notion of living in a snowbank for the next few months." Taking out his knife, he stropped it against his boot as he thought and then slipped it back into the leather holster sewed to the inside of the boot pipe. "Might pick us up an outfit ready to roll. If it's already loaded with tobacco or flour or such, then we'll just take that on up to Dodge and maybe turn a profit."

Pulling his knees up against his chest, Creed picked the sticktights off his pants and let them float away in the breeze.

"I've never been in a city," he said.

"Ain't much to miss," Renfro said. "Just people squeezed up until they're noisier, smellier, and meaner than they otherwise would be."

"Why don't we go on to Santa Fe like the others?"

"Could," Renfro said, easing down on his side, propping his head on his hand, "but this is the country I know, and figure passing through now and again might be a comfort." On the hill he could see the jack where Creed had lost sight of him, sitting as still as death. "Course, then maybe you'll want to get educated and amount to something more than mule skinning. What with shorter runs, I wouldn't be gone at such a stretch, and figure you'd less likely dry up on me."

Creed didn't say, but he knew what his father meant, about coming through again. This is where she was, her spirit and sum right here in these grasses and prairie winds.

"What I want," Renfro said, without waiting for a reply, "is two hundred J. Murphy wagons, sixteen-footers, made from seasoned wood and with shoe brakes, each one. They'll carry five tons, big enough to range hogs in, and drilled with hot iron so's they don't split. I hear tell they're paying a hundred and eighty a ton for freight, and that's just one way. Seems a fair living, riding out your days under the warm sun, sleeping under the stars at night. Whatever don't suit you can be left in your dust next morning."

Turning on his back, Creed let the sun shine on his face, and he could see blood the color of sunset in his eyelids. Beyond, he could hear Buck twisting off grass close to the sand, where it was still green and squeaky, and he knew that his life was about to change forever.

By midafternoon, the day warmed, and the saddle again wore at Creed's legs. Twice they stopped to drink, the first at a clear spring that caused Creed's teeth to ache, the second in a backwash where the water was warm and red like blood and smelled of moss and rotted leaves. It was best, Adam said, to take water when it was there, because it may not be there again farther on. It was a lesson, he said, that he'd learned the hard way and never forgot. Buck drank on both occasions with equal enthusiasm.

They rode on, their shadows stretching as the sun lowered, strolling like black giants across the prairie. At the base of a hill a cottonwood rose, its waxy leaves fluttering like yellow flags, its thick bark bearing the scars of endless lightning strikes. Roots twisted into the earth, ever deep into cold, crystal waters. A small creek no bigger than a step trickled from the side of a red bank, cutting across the valley.

"Look there," Adam said, pointing to the sand that gathered at the leeward side of the meander. "Tracks." Dismounting, they took a hard look, pushing their hands into the mud to see how fast the moisture rose into the impression. "Danged if it ain't a cow track, Creed, by itself, too, like it was dropped from the sky."

"Maybe it got lost or run off from the herd," Creed said.

The tracks led straight to the cottonwood, where they circled the base. Dirt spewed out in all directions where the animal had circled the tree countless times. Hair and blood clung to the bark of the tree. In the brush beyond were cow pies and wallows, as if it had lain in wait.

"Never knew a cow to tree like a dog," Adam said, pausing, "or a dog to milk, for that matter."

Soon they spotted where the tracks broke through the brush, heading southwest. Every hundred feet or so, there was a splash of blood in the sand, black, and big as a man's hand.

Adam smelled it before he saw it, bloated to a strut, its legs poked in the air, its head thrown back.

"What is it?" Creed asked.

"A cow, I think, or a camel, 'cept I don't recall camels this far south. I ain't never seen a worse-looking critter though, dead or alive. What's that coming out of its mouth?" he asked, bending over for a closer look. "Danged if it ain't swallowed a blue snake."

"That's its tongue," Creed said, holding his nose.

"I'll be, and there's what finished her off," he said, pointing to the two arrows that protruded from her chest. One arrow had shanked to the feathers. The other had taken a more sidling course, but both, mortal wounds on the best day. "Never saw an animal make it so far with its heart shanked, and look there, eagle feathers, Cheyenne Dog Soldier's by the looks of it. I'd say that warrior was pretty nerved up to use his sacred arrows on a cow."

Two tumblebugs with balls of fresh manure worked their way from under the carcass. Sand from Adam's boot turned them onto their backs, their angular legs pumping in the air. With the toe of his boot, he flipped them right side up and knelt for a better look at the cow.

"This old doll should've been blessed with a little less tongue and a little more teat," he said, tugging on the brim of his hat, "and maybe a little less grit."

Determined to get some distance between them and the stench, they rode until dark, making camp in the open. They made do with corn pone and water, slipping under their blanket without the comfort of fire. Stars spilled into the sky, and the night grew silent and still. Both fell into uneasy sleep.

At dawn a wind woke them, a cold and moisture-laden gale that spun sand into their faces and bled away the heat from their bed. When they could stand it no more, they rose, shaking as they searched for warmer clothes from the parfleche, while tumbleweeds raced past them in retreat from the rising dawn. Draping the blanket over Creed's shoulders, Adam spiked his own hat down against the wind.

"I'll go get the horse," he said. "We'll take an early lunch when we can get out of this wind."

Buck was a quarter mile away, his head down, his rump windward. By the time he was saddled and they were on their way, the sun rose clear and cold in the east, but the wind still blew, piercing their clothes, burning their skin, flapping their collars against their ruddy cheeks. They did not speak, not against the bitterness of the day, nor the darkness of their spirits, as they rode on.

At noon Adam pointed to a grove of oak that nestled in the valley ahead. There was a stream that entered the grove from the east, and the hills to the north provided a natural protection against winter winds.

Pointing to the stand of trees, he dropped the scarf from his face to speak.

"Let's eat there," he said to Creed. "Looks like plenty of wood and water, and we'll fry us up some corn mush and make hot tea."

Sunlight, mottled as if strained through a sieve, danced through the limbs. The soil was black and rich, and mushrooms sprouted like white fingers through the rotted leaves. Here, the winds vanished, quiet as a cathedral, with only the sound of fallen leaves under Buck's hooves.

"A good place for a winter camp," Adam said, more to himself than to Creed.

Overhead, a breeze swept through the trees, leaves dipping from the tops in surrender to the inevitability of winter, whispering, falling like snowflakes on a still dawn.

"It's so quiet," Creed said.

"We'll walk from here," Adam said. "It's a bad feeling I have."

Neither spoke as he moved into the heart of the grove, nor cried out at the horror, nor fell to his knees in disbelief, nor wept at the carnage scattered among the trees, its evil too dark, too desperate, too shattering even to acknowledge.

Bloated and distorted bodies lay scattered among the leaves. A black crow watched them from the corner of its eye as it picked at the bloodied ear of a corpse. The air was heavy with smell, a liquid, sodden smell that clung in the nose, a smell that permeated the clothes, the memory. The slumped body of a warrior leaned against a tent, his spilled bowels buzzing with flies. It was as if the camp had frozen in time, as if on another day they would've risen to go about their work, children laughing, the smell of meat cooking, women chatting among themselves, but on this day their lives were stilled.

Paralyzed by the spectacle of death before him, Creed stood at the body of a young boy. It was too soon, too close upon the heels of his mother's death.

"It's a terrible thing we do to each other, boy. There's no explaining it away or forgiving it, but we have to go on. We always have to go on."

On the far side, they came upon a squaw lying in the ashes of her fire, her dead child in her arms. Kneeling, Adam pushed away the leaves and looked into her face. She had been a beautiful woman once, an important one, too, by the looks of it.

"See the red stripes in her hair, Creed? Her husband counted many coup. See there," he said, pointing to the missing strips of skin on her arms. "She has wounds from sacrifice, and the child, just a babe, and its life snuffed out even before it began."

"Look," Creed said, regaining his composure, "an arrow, eagle feather like those in the cow."

"Guess we found who took on ole teatless back there. You're going to make a fine tracker someday, boy. You got the eye for detail." Walking the perimeter, Adam studied the scene. "Looks like that child was laid in its mother's arms by someone else, and see there where the grass is dragged down and that blood there. Maybe someone survived this disgrace, but he's bad hurt if he did, and as alone as a man could be." Dropping to one knee, he picked up a small stick and scratched at the bloodstained ground. Bits of flesh and bone sifted out from the sand. "Teeth." He shook his head. "Looks like he took a ball in the face, and hard, too. And those horses that rode in are shod. That probably means white men, or stole horses, maybe. With all this blood I'd say someone had the misfortune of stepping too close, too soon."

"Where do you suppose he is now?" Creed asked.

"Don't know," Adam said, "but it would take a mighty strong man to walk from this, or an angry one. In any case, I'd hate to be the one who crossed him today."

Turning his back, Creed paused before going after Buck.

"Let's go," he said when he returned. "I'm no longer hungry."

Even as night fell, they rode on, talking little as Buck plodded across the prairie in a tireless gait. Soon the moon rose like a sterling coin, its light casting the prairie in a silver glow. Down a distant canyon, frenzied coyotes ran a trail.

As the distance widened, the reality of their discovery softened, the vivid and cutting images still there, but fleeting, transitory, coming and going like a bad dream. Both sighed inwardly. Both knew now that with time, the memory would fade, no less than the carnage behind them faded. Soon enough, time would do what words nor understanding could never do, remove it from reach.

"I'm hungry," Creed said.

With the moon high overhead, they made camp, building a fire from buffalo chips and sage root. Supper was fried corn pone and a few leftover pieces of jerk meat. Soon they would have to replenish their supplies. Digging through the parfleche, Adam found honey that Twobirds had stored for emergencies, drizzling it over the corn pone, eating it down. Neither had realized the extent of his hunger or his fatigue.

While Creed finished eating, Adam led Buck into an open area where grass was available and hobbled him. Hanging his arms over his back, he looked at the moon and pondered the day's events. What he hadn't told Creed was that those tracks back there were made by Army horses, a small detachment by the looks of it and none too skilled at warfare. He hadn't told him because he was ashamed, ashamed at what they had done, and how they had done it.

As he made his way back, he could see the wink of the fire and smell its smoke in the wind. There was a deep and gnawing fear in him, a fear of what Creed would face out there in the world. It was a day he'd hoped would never come, but it had come. Now they must learn to live it.

By the time he returned, he found the fire was spent.

"Creed," he said, looking about. "Stoke the fire, boy, or we'll be in the dark." But there was no answer, the fire gurgling low in the darkening ashes. "Creed," he said again, a chill racing down his back at the silence.

When he saw the man standing in the shadows, his first impulse was to charge, but the cocked carbine lying across the man's arms caused Renfro's hands to drop in resignation.

Thirteen

By noon the river had edged higher, water seeping from under the door of the soddy, McReynolds watching it with controlled alarm.

"Here," he said, pouring another dose of the quinine.

"Not another," Sarah moaned, pushing her hair back from her face. "I'm fine, I tell you, but if you keep feeding me that terrible stuff, I won't be."

"The rain is slowing, don't you think?" he asked.

Turning her head, she listened.

"Maybe. I don't know."

"I think it's lessening," he said, "the slightest bit. You should rest now."

"But I'm not tired."

"I know, but we don't want it to come back on you. Plenty of rest is essential."

"Look, Dr. McReynolds," she said, putting her legs over the edge of the bed. "I'm feeling much better, and I don't need to sleep. Let me fix something to eat."

"No," he said, screwing the lid back onto the bottle of quinine. "It's too soon. I'll fix something to eat."

Bumping her forehead with the heel of her hand, she looked up at him through her hair.

"Fine, then. You fix something to eat."

Shrugging, McReynolds smiled.

"Sorry, I don't coddle my patients as a rule. It's just that I had a bad experience with an epidemic when I was a young doctor."

Folding her hands in her lap, she leaned forward and looked up at him with jade eyes, the weight of her breasts filling her gown, spilling forward like wind-swept snowdrifts.

"I thought maybe I was a special patient," she said. Before he could answer, she slipped on her shoes and her robe. "You rest. I cook. That's the way it's going to be. You've been up for hours taking care of me."

Seeing that she was determined, McReynolds propped his feet up, hands behind his head, and allowed himself to relax. Waves of fatigue swept over him as he watched her stir about, reaching for goods on the top shelf, the exquisite line of her back, the delicacy of her ankle, the fall of her honey-colored hair. Once, she turned and smiled, and then turned again to her work, humming as women are want to do. The irresistible call of sleep beckoned.

"You'll watch the river?" he asked.

She didn't answer, nodding her head instead, as she dusted the flour from her hands.

Sleep approached with impudence but entered with stealth, and when McReynolds next opened his eyes, evening light the color of molten iron seeped from under the door. Disoriented, he rubbed at his face and stretched his arms above his head.

"The rain has stopped," she said.

"How long have I slept?"

"Hours." She smiled from the chair next to the fire. "And these crickets and I have nothing left to say to each other."

"The food," he said, sitting up straight, "now I've ruined your dinner."

"Quite," she smiled, "but it's only soda biscuits and plum jelly, a little sugar-cured ham. I can reheat it. How about black coffee to top it off?"

"I'd like that fine," he said.

While Sarah warmed the food, he opened the door to check the river. The sun was down now, its color still sprinkled among the clouds like paint on canvas. The river rushed through the valley, a shimmering line of quick silver in the fading light. The air was cold and dry, and the soldiers' lights reflected from across the water. Kneeling, he checked the waterline at the door. It had receded a couple of inches.

"Looks like it's over," he said, taking his place at the table.

"Yes," she said.

Eating in silence, he tried not to rush his food, but he'd forgotten how delectable it was when prepared in small quantities, seasoned by a woman's hand, served in the sanctity of her home. Afterward, they drank their coffee and listened to the crickets welcome the night. Firelight flickered in the green of her eyes.

"You're certain to take a little ribbing about this when the river drops," she said.

"Let them," he answered with a smile, sipping at his coffee. "They would give their stripes to be where I am right now."

"It's good you came," she said. "I think I needed to be rescued."

Setting down his cup, he looked at her, and then at his cup.

"I received a dispatch from General Sully. He's decided to build the redoubt at the Cimarron crossing at Deep Hole Creek and has put me in charge of a detachment to assist with construction."

"I see," she said, brushing at her lap.

"Your husband will be assigned as commander of the redoubt."

"David?"

Reaching for his cup, he swirled the contents before answering.

"Yes, and the General's indicated there will be quarters built in the event you care to go, but he's cautioned about the lack of female companionship. It would be a lonely place, you see."

Falling silent, Sarah studied her hands.

"Loneliness isn't a place," she said.

There was something in her voice, her eyes. He'd seen it at the General's dinner, a wound too deep to heal.

"Sarah," he said, "what is it?"

Tears filled her eyes, deepening their green to olive, and raced down her cheeks. Brushing them away, she turned her head so that he wouldn't see.

"I guess I'm a little fragile still, you know, from the fever."

"It's you and David, isn't it?" he asked. "I don't mean to pry, but I thought at the General's dinner that something might be wrong."

Picking up the cups to wash them, she turned her back. Some time passed before she spoke.

"I'd had this dream, you know, that someday this wonderful man would find me, fall in love, and from that moment on, my life would be ordered and perfect." Turning, she looked at him. "I know how silly that must sound, but that was my dream."

"We all start with perfect dreams," he said, "but life has a way of rounding away the corners until all that's left is a tiny core of hope. When that's gone, then there's only the looking back, I suppose."

Walking over, she sat down, her hands on the table in front of her, symmetrical and delicate hands, white,

like the white of bone china, and she clasped them
together as if to hold in her pain.

"David was to be that man," she said. "In my mind,
he *was* that man, and when he did not measure up, I
was crushed. It was not all his fault," she added, looking up at him, "because no man could have lived up
to that dream."

"Living up to perfection is a difficult task. There
was a time I thought I could do it, but I couldn't."

"You were married, then?"

"Yes," he said. An old pain rose in his throat. "She
died on the operating table with hemorrhaged appen-
dix not long after we were married."

"How terrible," she said.

"Under my hand," he said. "My first lesson in im-
perfection."

Dropping her fingers into his, she said, "I'm sure
you did everything that could be done."

"It took me many long years to forgive myself," he
said, taking a deep breath. "One must forgive oneself
for being human. But then we're not talking about
me, are we?"

"David," she continued, "was determined to follow
in his father's footsteps as a military man. So I went
along wherever it took us," she paused, "even here.
David sensed my disappointment, of course, and I
sometimes think that's when it began. With each passing day, he grew more distant, aloof, staying away long
hours at a time. At first I thought there was another
woman, but then I realized it was more, something
deep and forbidding. I was," she paused, "*am* frightened by it, because I don't know what it is. You can't
fight what you can't see."

Beyond the cabin, frogs awoke and acclaimed the
flood with swelling voices.

"Go on," he said.

"Sometimes he would go days without sleep, darkening the whole time, charged, wounding anyone who dare step in his way. Still, it was never dull. Even his superiors were in awe of his unbounded energy. At those times nothing could stop him from what he wanted," she said, dropping her eyes, "nothing at all. I was at once drawn to his energy and frightened by it. At its worst, he hardly knew I was there, like a cyclone from a black sky, a whirling and uncontrolled storm. There was a coldness in him at those times, an evil, I think."

"Ambition," he said, "can be as ugly as greed."

Pulling her wrap about her shoulders, she shivered. "It's getting colder, I think."

"Here," he said, "I'll stoke the fire."

"We've used all the wood. There's some stacked at the side of the cabin, if it's not under water."

Lighting the lantern, he opened the door. The waterline had receded, now several yards from the cabin door.

"It's going down," he said.

"Be careful," she said.

Within moments he was back, his arms stacked high with wet wood. Unloading his arms, she brushed the dirt from his chest with her hand.

Soon the wood dried atop the hot coals, a yellow flame bursting through the column of gray smoke, and the room warmed.

Back at the table, she slipped the robe from her shoulders, lifting her hair with her fingers.

"It was not ambition," she said, picking up where she'd stopped, "but obsession. David would suddenly withdraw, not talking, not sleeping, not eating. For hours he would sit and stare. When he did sleep, he slept for days on end. No discussion was permitted, no reasoning nor talking allowed. It was maddening, more difficult than I can express."

In the lamplight, her eyes glistened, flecks of opal flung into liquid pools of green. The smell of smoke from the fire filled the room like a fragrant spice.

"But at the dinner, he was so confident, so sure," he said.

"I thought his assignment here might be the answer," she said. "It was his chance to soar, as he put it, but it's always that way at the beginning."

"It must be hard for you, so far away from everyone."

Sitting up straight, she gripped the edge of the table.

"You mustn't be too sympathetic, Doctor, or I'll shatter right here before you."

Rising, he lifted her into his arms, to protect her, to comfort her, to come between her and the pain. Arms about his neck, she fell into him, warm, liquid, vulnerable.

"Things will work out, Sarah," he said. "You'll see."

But she did not answer—her searching mouth, her searing kisses, her flowing tears. The ice within him moved, a jolt, like the beginnings of an earthquake and then the shearing away as it slid and spewed into the molten core. No ice, no man nor god could endure the arc and flare of the sun, nor the blue heat of his passion, the touch of her, the taste of her, the smell of her, like freshly turned earth in the spring.

"Oh, my God!" she cried, her hands against his chest.

But there's no stopping the shear, not once started, the crushing weight, the eons, the inexorable slide into the sea's warm belly.

"Wait, oh, my God!" she cried again, squirming in his arms.

"But Sarah," he choked, numbed with passion. In hysterics, she tore from his grip and clawed at her front, panic in her eyes. "What?" he yelled, the hair prickling on his neck.

"Oh, my God!" she squealed, thrusting her hand into her gown. "A cricket's down my front." Bouncing on one foot, she squealed as she fished it out, its gleaming black eyes, its gnawing mandibles, its twisting antennae like some monster from the deep.

Flinging it into the dark recesses of the room, she collapsed in her chair, her green eyes flashing, her pearl-colored hand covering her mouth. The absurdity of the moment convulsed them in laughter until they gasped for breath. When at last they fell silent, exhausted and content, they knew that something strong and noble within them had been spared.

Even as a cold moon arced over the prairie and dropped below the horizon, they talked, as old friends talk, with truth, and wonder, and vulnerability.

Nothing was said of the indiscretion, of the embrace, of the moment shared. Not then.

Fourteen

Even with the bandage pulled tight around Lieutenant Roland's leg, the blood gathered beneath Sergeant Wilson's hand. The lieutenant moaned, rolling his head from side to side, clenching his teeth against the pain. The knife had entered the large muscle of his leg, glancing off the femur in a wicked downward slash. Now a fire coursed up his groin with each beat of his heart and set white searing lights to flashing behind his eyes. Getting wounded had not been in his plans, had not even occurred to him.

"Half that Cheyenne's face was blown off," he moaned. "I thought the son of a bitch was dead."

"Not dead enough." Sergeant Wilson shook his head, tugging on the bandage. "It's still bleeding, sir," he said, wiping his hands against his chest, "no matter what. You're bone-white and cold as death."

"Oh, Jesus," Roland groaned, "I'm dying."

"Yes, sir," the sergeant said, looking up at the men who stood over them. "That's a possibility."

Roland's eyes widened.

"Well, do something!"

Sitting back on his haunches, the sergeant relaxed his grip on the bandage. Blood oozed from under his fingers and dripped into the sand.

"I'm just a sergeant, sir, and got no notion in the

least about medicine. I never saved a wounded man in my life, and I've tried many. You men got a notion?" he asked, looking about.

The men lifted their shoulders and shifted their feet like chickens scratching in the dirt.

"Saw Dr. McReynolds sew a man up once," Lance Corporal Inman finally said, "like a sack of flour, but he died anyway."

A hot pain shot up Roland's leg, taking away his breath. The plan had been so simple: attack the small band of Cheyenne in their winter camp while they slept, destroy them to the last soul, and take the glory right out from under Sully's nose. From the start it was obvious that Sully had no stomach for battle. A man didn't make it to the top in the Army hauling supplies or sitting on his ass in some remote redoubt, and it was not something Roland intended to do. Of this he was certain: What counted in the military was audacity and fearless contention, and that was his plan. But he hadn't counted on the wound, the pain, the lack of a bloody doctor. Now he was at the mercy of these malcontents.

Twisting up the bandage again, Sergeant Wilson looked out across the prairie in thought.

"Know how to sew on a button, I guess. Been doing it myself for near twenty-five years now. Course, it's up to you, sir, if you want me give it a go."

Roland looked into the sergeant's huge face and then at the bloody bandage wrapped about his hand.

"And the pain?"

"Sir?"

"I want some laudanum, you fool, something. You don't think I intend to let you sew me up without something."

"I don't have none of that you say. Any you men got any of that he says?"

Shrugging their shoulders, the men looked at each other.

"They don't issue that to enlisted," Inman said.

"Whiskey, then," Roland said, "a little whiskey to take off the edge."

"No, sir," Sergeant Wilson said. "Whiskey's against regulations, and I'd have these men's hides tacked if they was carrying whiskey."

"You can't sew me up without something," Roland said, clutching at his leg.

"No, sir," Wilson said, "but it ain't likely to stop bleeding 'less it's sewed up."

A north wind swept through camp, ashes gathering on the blood-soaked bandage and in the corners of Roland's eyes. Squinting against the sun, he cursed under his breath.

"I don't see as I have a choice, do I, but I want that needle seared in the fire first and a bridle rein for biting on." Looking up, he held his hands over his eyes. "What the hell kind of men wouldn't have whiskey?" he said through gritted teeth.

Shamefaced, the men looked at their feet before shuffling off to find needle, thread, and bridle rein.

A fire was built and the needle seared black before Sergeant Wilson squatted to perform his task.

"Here's that rein, sir. It's got a bridle on the end of it but should serve the purpose."

Gathering about to observe the operation, the men hooked their thumbs in their belts with importance. The wind had tuned sharper, causing them to hunker their shoulders like buffalo in a snowstorm.

Shivering, Roland cast his head from side to side in pain.

"Well, get on with it," he moaned, "before I freeze to death."

"Yes, sir," Sergeant Wilson said, pushing back his

hat and picking up the needle. Wetting his thumb and finger, he guided the black thread through the eye of the needle. "Well, here goes," he said.

With the first stick, Roland yelped with surprise, causing Sergeant Wilson to drop the needle in the dirt.

"What?" Roland said from behind the leather rein.

"Nothing, sir," the sergeant said, fishing the needle out of the dirt. "Here we go."

At first Roland's face turned crimson, his breathing labored, huffing through his nose like a rutting bull, and then he commenced to howl, the leather rein dropping onto his chest, the blowing sand sticking to the roof of his mouth, gathering in the wetness of his nostrils. By the time Sergeant Wilson tied the first knot, the lieutenant's scream was at such a crescendo that the men looked at each other with sheepish grins on their faces and kicked at the dirt with the toes of their boots.

"Goddamn it, hold him down," Wilson said, "before he kicks my head off."

With reluctance they placed their knees against Roland's wrists, held tight his feet while Sergeant Wilson stitched. Blood poured from the open wound, gathering black in the callused fissures of the sergeant's hands, and there was a red smear across his forehead where he'd wiped away the sweat. The smell of blood and body heat rose into their faces. Circles of white spread about Roland's eyes and his mouth before at last he fell silent.

"He dead?" Inman asked.

"No, he ain't," the sergeant said, "though when Sully finds out we kilt' the whole of a Cheyenne village, he'll wished he was. Turn him on his side so I can finish up here. I'm freezing my hands off in this bastard's blood."

"I ain't never shot women and children before," Inman said, "some right in their mother's arms. Seems a hard thing, even for Cheyenne."

"Well, you have now," Wilson said, "and you will burn in Hell for it, won't you? Get that saddle blanket and throw it over this son of a bitch. I don't want no one saying I let an officer freeze to death."

When finished, they built the fire higher and dragged up limbs from a dead elm to sit on. Under the saddle blanket, Roland lay in a pool of blood, scumming dark from the wind and the heat of his body.

Inman poured water from a canteen over Sergeant Wilson's hands and watched as he worked at his nails with his knife.

"What we going to do now?" he asked.

"I don't know, do I?" Sergeant Wilson said, snapping closed his knife and slipping it into his pocket. "Depends on whether he lives or dies, I suppose. Either way, they're likely to hang us all for stirring up depredations." Squatting before the fire, he warmed his hands. "You men got whiskey?"

The soldiers exchanged glances. After a time, Inman walked over to his saddlebag and untied the flap.

"I'll be," he said, "a quart poking right out of this here saddlebag."

"Ain't that a sight," Wilson said, "and there all the time. Guess if we'd known that, the lieutenant's sewing job wouldn't have been such an ordeal on us all."

As the bottle was passed among them, the men warmed the bottoms of their feet against the fire and talked. Roland lay still under the saddle blanket, his bleeding stopped, encrusted now from the blowing dirt and ashes that swirled about camp. The bottle was passed a second time, the men laughing among themselves, sharing a plug of tobacco all around.

"It's a fine-looking woman he's left behind," Inman

said. "Can't figure trading that for shooting Cheyenne, 'less she won't stand. Couldn't blame her for that, could you?"

Turning on his side, Wilson propped his head on his hand, looking into the fire.

"Sully's going to scream all the way from Dodge when he finds out about them kilt' Cheyenne. Course, we was just following orders and had no choice in the matter. But, who's to say Sully will see it that way? I'm not big on losing my stripes 'cause some green lieutenant thinks he can jump harness." Sitting up, he dusted the sand from his elbow and spit into the fire. "Course, if the lieutenant don't make it, God forbid, we'd sure enough be in for trouble, unless we'd agreed not to bring it up, so to speak. Who's to say but what it wasn't just another Indian raid? Ain't they forever killing each other so's they can hook another scalp on their lance? Who's to say, if we don't?" The men looked at each other and nodded their heads. After a few moments, he turned to Inman. "Any more whiskey?"

"Might be a case of bourbon left we confiscated from that ox train couple days back."

Wilson looked at him.

"I thought I told you to destroy that."

"And I'm certain that's just what I did. Course, I didn't take a double look 'cause of the blustery weather."

"Well, suppose you take a double look now."

"Yes, sir," he said, lumbering away. Within moments, Inman returned, toting a wooden box with an American eagle painted on its top. "Blow me down," he said, "there it was tucked away in the mess gear out of sight. Guess a double look was in order."

"Guess so," Wilson said, scratching at the whiskers that grew white from his chin. "Don't make sense to destroy it now, what with the weather turning and the lieutenant down. Suppose he'd wake up and want to take the edge off or need a stitch tightened or screw-worms dug out, and there we'd be with no relief."

They all nodded their heads in agreement again and spit tobacco juice into the sand between their legs.

Two more bottles were opened and passed around. The men laughed and slapped each other on the back. It was a turbulent laughter, fed by alcohol, intensified by guilt, confirmed by the darkness of their deeds. By afternoon the whiskey was nearly gone. Undaunted, they sang a raucous chorus of "Whiskey in the Rye" and then cheered Private Tanner on as he upchucked his share of the bourbon into a dead thistle on the edge of camp.

"I'm hungry," Sergeant Wilson said, "and not for hardtack and jerk. I want a deer steak the size of a mule's ass, and I know just where one is. We passed 'em coming in, not five miles back. Come on, Inman, get your carbine. We're going hunting."

"Aw, Sergeant," Inman sighed, "there's two more bottles of hooch, and the day's young."

"Get up, soldier, or you'll wear those stripes where you least expect, and take care not to step on the lieutenant there." Kneeling down, Wilson looked at Roland and shook his head. "That Cheyenne cut a mean knife. Been a foot closer, the lieutenant here wouldn't need no wife."

Opening his eyes, Roland tried to focus.

"Now never you mind, sir," Wilson said. "The bleeding's stopped. We're headed out to get you some fresh meat, to build you back up. Everything's under control. Yes, sir. No need to worry, 'cause everything's under control."

As they rode out of camp, the sun moved from behind a cloud, its brief light falling warm on their backs before slipping away once again. A cold and determined wind blew in their faces, and their eyes watered in protest.

Within an hour, they approached the oblong clearing where Sergeant Wilson had seen the deer grazing the day before. Already the sun's light faded, a gray shadow stretching across the valley. To the east a grove of cottonwood twisted from the banks of a dry gulch, their branches filled with a thousand blackbirds. Dismounting, Wilson and Inman led their horses to the rise where they could get a full view.

"There," Wilson said, "just to the right of that skunk brush. Looks like a buck and a couple of doe."

"Yup," Inman said, "big and fat, too."

Half-bent, Wilson worked his way back to his horse, unholstering his carbine. Wetting his thumb, he put a shine on the site, lowering himself onto the ground. With a deep breath, he brought the barrel down, leveling it to the right of the buck's front leg. Lifting his head, the buck dipped his rack, big as a field cot it was, his coat the color of saddle leather, and then he fell still, except for the random twitch of his ears.

Just as Wilson squeezed his trigger finger into the palm of his hand, all three deer bolted into the grove of cottonwood, the blackbirds rising into the air like a cloud of smoke.

"What the hell," he said, throwing his hat onto the ground.

"Look there," Inman said, pointing to a lone rider loping across the opening.

The rider headed straight to them. As he started up the rise, they could see the gold of his chevrons and the blue of his uniform.

"It's a Cavalry sergeant," Wilson said, "come from somewhere. You let me do the talking."

Dismounting, the sergeant tipped his hat and dropped his reins so that his horse could graze.

"You boys are hard to catch up with," he said.

"What brings you to ride alone in these parts?" Wilson asked.

Lifting the canteen off his saddle, the sergeant tipped it up until water dripped off the end of his chin, hooking it back over his saddle horn.

"I'm Sergeant Westhoff," he said, "courier for General Sully out of Dodge. Been trying to locate a Lieutenant David Roland who's got a detachment in these parts. I'd guess that must be you boys."

"Looks like you found us, Sergeant. What brings you all the way from Dodge?"

Reaching into his saddlebag, Westhoff retrieved a paper and handed it to Wilson.

"General Sully wants that redoubt built at the Cimarron crossing at Deep Hole Creek. There's another detachment on its way out of Camp Supply with men and munitions. It says there in that paper that he wants it built without delay while things are peaceful."

"I see," Wilson said. "Well, we were just about to shoot ourselves some supper before you scared 'em off."

"Sorry, Sergeant. Didn't see them before it was too late."

"Couldn't be helped. Don't you worry. I'll see the lieutenant gets this soon as we get back."

Tipping his hat, Westhoff mounted his horse, pulling him around.

"Just one problem, Sergeant," he said.

"What could that be?" Wilson asked.

"Came upon a massacre a ways back. Whole village of Cheyenne kilt' right in their beds, women and children, too, as sickening a thing as I've seen. Cheyenne don't let something like that go, do they? The General ain't going to be happy, I can tell you."

Lifting his carbine, Wilson laid it in the cradle of his arm, and looked back in the direction where Westhoff had pointed.

"You know how them Cheyenne are," he said, "killing each other, stealing horses, counting coup. Ain't no end to it, that's sure."

Shifting his position, Sergeant Westhoff leaned forward on his saddle horn.

"Just one problem," he said. "Them tracks was shod, Army shoes, too. That would be you boys, wouldn't it, and I can tell you heads will roll." Sitting up straight, he looked Wilson in the eyes. "In fact, I hope you sons of bitches hang from the fort gate for it."

There was a still and cold moment as the two men's eyes locked. Without warning, Wilson lifted his carbine, firing with a deafening roar into Westhoffs face, the ball catching his upturned chin, pitching him backward from his horse. From the purple hole under his chin, blood dripped into the dirt.

Hopping on one foot and then the other, Inman circled the body of Westhoff like a black crow.

"You kilt' him dead," he cried. "You kilt' him dead. They'll hang us sure now."

Pumping the empty cartridge jacket out, Wilson dropped the carbine back into the saddle holster.

"Ain't no one taking my stripes," he said.

"They'll hang us sure," Inman wailed, "just like Westhoff said, right off the fort gate."

"Shut your mewling," Wilson said, slipping his pocketknife from his pocket and tossing it to him, "and take his scalp."

Stunned, Inman's chin dropped.

"I can't take a white man's scalp," he said. "It ain't right."

"Ain't right for a man to spend his life earning rank just to have it snatched away 'cause some lieutenant wants a little glory, is it? Now take his scalp, and dust out those tracks. Ain't no one to ever know but what the Cheyenne took him, riding across the country by hisself like that."

With trembling hand, Inman sawed at a patch of Westhoff s scalp.

"Ain't got much hair," he said, lifting the scalp lock with the tips of his fingers.

"Not the point, is it?" Wilson said. "It's the taking that matters. Now go bury it and be smart about it. We been gone long enough."

As they rode back to camp, the evening sun dropped cold in the west. A gray fog rolled down the valley, interring them in its silence, complete except for the clop of their horses' hooves, and the hot beat of their own hearts. Within the hour a rain commenced, and they soon shivered under its chill.

"I been thinking," Inman said, water drizzling from the brim of his hat, "about them Cheyenne."

Pulling up rein, Wilson wiped the water from his face.

"Thinking don't change nothing, does it?" he said.

"I been thinking about them tracks left behind," Inman said. "What's to keep someone else from seeing?"

Pushing back his hat, Wilson let the rain fall on his face, silver rivulets racing down his cheeks into his gray beard.

"This here rain, Inman, washing away our tracks and our transgressions. It's time you let it go, boy. We did what we had to do, that's all."

By the time they reached camp, the men had sobered, huddling forlornly about the fire. Lieutenant Roland groaned from under his blanket.

"Where's the deer?" Corporal Wheeler asked.

"Bad luck," Wilson said, shrugging his shoulders. "How's the lieutenant?"

"Drunk as a lord," he said. "Private Tanner gave him our last bottle of hooch, and he drank the lot."

Even a hot fire failed to raise their spirits or warm their bodies as the rain worsened, the night falling black, evil lurking at the edge of the firelight, the vast and forbidding prairie at their backs.

"It's like this," Wilson said, twisting his mouth to one side as he thought, "someone's going to pay for them Cheyenne back there. If the lieutenant lives, then he can step forward; if he dies, then that leaves only us to blame."

"But we was following orders," Tanner said, checking the faces of the other men. "They wouldn't hold us responsible, would they?"

"Don't make no difference far as they're concerned," Wilson said, turning his face into the light of the fire. "We done it, and so it is. Now, if the lieutenant don't make it through the night, then we'll just say it must have been a war party, taking coup and stealing horses. Who's to say otherwise?"

Taking off his hat, he looked at each man in turn. Above his hat line, his head glowed white in the light of the fire.

"But what will we say happened to the lieutenant?" Tanner asked.

Putting his hat back on, Wilson bore down, his eyes fiery.

"Horse bolted, drug him off under a cottonwood limb. Must of broke his back cause he never uttered a sound or opened his eyes. The important part is we stick together. No need we take the blame for another man's ignorance. Course, if the lieutenant makes it through the night, then it's him can do the explaining. Agreed?"

Nodding their heads, the men moved into the darkness, to their wet and cold beds, to their own unsettling dreams.

When all was silent, save the nuzzle of rain in the darkening ashes of the campfire, Sergeant Wilson stood next to Lieutenant Roland, who snored now in a drunken stupor, his bloody bandage soaked from the rain. Hooking the toe of his boot under Roland's blanket, he sent it spiraling into the blackness.

When the cold dawn arrived, the world was covered with ice, each limb, each saddle, each blade of grass.

Gathering about, the men talked in hushed tones, shaking their heads, looking into the frozen face of Lieutenant David Roland.

Fifteen

The wagon was home to Nurse Cromley, and she liked it, liked the privacy it afforded, the quiet of the night, the stars like jewels scattered across the sky. What few belongings she had, fit into the wooden box at the back, with room to spare, and her bed was warm against the cold night. Even though the monks were willing to share their quarters, she knew her presence would make them uncomfortable. In any case, she preferred to be alone. As a white woman among the Indians, she'd spent most of her time alone, came to prefer its pleasures, to understand the allure of solitude, perhaps even more than her monkish friends realized.

Dawn rose cold, and she shivered as she dressed. Meals were still cooked on the campfire, the monks' quarters little more than a half-built soddy with no chimney nor door. Food was scarce, too, the cold weather having decimated all but a few of the fall vegetables they'd managed to plant. There was still cornmeal for mush, flour, sugar, and the occasional rabbit or quail. Brother Jacob was a fair shot, spending much of his day hunting, while Brother Alexander was forever hopeless, closing his eyes, pulling his shot, cringing at the last moment. Dejected, he resigned himself to the quarry and to the keeping of the garden.

Help from the monastery was meager, a single load of woolen blankets, and a case of sacramental wine brought in by hired wagon. Since then, there had been no word, no supplies at all.

"Good morning, sister," Brother Jacob said, rubbing at the stubble on his chin.

"Good morning."

"I'll get some wood," he said.

"No, no. It's done. Here, have some sage tea. I wish it were coffee but then . . ."

"Oh, I like it," he said, sipping at the cup. "I think I prefer it actually."

"No one prefers sage tea over coffee, Brother Jacob, not even the saintly."

Smiling, he dropped his eyes and let the steam warm his face.

"Thought I'd hunt rabbits this morning. They come out at daybreak and graze on Brother Alexander's garden."

Nodding her head, she poured herself a cup, taking her place on the camp chair. Sitting was difficult with the splint, her leg awkward and stiff as a log, her toes blue from the cold. Even though there was no pain, the leg had not healed, and on the best day would not sustain her weight. But it was the lack of pain that worried her the most.

"I should be wild with the itch by now," she said.

"Perhaps it is time we removed the splint."

"Not a chance," she said, tossing the remains of her tea into the fire. "What if it isn't set? No horse doctor is getting hold of me again, not in this life."

From across the way, Brother Alexander exited from the soddy, his hair tousled, his robe wrinkled and dirty, his beard peppered with gray. The prairie had taken its toll on him. There was so much he feared, the distances, the brutal weather, the formless days that emp-

tied his mind and his soul. But it was food, or the lack
of it, that troubled him most, shriveling his corpulent
figure until his robe hung over his frame like a camp
tent. From the time he awoke until he fell exhausted
into his bed at night, he thought of food. Even in his
sleep, he dreamed of food, ravenous, voracious dreams
awakening him in a cold sweat. Prayers offered little
relief. The moment his mind fell quiet, visions of food
flooded in, his stomach growling like a caged animal.

"Good morning," Nurse Cromley said.

"Morning," Brother Alexander said, perching on
the locust log that had been hauled in for a bench.

"We're having fried mush this morning," Nurse
Cromley said, "and I've melted some sugar for syrup.
It will be sweet and filling."

Shrugging his shoulders, Brother Alexander looked
at the ground, his bowels frozen with fried mush. Just
the thought caused his stomach to churn.

"Perhaps I should cultivate the garden today," he
said, sticking his hands up his sleeves to warm them.

"Perhaps," Nurse Cromley said, dropping the slabs
of corn mush into the hot pan, "but there is so little
left to cultivate. Only the turnips thrive in this cold
weather, and no amount of cultivation is going to
change that."

"Maybe the monastery will send us food," he said,
"maybe a sugar-cured ham, brown eggs, potatoes to
boil."

Serving up the slabs of mush and pouring the clear
syrup over them, she handed him his plate.

"It's sacramental wine they've sent and enough blankets for the Cavalry."

"Food for the soul," Brother Jacob said, cutting his
mush with his fork. "Our Lord spent forty days and
forty nights without sustenance. Surely, we can manage
on corn mush and syrup."

Holding the mush up on the end of his fork, Brother Alexander turned it.

"Last night I dreamed that Blue Tongue returned," he said, casting a glance at Nurse Cromley, the subject of Blue Tongue still being a sensitive one. "She was standing on my foot," he said, "her breath smelling of green thistle and gourd, and great strands of yellow hung from her nose. Every time I called out in pain, she thrust her blue tongue down my throat to choke off my cries. It was awful," he said. The syrup from the corn mush dripped onto his robe like dots of glass. "When I awoke, my head was over the bunk rail, and I was all but suffocated."

"You've been working too hard in the garden," Brother Jacob said. "Take the day to refresh your mind and spirit."

"Yes," Nurse Cromley agreed, wiping the pan free of grease and storing it in the wooden box. "Brother Jacob and I will handle the chores and, with luck, we'll have fried rabbit for supper."

"I've been thinking of carving a cornerstone, the date of origin, a stone fit for *Bueffel Au* Monte Cassino," he said. "There's a wonderful piece of limestone I've uncovered in the quarry."

"Yes, do," she said, "a perfect idea, a cornerstone to proclaim the birth of our new monastery, 'A Grove for Buffaloes.'" With her walking stick, she pushed down the lid of the larder. The stick had taken on an amber patina from the heat and oil of her body, and she was adept at using it as an extension of her arm. "Now go," she said, shooing him away. "Hitch up Shorty and take the wagon to bring back the cornerstone. Cody's taken up lame, but without a load Shorty can handle it, although he's likely to object. You can carve the stone by the fire here in the evenings. And you, Brother Jacob, go shoot us a big rabbit for frying."

By the time Shorty was harnessed, the sun broke across the prairie and fell warm on Nurse Cromley's face. Sitting down, she listened to the wagon rattle away in the distance. Keeping Brother Alexander motivated was a burden, a burden endured by both Brother Jacob and herself. Rubbing at her leg, she wiggled her stiff toes. At times they felt detached, as if they belonged to someone else.

"His distress grows each day," Brother Jacob said. "I worry that it's too much for him." Reaching for his rifle, he checked the chamber, and then laid it across his arm. "There is no sustenance here for him, neither for his stomach nor for his soul."

"I was the same," she said, "when I first came, alone, as if cut off from all of humanity."

"It is different for me," he said. "In this place there's only truth, a window opening on the face of God. In its harshness there is a cleansing and freeing of the spirit. Here, I think, resides the glory of exile." Reaching into his robe, he pulled out a handful of shells and counted them. "And there are no children to abide," he said, waving as he walked away.

She watched Brother Jacob amble off, his cowl fluttering in the wind, reminding her of the birds that waddled across the prairie in such great numbers.

By noon, rock dust clung to Brother Alexander's eyelashes like spiderwebs, his hands white with limestone. Brushing away the dust from the face of the stone, he wet his thumb, swiping it across the surface. It was perfect, a smooth and translucent tablet for his carving. There was a permanence about the quarry that he loved, the smell of it, the dust, the layers of stone jutting from the earth. Even the stone he loved, its permanence, its endurance, its transcendent reach into the past.

With wedge and hammer, he drove the layers apart, each blow loosening the slabs into faultless symmetries. With great care he stacked them, one upon the other, conical structures visible for miles away. When there was enough, he would begin the monastery.

The cornerstone was to be perfect, taken from the heart of the quarry where the layer was dense and pure, protected by overburden from the effects of weather, and on it he would chisel the date for all to see when this great work began.

Standing, he dusted off his robe, clouds of lime bellowing about his head. On the horizon a wagon approached like a slow-moving ship, trekking at angles across the rolling prairie. To see another human here was rare, though there was the occasional squatter or whiskey rancher to be seen. Most never stopped. Those who did were often aloof and secretive, revealing only the barest of information about themselves. At first he thought they were to pass him by unnoticed, but then the wagon changed bearing and headed his way.

A man drove, his hat lodged over his ears, and a woman sat next to him, her cotton dress tattered and dirty. In her arms was a baby wrapped in a flour sack, suckling her breast. Between them a blond-haired boy leaned against his mother. At the back of the wagon a pig was tied by its neck with a length of rope. Every so often it would set its feet and throw its head to the side as the wagon pulled it along.

" 'Lo," the man said, wrinkling up an eye against the sun.

"Hello," Brother Alexander said, dusting off his hands.

"We're the Johnsons," the man said, "my wife, May, and the two boys here."

Adjusting the baby, the woman pushed back her hair and nodded her head. With a pop the baby released her nipple, the brown rim shining with milk in the morning sun.

Regaining his composure, Brother Alexander held out his hand.

"I'm Brother Alexander," he said.

The man grinned, a single tobacco-stained tooth hanging like a fence post from his top gum. The blond-haired boy's finger disappeared into his nose as he looked at Brother Alexander's skirt.

"Ain't never seen a man wear a dress before," the man said.

"I'm a monk," Brother Alexander explained, "here to build a monastery."

"Making water must be a inconvenience," he said.

"What he say?" the woman asked.

"Says he's a monk, like a preacher, 'cept he wears a dress."

"Don't seem natural, does it," she said, tucking the baby closer to her breast.

"It's a habit. All monks have them," Brother Alexander said.

"Says it's a habit, May. All of 'em got it." Seeing the look on her face, the man lifted his brows, shaking his head. "Now don't go faulting nobody for their habits. Ain't I chewed twist since I was six, and what about your coffee drinking, morning, noon, and night?"

Pulling the flour sack up to cover the baby's face, May looked at Brother Alexander out of the corner of her eye.

"Seems like his ma would've known better," she said.

Resigned, Brother Alexander turned his hands up.

"What brings you folks this way?" he asked, changing the subject.

"Starved out," the man said, "waiting for the government to clean out the Territory. We're going back to Kansas City to live with May's kin until some work comes up. Course, we're a tad short as you can see, what with the new babe and all. Wouldn't have a little money to get us on our way?"

"I'm sorry, but monks take a vow of poverty and celibacy. We'd be happy to share our camp and what little food we have, though."

"What he say?" the woman asked.

"They don't have no money nor women about," the man said.

"Well, I ain't surprised," she said.

Scratching at his chin, the man looked at the wagon and at Shorty, who napped in the shade of the limestone outcrop.

"Maybe you got something to trade, like that horse there? I got a good hog tied on back, but he don't track so good. Hogs ain't known for following directions, and I ain't keen on dragging him clean across Kansas."

"Shorty? No, Shorty's all we have for pulling the wagon."

When Shorty heard his name, he opened his eyes and flagged his ears before dropping off again.

"Come take a look," the man said, climbing down from the wagon.

The blond-haired boy followed, his finger ensconced in his nose.

"It's a fine hog, ain't it?" the man said, slapping him on the rump.

Dust boiled into the air, and the hog backed against his rope, his black eyes crackling from under his ears.

"Chopper's his name. Just look at them hams. Smoke those up, and you'd have good eatin' come snow. Course, I admit he's a tad randy and a bit stubborn, but then, ain't we all?" He winked. "Still, he'd beat hardtack on any day."

"I don't know," Brother Alexander said, his stomach growling at the thought of ham. "I'm not all that good at picking livestock, although he appears to be a healthy specimen."

"Oh, healthy's it, ain't it?" the man said, taking out a twist and cutting off a chew with his knife. "Topped ten sows in a week, he did, and that, on kitchen slop and watermelon. Guess he'd burn 'em to the ground on corn."

A cool breeze swept Brother Alexander's ankles. When he turned to look, the little boy's head was under his robe.

"Here, boy," the man said, dragging him out, cuffing his ears. "Ain't decent looking up a man's dress, least I don't think it is. Now get on up there with your ma. Maybe there's some titty left."

Skipping back to the front of the wagon, the little boy climbed the wheel, disappearing from sight.

"What do you think you'd have to have for the hog?" Brother Alexander asked.

"Depends," the man said, spitting a stream of tobacco juice at Chopper's feet, "seeing he's kind of a member of the family, if you know what I mean. What you got to trade?"

"The monastery sent some wool blankets."

"Let's take a look," the man said.

As they walked past the wagon, the little boy buried his face in the warm mound of his mother's breast and watched them pass, his finger entombed in his nose, his legs dangling from her lap.

Laying aside Nurse Cromley's belongings, Brother Alexander dug down, locating the wool blankets that she'd used to line the bed. Unfolding one, he held it to the sun for the man to see the weave.

"The monastery provides only the best woolen blankets," he said.

"Oh, yes, yes," the man said. "They're good blankets, sure enough, if a man had a use for 'em. They're kinda like wives, though, ain't they?" He grinned. "Nice to have one, but what you going to do with three?"

"Perhaps you could sell them for money, or barter them for other things."

"But it's a heap of trouble, ain't it?" the man said. Rolling his cud, he peeked into the wagon. "Sure you ain't got something else in there?"

"Well, there's the sacramental wine, but I couldn't trade that."

"Wine, you say."

"But it's sacramental wine and not for trading."

"Well, now," the man said, lifting up on his toes to see into the wagon, "if you wanted to sweeten the bargain with a few bottles of that wine, I just might do some serious consideration."

"Oh, I couldn't trade the sacramental wine. It's strictly for religious service, you see."

"I'm 'bout as religious as the next man, take to praying now and again, especially when the wife gets on a tear. That'll bring a man to his knees soon enough."

"I don't think so," Brother Alexander said, reaching for a bottle of wine, holding it to the sun. "It wouldn't be right, I'm sure."

"Course," the man said, "you gotta do what you gotta do, but seems to me that ole Chopper would serve you more good than this here wine, what with slabs of bacon, pork chops, sugar-cured ham, and hog's headcheese, not to mention redeye gravy and the like. Man eat like a king for a good part of the winter, wouldn't he?"

"I don't know," Brother Alexander said, folding his arms across his stomach.

Looking over his shoulder, the man checked the whereabouts of his wife.

"Tell you what," he spat, "seeing as how you're a godly man and all, I'll throw in a bolt of calico and enough corn for the week."

"Three bottles of wine," Brother Alexander said.

"Four."

"Three, and half the blankets."

"Done," the man said, sticking out his hand.

With Chopper at the end of the rope, Brother Alexander watched the wagon lumber down the trail. A hundred yards out the little boy appeared at the back, his blond hair blowing across his eyes as he peed into the dust that boiled up from the wheels.

No sooner were they out of sight, when Brother Alexander's soul darkened with guilt, his heart aching with regret, falling so low as to sell the very blood of his savior for a hog.

When he looked down, Chopper's black eyes snapped, his snoot twisting first one way and then the other. Powerful mandibles smacked with a chop-chop sound, and every few seconds he grunted, his tail winding like a tight and coiled spring.

"Come on, Chopper," Brother Alexander said, pulling on the rope. There was an instant and equal resistance as Chopper's legs stiffened, his feet planted in the soil. Drool glistened from the corners of his mouth, his yellow tusks pushing his lip into a snarl. "Come on," Brother Alexander said, leaning into the rope.

Lowering his head, Chopper grunted, the rope disappearing into the folds of his neck. Thirty minutes passed, and then an hour, as Brother Alexander coaxed, pulled, pleaded, but to no avail. No amount of persuasion or pushing made a dot of difference. Chopper was as immovable as the rock quarry.

Sweat dripping from the end of his nose, Brother Alexander grabbed Chopper's tail, twisting it tight, pushing with all that was within him. With a contented grunt, Chopper sat down.

Looking skyward, Brother Alexander prayed for the strength as given to Solomon, but even as he prayed, he knew the odds were against him, a man so lowly as to sell sacramental wine.

Grabbing Chopper's tail, he pushed again, his cheeks bulging, his legs trembling, but Chopper was intractable, an unyielding wall of pork, unmoved by power or grace.

"In another life you would be a bishop," he choked.

Rising, Chopper squatted and produced a foul-smelling rope that curled behind him. Satisfied with his production, he made a slow turn before lying down again to sleep.

Taking up a seat on the back of the wagon, Brother Alexander pinched his nose from the smell as he thought. The idea first was scattered, but as he watched Shorty nip grass from under the rock ledge, it began to clear. Why couldn't he leave the wagon here, tie Shorty to Chopper, and drag him back to camp? Trail hands pulled cows in such a way all the time, and they were a sight bigger than Chopper. Tomorrow he could return for the wagon and the cornerstone.

Shorty's ears perked and his tail twitched as Brother Alexander led him to where Chopper slept. When the fulsome odor made its course, Shorty's nostrils flared in alarm, and he reared up.

"Whoa," Brother Alexander said, trying to calm him.

Front legs pegged, Shorty dropped his head to appraise Chopper's unholy deliverance. Blowflies rose into his nostrils with an alarming buzz, and he reared off the ground again, lip curling in disgust.

"Whoa, boy, whoa," Brother Alexander said, leaning back on the reins. "It's just an ole pig. Easy, boy. Easy, boy. There, let's just tie these two ropes together and take a little walk with ole Chopper."

No sooner was the knot tightened when Shorty's body commenced to tremble, the rope now a nerve between them, a personal and revolting nerve connecting each to an abhorrent other. When Shorty hit the end of the rope, Chopper grunted, skidding across the ground and knocking Brother Alexander on his back. By the time he recovered, Chopper was running a sweeping circle, at remarkable speeds for one who moments before had refused a single step. By now, Shorty was beyond control with fear and aversion, kicking and pitching in blind panic.

"Whoa, whoa!" Brother Alexander yelled, but even as he yelled, the rope wrapped about Shorty's legs, tying them together with the able certainty of a cowhand's loop. Teetering, Shorty looked at Brother Alexander for help before toppling in a dispirited heap. Only then did Brother Alexander smell the reek emanating from his clothes, a telling smear of brown across his sleeve. A loathing beyond all reason seized him in that moment.

"Damn you!" he shouted, spit flying from his mouth.

Ears swinging from side to side like canopies, Chopper approached, sniffing Brother Alexander. Satisfied with the telling smell of family, he gave an approving grunt before lying down to nap.

That night as Brother Alexander made his way back to camp, a cold fog quieted the prairie, mist clinging to the grass, the enormity of his sins bearing in on him. What sort of man, much less a man of God, traded away his soul?

When arriving at camp, he watched from the protection of darkness as Brother Jacob and Nurse Cromley busied themselves with chores. It was right for him to hide in the darkness, expelled from the garden, shunned by his own.

"What is that wretched smell?" Brother Jacob asked, staring into the shadows.

"It is I," Brother Alexander said, stepping into the light, covering his face in shame.

As they gathered about the fire, his story poured forth, the tenets and power of confession driving him on.

"The sacramental wine?" Brother Jacob asked.

"Really, Brother Alexander," Nurse Cromley said, "how could you, and you don't even have the pig to show for it."

Holding up his hand, Brother Alexander showed them his blisters.

"No amount of pleading or pulling would move Chopper one iota," he said. "For hours I begged, but to no avail. There was only one thing left to do."

"And what could that have been?" Brother Jacob asked with caution.

"I built a fence around him as he slept, one stone at a time. Chopper is living within the walls of our monastery," he said, burying his face in his hands.

It was midnight by the time they'd heard the story again. Inconsolable, Brother Alexander refused to eat or drink, and it was only when Brother Jacob pointed out that perhaps God had simply answered his prayer, that Brother Alexander agreed to have some tea. After all, hadn't he prayed for ham and hadn't God provided him a way to procure it? It was all no more than answered prayer.

This seemed to comfort Brother Alexander, and so they hung his robe to air in a tree, sending him off to bed with two of the remaining blankets.

Stirring the fire, Brother Jacob and Nurse Cromley warmed their hands as they contemplated the day's events.

"He's a good man," Brother Jacob said, "but with great appetites."

"It is hard for him here," she said.

Rubbing her leg, she listened to the whisper of the flames.

"I've been thinking about the splint," she said.

"I know," he said, pulling his hands into the sleeves of his tunic.

"Maybe it's time now."

In the yellow light of the campfire, Brother Jacob cut the wrappings, laying them aside one by one. Before easing away the slats, he crossed himself.

With eyes closed, Nurse Cromley waited in vain for the touch of the night mist to fall clean and cool on her leg.

Sixteen

Clouds raced down the valley like white ghosts, and water droplets gathered in Little Dog's black hair. Through bruised and swollen slits, the world was a blood dream, his features so distorted that no man would have known him, lips puffed and contorted, teeth jagged and broken, features shoved and torn askew by the bullet's ferocious impact. Pain throbbed in his face like the beat of a drum, his mouth a crushed and bloody maw.

Naked and cold, he lay shaking in a patch of briar, body jerking and trembling in the dampness, still clenched in his hand, his bloodstained knife. Fall leaves pitching from the tree above covered his legs.

Lifting himself with his arms, he tried to stand, head spinning, nausea sweeping him in a tepid wave. Like a dark dream, the events unfolded; Owl Talker thrown across the burning embers; the baby, cold and silent in her arms; Walking Horse at his teepee. But where was Crooked Leg? He could not remember, but there was a lot that he could not remember about those moments.

The sun broke through the clouds, filtering through the limbs onto his back, and fatigue washed over him.

When next he awoke, the night was black. In the distance coyotes quarreled over prey, a sound he'd known often as a boy. But in that moment he knew what lay in the grove of trees, knew the stillness among the oak leaves, and knew the carrion they now dispatched.

Whether he lay for a day or week, he knew not, but when he woke next, the morning sun was warm, and birds sang in the tree above him. When he moved, his muscles cramped from stiffness, his head whirling from the loss of blood. Taking hold of a nearby limb, he pulled himself onto his feet—a little at a time to regain his balance, his confidence in the living world—realizing then his nakedness, the dried blood, the briar scratches like the marks of a lash.

With the first step, he was seized with suffocation and panic, falling to his knees as blackness dropped across his eyes. Moments passed before his thinking cleared, his ravaged face, the grisly wound, the air passages swollen and caked with dried blood. Even the slightest exertion wrenched him close to unconsciousness.

With slow and deliberate movements, he pulled himself forward, no matter the pace or distance, because this was the way of the Cheyenne, their strength and courage. Hours passed as he crawled, inching through the endless grass. At times he slept, dreamed, awakened to find that even as he slept, his body had moved forward, his spirit moving as a thing apart. Each time he rested, he held tight the knife, his only hope in a hopeless world.

The evening sun hung suspended in the stream, a churning mass of gold, a fuming cauldron of heat and fire shimmering in the cold waters as Little Dog peered over the moss-covered bank. What looked back stilled his heart, the fractured and misshapen jaw, the crushed mouth, the white maggots writhing in the black depths of the wound. There was no scream of terror, of disbelief, nor curse thrown at the feet of life, not that could be heard. But in his soul, gods howled in despair, and hope shattered into broken and useless shards. There was no hold, no center, no lifeline as he fell away into the darkness.

Dawn broke in the clear, cold morning. With each awakening, his energy dimmed, chances fading, paling against the enormity of his condition. Peering into the pool, he held his breath. Were they still there, legless, blind, ravenous? They were, as he knew, worming at the bloody edges of the wound.

Struggling against fear and revulsion, he searched for a stick, culling, discarding, trying again until satisfied. Peering into the waters, he steadied his hand, thrusting the stick into the wound, pain coursing through his body. Like angry bees from a hive, the maggots boiled out, blood dripping from his chin into the mirrored water.

Leaning close, he held open the wound, washing it in the water, the edge bright and raw from the intruders' appetites. With cupped hands, he splashed water onto his face, cleaning away the dried blood. When all was done that could be done, exhausted, he curled against the bank and slept.

Sometime in the night he awoke, the swelling down, his breathing opened. Wrapping his arms about his legs for warmth, he thought back over the passing hours. For the first time his thinking was clear, the events rushing back in their enormity. In the loneliness that was his in that moment, he spoke Owl Talker's name for a final time, reaching into the night to touch the cold cheek of his infant son, swearing vengeance for the dishonor he now bore.

By late morning, the sun brightened, a warm breeze picking up from the west. Even though weak from hunger and cold, his walking was steady, and soon he'd reached the westernmost watering hole of winter encampment. Sometimes, with luck, buffalo drank here before bedding down in the afternoon heat. But with only a knife and trail-weary feet, the chances for a kill were small enough.

Dropping to his stomach, he crawled the last few yards through the tall grass that rimmed the knoll, listening for changes in the prairie sounds, for the shifting wind, for the knowing that comes with the silence. Reaching the top of the knoll, he parted the grass. Below, a buffalo bull snorted, lifting his nose to the air.

Something was wrong, his stance, his shoulders awkward and off center. Crawling to the far side of the knoll, Little Dog could see then; the bull's front quarters were bogged in the mud, a swath cut from the swing of his great head as he struggled to free himself.

Maybe there was a chance, if his own strength held, if the bull were exhausted from his struggle. How many times he'd seen them charge in a blind and unstoppable rage when their great fear and strength were unleashed at the sight of man.

Making his way down the knoll, Little Dog stopped to gauge his adversary, big, a ton, maybe more, his strength and will intact. Even if he could get to him, the hunting knife was insufficient for a kill, maybe with a jugular cut, or a vital organ, maybe then.

Half-bent, Little Dog broke into the open, moving fast, knife leveled, and just as he was upon him, their eyes met. With a roar, the bull lunged against the mud, his eyes rolling white, tongue lolling and slobbers flying as he flung his great head from side to side. Again he lunged, bellowing with quivering and terrifying power. In that moment Little Dog leapt onto the bull's back, plunging his knife again and again into his great ruff. Even as the bull relaxed under him and the waters darkened with blood, Little Dog did not move. Not until the bull's head dropped and the heat bled from beneath him, did Little Dog begin his task.

Standing knee deep in the mud, he skinned the buffalo, rolling the hide, hair down, on the bank of the watering hole. From the back and hump he took the choice cuts of meat, and from the head, he took the tongue. When finished, he rolled the meat into the skin, tying the ends with strips of the hide. High above, black specks dotted the blue sky in a silent wait. Thanking him for his skin and for his flesh, Little Dog bid farewell to the naked buffalo that watched him with wide eyes.

Heading west, Little Dog put miles between himself and the watering hole, reaching a muddy creek that meandered through a shallow valley. Where the water pooled in a turn of the creek, a stand of cottonwood grew, shelter, cover, fuel, and he unloaded his burden. Stripping away the spiny leaves of a yucca, he formed a twirling stick for his fire. Greasewood was better, but this would do. From a fallen cottonwood, he tore away the bark, peeling away the strands of paper from the backside, crumpling it with his hands. With expert skill, he twirled the stick until spots of black curled at its end. Blowing, he nursed them into an ember and then a flame and then a fire that crackled hot against his face.

Once the fire was secure, he cut slices of meat from the hump, skewering them on the yucca stick and placing them over the fire. The aroma of blackened meat filled his camp. Ignoring the pain of damaged teeth, he chewed the meat, each piece returning his strength.

Throughout the day, he jerked the remaining meat, fashioning a robe from the skin, and crude moccasins for his feet. They would stiffen soon enough from lack of tanning, but for now, they must do. Once, they would have been tanned with soap weed mixed with the brains, liver, and grease from the buffalo and chewed soft by the women, but that was another life. For now, this must do.

Afterward, he sat at his fire, and for the first time in many days, did not tremble from the cold.

The next day broke warm, and Little Dog's strength was renewed with rest and food. At the creek he checked his wound, swollen and sore, but draining well. The maggots had not returned.

A careful search turned up a bois d'arc clinging to the side of the creek bed, dense and strong and straight. From it he fashioned a lance, scraping it with the blade of his knife until it glistened in the sun. To kill with a lance, to stand arm's length from death, took much skill and bravery, and with it the greatest honor. With this lance, he would take his revenge.

As Little Dog prepared for his walk, the wind blew from the west and smelled of the desert. Over his shoulder he hung the strips of jerked meat on a string of rawhide. With luck, it would last a few days, but it was the lack of water that worried him most, the long distances and brutal miles, the uncertainty of watering holes.

As he studied the horizon, a loneliness pressed in. Behind him was all that mattered, ahead the boundless and empty prairie. After a moment, he lifted his chin, adjusting the rawhide across his shoulder, and headed west into the sun.

For two days he walked without water nor sign of water, the jerked meat scalding his throat, his thirst doubling and redoubling with each mile. At night he slept on the ground or on piles of dried tumbleweed to ease his aching bones as the sun dropped away and night set in. The wound on his face crusted, stiff as the moccasins on his feet, and his robe reeked of rotting flesh.

Approaching the break, he could see the buffalo cow, belly swollen, feet strutted, head twisted from heat and contracting muscles. Unmistakable, too, was the scent of death, skulking from the shadows, circling overhead against the warm columns of air. By her horns, he turned her head to look for signs of wounds, for gunshot or arrow, finding instead a single bois d'arc apple lodged deep in her gullet. Squatting on his haunches, he studied her. By the looks of her extended belly, she'd been to water not long ago.

Just beneath her breastbone he inserted his knife, bringing it around in a shallow cut the length of her body. With the keen edge of the blade, he separated the thin layer of fat, the muscle, the sinew, until the white of her cavernous stomach bulged through the opening. Reaching in with both arms, he worked out the stomach paunch with its telling slosh, its fetid smell. Leaning the paunch against the carcass, he cut away its top, pitching it into the clump of goldenrods that shot from the sand like yellow flames. Kneeling, he lowered his head into the paunch and drank of its contents.

When rested, he headed west once more, crossing a set of horse tracks disappearing up a dry gulch, a cold but clear trail, Army shod, a dozen or more. The decision to follow was an easy one. For the first time in many days his destination was certain.

Within the hour he found their camp, pushing his fingers into the ash of the cold fire. Scattered about were empty whiskey bottles, a yellowed bandage blown into the weeds, a spot of blood dried in the sand. Beyond in the brush was a horse blanket and not far from that, a shallow grave. The partial remains of a body lay in the drifting sand. One pant leg was cut away from the faded blue uniform, and the signs of a knife wound were still visible on the soldier's leg.

The wind fell clean against Little Dog's face, and a white cloud sped across the sky. Raising his lance, he thrust it into the body of the soldier, and with his knife he cut away a scalp lock, tying it with strands of rawhide to the end of his lance.

Even though the tracks were days old, Little Dog followed them with ease. As dusk fell, Chimney Rock rose on the horizon. Beyond that lay the great canyon, and there he would find water. Abandoning the tracks, he turned north. There was time, and tomorrow he would pick up the tracks again.

The canyon stretched out below him, a great and yawning rift. Working his way down the narrow path, Little Dog used his lance to secure his hold. As a boy, he'd been here, knew that water sprang eternal from the reeds below. It was said that somewhere beneath, a great cavern wound into the heart of the earth.

The air dampened and grew heavy as he descended, the smell of water and vegetation seeping from the crannies of the canyon wall. From the spring he drank long, cupping the icy water onto his face and throat. Slipping from his garment, he dropped into the pool, its frigid waters stealing his breath. Overhead, the moon hung in the black sky like an earthen pot, burnished smooth and silver with river stone.

Trembling, he rose from the pool to let the night air dry his body. Too tired to build a fire, he ate from the jerked meat, still tasting of dust, and crawled under an outcrop to sleep.

As the moon dropped below the horizon, and blackness poured into the chasm, Little Dog sat upright, his heart pounding. Something had awakened him, a sound, a feeling. Rubbing his face, he listened again, searching for his knife, heart calming with its touch.

Certain that he was not alone, he stood, moving into the darkness, an inch and then another, each step chosen and placed with caution. The pungent odor of mud and rotted leaves rode the currents and in it the smell of smoke. There in the blackness of the canyon, he could see the light from a fire.

Crouching at the edge of the camp, Little Dog readied his knife. A figure hunkered near the fire, a blanket pulled over his head and about his shoulders. With a terrifying war whoop, Little Dog charged, his toe catching under the root of a tree, throwing him to the ground.

"Yeow!" the figure screamed, pitching his blanket into the air.

Recovering his knife, Little Dog rose. Circling the tiny fire, their eyes locked, pitched in combat. Perhaps it was the way his foe moved, hip cocked and slow, that Little Dog first recognized.

"Crooked Leg?" he said, lowering his knife.

"Is it you, Little Dog, or the *mistai* come to take me away?" Crooked Leg said.

Grasping each other's hand, they held tight, neither speaking for a moment.

"I thought you were a soldier," Little Dog said. "If I had not fallen, your throat would be cut."

"Your face is even more ugly than I remember," Crooked Leg said. "For a moment I thought you were the blue-tongue spirit come to paw open my skull."

"But you were dead, surely," Little Dog said. "All of the camp was slain."

Putting the blanket over his shoulders, Crooked Leg looked into the fire.

"I rose that morning, unable to sleep. The dogs had not yet come in, so I took my horse to find them. When I returned, my heart broke with what I saw. I searched among the bodies for my friend, Little Dog, but he was not there. Still, there were many I did not know." Looking into the darkness, he shrugged his shoulders. "Already the coyote had come."

"I have no horse, no bow, not even clothes," Little Dog said.

"Yesterday I came upon a soldier's horse, a bay," Crooked Leg said, "with its saddle hanging under its belly. There were clothes in the saddlebags, which I took, but there were no weapons."

Poking the coals with his knife, Little Dog watched the embers flash in the fire.

"They kill each other now," he said. "Today I found the body of a soldier who bore the wound from my knife. I followed the others' tracks leading west." Pulling the blanket up around his neck, Little Dog studied the fire. "The Dog Soldier Clan is no more," he said. "The Cheyenne now is gone. There is Black Kettle on the Washita with a few warriors, others starving on the reservation, some hiding in the hills like us."

"Tomorrow we follow," Crooked Leg said, curling close to the fire to take his sleep. After a moment he lifted himself up on an arm. "You are wrong about the Dog Soldier Clan. There is still you and me, my friend."

The next morning Little Dog put on the soldier's pants from the saddlebag and cinched them tight with a length of rope. From the shirt he tore a strip to tie back his hair. The bay horse was strong and spirited under him as they rode out of camp.

The sun was high overhead by the time they climbed the knoll overlooking the Cimarron crossing at Deep Hole Creek. On the far side of the meander the soldiers sat around their fire. To the east a corral built of cedar logs held their horses. In the stand of cottonwood beyond, tents cropped up like mushrooms, and clothes hung in the limbs to dry.

Muscles trembling, Little Dog lifted his lance.

"No," Crooked Leg said. "We must wait." Not hearing, Little Dog rose to a crouch, eyes and mind trained on the men below. "We must wait," Crooked Leg said again, taking hold of his arm. "There are too many to kill. Their camp is here to guard the crossing for their wagons. We will come back with others."

Lowering his lance, Little Dog stared up into the burning sun, into the dark eyes of Owl Talker falling in a cool shadow across his face.

Seventeen

"Who are you?" Renfro asked, his voice cold.

"I might be asking the same question, sir, seeing as how I got this here carbine aimed at your belly," the man said.

"This is my camp, and that's my boy you got hold of," he said.

"Well, now, is it?" the man said, letting go of Creed's arm. "Thought you might be one of them whiskey ranchers or squatters come sneaking up in the dark." Lowering his carbine, he stepped into the light of the fire. "James Elliot," he said, sticking out his hand.

With hesitation Renfro shook his hand, looking him over in the light of the fire. He was a big man, six feet or over, with a chest like a beer keg. White whiskers sprouted from his chin, eyes watery, brows sweeping up like the tail feathers of a peacock. He sported buffalo-hide boots, rough trousers, red shirt, and a sweat-ringed Mexican sombrero pushed to the back of his head. Strapped about his waist were a revolver and the biggest bowie knife Renfro had ever seen.

"Adam," he said.

"Well, now, Adam, you wouldn't happen to have a little grub you could share with a fellow traveler?"

"It's poor fare," he said, "but you're welcome.

Creed, get some of that pone for Mr. Elliot and heat up some of that tea."

Sitting down at the fire, Elliot laid his carbine across his lap, pulled off his sombrero, and ran his fingers through his thin hair.

"I'm right fond of sage tea," he said, "but even more so of whiskey. Guess you wouldn't be having some of that to share?"

"No, sir. Whiskey's not something I've got, for sharing or keeping, neither one. What brings you to be walking these hills alone, Mr. Elliot?"

"Seems like the whole world's walking these hills, don't it?" he grinned, exposing a missing tooth. "Guess I could ask the same of you."

Kneeling between them, Creed placed the pone on the fire to heat, glancing up to meet his father's eyes.

"Guess you could, Mr. Elliot, but, then, this is my camp, and that's my pone you're fixin' to eat, ain't it?"

Leaning back, Elliot laughed, a deep roar that rolled about the camp before disappearing into the dark.

"You got a point there. Let's say I've had a run of bad luck. Lost my wagon, my team, and damn near my life in this godforsaken country."

"That right?" Adam said. "Ain't that a bullwhacker's outfit you're wearing there?"

Pouring the tea, Creed handed a cup to Elliot and then to his father.

"A bullwhacker it is. Keen eye you got there, mister. Worked for the Hampton Company on the Santa Fe Trail for near three years," he said, taking a sip of the tea, looking off into the dark, "till one day my wagon backed over me, five tons of tobacco and calico right over my leg, making powder out of my kneecap and stew meat out of my thigh. I's screamin' 'whoa' so loud, milk wagons stopped far away as Kansas City but not them damned ox. No, sir, not them ox. They just kept backing on up with me a-screaming and hollering like a man on fire, but didn't make no difference. Course, as you know, man with a stiff leg can't keep up with a train, even if it is ox."

"What's a bullwhacker?" Creed asked.

"Why, they's the toughest, meanest critters this side of Hell," Elliot said, before Adam could answer. "They's the ones keep them oxen pulling Conestogas and J. Murphys where no sane man would go, sometimes fifteen, twenty head in a single team, the dumbest creatures God ever made, and the whacker with no more'n a bullwhip and a life collection of cussing to keep 'em going. Ever' step them ox take, the whacker takes three 'cause he's got to work the whole line and then back again. At the end of the day, he's still got two men and a tornader to fight 'fore dinner. It's a good job, though, if he don't get struck by lightning or kilt' by Cheyenne, or," he paused, "backed over by a Conestoga." Reaching into the pan with his bowie, he speared a piece of pone, biting off the end and looking into the fire. "Weren't never a wagon master like J.B. Hampton, I'll tell you, the meanest son of a bitch for a white man I ever knew."

Looking at Creed, his dark eyes, the straight black hair that glimmered in the firelight, he turned back to his pone.

"Remember once, ole J.B. came back from a scoutin', wanted the whole train to take a well-earned rest, he says. 'We'll just hole up here in the shade,' he says, 'out of the afternoon heat and take ourselves a little rest.'" Slapping his leg, Elliot let out a roar. "Well, by God, we looked at each other like he'd gone crazy. J.B. never took no rest in the worst of weather, let alone no peak of the day." Wiping off his bowie, he slipped it back into its holster. "Come dark, J.B.

says, 'Alright, boys, let's hit the trail. We got to make up for lost time.' Come midnight, here we were heading down this canyon trail in the dark. At the bottom, I stops and says, 'J.B., what the hell we sleeping the day away and then traveling in the dark for?'

" 'Well, by God, Elliot,' he says, looking me straight in the eye, 'no man in his right mind would've come down that canyon trail in the daylight.' "

With that, Elliot threw his sombrero on the ground and laughed, bits of corn pone spewing from his mouth.

"Oh, he was a fine one," he said, cleaning his beard with his fingers. "Gave ever' man a brand-new Bible and a blanket the day he signed on, after that, nothing but twelve-hour days, lard biscuits, and a weekly cussing."

The wind shifted to the north, spiraling dirt and smoke into Adam's eyes. Rising, he hooked his hands in his back pocket and let the fire warm his front.

"How was it you walking these hills with nothing but shoe leather and a carbine?" he asked again.

"Pour me some more of that tea, boy." Elliot held out his cup to Creed. "Ain't whiskey but ain't half bad, neither." Lifting the pot with his shirttail, Creed poured the tea. "Thanks, boy. A damn good hand, ain't he?" he said, looking up at Adam. "Kinda on the quiet side, but then that ain't all bad, is it?"

Sipping at his tea, the firelight lit up his brows like white plumes and flickered in the black of his eyes.

"Well, sir," he continued, "ole J.B. gave me a choice. 'Elliot,' he says, 'you can take the pay you got coming and stump it on back to Dodge, or you can take that Dearborn and a team of ox, and we'll call it even.'

" 'Ox,' I says. 'Hell, J.B., at least a couple of mules would get me back 'fore I die of old age.'

" 'That's true enough,' he says, 'but then a man with

a stump ain't in no hurry, is he? 'Sides,' he says, 'you can eat them ox or turn 'em into breeding stock if you take a notion.'

" 'At the rate they move I could turn 'em into a statue,' I says. But, in the long run figured getting back was more important than pay, so I took him up on his deal."

Sipping on his tea, he reflected on his ordeal. "Hadn't gone a hundred mile when one night the coyotes slipped in and ate the harness right off the wagon bed, leaving me with one Dearborn and no way to pull it. So's I took to riding ole Roan, didn't I, if you could call it that, and leading Snort on a short rope. Riding a ox is like squattin' over a three-foot pear cactus. Once on, you can't get off." He grinned.

"We're getting our own freight outfit someday," Creed said.

Tossing the remaining tea into the fire, James Elliot looked up at Adam.

"That a fact?" he said. "Takes a fair amount of money to buy a freight outfit."

"Just a dream," Adam responded, looking over at Creed, "something to think on."

"And a fine one it is, too," he said.

"Now," Elliot continued, "I didn't get ten mile down the trail when Snort threw a shoe. Know how many men it takes to shoe a ox, boy?" Riveted with the tale, Creed shook his head no. "One enlisted regiment and a two-star General," he said, "and thirty days with no rain. They got to be caught, throwed, and tied. Catching 'em is the easy part 'cause a ox ain't going nowhere anyway, not ever, but throwing one is like trying to push over a granite mountain with your pecker. And then he's got to be tied. Ever tie up a bobcat, boy?" Shrugging, Creed looked at his father. "Well, tying up a ox is like roping a bobcat with barbwire and bare hands.

"And the worst part is, you ain't even got around to shoeing him yet, all four feet stuck in the air like a dog on its back. Guess there was slim chance me getting all that done by myself and me with a game leg."

"What did you do?" Creed asked.

"Didn't do nothing." He shrugged. "Texas tick fever kilt' Snort that day and Roan the next. Been stumping it ever since."

Sitting back down, Adam leaned against Buck's saddle and studied on Elliot's words.

"You're a far piece south from the railroad, ain't you?"

"Lost," he said, "walking circles mostly, I reckon, trying to figure what to do, if I didn't get kilt' or starved." Tapping his shirt pocket with his hand, he said, "Ain't got any makins', have you?"

"Sorry." Adam shrugged.

"And then it occurred to me," he said, "sitting on the edge of a cedar canyon thinking 'bout cherry pie and other unmentionables. There's a railroad coming this way, coming as certain as sunrise, and ain't no freight wagon going to keep up with no steam engine."

"What's a steam engine?" Creed asked.

"Boils water to make steam and runs down a track of steel at forty mile an hour, day in and day out."

"No," Creed said, looking at his father in disbelief.

"Pulls twenty, thirty cars behind it. Once that track's laid, wagon freighters are done for, that's certain. Coming south a mile a day, they are, five hundred workers, earning a dollar seventy-five a day, rooting and cussing and digging their way to California. Three million a year in trade, and it's all going to be theirs."

"Where's all that steel come from?" Adam asked.

"That's just it, ain't it? Three thousand tons ordered from England, hundred dollars a ton it is, twelve thousand dollars a mile, but once it's done, there won't be no stopping them. They'll haul freight so cheap that J.B.'s likely to be hunting buffalo bones for a living, God willing."

"Maybe dreamin' on a freight line ain't all that practical," Adam said.

"Well, sir," Elliot shifted positions, "it's all in the timing, I'd say. What else a railroad got to have, cross ties, that's what, big timbers that won't rot, and the farther west they go the fewer timbers there is. And there I am sitting on top this cedar canyon thinking about cherry pie, and down there below like a green ocean is the biggest, finest cedar in the country. Why, a cedar post will sit in the ground till Armageddon without rotting, all down there below me just waiting to be sold to the railroad. All it would take is a little money, a few wagons, and some strong backs, a man with a dream, maybe?"

"Dreams are only dreams, Mr. Elliot, and don't move cedar posts out of canyons. I ain't so certain they should, in any case. The land ought to be for the Indians, little enough as it is. Ripping out their trees and hauling them off don't seem quite right to me."

Reaching for his sombrero, he put it on his head, pushing it back until it framed his face.

"Maybe," he said, "maybe so. I ain't here to argue that point. Don't matter, does it, seeing as how it's only dreams?"

Standing, Adam brushed off the seat of his britches.

"You're welcome to stay the night, Mr. Elliot, and share breakfast for what it is. There ain't much beyond that, we got. Come on, boy," he said, motioning for Creed to follow.

"Good night, Mr. Elliot," Creed said.

"Good night, boy," Elliot said, his white beard reflecting the orange glow of the fire.

Making their bed under the shelter of a big elm, Adam and Creed lay under their blanket and watched the stars. From there, Adam could see the campfire and could see James Elliot sitting at it like a great and lonely bear.

The night air was thin and clear, and the stars flickered like signals from the depths. Pulling the blanket up around Creed's shoulders, Adam let his hand linger on his shoulder.

"Night, boy," he said, turning onto his back.

Some time passed before Creed spoke.

"Mr. Elliot's been a lot of places, hasn't he?" he asked.

"Seems so," Adam said.

"And knows all about steam engines, and oxen, and the Santa Fe Trail?"

"Yes," Adam said. "He's been around some."

"Someday I, too, will have been around some, and someday I'm going to ride one of those steam engines at forty mile an hour down the steel tracks," he said with determination.

"There's a whole world waiting on you out there, boy, and I got a notion you'll experience your share of it. Now, go to sleep."

When morning came, frost glistened in the tree above, and the morning sun shimmered cold across the prairie. Rising on an elbow, Adam rubbed the sleep from his eyes. Across the way the campfire smoldered, a cold curl of smoke twisting into the still morning air. On the far side, James Elliot still slept, his blanket pulled over his head from the cold.

Rising, Adam dressed, pulling the covers over Creed. Wouldn't hurt for him to sleep a little more while he caught up Buck.

Even in sparse grass, Buck could seldom cover more than a quarter of a mile under hobble. Being accustomed to the rope, he rarely ventured that far. But Buck was not to be found. Concerned, Adam circled again before making his way back to camp.

Still sleeping, Creed snored softly as Adam approached, and James Elliot lay unmoved under his blanket. Only then did he see the saddle gone, the food, and the bags of silver, too, all gone as certain as his own hopes and dreams. Kicking at the blanket where Elliot lay, sent clumps of tumbleweeds spinning into the air.

Sitting next to the cold fire, he wrapped his arms about himself and cursed. How could he have been so foolish? How could he have not known? Now, there was nothing left. Without the silver, there would be no future for Creed. Without food and horse the going would be tough, even for a trail-hardened man, it would be tough.

But with a boy along and winter setting in, it could be even worse than that.

Eighteen

Finishing the diary entry, McReynolds laid it aside and checked the supply list for the redoubt. Much of the nonperishables were loaded, flour, sugar, coffee, barrels of bacon packed in bran. At the last moment Cookey would load fresh meat, cabbages, and turnips to be consumed early in the journey before they spoiled. Thereafter, barrels of salted pickle would be their only defense against scurvy. While not life-threatening early on, scurvy resulted in a softening and bleeding of the gums. Without treatment, however, uncontrolled hemorrhaging could result.

In addition to the wagons, he'd procured horses and mules, a bell-mare, and Grimsley packsaddles. A burden of 125 pounds could be maintained on the average, and once arrived, the animals could be used for clearing of timber and for the construction of the parapet. One wagon was filled and secured with camp chairs, tables, field cots, mess chests, camp bureaus, and Cookey's field oven.

With some objection from the quartermaster sergeant, McReynolds was able to acquire an entire wagon for Sarah's household goods, as well as a private Sibley tent for her comfort.

The only thing missing were the mountain howitzers for defense against major attack. Having none available, McReynolds dispatched a message to General Sully at Fort Dodge, requesting that the howitzers be sent along on the next available wagon train, to be left off at the redoubt. With Custer's winter campaign in full swing to the south, there was little reason to be concerned about depredations as far north as the Cimarron in any case, especially with the onset of winter. A few weeks without large artillery should be no problem.

Sitting back, he lit his pipe and looked out over the compound. The only thing that remained was to fill the water barrels. The carpenters had built new ones of cedar slats, tied them together with rope and threw them in the river to swell. Until that process was complete, they would be unable to leave. There was also the matter of picking the men to go along. This, with a few exceptions, he'd left to Wallace and Cookey. His main request was that Sergeant Number accompany him. He depended on Number, trusted him, not only as a valuable medical assistant, but as a trailwise source of information. There was something to be said for Number's company, too, for his irrepressible personality and his friendship.

Folding his check list, he walked to the door of the new infirmary and waited for Sergeant Number as he strolled across the compound in his carefree manner. There was a slight hitch to his walk from where the scar tissue had thickened after his burn. Like himself, Number was not getting any younger.

After the flood, and his night stranded alone with Sarah, McReynolds had taken some ribbing from the other officers, in the manner of winks and knowing glances. The enlisted, on the other hand, said nothing, as was in keeping with their station. Most considered Army surgeons as asexual at best, indifferent to anything as frivolous as the opposite sex.

"Morning, sir," Number said, saluting.

"Morning, Sergeant. Everything under control?"

"Oh, yes, sir. Mosley's complaining of backache again, and Fortenberry's got an abscessed tooth by the looks of it. Roscoe Weedling's nose is broke, fell off the barracks steps, he claims, and Rutledge's piles are bleeding from sitting mules too long, he says. Everything's as under control as it ever gets around here." Taking off his hat, he scratched at his head and looked up at McReynolds. "What's going to happen to these scammers when you leave, sir?"

"There's a surgeon scheduled to visit from Fort Reno, although I'm not certain when he's due to arrive."

"Well, by the looks of it, there's whiskey about and trouble at the gate."

"What do you mean?" McReynolds asked.

"I hear tell Roscoe Weedling got his nose poked over that laundress, the redheaded one, and that trouble is brewing between him and Stable Sergeant Kingston. Rumor is that Weedling's got the notion that she's his own personal laundress and don't want her washing no one else's clothes. Turns out, the stable sergeant's been getting his duds washed while Weedling's growing old on ox-train patrol."

Scratching at his chin, Number gave it some thought.

"Normally, I wouldn't care much one way or the other, sir. It's something can be worked out behind the barracks, except when you add corn liquor and lots of it, then I begin to worry."

"Perhaps I should bring it to the commander's attention, Sergeant?"

"Maybe, sir, except I thought it might be something we could handle ourselves. I mean, maybe we wouldn't have to bother the commander, and someone lose their stripes and all."

Walking around his desk, McReynolds put away the diary and knocked the ashes out of his pipe.

"I'll do some checking around, Sergeant. In the meantime, pack your gear. I assume you understood that you'd be going with us to build the redoubt up on the Cimarron."

"Well, yes, sir. I thought as much."

"I've got to go see the ordnance sergeant and then Captain Wallace. Pack the medical supplies, too, thirty days' or so, and both sizes of those forceps. No need making little wounds into big ones with the wrong-size forceps." Pausing, he looked around the room. "Put in ample chloroform and the rest of that quinine. I've done all the surgery without anesthetic that I intend to."

"Yes, sir," Sergeant Number said.

As McReynolds made his way across the compound, the effects of the flood were still visible, a thin film of mud still clinging to the grass and up the sides of the lower-lying buildings. Sticks and mud wrapped the trunks of trees, left there by subsiding waters. Hanging in the air was the dank smell of river mud and fish.

Even with the door open, the munitions shed was dark, smelling of oil and gunpowder. Leaning over an oil-soaked bench, the ordnance sergeant spun the chamber of a side arm, holding it close to his ear, measuring its whir against some standard buried deep in his brain. Black grime ringed his fingernails and filled the creases and crevices of his hands like the lines of a map. Glasses sat on the end of his nose, magnifying his eyes and the black mole that sprung from his cheek like a mushroom. But in his eyes wisdom shinned through the dimness like a faint star.

"Morning, sir," he said, laying down the firearm.

"Morning, Sergeant. I'm Major McReynolds."

"Yes, sir," he said. "Had reason to meet you once, when a pistol hammer took off the end of my finger."

"Oh, yes," McReynolds said, his eyes adjusting to the darkness of the shed. "I remember now. So how goes it?"

"Oh, just fine, sir. Course, I miss it now and again, but that's getting old, ain't it, one adjustment after another?"

"Yes," McReynolds said, putting his foot up on the chair, "one thing after another."

"Can I help you with something, sir?"

"About this redoubt business," McReynolds said.

"Yes, sir," he said. "Have already issued the small arms, pistols and rifles both, according to the request, and enough ammunition for a healthy attack, God forbid. And of course you know there's no howitzers, sir. That, we don't have."

"I understand and have already sent a message to Fort Dodge to have them sent along on the next train. What I need to know," he said, putting down his foot, "is if there's anything else ought to be taken, in your opinion?"

Pleased at being asked, the ordnance sergeant pulled up a munitions box and sat down. A smear of dirt ran across his cheek like Cheyenne war paint, and a column of light from the doorway fell across his face, lighting up a patch of white whiskers that had escaped the morning shave.

"Well, sir, now that you asked, there are arms for a camp, and there are arms for a fort, each serving a different function, you see. But a redoubt ain't a camp and it ain't a fort, so's it's got to have particular thought. Seeing as how I've done this for near twenty-five years, I've give it particular thought."

"And that's why I'm asking," McReynolds said, finding himself an empty munitions box to sit on. "I've got twenty-five men to worry about, Sergeant."

Taking off his glasses, the ordnance sergeant cleaned them with the tail of his shirt, his eyes receding into black dots under his bushy eyebrows.

"Seems to me, force invites like force, sir. If it's a camp to attack, small arms is sufficient. If it's a fort, well, then, it's a fort, ain't it, and you bring all you got against it. Now, a redoubt ain't exactly a fort, but it damn sure ain't a camp. It's got walls, parapet, head log, sandbags, corrals, sentries, and sits out there in the middle of the prairie just inviting trouble. I wouldn't bring no camp force against a redoubt if I was a Cheyenne. So if I was in charge of a redoubt, I'd damn sure want fort guns to do it with." Slipping his glasses back on, he looked at McReynolds. "You don't build a redoubt without howitzers, sir, at least two."

Standing to leave, McReynolds turned.

"I'm inclined to go along with your logic, providing there's an imminent threat, and the availability of munitions. Seems I'm lacking in both.

"By the way," McReynolds asked as an afterthought, "what's going on with Weedling and the stable sergeant?"

Picking up the side arm, the ordnance sergeant spun the chamber again, assessing the oiled hum of the cylinder with his ear.

"Rutting season, sir."

"Whiskey?"

"Whiskey ain't allowed," he said.

Making his way down the path, McReynolds found Cookey outside the mess supervising a couple of soldiers, their sleeves rolled to the elbows as they worked over an enormous kettle. The ever-present coffeepot sat at the edge of the fire. Seeing the major approach, Cookey snapped a salute and flashed a smile.

"Morning, Major," he said.

"Morning. What are we cooking today?"

Wiping at his forehead with his sleeve, Cookey pointed to the kettle.

"Yeast, sir. What with going on the trail, we'll need extra yeast. These boys don't get their bread allowance, they're likely to falter on the first hill."

"Weren't for your bread, Cookey, there'd be no reason for any of us to rise out of bed."

"Yes, sir," he answered with a smile, "and it all happens right there." He pointed to the kettle. "A man's got to start with boiling water, springwater when it's possible, and then three or four handfuls of good hops. Stir in your stock yeast, some cracked malt, and let her cook until she's just warm. Boil up some new taters for a ferment, mash 'em up with your hands, got to be your hands, sir, the human touch, you know. Put it in a sugar barrel, add your yeast, and give her lots of time to grow. Two days and you got the best yeast this side of the Mississippi, if the Cheyenne don't ruin it."

Peeking into the kettle, McReynolds took a whiff of the earthy aroma.

"Well, there's no denying your bread, Cookey."

"Yes, sir." He grinned. "She's saved me from many a harmful duty. Long as there's hot bread waiting, no man nor officer has a carp with the Cookey."

Pouring himself a cup of the thick coffee, McReynolds leaned against a wagon wheel and watched the men work.

"Picked out your boys to go along?" he asked after a while.

"Why, yes, sir, I have, right afore you. This here is Private Benjamin and Private O'Ryan." The men looked up from their work, dipping their heads in greeting. "They ain't the smartest we got," Cookey continued, "nor the best-looking, as you can see, but they're hardworking and have a good nose on them."

"Glad to hear it." McReynolds smiled. "Best be on my way. Need to find Captain Wallace. We'll be moving out soon as those water barrels are sealed."

"I'll be ready," Cookey said. "Captain Wallace is digging the new well, I think. Said he was tired of drinking frog droppings in his coffee."

Tossing the remains of his coffee onto the ground, McReynolds handed his cup to Cookey.

"By the way, you wouldn't happen to know what's going on between Weedling and the stable sergeant, would you?"

"Just a mix-up over washing day. That redhead laundress told Weedling he'd have to wait, that the stable sergeant's wash took more time and attention, so to speak. Guess Weedling took offense and got his nose broke in the process."

"Any whiskey involved, Cookey?"

Crossing his arms, Cookey looked toward the barracks.

"Whiskey ain't allowed, sir."

Muffled voices rose from the bottom of the dug well, the smell of mud hanging in the air.

"Hello," McReynolds called, leaning over the edge.

Looking up, splotches of mud streaking his face, Captain Wallace called back.

"Well," he said, "if it isn't the good doctor."

"Think you could come out of your lair long enough to talk?" McReynolds asked.

"Oh, yes, sir," Wallace said, taking off his hat, wiping away the sweat with his sleeve. "We'll just shut 'er all down. Just 'cause there ain't a decent swill of water to be had, and just 'cause half the fort's sick from swamp fever, ain't no reason we can't shut 'er down so's we can have a chat."

Muttering as he stepped from the ladder, Captain Wallace looked him over.

"Know your business is mighty important," McReynolds said, "but thought you might spare your new commander a minute."

"Oh, all the time you need," Wallace said, taking out a plug from his sweat stained shirt. "Hope you didn't get them boots muddy or perhaps soil your hands. Life out of the infirmary can be mighty trying, sir. Maybe you ought to send a runner next time, that way we can bathe and clean up so's we don't spoil your day or take away your smooching time."

"No, no," McReynolds shot back, smiling, "I'm one to keep in touch with my men, if you know what I mean, to mingle with the common man, to make better decisions, you know."

Spitting a stream of tobacco across the opening of the well, Wallace grinned.

"And ain't we honored, sir, and what man wouldn't be, a visit from the camp doctor in his spiffy uniform and clean hands, come all the way from his hospital to tell us how to run our business."

Taking out his pipe, McReynolds filled it, striking a match on the side of his boot.

"Think nothing of it, Captain. Just checking to see if things were ready to go."

Turning serious, Wallace tilted his head in thought.

"As ready as I can get them, tools and men mostly. We'll build with the materials the area provides, which will be precious little, of course. But with soldiers there to keep guard, it should move right along once started."

"How's that thumb?" McReynolds asked.

Holding it up for McReynolds to see, he turned it this way and that.

"Been healed a long time ago, if most of it hadn't been whittled away."

McReynolds clapped him on the back.

"Thanks for your vote of confidence, Captain. Soon as those water barrels are tight, we're pulling out."

"Yes, sir," Wallace said, starting back down the ladder. Pausing, he looked up at McReynolds. "Careful you don't get caught up in no flood, sir. The men hardly slept a wink, what with you being stranded with rising waters and no way to protect yourself."

Before he could answer, Wallace's head disappeared into the well.

Making his way back down the path, McReynolds could see Sarah's soddy, remnants of the flood still evident. A wagon had been backed in, and several soldiers were loading her belongings. Stopping under the shade, he waited, hoping for a glimpse of her. Their night together was still vivid, their kiss, their laughter at the cricket.

As he'd hoped, Sarah stepped from the door, her hair loose, falling about her shoulders, an apron tied about her waist. Pushing her hair back from her face, she looked in his direction, and a tingle raced through him. Stepping into the shadows, he watched her as she swept her threshold, as she tied back her hair with a bandanna taken from her pocket. Leaning against the doorjamb, she turned her face to the sun for a moment before disappearing inside.

Coming up the hill, he could see a number of the men gathered about a wagon near the gate. Their voices were animated, and he could see Cookey talking to a man and a woman who were seated on the wagon. There was a babe in the woman's arms and a child at her elbow.

"What is it?" McReynolds asked Cookey as he approached.

"Says he wants food, sir. Says it's the duty of the U.S. Government to provide it to him. Says that we're feeding them Indians good food whilst he and his family are starving to death. I offered to feed him, but that wouldn't do. He wants enough to get him through to Kansas City."

The man on the wagon shook his head in confirmation, his hat pulled down low over his brow. The woman rocked the baby in her arms. It was wrapped in a dirty flour sack, and its mouth was red and chapped from nursing. The boy at her side picked at his nose and swung his foot off the side of the wagon.

"What you doing in the Territory, mister?" McReynolds asked. "It's against the law and dangerous for this young family of yours."

"Territory?" he said, tugging on his hat. "Hear that, May? He says we're clear down in the Territory."

Extracting her breast, May guided it into the baby's mouth.

"It's Kansas City we're headed to," she said, "if we don't starve or get kilt' by the Cheyenne first."

"We'll feed you, and you're welcome to the water," McReynolds said. "Then you head north to the border. By rights, I should arrest you."

Tearing off a twist of chew, the man rolled it into his cheek.

"Maybe a trade," he said. "I got fine wool blankets in the back, for some food, or whiskey per chance."

"No whiskey," McReynolds said. "Where you get blankets, mister?"

"From a monk." He grinned.

"You mean Indians?"

"Monk." He shook his head. "Ain't it so, May? Wore a dress, he did, and traded them blankets for a prime boar hog."

Maybe it was the way he sneered when he talked, or

maybe it was just instinct. Whatever it was, McReynolds didn't like them.

"Give 'em a hindquarter of salt pork, Cookey," McReynolds said, "and escort them to the gate."

"A hindquarter would be a fine start," the man said, "but ain't likely to get us to Kansas City, especially with no babe on the breast. Maybe you got some womenfolk about wouldn't mind taking care of the baby here, just for the time being, until we got on our feet. Soon as I get work in Kansas City, we'd be back immediately."

"Give them a sack of sugar, Cookey, to make sugar water for the baby in case she dries up." Looking up at the man, McReynolds's eyes narrowed. "Can't say I think much of a man who'd leave his baby behind, mister. You move on outta here, soon as you get your goods. There's depredations in the south, and who knows when they'll move this way."

Not waiting for an answer, McReynolds headed for the infirmary. There was a cold and hard knot in the pit of his stomach as he made his way down the path.

Sitting on the porch of the infirmary, he watched the sun drop below the horizon. When darkness fell, a chill descended from the north and set him to shivering. As he smoked his last pipe, lantern lights blinked from across the compound, and the beat of the Arapaho drum thumped in the distance. A foreboding swept him, something disturbing and indefinable.

No sooner had he risen to go inside, when shots flashed through the darkness, spits of yellow and blue followed by the crack of pistol reports. Waves of dread washed over him as he raced through the darkness toward the barracks.

Pushing his way through the circle of men, McReynolds knelt next to Number, whose hands lay open and bloodied at his side. At the bottom of the steps, Roscoe Weedling lay dead, a hole blown through the back of his uniform. Next to him Stable Sergeant Kingston lay facedown across the bottom step.

With trembling hands, McReynolds lifted Number's head into his lap.

"It's going to be okay," McReynolds said. "Don't you worry. What happened?" he asked, looking up at Cookey.

"Weedling came out of the mess carrying a pistol and shot Kingston dead center without so much as a word," he said. "Sergeant Number grabbed Weedling from behind, to pin down his arms. That's when Kingston opened fire from right there where he lay by the step, Lord knows how with a bullet hole in him. No more than a few feet away, he was, and hard to miss. Liked to have tore my eardrums out." The other men nodded in agreement. "Reckon the bullet passed clean through Weedling, striking Sergeant Number here."

Opening Number's shirt, McReynolds examined the wound, his heart sinking.

"Take him to the infirmary," he said.

Once at the infirmary, they lay Number out on the table, and Cookey helped McReynolds strip away his shirt. Reaching for McReynolds's hand, Number tried to speak.

"Kilt' by my own," he whispered.

"Take more than a bullet to end someone tough as you," McReynolds said. "Get the chloroform, Cookey, and the large forceps out of that bag. The rest of you men get on out of here."

"It's death come on me," Number said, "like a cold hand. There's a little money in my trunk and an address."

"That's a good many years down the road," McReynolds said.

"I ain't afraid," Number said. "A man thinks on

dying his whole life, and when it comes, it ain't nothing at all."

"Bring the carbolic acid over there," McReynolds said to Cookey, "and sprinkle some chloroform on that gauze. Don't get too close, or I'll be picking you off the floor. There, good," he said. "Now hold it over his nose and mouth until I say 'stop.'"

"I ain't afraid at all," Number said, "now that it's come."

Moments passed before Number relaxed, his breathing steady and slow.

"He's under," McReynolds said. "Sprinkle my hands with that carbolic acid."

Doing as directed, Cookey watched McReynolds scrub at his hands with the harsh acid.

"What's his chances?" he asked.

"It's a chance," McReynolds said.

What he didn't say, was that it was a sixty-two percent chance of dying, on the average, and this wasn't the average. If Number didn't bleed to death, surgical fever would probably get him, pus gathering in the wound cavity and racing through his veins like hot lead. The chloroform itself would bring him as close to death as the wound. If he were lucky enough to survive all of that, he'd probably addict to the opiate painkillers and stumble through the rest of his life in a half-conscious stupor. Those were the things he could have said, but didn't.

Drawing the scalpel down, McReynolds judged its depth, a slight tearing sound as the skin parted, the white layer of fat opening under his hand, blood oozing from the edges of the incision.

"Step back," he told Cookey, whose face had whitened. "Don't go down on me. I may need you."

"Yes, sir," Cookey said, rubbing at his face. "Just

never saw the inside of a man before, especially one I know."

"Inside's no different than the outside. It's the same man. Now, give him a little more."

"It's a disappointing sight," Cookey said, holding the chloroform close to Number's face, "no more than the inside of a hog or a side of beef, is it?"

Pulling open the incision, McReynolds probed with his fingers, tracing the bullet's trajectory, following the bits of blue uniform strewn along its path, the ruptured liver, the bit of lung dangling from the left lobe, the rib cage shattered like a broken dish.

Tossing the spent bullet onto the table, he looked up at Cookey, to tell of the hopelessness, to tell of this unfortunate dying, of this man who'd worked at his side and who'd stood between him and death on the trail so many times. But there would be no telling, no explanations nor reminiscing; Number's heart fluttered like a weak and dying sparrow.

From McReynolds's own life, something broke and slipped away in that moment, like a drifting leaf turns in the shallows as it moves into the irrevocable turbulence of the river.

Nineteen

Once the splint was removed, Nurse Cromley could not bear it replaced again, so she spent much of her time sitting at the fire, foot propped on a camp stool. With considerable difficulty, she managed to cook, what little there was, an occasional rabbit or ill-fated rodent.

Whatever Brother Jacob brought in was dumped in the pot and eaten without question. Theirs was a slow and protracted starvation, a matter of too little too late, and as the fall deepened into winter, food plummeted in proportion to the cold.

The garden failed, turnips shriveling in the ground like pathetic, wrinkled prunes. Determined, Brother Alexander tilled the dying plants, mounding the earth about each one with cold, blue fingers, until in exasperation Brother Jacob pulled them up, dumping them in a heap at the end of the row. Brother Alexander watched on with grim abandon.

Soon the sugar ran out and then the flour. When the grease bucket turned up empty, and the last of the corn meal dribbled from the burlap bag, Nurse Cromley approached Brother Alexander around the evening camp.

"It's too soon," he said. "I've carried pigweed from the canyon and fresh water by the bucket every day, a mile down and a mile back, but nothing appeases him. Around and around he runs, day and night, around and around with his nose in the air, squealing as if possessed. With his snout he digs great holes under the stones, and when I fill them up, he digs them again until his snout is bloody, and his ribs poke through his skin like wagon slats."

The firelight glistened in his beard and in his eyes as he thought on Chopper.

"It's God's vengeance," he said at last, "for the evil done, for the blasphemy and doubt I carry with me. It's a plague and sickness I've brought upon us for trading the sacramental wine."

Leaning over from her chair, Nurse Cromley stirred the pot. A foul smell rode up the column of steam. Whatever boiled in the pot, had been skinned, quartered, and handed to her on a bloody plank. She didn't have the heart to ask what it was, and Brother Jacob didn't volunteer.

"All the more reason to do it now," she said, "before there's no meat left on his bones."

"She's right," Brother Jacob said. "If we wait much longer, there'll be nothing left to eat."

"I've prayed that the abbey send us a wagon," Brother Alexander said, shaking his shaggy head, "that they do not abandon us in our hour of need. But there is no wagon, and there is no hope, and why should there be?"

"Nurse Cromley's right," Brother Jacob said, his voice strong, certain. Even as the others' will and strength waned, his own grew stronger, feeding on the loneliness and hardship of the prairie itself, like a cactus blooming from the hard, baked earth. "It's time Chopper served his purpose."

A man in deep and painful thought, Brother Alexander rolled his head from side to side.

"I've been sent a sign twice now in the wilderness," he said. "First there was Blue Tongue to test my will and then Chopper to tempt me, and I've been found lacking, His eyes, His voice, His sign against the evil and weakness that corrupts me."

"Now listen to me," Brother Jacob said, taking hold of his shoulder. "God doesn't need to talk to you through the tongues of animals or watch you through their eyes. Animals were put on Earth to serve man, and it's high time that hog stepped up and made his contribution. Come morning, you and I are going to the quarry. By tomorrow eve we'll have pork chops for dinner, and things will look a sight cheerier for the lot of us."

Unconvinced, Brother Alexander shuffled his way to the soddy, shoulders hunkered, head down, as if under some great weight.

Darkness dropped black and cold about them, and Brother Jacob stoked the fire to ward off its bite.

"I'd fix you some sage tea," Nurse Cromley said, "but it's dry on the bush and bitter as gall. Maybe some hot water to ease you?"

"Hot water would suit me fine," Brother Jacob said, rubbing his stomach. "Calms a man's hunger like nothing else."

As she worked at the kettle, he could see the pain in her eyes. The leg was getting no better.

"Hot water," she smiled, handing him the steaming cup."

Wrapping his hands about the cup, he sipped at the water.

"With a little imagination, I can smell roasted coffee coming right out of this cup."

Smiling, she poured herself a cup, arranging her leg on the camp stool.

"It isn't getting any better, is it?" he asked.

Tears filled her eyes, and she looked away into the darkness.

"The feeling is gone now. I think I'm running a low fever."

"What will we do?" he asked, sipping at his water.

"I've lived with the Osage these many years," she said, "and have seen hard things. This I know with certainty: One is born, lives, and dies. These are of equal value, and none can exist without the other. When it is time to die, one must embrace it with the same energy and belief that one faces life." Shrugging, she smiled at him. "I don't know what to do, to answer your question."

"But there is God," he said, "and so hope."

"Yes," she said, "and there is God."

As they went to their beds, a silence fell in the camp as complete and empty as their hearts. A silver moon, suspended in the blackness of the sky, cast the prairie in sterling; while ghosts, standing hand in hand, murmured in the winds that blew from the cottonwood grove.

Morning came with a bitter wind sweeping from the north, a relentless and icy blast that penetrated their clothes and turned their faces the color of blood. Brother Jacob sat close to the fire, his rifle in his lap, a scarf wrapped about his throat for warmth. Standing at the edge of camp, Brother Alexander stared at the horizon.

"Have some meat, Brother Alexander," Nurse Cromley said, dipping the gray morsel from the thin soup.

"No, no, thank you," he said, turning his back to them once more.

"Well, it's time to go," Brother Jacob said, slinging his rifle over his shoulder. "We'll take Shorty and build a travois to bring back the meat. Cody's next to useless, and he's developed an ulcer on his neck where the collar rides. Appears to me he's got a sickness, Texas Tick Fever probably, from the cattle coming down these trails.

"What *are* you looking for, Brother Alexander?" he asked, exasperated.

"I prayed for the wagon from the abbey to come, filled with meat and flour and dried apricots for our biscuits. It will come from that direction," he said, his beard feathering against the wind, "and bring us bounty, and then I will free Chopper. What was bought with the blood of our savior should not be consumed by us."

After catching up Shorty, Brother Jacob threw an extra length of rope over the saddle horn, bringing the reins up under Shorty's chin and leading him to where Brother Alexander stood.

"Take Shorty," he said, "case I get a shot at something on the way to the quarry."

From camp, Nurse Cromley watched them walk down the trail, Shorty between, head down, ears back in protest at the prospect of work.

Even before Brothers Alexander and Jacob saw Chopper, they heard his squeal, a high shriek emanating from behind the rock fence. Shorty danced with anxiety as they tied him to a tree, eyes rolling in anticipation of being thrown onto his back.

Tossing his abraded nose into the air, Chopper snorted at the men. Deep holes pocketed his rocky confines, and there was a path worn about its perimeter.

"Now," Brother Jacob said, laying his rifle on top of the rock wall, "go get the knife and a piece of charcoal from the saddlebag."

"Charcoal?"

"And the knife."

Loading his rifle, Brother Jacob waited for Brother Alexander's return.

"Here's the knife and charcoal," Brother Alexander said.

"Draw an X from ear to eye on his forehead. He's used to you and less likely to bolt."

"I can't," Brother Alexander said, holding the charcoal out to Brother Jacob.

"Do it," he said. "God expects us to take care of ourselves."

"It's a sign, isn't it," he asked, "to ward away demons, to thwart the powers of darkness?"

"It marks the exact spot where I'm going to shoot him," Brother Jacob said, wetting the sight of his rifle. "Soon as he drops, we cut his throat so the meat will not taste of bore."

Reaching over the fence, Brother Alexander marked the X. Chopper blew water from his snout in protest.

Crossing himself first, Brother Jacob drew down, waiting for Chopper to lift his head. When at last he looked up, his dark eyes snapping from under his ears, Brother Jacob began the slow squeeze of the trigger into the palm of his hand, a technique learned at his father's side, and it rarely failed him.

"No!" Brother Alexander shouted, shoving the rifle aside just as it exploded in a gray cloud of smoke.

Chopper jerked in disbelief at the hole that appeared in the top of his snout, a geyser of blood spewing from it, raining down on his back. Pitching his head in terror, he commenced to run the circumference of the pen, his squeal penetrating the very core of the brothers as they looked on in disbelief.

In desperation Brother Jacob circled the pen, trying for another shot, but Chopper's squeal destroyed his concentration and resolve.

"We've got to do something," Brother Alexander cried.

"Cut his throat!" Brother Jacob yelled, tossing the knife at his feet.

"What?" Brother Alexander's face paled.

"Do it now."

Picking up the knife, Brother Alexander looked over the edge of the pen at the fury below. The walls were blood splattered and caked with sand, the smell of slaughter rank in the air as Chopper charged about his pen.

All attempts by Brother Jacob to sight were foiled by Chopper's frenzied pace, his head lowered to block another murderous shot.

"Do it!" Brother Jacob yelled.

Hovering atop the stone wall, Brother Alexander waited for Chopper to circle the pen, and then like a great, black vampire, leapt upon his back, driving the knife into the deep folds of Chopper's neck. Terrorized by the thing on his back, Chopper raced about the pen in a final burst of adrenaline, dragging Brother Alexander along. When at last Chopper weakened, he swayed to and fro as if to some distant tune, his knees buckling in a final grunt.

"If you hadn't shoved me, this would not have happened," Brother Jacob shouted.

Without a word Brother Alexander walked first to the creek, where he washed his hands of Chopper's blood, and then to the top of the quarry, where he sat down on a great rock that overlooked the valley. There he remained, and no amount of pleading could bring him down to help.

Saying a prayer, Brother Jacob asked God to forgive him, for at that moment he wanted nothing more than to draw an X on Brother Alexander's forehead.

Tying Chopper's back feet with the length of rope,

Brother Jacob tossed it over the lower limb of the elm that grew out of the rock overhang near the pen. After considerable coaxing, Shorty pulled Chopper off the ground where Brother Alexander secured him with a half hitch around the trunk of the tree. First came the gutting, and then the scraping of the hide until clean of all bristle. With great care he stripped fat from the entrails, removing the heart, liver, kidneys, and wrapped them in burlap.

By late afternoon he'd built the travois, lowering the carcass into place, covering it with the woolen blankets that had been sent by the abbey.

The trip back was a dirge, the scrape of the travois as they plodded through the night. Attempts at conversation were met with heavy sighs from Brother Alexander, so they fell silent as the night drained away the day's warmth, and Shorty's breath rose in clouds of steam in the chill.

"It's done?" Nurse Cromley asked, rising to meet them.

"We'll hoist him into the tree away from the varmints," Brother Jacob said. "It's cold enough that curing won't be necessary."

Hooking her crutch under her arm, Nurse Cromley pulled a pot from the back of the wagon.

"Take a ham," she said, "and some of that lard. Tonight we eat."

"We are damned," Brother Alexander said, pulling his collar about his ears, "damned and abandoned. I go to finish my stone. It is all that is left."

As he trudged away into the darkness, Brother Jacob and Nurse Cromley looked at each other.

"He'll come around," Brother Jacob said. "It's the loneliness."

Grease glistening on their lips, they sucked at their fingers as they finished their third helping of pork.

With stomachs full, they lay back, content for the first time in many days, the red embers of the fire warming their faces.

Above them in the outstretched arms of the blackjack, Chopper twisted at the end of the rope. In the distance Brother Alexander worked under the light of the moon, his chisel ringing against the stone like the peal of bells.

It turned out that Brother Jacob was wrong about Brother Alexander. Nothing could dissuade him from his fast. Crossing his arms, he stared at his feet with determination.

"But you must eat," Nurse Cromley pleaded. "The days are cold, and you have lost too much weight."

"That poor creature died under my hand," he said, "and I'll not eat of its flesh."

"But there is nothing else."

"It's in God's hands."

And so the days passed, cold, bleak days, beginning and ending with mind-numbing monotony. Each day was colder, more bitter, than the next, incessant winds racing down from the north. Blankets and coats were no match as the cold wormed into the smallest openings of their garments. Trembling under her pile of blankets, Nurse Cromley doubted that she would ever again be warm.

Ever resolute, Brother Alexander worked at his cornerstone no matter the weather, but it was soon clear to all that he was starving, the gray pallor, the sunken eyes, the extravagant smile from behind his gaunt face. With nothing else for them to eat, Chopper's carcass soon dwindled to jowl and head, twisting in the tree at the whim of every breeze.

Her leg useless now, Nurse Cromley hobbled about from camp stool to bureau, to wagon hitch and back again, as she prepared the meager meals. An ominous black invaded her toes, and she was never far from her fever. If not for Brother Jacob's unflappable optimism, her will would have broken.

On a clear and bright day as Brother Alexander poked at the fire with a cedar stick, Nurse Cromley noticed the red spots in his thinning hair.

"Come," she said, flexing her finger.

"What is it?" he asked, looking up with hollow eyes.

"Let me see."

"What?" he asked, touching his head.

Parting his hair with her fingers, she examined his scalp.

"Now, open your mouth. Like this," she said, showing her teeth.

"They're filthy, I know," he said.

"They're bleeding," she said, "and there's blood around your hair follicles, as well. Brother Jacob," she motioned, "you too. Let me see your scalp. Yes, just as I thought. Now, look at mine." She parted her hair with her fingers. "What do you see?"

"A roach," he said, "with antennae and green eyes."

"No," she giggled, slapping at his hand. "What?"

"Specks at the base of each hair."

"And my gums?"

"Very red, like Shorty's."

"Of course," she said, pitching her crutch onto the ground.

"What?" Brother Jacob asked, studying her face.

"Scurvy."

"Is it dangerous?"

"Sooner or later. We need vitamin C, fruit, vegetables," she said.

"What do we do?"

"Do you think the wagons will come from the abbey?"

Some time passed before he answered.

"No," he said.

"We must have fruit or vegetables, even pickles would do."

Folding his arms, Brother Alexander studied the horizon. "I must finish my stone," he said.

Lifting her crutch from the ground with her good leg, she stuck it under her arm.

"Wait," she said. "Is there any sacramental wine left?"

"No," Brother Alexander said, turning.

"Yes," Brother Jacob said, "several bottles, I think."

"Grapes are rich in vitamin C, perhaps even enough to prevent further hemorrhage."

"I shall not participate in such a sacrilege again," Brother Alexander said.

"God gave you a brain for a reason," Nurse Cromley said.

"She's right, you know," Brother Jacob said. "To use the wine in these circumstances would be no sin."

Tucking his hands in the cuffs of his robe, Brother Alexander walked away.

As the days passed, the temperatures dropped, until even Shorty and Cody acknowledged its bite, their rumps turned northward, their heads drooping in resignation. The colder it became, the less game could be found. On a bitter cold morning, Brother Jacob laid his rifle under the seat of the wagon and picked it up no more.

Refusing to eat, Brother Alexander soon faltered; a falling away, a collapsing of his life and the interests that sustained it. Veins rode the tops of his hands like blue ropes, blood seeping into the whites of his eyes, gathering in the cracks of his teeth and in the pores of his skin. Threats gave him no pause nor consideration of his dire circumstance.

First his conversation stopped, and then his prayers.

Time at the stone grew less each day, his flagging energy apparent in the faint ring of his hammer. Each night before retiring, Brother Jacob would pour two glasses of wine, one for himself, one for Nurse Cromley, but Brother Alexander steadfastly refused.

"See," she would bare her pink gums to Brother Alexander, "a little vitamin C, and the world is a different place."

Picking up his hammer, he would rub his thumb over its worn end before turning back to his stone in silence.

Dipping out a cup of boiling water from the pot, Nurse Cromley mixed it with a daub of molasses she'd found stored under the wagon seat. It was the only sustenance Brother Alexander would take and only then if she insisted. Lifting the remains of Chopper's head by the ears, she placed it into the water to boil, the eerie bob of his snout above the rim of the pot.

After calling twice with no answer, she sent Brother Jacob to roust Brother Alexander from his bed.

"Still in his bunk," he said, when he returned. "I fear that he's given up hope entirely."

"I'll go," she said, "placing her hand under the cup to steady it. "Soon as that head's cooked, strip away the meat and fat. Do a good job, Brother Jacob. It's all there is between us and starvation."

Like a frail child, Brother Alexander lay curled on his bunk. Balancing the cup, she nudged his shoulder, so weak and yielding under her hand, the sodden smell of old clothes, the rawness of his breath. From the open door, a column of light fell on the rubble left by his stone carving. "You must get up," she said, shaking him again. "I've brought you water and molasses, and you must promise to drink it. Drink it now," she scolded, setting it on the small table at the head of his bed, "and then join us at the fire."

Turning over, he rubbed at his face.

"A little later," he said. "I've finished the stone, and I'm very tired now."

Standing at the door, she waited until he drifted back into sleep.

At camp, Brother Jacob worked at Chopper's skull, which he'd secured between his knees, a growing mound of morsels on the board next to him.

"Brother Alexander won't stir," she said.

"We'll make the hog's headcheese," he said, "for supper. Who could resist that?"

So while Brother Jacob gathered firewood, she prepared hog's headcheese, boiling the meat into a glutinous gel, pouring it with great care into the bread pans, setting it to chill in the back of the wagon. Later, they moved the horses south near the creek, where the grass was better, in hopes that Cody might regain some strength. After that, they probed the barren garden for a few remaining turnips.

When the evening meal was finished, she sliced off a thick piece of the hog's headcheese for Brother Alexander. But when she stepped into the soddy, she knew that it was over, that his temptations were past, his trials ended. Fading into the folds of his massive robe, he lay next to his chiseled stone, the finality of death's repose filling the tiny room.

The next morning they dug a hole in the hard packed earth of the compound and buried Brother Alexander, graced by neither casket nor cross but laid down in the clothes he wore. First she wept for him, and then for herself, for her own lost soul, and then for the loss of love and promise of life itself.

After Brother Jacob's prayer, a towel was draped over Brother Alexander's face against the rudeness of the grave, and they covered him with dirt. When finished, they lay his cornerstone at the head of his grave, and then they rested.

Rifle in hand, Brother Jacob walked to the south meadow, where he shot Cody, who could no longer graze, his body racked with pneumonia, his nose running with mucous.

That night Nurse Cromley did not rise from her chair to prepare meals as was her way, but sat instead at the edge of the fire, her blanket wrapped about her shoulders. White flurries of snow streaked across the darkening sky and gathered in the tangle of her hair. When Brother Jacob returned, she heard him stop behind the wagon before coming into the light. The day had been hard.

Kneeling at the fire, he warmed his hands but did not look at her. Snow flurries turned to water in his beard.

"We must leave," he said.

"But where?" she asked.

"There is a place at the Cimarron," he said, "a crossing for wagons called Deep Hole Creek. Maybe someone will come along there."

"What if no one comes to the crossing?" she asked.

But he did not answer, his thoughts lost in the silent grave beneath the cornerstone next to the soddy.

Twenty

First, a light snow fell, plump soft flakes that floated onto the top of Renfro's hat and across his shoulders. But within the hour a bitter gale dropped from the north, changing the snow into hard white pellets that stung their faces and rattled against the dead leaves of the trees.

Standing atop a hill, Renfro turned in a slow circle until he spotted the crush of dry grass to the west.

"There," he said to Creed, "just beyond that yucca."

In silence they made their way down the slope, Creed following in his father's footsteps.

"See," Renfro said, pointing, "where the earth dampens in that draw. Those are Buck's tracks. I'd know them anywhere."

"We'll never catch him," Creed said, rubbing at his cold hands. "We could never keep up with him without horses."

"Over there," Renfro said, "where he's taken his rest. See his tracks, one heavy, the other twisted." Pushing back his hat, he looked at Creed. "He's a bullwhacker, ain't he, and comes to think like a ox. Soon enough we will find him."

"If we don't freeze to death first," Creed said, wrapping his arms about himself.

Stooping, Renfro dug through the parfleche.

"Here," he said, tossing Creed a blanket, "least he didn't get off with our bedding. Wrap this around you."

Looping the blanket about his shoulders, Creed nodded.

"Better," he said.

"Then we best be on our way if we're going to catch this bullwhacker and give him what he deserves."

With the blanket about his shoulders, Creed reminded Adam of Twobirds, the way she had stood, the same determination in her face. Creed was like her in most ways, and of this he was glad.

The hours passed in silence as they trudged throughout the cold day. The quiet was broken only by the sound of their boots against the rocks, or the occasional caw of a crow. By noon the winds swept down from the north, swirling the skiffs of snow into the cracks and crannies of the rugged terrain.

Whenever they crossed a ravine or low area, Renfro would drop to his knee and study the tracks, assessing the rate, the direction, the strategy of his foe.

"Always takes the easy path," he said, looking up, "like water flowing downhill. See where he's followed that dry gulch instead of taking the shorter route over that butte. It's hours on, ain't it, 'cause for every easy decision he makes, we'll make the hard one." He paused. "Ain't taking care of Buck like he ought, either, too short of rope, not enough grazing range, or resting time. Sooner or later it'll take its toll."

Standing, he took a look at Creed.

"How you doing, boy?"

"Fine," Creed said, tucking the blanket up around his ears. "Could use something to eat, though."

"You been seeing those rabbit pellets?"

"Runs, too," Creed said, "mostly cactus runs."

"Good eye." Renfro smiled. "I figure one will stick

his head up and volunteer for supper sooner or later. Meanwhile, we got to get started on this butte. We'll pick up our bullwhacker's tracks on the other side."

The climb sharpened as they made their way up the butte, rocks cluttered and strewn about like giant eggs, cracked and worn from the ceaseless winds. Cactus sprouted from their crevices like spiny tumors, shriveled into themselves from the onslaught of winter. Below, the sounds of the prairie faded, replaced by the rush of wind like the flow of a great and distant river, air thinning, sterile and void of the pungent aromas of the prairie. Overhead, clouds rushed across the sky, their gray bellies churning from the winds.

As they approached a rock ledge, Renfro motioned Creed down. Bringing his rifle about, he eyed in the sight and squeezed off a shot. A jack sprung into the air, flopping and kicking down the slope toward Creed. Lifting him by his ears, Creed estimated his weight.

"A little on the skinny side," he said.

Ejecting the spent cartridge from his rifle, Adam counted the remaining shells.

"We'll have to make him do, boy. That bullwhacker got off with the ammunition."

"I'll watch for tortoises," Creed said.

"And you don't have to run 'em down," Renfro said, "least not far."

By the time they pulled themselves up the last few yards of caprock, the snow had retreated, and the sun lay cold on the horizon. Below them the prairie swirled in muted and abstract tones.

Wood was scarce on the top of the butte, a few twisted cedar clinging to the gypsum caprock, but soon Creed returned with his arms full. After building a small fire among the rocks, he skinned and cleaned the rabbit, spearing the carcass onto a yucca stick for roasting. Squatting on his haunches, he turned the rabbit over the fire and watched his father walk the rim of the butte, the wind blowing his graying hair across his face. It was as if the years had spun forward after Twobirds's death, aging those she'd left behind. There was in his father's face an emptiness, and there was nothing Creed could do to ease it.

Hunkered in the shelter of the rocks like ancient hunters, they broke the rabbit carcass in half. From a charred stick, Adam scraped charcoal onto the halves with the blade of his knife.

"It ain't salt," he said, "but it ain't bad."

Night fell clear and cold above them, stars bursting across the blackness in a dazzling array, but they did not speak in their weariness. Soon Creed slept, his knees pulled up for warmth. Laying the blanket across Creed, Renfro made his way onto the rock ledge that jutted westward from the butte. From that vantage the sky opened onto the infinite vastness of the universe.

Pulling his knees into his arms, he fell into the night sky, her presence and breath against his face, her hand in his own. If not for Creed, he would go with her now, but there *was* Creed, asleep in the rocks by the fire, and so much he hadn't been told. The promise was made, and he would keep it. The silver was Creed's only hope in the white world, and it was gone because of his own stupidity. Too long in the peace of the wilderness, he had grown careless and trusting.

Lifting his arms into the sky, he chanted her song, the Kiowa song, and his heart stilled with loneliness. With a jagged rock he slashed at his arms, his blood mixing with the ancients who'd mourned before, and his cry rose into the boundless night, a lament for the only thing that had ever mattered to him, for the only thing that ever would.

As he made his way back to the camp, his breath rose into the cold, the heat of life like a wall standing between him and Twobirds. Stopping, he turned into the night to gauge its temper, its mood and intensity. It was the absence of sound that was the most revealing on the prairie.

Something caught his eye from behind him, moon-light shooting through the night, a single refracted beam caught in the eye and spun askew into the darkness. Dropping down, he quieted his breath, his eyes absorbing the blackness, searching for the small-est movement. At first he wasn't certain, but then the coyote moved again, fixed in its disguise. With ears back, legs crouched, nose to the ground, it lapped at Renfro's spilled blood. Lifting its head, it watched him with luminous eyes. They did not avert nor know fear, and in them was affirmation and hope. Throw-ing its head to the side, it loped away into the dark-ness.

Adding wood to the fire, Adam moved in close, rifle across his lap, and watched as Creed slept. This night was as no other. This night he'd seen and heard and knew. This night he was not alone.

Tomorrow they would walk again. Each butte the bullwhacker skirted, they would climb; each creek he did not ford, they would ford; each rest he took, they would walk on. Mile by mile they would gain because the bullwhacker was like the aimless ox he drove. As to the men who followed him, their path was straight, their hearts strong and unconquerable.

When morning came, the sun rose into a brittle sky, pushing the night into the retreating shadows of the butte. Dried blood caked Adam's arms, hiding the slashes that covered them. Turning his head away, Creed did not look at nor speak of the wounds.

"Without ammunition, how will we hunt our food?" Creed asked, wrapping his blanket about his shoulders.

"Let's go, boy," Adam said. "While that bullwhacker sleeps, we'll be gaining."

Just as Adam predicted, they picked up the bullwhacker's tracks in the dry gulch that cut in a wide meander around the butte.

"Buck's taken on a rock," Adam said, checking the track. "See how he cuts that right hind leg out? Go lame, likely, if it ain't taken care of."

They pushed hard, walking steady with no time taken for a noon break. Without complaint, Creed followed behind, concentrating to maintain Adam's pace. Late afternoon they crossed a dry creek bed where Buck's tracks were clearly visible. Beside them were the boot tracks of the bullwhacker.

"He's walking," Creed said.

"Buck's pulled up lame," Adam said, blowing sand away from the tracks. "See how he's dragging that hoof?"

"Maybe they're close."

"Closer, for certain, but he's had a fair head start on us, boy. It'll take some doing yet." Sticking his hand into the sand, Adam checked for dampness. "Might be water here. Best we find out."

"Won't we lose time?"

"There ain't nothing ahead but sage, sand, and dust. Take water when it's there. It's a lesson you'll never forget. Here"—he handed his knife to Creed—"go cut some stakes to hold back this sand while I scoop out a spot."

By the time Creed returned with his arms full of yucca sticks, there was a considerable hole dug in the sand. With a rock Creed drove in the stakes to encase the hole, to keep it from collapsing. Using the coffee-pot, Adam dug out more sand while Creed maintained the integrity of the stakes with periodic blows of the rock.

"There," Adam said, "that ought to do it."

"What now?" Creed asked, stepping back to examine their work.

"Everything makes water sooner or later, boy, even this ole earth we live on. We just got to give her a little time to relax, that's all."

Taking out his blanket from the parfleche, Adam threw it about his shoulders and leaned against the bank to wait. The first hour there was little more than a dampening of the stakes from the sand, but soon a small puddle gathered at the bottom of the hole. An hour later it was an inch deep.

"Sure muddy," Creed said, looking into the hole.

"Course," Adam said, "but she'll settle out soon enough and wet's wet, ain't it? I've seen the time I'd give my arm for a single slurp of that water."

Another hour and the water had increased to four inches, an uninviting white foam floating on its top. With great care he skimmed away the foam and filled their containers, securing them in the parfleche.

"We could make camp here," Creed said, handing the knife back to his father, "seeing how it's late."

"Could," Adam said, "but then we'd be thinking like that bullwhacker, wouldn't we? There's several hours of daylight left, and we need to make the most of it. I know you're wore out but . . ."

"No," Creed said. "I'm fine."

"Keep your eye out for food while we walk. It's a hard camp without supper."

As they moved into the open prairie, the hills rolled before them like swells on the ocean, their steps falling small and feeble against its immensity. Unhindered, the north wind swept across the plains, their faces stinging, their eyes watering, their heads down against its bitterness.

Twice, Creed reached into the grass to retrieve tortoises, dropping them into his pocket where they struggled with audacity.

By nightfall the sand turned to clay and the sage to rock, and the tracks of the bullwhacker were no longer visible.

"We best stop here," Adam said. "The tracks are too poor to follow in this light."

"Alright," Creed said, averting his eyes so that his father could not see the relief in them. "I'll get the fire started."

"No," Adam said, tossing him his knife, "I'll gather wood. You dispatch those turtles and take a rest. It's been a hard day."

Setting the turtles on the ground, Creed waited for them to inch out of their shells with inevitable curiosity. A quick snap of his knife removed their heads, their eyes blinking in disbelief, their legs grinding on, ignorant yet of their demise.

Both Adam and Creed stood close to the crackling fire, their hands extended to absorb its warmth and solace. When the coals glowed, undulating and whispering against the wind, Creed lay the turtles, shell and all, on their backs in the fire. Soon the smell of roasted meat filled the air and sent Creed's appetite soaring. Roasted turtle was delicious but exasperating, the small strands of meat woven through a maze of bones and joints and nearly impossible to retrieve.

With a pair of sticks, Creed gave them a periodic turn, shells blackening, juices bubbling and sizzling into the coals. With their shirttails they held the hot shells, prying off their lids with the knife to get at the succulent bits of meat.

Grease glistened on their lips and fingers as they sucked the tiny bones clean and tossed them into the fire.

"Better to starve all at once, than a turtle at a time," Creed said.

Leaning back, Renfro locked his fingers behind his head and looked at him. Creed had grown into a good man, more even than he'd realized. There was a kindness that emanated from his eyes, but a toughness, too, a mettle and resolve that would strengthen with age.

"Tomorrow, I must go on alone," Adam said.

"But . . ." Creed started to protest.

"I know you will not be afraid to stay alone. We are closing in fast, I think. Two people make surprise more difficult, and then there is only the one rifle. I can't take you in unarmed. Your mother would never let me rest."

Crossing his arms, Creed looked at his father.

"I must be a man someday," he said.

"You are a man," Adam said, "and with much time to prove it." Tossing the stick into the fire, he looked up at him. "Tomorrow I want you to hunt for food. There are berries back there where the sand gives out and mesquite beans a mile or so to the west where that ravine cuts through. When you're finished with that, there's a rabbit run in that cactus patch we crossed through, a half mile or so back. With a rock and a little patience, you just might bean one. Find what you can to eat, and I'll be back in a day or two. Remember, that water is of first concern, and don't let this cold weather fool you. Water's first, always first." Pulling the blanket up around his shoulders, he said, "The weather is colder each day, and soon winter will be upon us. It will be harder then, much harder."

"What if you do not return tomorrow?"

"Wait three days. If I have not returned by then, follow the sun until you come to the trail. Cut to the Cimarron crossing at Deep Hole Creek. Sooner or later someone will come."

"I don't know," Creed said, unease in his voice.

"We must sleep now," Adam said, turning over and pulling the blanket about his ears to avoid seeing the look in Creed's eyes. "I must rise early to catch this bullwhacker."

At sunrise, Adam rose and stoked the fire. Laying his blanket on Creed's shoulders, he looked on for a moment before leaving.

At the ravine he picked up the bullwhacker's tracks.

"Like water," he said, "moving downhill." Buck's tracks were deep and stressed, his left front hoof splaying to the side as if under a burden. "What kind of a son of a bitch rides a lame horse?" he said to himself.

Head down, he struck out north to cut across the meander. With luck, he'd pick up his tracks again on the back swing and gain a few miles. If not, he'd double back and pick them up here.

When he got there, the tracks were easy enough to find, as they pushed down the center of the creek bed, but they were dry, old yet, and the bullwhacker was nowhere in sight. So far, Adam was no closer than ever, and there was a price to pay in energy for his relentless push, a weariness that spread across his shoulders and down the backs of his legs. Perhaps he'd misjudged the jump the bullwhacker got on them, or perhaps Buck was not as lame as he thought. Doubt dogged him as he considered the possibilities where he could have gone wrong.

At nightfall he crawled into a break. Exhausted and

half frozen, he curled into a ball to conserve heat. As he dropped into a troubled slumber, he wondered about Creed, alone, too, on the prairie, and he wished that it were not so. But wishing had paid small fare in his lifetime, and there was little reason to believe that now would be different.

At some point in the night, he awoke and rose into the cold, black silence. Trembling, he rubbed at the stiffness in his muscles and brushed away the frost that had gathered on his clothes. Too cold to sleep, he considered his options. Tracking would be impossible without moonlight to help. The dry riverbed would be easy enough to follow in the dark, but then he would not know if Elliot had changed paths, and he might go miles in the wrong direction. Burying his hands in his pockets, he plunged into the darkness. Whoever heard of an ox changing its mind?

Even in the dark, the riverbed was an easy trail. Mile upon mile, Adam pushed forward at an unwavering clip. With each mile his muscles warmed and grew stronger, and the deep chill within him faded.

By the time the sun rose in the morning sky, he had covered many miles. There in the sand, as certain as day, were Buck's tracks—fresh too, hours, maybe minutes. Dropping to his haunches, he listened, closing his eyes, ticking off the morning sounds. There were no birds, no mourning doves, no mockingbirds or blue jays arguing over breakfast. Tilting his head, he separated the smells, isolated each from the myriad flavors that hung in the morning air, the earthy fungi sprouting from the rotted cedar that lay half buried in the bed of the river, the pungent goldenrod that shot from the earth like streaks of fire, the metallic smell of winter sitting beyond the horizon like an angry white god. But there among the mix was an imposter.

"Campfire," he said.

Adrenaline pumped through him, quickening his pulse. Opening the breech, he checked the rifle chamber, one cartridge, one cartridge between him and the bullwhacker. It had served no purpose to tell Creed how few shells were left.

As he worked his way along the bank of the dry gulch, he stopped often to check the sounds, the smells, and then moved on again. Half-crouched, he traveled as silent as the Kiowa with whom he'd lived, forward a few yards, listening, forward again. How long, he couldn't be certain, but the sun bore down hot on his back through the thin, cold air, and perspiration gathered on his brow.

And then there he was, his broad back hunched over his fire. Buck, still saddled, stood with ears down, his back-leg hip shot from exhaustion. The bags of silver hung over the back of the saddle. Elliot's hat was tossed over the saddle horn, and his long gray hair fell in twists down his back. Buck opened his eyes, lifting his nose against the wind.

Dropping back against the bank, Adam checked his carbine. Snaking his way along the bank, he positioned himself with full view of the bullwhacker. Bringing down his carbine, he sighted in at the base of Elliot's neck. A head shot was always hard, but with only one cartridge, his options were limited. Taking a deep breath, he let it out slowly, relaxing the muscles across his shoulders. With a slow and deliberate squeeze he brought the trigger into the palm of his hand. At that moment Buck caught his scent, throwing his head, shying into the line of fire. Instinctively, Adam jerked his arm, the shot plowing into the dirt beneath Buck's belly.

Spinning about, Elliot leapt for his weapon, leveling

it at Adam. Hair fell across his eyes, his face red and swollen from the cold.

"Climb out of there," he said, " 'fore I blow off your head."

Tossing down his carbine, Adam stepped out.

"Morning, bullwhacker," he said.

"Ain't you the son of a bitch," he said, "catching me afoot."

"Ain't hard to outthink a ox," Adam said. "Had I one more cartridge, you'd be facedown in your campfire."

"Well, I ain't, am I; so me and your silver there's going to St. Louis."

Bringing around the butt of his gun with the full force of his weight, he caught Adam across the eye, dropping him into the dirt at his feet.

"Guess I should've shot you and that half-breed kid when I had a chance."

Blood spilled from Adam's scalp as he sat up. Fighting to clear his head, he mopped at his eye with the sleeve of his shirt just as Elliot brought the rifle up to his shoulder.

Instinctively, Adam slammed the heel of his boot into the bullwhacker's knee with a crushing blow, his rifle skittering into the campfire.

Blood narrowed Adam's vision to a slit, but it was enough to see Elliot's bowie knife flashing in the morning sun. Unsheathing his boot knife, Adam rose to face his enemy, and formidable he was, too—the colossal bowie, the massive strength of his shoulders.

With a ferocious swing, the bullwhacker opened the skin of Adam's chest with a crack. A hot pain shot up Adam's arms, settling in his chest, legs buckling under him.

"I'm going to hang your balls over my saddle horn," the bullwhacker said, "along with that silver."

Ignoring the scalding pain, Adam drove his foot into Elliot's other knee, Buck rearing into the air at the bullwhacker's scream. Bewildered, the bullwhacker searched for his bowie but too late as Adam set the boot knife under his rib cage. There was a whoosh of air as his black heart seized, and he fell forward into the dirt like a downed tree.

"Only a ox would go for the same trick twice in a row," Adam said.

Cutting a strip off the bullwhacker's shirt, Adam tied it about the wound on his chest to stop the bleeding. After that, he took the saddle off Buck, rubbing him down with a handful of sage, hobbling him out to graze. At the riverbed he found a puddle of water from which he drank, washing the blood from his face and arms. On the way back he gathered sticks, stoked the fire, and finished the breakfast the bullwhacker had started. Then he lay down to sleep, a hard and deep sleep without dreams or worry or caution.

When he awoke, the sun was low in the sky. Even though his eye was swollen to fist size, and the slash across his chest burned with every movement, his energy was strong, and his spirit was high. While saddling Buck, Adam scratched the horse's ears, and let him nibble the back of his sleeve in way of welcome.

As they left camp, a buzzard settled atop the bullwhacker's chest, lifting its wings with indecision before dipping its head to feast.

Heading up the riverbed, he struck a steady and fixed pace. To the west the sunset burst into a pageant of colors, reds and oranges lapping against the horizon, crimson waves rolling across the darkening sky.

It was nearly midnight when he broke out of the

valley to climb the butte. As he approached Creed's fire, he called out, "It's me, boy."

Stepping from the darkness, Creed's face lit up.

"You okay?"

Slipping the saddle off Buck, Adam jingled the bags of silver so that Creed would hear.

"You get something to eat?" he asked, dropping the saddle to the ground.

"Beaned a jack, a big one, too."

"That's good, boy, 'cause I could eat a boiled boot right now."

"You've been hurt," Creed said as Adam stepped into the light of the fire.

"Took a lick across my chest and eye, but it looks worse than it is."

Threading the jack onto a stick, Creed held it over the fire.

"Is Buck alright?" he asked.

"Feelings are hurt," he said.

Warming their feet against the fire, they ate the rabbit, neither speaking of the bullwhacker's fate. Rising, Adam dug through the saddlebags until he found the bullwhacker's bowie.

"This is yours, boy," he said, handing him the knife.

"It's the bowie," Creed said, "the bullwhacker's bowie."

"Yours now."

"Where do we go from here?" Creed asked, tucking the bowie into his belt.

"Cimarron crossing at Deep Hole Creek," Adam said. "Time you and me met up with civilization."

"Are they all like him?" Creed asked.

Taking out his blanket, Adam threw it over his shoulders and lay down next to the fire.

"Some are and some ain't," he said. "It's like that

knife there. Was a mighty big bowie carried by a mighty small man."

"I don't understand," Creed said, thumbing the handle of the bowie.

"It ain't the knife that makes the man, Creed," he said, closing his eyes in sleep. "It ain't never the knife."

Twenty-one

Word came of the desertions while McReynolds was busy making his final entry into the camp diary. On most days desertions would not qualify as news, except that now he was going to be three men short. Even worse was the shortage of experience among the men he did have, no depth, no one he could rely on if things turned sour. The thought of going into the prairie without Sergeant Number at his side filled him with uncertainty. As a surgeon McReynolds was secure, but years of experience in the Army had failed to make him a confident soldier.

"This morning?" he asked.

"Yes, sir," the regimental sergeant major said, tucking in his chin, "after they had breakfast and 'fore roll call."

"Which way they go?" McReynolds asked, closing the camp diary.

"North, most likely."

"Send anyone after them?"

"Wouldn't, just for French leave, except they took three good mounts."

Circling around his desk, McReynolds looked out over the compound.

"Can you provide me replacements?"

Scratching at his beard, the sergeant studied for a

moment. "Not if I have to send out a detachment to bring them in. Otherwise, I guess I could spare a few. Course, they'd have to settle for culls, smooth mouths, and a hammerhead roan."

"Well," McReynolds said, putting on his hat, "give me the replacements, and we'll let the prairie take care of our deserters."

"Yes, sir," the sergeant said, "and likely so. There ain't brains enough betwixt the three to find the fort gate on a spring morn."

From across the compound, McReynolds could see Wallace loading a supply wagon. Work was Wallace's heartbeat, his soul, and he thrived on it. It was the rare man who did more, or did better, than Wallace.

"Will there be anything else, sir?" the sergeant asked.

"Nothing else. The expedition is leaving, daylight. We'll need those mounts outfitted and the men briefed."

"Yes, sir," he said, stepping past McReynolds and onto the wooden deck of the infirmary. "It's a comfort knowing them Cheyenne are in the south, ain't it? Best of luck to you, sir."

The sergeant major trudged away, a slight gimp in his walk, thrown from a horse, no doubt. Almost everyone in the Cavalry took a serious bone break sooner or later. Growing bones back was no problem. Growing them back straight was another matter altogether.

Stepping out of the door, he started across the compound, to talk to Wallace, to check on Sarah, to make certain Cookey's supplies were set to go. Halfway across, he changed his mind, turning back to the infirmary. Tomorrow would be soon enough. Everything that could be done in way of preparation had been done. Once the expedition started, privacy was no longer a choice. At this moment it was, and he was going to take it.

The next morning as reveille sounded over the camp, its siren call striking dread into the sleepy hearts of the soldiers, McReynolds was making his rounds.

It was Wallace he found first, of course, double-checking his supply wagons to make certain he'd forgotten nothing.

"Captain Wallace," he said, walking around the wagon.

"Well, morning, Major. Guess it must be coming on noon if you're up and about."

"Do my planning *before* the day I leave, Captain. Others would do well to follow that example."

Squinting his eyes against the rising sun, Wallace looked at him from under his bushy brows.

"Well, now, seeing as how I got to follow a sawbones into the wilderness, and seeing as how he's got my life in his hands, so to speak, and seeing as how I ain't likely to get out of any of this alive, guess I'll just keep my mouth shut."

"And the sun won't rise across the sky ever again, Captain Wallace."

"Well, now," Wallace pushed back his hat, "I guess people who walk on water and such ain't likely to be surprised by a trifling miracle as that."

"Wouldn't be the biggest miracle I've made, but then every miracle is special in its own way."

"It's a miracle more ain't kilt' or gone mad from the spectacle of army life, I'd say."

McReynolds laughed. "We'll move out at eight. I've gone over everything three times. Hope I haven't missed anything."

Adjusting his hat back down, Wallace shrugged.

"I figure you'll do just fine, Major. It's a short trail as trails go, and depredations been pushed south from what I hear. We'll build that redoubt and be back home before Santa can hitch up his mule team." Checking the tautness of the ropes, he looked up at McReynolds. "I have been wondering," he said.

"What's that, Captain?"

"Why there's no howitzers."

The bray of complaining animals rose from the barns as the men hitched up harness and wagons, the smell of fried fatback and boiled coffee drifting from the mess.

"Sully's assured me howitzers from Fort Dodge on the first train."

"Oh, well," Wallace said, "that's a comfort, knowing Sully as we do, what with him safe in Kansas while Custer does his dirty work down south. Makes a man wish he'd paid more attention to smooching etiquette when he had the chance." A rush of cold wind swept the trees, their bare limbs clawing at the blue sky. Hunkering his shoulders against the cold, Wallace shivered. "And about that girl," he added.

"Sarah?"

"That one," he said, pointing his chin toward her cabin. "She's got no business going to that redoubt. It's a hard life out here at best, and it'll be gut-hard living in a redoubt. Seems a damn fool thing."

"You tell her that?"

"I ain't been in the Territory *that* long, Major."

Checking his watch, McReynolds looked up at the rising sun.

"Cookey will be driving her team," he said. "He's a fair hand with the horses and has a calming way with women." Scraping at a piece of mud clinging to the wagon wheel, he paused. "It's that husband of hers. It isn't right for a man to beat a woman down so."

When he looked up, he saw the expression on Wallace's face. "What's wrong with you?" he asked.

Wallace lifted his brows. "With me?"

McReynolds stiffened. "She's a married woman, Captain." When Wallace didn't answer, McReynolds shrugged and gave a turn. "Well, then," he said, "that's that. We're pulling out within the hour."

As the small band of wagons rumbled from Fort Supply, a chilling wind swept from the north snapping the canvas covers of their wagons like whip tails. Soldiers from the fort held onto their hats and took shelter as they watched the departure.

Within a few miles the train passed the Indian encampments, a tired and defeated people waiting for the rations to be brought each day from the fort. They did not speak nor wave nor smile but looked on with sad and deserted eyes as the wagons passed by. From somewhere deep within the encampment came a drumbeat, a singular and disturbing throb that struck the hearts of those who heard.

Riding back to check the wagons, McReynolds spoke to each driver and smiled in an effort to raise his spirits. There was no loneliness so complete, no moment so abject or contrary to reason as riding into the dangers of the prairie.

Pulling his collar up against the wind, McReynolds rode along side Cookey and Sarah's wagon.

"Morning, Cookey," he said, glancing at Sarah.

"Morning, sir." Cookey saluted.

"Morning, Sarah," McReynolds said, touching the brim of his hat.

"Major," she said, a quick smile sweeping her face.

"I take it, all is well."

"Why, yes, Major," she said, pushing a strand of hair back. The morning sun lit her delicate upturned mouth. "Aside from the chill, everything is fine. I do wonder how long it will take?"

Reining up, they waited for the wagon ahead as it

crossed a dry gulch. As soon as the wagon moved up the other bank, he spoke.

"A few days, if the weather holds, and we have no major breakdowns."

"Days?"

"But the trail is well marked," he added, "and the depredations are to our south. It should be an easy journey. There is nothing to fear."

Lifting her chin, she dropped her eyes until they locked onto his.

"I'm not afraid," she said.

"I am," Cookey piped up. "I hear tell the Cheyenne shot an arrow straight through a guard's ear at Fort Reno. Kilt' him so fast he didn't even fall. There he was, still standing, dead as a carp, with a cigarette burning between his fingers. Wasn't until they found a piece of feather clinging onto his earlobe that they even knew what kilt' him. Course, it's the way to go, I reckon, if you have to go."

"Pay him no mind," McReynolds said, "too many years of Army beans and bad hooch."

"Sorry, ma'am," Cookey said, pushing back his hat, "no mind at all."

As the drumbeat faded, the wagons pulled onto a vast expanse of sage, and the men's spirits lifted. At noon Cookey fed beans and bread, along with a special treat of cold milk packed in river ice and sawdust. The men joked and lay about on the ground, their hands behind their heads like great birds. Everywhere Sarah went, eyes followed, and men fell silent at the feline curve of her back, the soft mound of her body through the cotton dress, the gurgling richness of her voice when she spoke.

But it was McReynolds who watched her the most, the way she combed her hair, the way her breasts lifted and fell with each breath, the way she grew quiet sometimes as if haunted by dark memories. There was in her a disconsolate and irretrievable sadness, something broken, something damaged beyond repair. It was so in many women he'd known, a sense of loss that tempered and quieted their spirits.

That night they camped at the edge of canyons that twisted into the red clay hills beyond. Here, drought was perpetual. Even though rains swept down the canyons in a fuming rush, they left naught but a slick, red grease behind. So impenetrable was the red clay that even the tenacious mesquite could not survive. Still, there was plenty of firewood, washed by the flash floods and deposited in convenient stacks at every turn of the canyon.

Soon Cookey had his fires built, and the smell of corn bread filled the air. There was a general good feeling, a sense of purpose and community. They were a good lot of men, as soldiers go, but not a warrior to be found among them. None had been tested. This McReynolds knew with an uneasiness that lay in the pit of his stomach like a cold bar of steel.

The biggest and strongest was Hamilton, a boy from West Virginia who took considerable pride in his strength and in his carpentry skills, but was fearful of horses and walked afoot most of the day. And then there was Housman, an unlikely blacksmith, fairskinned and frail with large, sad eyes. Some claimed he could make a horseshoe out of a square nail, but he was timid and seldom spoke to anyone, preferring instead to scribble his thoughts in a writing pad that he kept tucked in his back pocket. Rumor was that he was pining for a girl back home, and that sometimes at night they could hear him weeping with heart sickness.

The last time McReynolds walked these trails he'd been surrounded by warriors: Renfro with his opti-

mism and courage; Twobirds with her supreme knowledge of the prairie; and, of course, Number, his loyal
and giving friend. They were warriors. But these were
mostly kids, uneducated, rough, escaping from places
with little promise and less hope, coming to this desolate and dangerous land in an irrational search for
themselves. But there were no warriors. None had
tasted the bitterness of war, the terror of the enemy,
the reality of death.

Tossing the last of his coffee into the fire, McReynolds rose to make his way to bed. As he passed Sarah's
wagon, her light glowed behind the drawn canvas.
Pausing, he watched her shadow moving through the
yellow cast of the lamp, an ephemeral and delicate
reverie vanishing as she extinguished the flame.

Exhausted, McReynolds pulled his blanket about
him. Above, the sky cleared, and the night fell cold,
still, a blue moon riding overhead. From the rope corral a horse stomped its hoof, and smoke curled undisturbed from the dying fire. On the distant horizon,
the solitary cry of a coyote faded away.

Dawn found Cookey chipping at the block of ice in
the water bucket, his ears red from the cold.

"Morning," McReynolds said, rubbing at the whiskers that had already begun to sprout on his face.
"What's the problem?"

"Froze solid," Cookey said, "Cheyenne probably,
casting spells and lurking about all hours of the night.
There ain't time for bread making, either."

"Can't be helped. Make it a quick breakfast, Cookey.
We need to make time today."

Truth was, he was worried about the weather. It was
colder than usual for this time of year, and the smell
of winter was in the air. He'd been caught by winter
before in this country, and it was not something he
cared to repeat.

"Seen Captain Wallace this morning?" he asked.

"Fine and dandy, he is." Cookey grinned broadly. "Working like there's no tomorrow."

Squatting at the fire, McReynolds held out his hands to warm them.

"And Sarah?"

"Yes, sir, her too."

"She manage alright?" he asked nonchalantly.

"Manage?"

"With the journey and all?"

"Yes, sir. I'd say she managed. Been helping with the cooking, too. 'That's the job for these here boneheads,' I said. 'If they ain't kept busy, they're likely to join up with the Cheyenne or get shot through the ear, no telling what.' But she wouldn't have it no other way, sir."

"Well, see to it she doesn't work too hard, Cookey. Things are likely to get harder."

"I'll keep an eye out for her, sir. Don't you worry."

"It's just that I feel responsible."

"Yes, sir," he said, looking up from his kettle.

Temperatures dropped all morning, a precipitous plunge that sent the men digging for winter coats and hats. Winds whipped through the canyons, burning their faces, stinging their ears, turning their eyes to water. Twice, ropes broke on the wagons, spilling their contents onto the ground. Kicking at the wagon bed, Wallace cursed and swore vengeance on the Army and the shoddy workmanship of its soldiers.

As was Housman's way, he bent to fill his arms with lumber, not one to shy from helping wherever it was needed. But Wallace, in a pout, refused the help, securing the load himself. Feelings hurt, Housman turned away, his hands buried in his pockets.

"Don't worry about it," McReynolds said as he passed. "The captain's under a little stress, that's all. The trail takes its toll."

"Yes, sir," Housman answered with a smile, ducking his head as he made his way toward the corrals.

At noon they rested on the south slope of a canyon wall. With sufficient fuel for a fire, Cookey prepared potato soup with the remaining milk and brewed up ample pots of hot coffee. Spirits rose as they warmed themselves with food and fire, and soon they were joking with each other. Bantering was never far from the surface, the proclivity of the boy within them bubbling out at the slightest opportunity.

Sarah filled their cups with coffee, and their hearts with joy, her smile lifting them even higher from the drudgery of their journey. With a delicate touch she steadied McReynolds's hand as she poured his coffee, the smell of her sachet, the brush of her hair against his face, the elegant turn of her mouth like the curl of a rose petal. The memory of that unguarded moment alone in the cabin caused his face to flush with heat.

By late that afternoon the canyons opened onto a broad plane, tufts of yucca and sage dotting the otherwise barren ground, winds sweeping unhindered down its face, pushing great swirls of sand before it like breaking waves. The going would have been easier, except for the chill, the unrelenting wind, the mind-numbing monotony of the terrain.

That night they camped in the open, their backs to the wind, and ate their meal in silence. Sleeping was nearly impossible, and when morning came, it came with a vengeance, icy winds, scouring sand that abraded their skin and set their tempers on edge.

Grumbling and complaining abounded as they gathered for breakfast. When they discovered that once again they were to be deprived of their bread rations, the complaints turned to Cookey.

"It's the Cheyenne, ain't it?" Cookey lamented.

"How's a white man going to make bread, what with half the Cheyenne nation dead set against it?"

"What kind of craziness is that?" Hamilton asked, throwing his hat to the ground. "The Cheyenne ain't got nothing to do with making bread. Seems to me it's the cook's job, to cook and that's that."

"Well," Cookey said with a puzzled look on his face, "anyone with a lick of sense knows we're smack in the middle of Cheyenne country, and that ain't the cook's fault, now is it?"

There was no reasoning with Cookey once his mind was set. Exasperated, the men ate their cold beans in silence and trudged off to harness the teams.

The decline in morale was predictable. McReynolds knew the pattern well. It was an established part of the seasoning process that took place on the trail. The antidote was equally well-known.

Noon came and went and he did not stop, driving them hard into the icy winds. A silence fell over the men as they turned energy into the task and their discontent against the pace. By afternoon there wasn't one among them who wouldn't have given a day's pay for cold beans and a moment's rest. But it was Sarah he watched, pleased to hear not a word of complaint as she huddled against the cold under the wagon tarp next to Cookey.

Four hours' push brought them to a river that meandered down the center of the plane, ice glistening across its expanse, frost crystals drifting in aimless circles over its surface.

Like crows on a fence, McReynolds and Wallace stood on the bank and studied their situation.

"Ain't that just fine and dandy," Wallace said, spitting tobacco juice onto the ice at his feet. "Two days out, and we're already standing at the edge of the Arctic."

"Doesn't appear to be deep," McReynolds said, "but if a wagon dropped through the ice, be a task getting it out."

"Still," Wallace observed, stepping out onto the ice and trying his weight, "it ain't running water, is it? Not so you can tell, at least. We could lighten a wagon and send it across for a test run."

"What if it broke through?"

Shrugging his shoulders, Wallace looked at McReynolds.

"Well, if I was a doctor, God forbid, I'd just say there was little to be done and wait for my problem to die so's I could cover it over with dirt, and everybody could forget about it. But I'm an engineer, ain't I, and if one thing don't work, then I try another and another until the problem is solved."

"I don't know," McReynolds said, pulling his collar against his ears. "Seems a tad risky to me."

"Well, if it's getting your shoes mucked up that's worrying you, Major, maybe the boys and I could carry you over on our shoulders. Course, if it's a red carpet you're wanting. . . ."

"Alright, alright, Captain, you're the engineer, but send one man with a lightened load. If it's too thin, we'll just hole up until tomorrow, then move upstream until it narrows or peters out."

It was Housman who stepped forward from the ranks.

"I'll take one over, Captain," he said.

"You boys empty the wagon and hitch up that hammerhead jack," Wallace said. "He's strong enough to do the job and dumb enough not to know any better." Wiping the water from his nose with the sleeve of his coat, Wallace put his hand on Housman's shoulder. "Take it slow," he said, "and keep her on white ice. If she begins to crack, jump off and let her go."

"What about the mule, sir?"

"The mule too, Housman. I ain't seen one yet couldn't follow orders better than a soldier. Course, I ain't tried to teach one smithing yet."

"Can't tell an upset from a draw, sir, no matter how many times they're showed."

"Don't be scared to turn back, soldier," Wallace said. "No one here blame you for that."

At first the mule refused to step on the ice, dropping its hindquarters in protest, its ears pointed forward on its head. Climbing down from the rig, Housman whacked him smart across the ears before tailing him up.

Back on the wagon, he popped the whip smart over the mule's head.

"Huh!" he shouted. With reluctance the mule stepped onto the ice. "Hitup!" Housman shouted again.

From the bank, McReynolds and Wallace watched and called out orders as the wagon creaked farther onto the ice.

Every few steps, the mule stopped, splaying its legs, and whickering, but Housman gave no quarter, urging him ever from shore.

Looking back, Housman waved, his face beaming with excitement. When a gust of wind lifted something in the air, he stood, reining up the jack, his smile gone.

"What?" McReynolds said.

"Don't know," Wallace said, stepping out onto the ice.

Dropping from the wagon, Housman began working his way around the bed, holding onto the side boards with both hands.

"Bring him in," McReynolds said. "He can't be stopping on the ice."

"Damn kid," Wallace said, waving for Housman's attention.

Making his way to the back, Housman reached through the rungs of the wheel, pushing his shoulder between the spokes as he stretched to retrieve whatever it was the wind had taken.

"Get him in," McReynolds shouted.

But even as he spoke, the rear of the wagon dropped through the ice, a sickening crack, like the crack of bone, and the braying of the mule as it was thrown to its side by the weight of the wagon, the terrifying thrash of water as Housman was yanked beneath the surface.

"Oh, my God!" Sarah screamed. "He's drowning."

"Get a rope," McReynolds yelled, "fast!"

Within moments Hamilton tossed a rope down the bank. Hands shaking, McReynolds tied one end about his waist and handed the other end to Wallace.

"Wallace," he said, "we're about to bury one of your problems out there. Stay as far back as the rope will allow. Won't do any good if we both go in the drink."

At first he went slowly, testing the ice to make certain of its thickness. Convinced of its strength, he moved on, edging his way to the wagon, turning to check Wallace's whereabouts, dropping to all fours as he approached the hole. The terrified mule brayed and struggled to regain its feet as McReynolds came closer.

What McReynolds saw struck hard, Housman's free hand reaching from the murky waters, fingers clawing for help, face inches from the surface. Grabbing his hand, McReynolds pulled with all that was within him, with all that man in his weakness could do, but Housman was pinned beneath the wheel, hopeless and irretrievable.

If only he'd brought his scalpel to amputate his arm, free him at least from certain death, but even as he turned to call, he knew that Housman could wait no longer, that no man could save him now. Bubbles rose from the water, bursting like whispers at its surface as he held tight the dying boy's hand.

It was nightfall by the time they'd freed the mule, roped the wagon into shore, and buried Housman on the knoll west of the crossing. Standing next to the grave, Sarah took McReynolds's arm while Captain Wallace read from the Bible.

As they made their way down the knoll, the men felt the reach and finality of Housman's death. If *he* could die, so could they. As Sarah and McReynolds fell in behind the procession, Sarah stopped.

"Why did he climb off that wagon?" she asked. "Why would he do such a fool thing?"

Reaching into his coat pocket, McReynolds handed her Housman's tablet, filled with his dreams and hopes, the pages still curled and wet from the icy waters of the river.

Twenty-two

The scar on Little Dog's face was a bruised and purple ridge where the savage wound had once been. Still tender, it ached as he and Crooked Leg rode into the cold wind, but it was a welcome pain, a reminder of the vengeance that burned in his heart. To feel the pain was to know there was still reason to move into the bitterness that was his life.

For days they had traveled south to the Washita, the winter encampment of Black Kettle. Only Black Kettle's band was strong enough to resist the soldiers, and Little Dog was certain that once he'd heard of the slaughter of the Dog Soldiers, he would rise against them.

"Soon we must camp," Crooked Leg said, rubbing at his ankle. The bone had not mended as it should, giving Crooked Leg much pain.

"There is timber over there," Little Dog said, "a stream, and shelter from the wind."

When something caught his eye, he fell silent, dismounting and studying the ground, turning in a slow circle.

"Shod," he said, "three, with one walking, a day, maybe more. The tracks are crusted from dew, and there are droppings from the horses. See where they stood figuring their way, and then following the sun."

"It is the wrong direction for us," Crooked Leg said.

"Still, there would be horses, and maybe rifles. These things we will need."

"But we must have more warriors," Crooked Leg said, "and they are south to the Washita."

Mounting his horse, Little Dog studied the horizon.

"The decision will wait," he said. "Now we will camp."

When they came upon a stand of locust sprouting from a sandy creek bottom, blackbirds swept skyward, banking against the sun. On the north a knoll broke the wind, the sand still warm from the sun's heat. Soon a fire crackled, and smoke rose into the reaches of the trees.

Threading the last of the buffalo meat onto a sharp stick, Crooked Leg turned it in the blue embers of the fire. The aroma of roasting meat silenced them with anticipation. As dusk set, they chewed their meat and looked into the flames. Many nights they'd gathered about the fire like this, bound by blood, by brotherhood, by kind. But this was a camp without solace, devastated by tragedy and an uncertain future.

Rubbing his ankle, Crooked Leg leaned back against a log and watched the last swatch of orange fade on the horizon. Even in the dusk, Little Dog could see the strain about his old friend's eyes, the hawkish cut of his nose against his thinning face. Since the beginning they had hunted these sweet hills, but they were old too soon, tired and dispossessed. Here on this cold night they sat out of time, out of place, two hunters thrown at the irreverent feet of a new world.

"I am weary," Little Dog said, tossing a meat gristle into the fire. "My rest does not heal as it should."

"I too," Crooked Leg said, leaning toward the warmth of the fire. "My bones have been hollowed and filled with sand."

"Each day I rise only for vengeance," Little Dog said. "Will it come?"

"Black Kettle will help," Crooked Leg said, wanting to bolster his friend's flagging spirits. "We will return in great numbers and with many horses. You and I will drive our lances into the ground and not retreat until the plains run red with their blood."

Smoke shifted from the fire as the north wind swept the trees above them. Leaning on his elbow, Little Dog looked at his ole friend.

"I tell you this," he said, "that my heart beats only for that moment. From then I wish to live no more."

Neither spoke as he prepared himself for sleep, backs to the dying fire, thoughts lost in the blackness of the prairie.

For Little Dog the dream rose like a feather into the north wind, lifting him ever higher into the cold, black sky, but he was not afraid, and his voice was full and resounded throughout all the prairie when he spoke. When he came to a great canyon, it smelled of cedar and sage, and Blue Tongue stood at the mouth of the canyon, her great tongue lolling in the dirt, her breath smelling of gourd, her teats full and strutted.

"Where am I?" he asked.

"Heammawihio," Blue Tongue said, "as everyone knows."

"I want to see Owl Talker," he said, "and my son."

"You must milk out my teats first," Blue Tongue said, "because they are swollen and painful."

But when he milked her teats, red streams of blood poured from them and splashed onto his bare feet and ankles. And then Owl Talker touched his shoulder, and his heart burst with joy to see her. Leaning over, she kissed his eyes, and he could see the great wound that had taken her life. Pointing to their son who played in the bloody sand at Blue Tongue's feet, she said,

"See how they have killed him because of their hatred for you."

When he tried to speak, his voice would not come, and he sat up, gasping for breath, the smoke from the dying fire burning his nostrils. In the stillness of the night he could hear the thump of his heart and the quiet snore of Crooked Leg under the saddle blanket.

When morning came, the cold was deep, and their breaths rose above them as they worked at saddling their horses.

Throwing the reins over his horse's neck, Little Dog turned to Crooked Leg.

"I will follow the horses."

"I, too, will follow," Crooked Leg said, swinging onto his mount, "for the Dog Soldiers will always be as one."

That day they rode west, following the tracks that turned first one direction and then another and then back again. The bitter wind that blew from the north numbed their hands and set them to shivering against its blast.

Standing on the bank of a creek, Little Dog pointed.

"They have joined others," he said, "a single wagon, four horses. And there," he pointed, "one has relieved himself behind the tree and smoked tobacco."

"There will be more guns now," Crooked Leg said.

Lifting his lance above his head, Little Dog yelped, a high-pitched wolf howl that sent Crooked Leg's blood hot.

"The more to kill," Little Dog said, reining about his horse.

Soon they had entered a narrow valley, a fast-moving stream twisting down its center, blackjacks and cedar clinging to life along its muddy banks. Even in the cold, their horses were white with lather and their nostrils flared from exertion. At a low spot they stopped to water, and it was there Crooked Leg spotted the wagon tracks cut deep where it crossed the stream.

Dropping his hand to warn Little Dog, Crooked Leg whispered, "They are very close."

Laughter rose then from somewhere beyond the trees, Crooked Leg and Little Dog crouching, moving into the darkness of the grove behind them. Laughter broke again, thick and drunken, caution lost in the moment.

From Little Dog's vantage he could see the south turn of the creek, a sweeping bank of red mud, a band of water grass sprouting from the undercut. At first he didn't see her sitting on the bank, her legs pulled beneath her, her hair swept over her shoulder, a baby suckling at her breast.

When he did, his breath shortened. With difficulty he stilled himself, steadied his eye, his hand, to quench the fire that burned too hot within him. Signaling Crooked Leg, he drew his knife.

With singular concentration he moved from behind, to smell the wetness of the child, to hear its contented grunt at the nipple. A breeze rippled the treetops as he reached for her, covering her mouth with the iron grip of his hand, her eyes wide with terror, her body trembling. Even as she struggled, he thrust the knife under her shoulder blade, a swift and immutable blow that left her body quivering, milk dripping from her breast onto the baby's face. Even as it opened its mouth to cry, Crooked Leg brained it with a rock, slinging it into the water, blood curling from its head into the back swirl of the stream.

Moving into the trees, Little Dog and Crooked Leg waited, their eyes fixed on the bend of the creek. First to appear was a boy, a wool blanket wrapped about his shoulders, a finger buried in his nostril as he strolled the shore of the creek. At first sight of the slain baby, he stopped short, his eyes widening in fear. The arrow from Little Dog's bow glanced askew, spinning into the boy's shoulder, his scream a crescendo of disbelief, but the second shot silenced him, and he crumpled from sight into the river grass.

"May, can't you quiet that goddang kid?" a voice called from around the bend of the creek.

When the old man stepped into view, he tossed up his hands, his jaw dropping, a single, yellow-stained tooth hanging from his head. The lethal whir of Little Dog's lance cut through the stillness, burying itself in the old man's chest.

Dropping back, Little Dog and Crooked Leg checked and rechecked their positions. It was Little Dog who first signaled, sweeping his hand in the direction of the creek.

Two men with rifles worked their away along opposites sides of the stream. One carried a wine bottle, which he tipped up from time to time. A third crept along the top of the bank, his straw hat bobbing above the river grass.

Lifting himself into a cedar, Little Dog braced against the fork of the tree and waited. Within moments, the man nearest him moved into range, his blond hair draped across his eyes, his skin burned red from the wind. Stopping, he took a pull from the wine bottle and wiped at his mouth with the sleeve of his shirt. Even though his clothes were that of a farmer, his boots were the black leather of a Cavalry soldier, a deserter, Little Dog figured, from the white man's camp. It was their way to rid themselves of the soldier's uniform as soon as possible, so as not to be caught and punished.

Pulling back the string of his bow, he let the quiver in his arm steady, a half-pace lead, a last second adjustment for arch and wind, a swift and flawless trajectory. The man grunted as the arrow tore through his rib cage and lodged in his spine.

On the other bank, the soldier struggled to bring about his firearm, but Crooked Leg's arrow drove deep into the soft folds of his belly. Falling to his knees, he grasped its shank in astonishment.

From above, the third man broke. It was in his mind to run, to race across the prairie with all that was within him, to flee the vile and bloody end of his mates, but Little Dog's arrow tore through his back, spinning him about in a pirouette of death.

When Little Dog and Crooked Leg entered the camp, they found the campfire still burning.

"Rifles," Crooked Leg said, "and ammunition."

"They were expecting a hard winter," Little Dog said, holding up blankets from the wagon bed.

Popping the cork, Crooked Leg tipped a bottle of wine.

"It was a good idea you had, to follow the tracks, Little Dog," he said, handing him the half-empty bottle.

Drinking deeply, Little Dog let the wine dull his pain. From behind the trees the sun set, a churning dollop of red.

"We will pack the blankets on one of the horses," he said, "and burn the wagon."

"But it will soon be dark," Crooked Leg said.

"There is a full moon tonight. We will ride for a while and find a clean place to camp."

Flames rose into the darkness from the burning wagon as they made their way down the creek bed, the string of horses dancing and blowing at their backs. As they passed the bodies of the soldiers, their horses shied with eyes wide at the specters floating in the water.

A moan issued from the darkness, and Little Dog searched for movement.

"Over there," Crooked Leg said.

Once again the soldier groaned, his bloodied hands still grasping the shaft of the arrow that grew from his belly. Reining about, Little Dog circled the dying soldier.

"Do you want me to kill him?" Crooked Leg asked.

"No," he said, burying his heels into his horse's sides.

That night they rode until the moon was high overhead. In a dry arroyo they camped without fire, sleeping on the blankets from the wagon, their horses staked between them and the canyon wall.

When they rose in the morning, frost covered the grass. They ate cold meat in silence and admired the herd of horses they had won the night before. Within the hour they rode south again with renewed energy and hope.

At noon they climbed high onto a ridge of hills that ran south along the river valley. Here, Little Dog gathered dried wood, stacking it knee-high in a tight weave. From the rock ledge he gathered cedar bough, placing them in a heap next to the wood.

"You think they are near?" Crooked Leg asked.

Spinning the yucca stick against the bark, Little Dog blew into the tender.

"It's time to find out," he said.

When the blaze was hot, he threw the cedar boughs onto the fire, waiting until the flames snuffed away. Sweeping back the boughs, a great ball of smoke rose into the sky. Twice more he did this, each time the smoke boiling into the cold, still sky above them.

"We'll ride the ridge," he said, pointing to the range of hills, "where we can watch the horizon."

For two hours they rode, stopping only to water the horses in an icy pool that gathered among the rocks.

Just as they mounted, Little Dog pointed to the south where a ball of smoke rode down the ridge of the hill.

"Black Kettle," he said. "They do not kill us yet."

But it was a small band who rode across the valley, twenty, maybe less, and women and children who waited beyond in the grove of cottonwood.

Holding up his hand in peace, Little Dog greeted their leader, a young man, eyes set deep beneath heavy brows. A fresh wound cut across his chest, and his horse's head hung low with weariness. There was no war paint nor shield nor fresh scalp on his belt. The young warrior stared at Little Dog. Only then did Little Dog remember his own disfigured face. Touching the scar with his hand, he spoke.

"We are what's left of the Dog Soldier Clan, slain in our winter camp by the soldiers. Now we must take our vengeance. We have come for Black Kettle because he is a great warrior. As for us, there is only what you see before you."

Dropping his eyes, the young warrior did not speak for some time. When he looked up, the pain of his story filled his eyes.

"I am Dragonfly," he said, "and for Black Kettle, he is dead, and there is only what you see before you. We, too, were attacked in our winter camp, a hundred slain, another fifty captured by soldiers." Turning, he pointed to the horizon. "They came from the hills beyond, riding into our camp, shooting even the children who played in the trees, and the women who cooked at their fires. There were many soldiers, and their rifles never stopped until the camp ran with blood. Even the horses they shot in the corrals, and then burned the teepees to the ground."

"But you gave them great battle," Little Dog said, searching the faces of the warriors.

"They killed us in our sleep," Dragonfly said, "and took our women to share among themselves. There is food at the fort, they say, and all we must do is come there."

"The Dog Soldiers will not take food from the hands of his enemies," Little Dog said, "nor sleep at his door."

"You are welcome to our camp," Dragonfly said. "Soon we must decide what we do. The winter is upon us. The buffalo are gone. Our camp is gone. We are but a few, and the soldier never ends."

"We come to your camp, Dragonfly, and bring with us many blankets that will keep you warm through the winter."

It was a quiet and sad place they entered, void of laughter, of the gentle teasing that filled Cheyenne camps. An uneasy silence greeted them instead, the women glancing at Little Dog's face, nodding a thanks as Crooked Leg distributed blankets. The children did not play, their eyes cast down, standing at their mothers' sides, clinging to their mothers' dresses.

As the sun set, the warriors walked the perimeter of the camp, like the coyote pacing its den, eyes trained on the horizon, waiting and watching for the blue of the soldiers' coats.

Beyond the camp, Little Dog and Crooked Leg built a small sweat lodge, heating the rocks, covering them with sage and cedar bough, pouring water over them from a heart-bladder cup stretched across the end of a forked stick. Stripping, they entered the lodge to sing their prayers, to make their offerings, to clean their bodies and their spirits.

When darkness fell, they gathered about the fire to await the drum. And when the drum spoke, its voice filled the night, and told of their misery. Soon they danced, moving to the beat of the drum, only their steps joined, their souls divided still against the fearsome enemy who killed them.

As the moon lit the night, Little Dog rose to speak. He told of the slaughter of the Dog Soldiers and of the death of his wife, whose name he no longer spoke, and of his son. He told of the killing, of the coyote who picked the bones of his people. He told of his crushed face, of the worms that cleaned the wound to save his life.

When finished, Little Dog walked to the edge of the fire so all could see the great wound that cleaved his face. With the edge of his hand, he cut across his arm, and took the pipe from Crooked Leg, holding it in front of him.

"I will drive my lance into the earth before the enemy and not move from it," he said. "This is the promise I make."

No more could be asked of a warrior, and each who smoked knew the seriousness of this oath.

Without hesitation, Crooked Leg took the pipe and smoked of it, holding it then in front of him. From across the camp, Dragonfly rose to smoke of the pipe, and soon every warrior smoked of the pipe.

And then they danced, as Cheyenne dance, as warriors, and the drums thundered unafraid into the night.

Twenty-three

Even with help, Nurse Cromley was unable to walk for more than a few minutes at a time. By hooking her arm over Brother Jacob's neck, she could swing her leg forward, leaning in with a downward pull. By noon a water blister rose on the side of Brother Jacob's neck, and his kidneys ached from the perpetual tilt of his body.

There was Shorty, of course, but he was packed with the few belongings they had and was in uncertain shape himself. The choice was simple, walk or starve. Even at that, they'd managed several miles a day by switching Cromley from one side to the other and by laying a horse blanket over Brother Jacob's shoulder for protection.

By nightfall of the second day, ruptured veins blackened Nurse Cromley's arm from elbow to shoulder, and the muscles in her neck quivered from fatigue.

"I'll build a fire," Brother Jacob said, rubbing the stiffness from his fingers, "and boil water to drink."

Collapsing on the ground, Nurse Cromley pulled the horse blanket about her shoulders.

"Take care of Shorty first," she said. "Without him, you and I won't last another day."

Working at the cinch, Brother Jacob spoke words of encouragement to Shorty.

"Whoa, boy. Good, boy. Easy, boy."

When the pack came off, Shorty dropped his head to pick at the nubs of dried grass. Pack sores wept down his sides, and patches of hair fell away from the cinch. Rubbing him down, Brother Jacob hobbled him out to graze.

After the fire was built, they moved in close, wrapping their arms about their knees to slow their trembling. As soon as the coals were ready, Brother Jacob put on the water, pouring a cup for Nurse Cromley when it was hot.

"See," Brother Jacob said, "it's not so bad. We have the fire, and the hot water warms the insides."

But Nurse Cromley was not to be cheered, her face drawn from pain.

"You should have left me," she said.

"At the crossing there will be people and wagons, maybe even a doctor. Sooner or later someone will come along."

A drop of water clung to the edge of Nurse Cromley's lip before racing down her chin. She neither noticed nor wiped it away.

"I remember my father," she said, "when my mother died. I remember how he looked that day."

"Sooner or later someone comes to the crossing," Brother Jacob said, "and we'll put you into a wagon. Sooner or later they'll get you to a doctor, and everything will be alright."

"Perhaps," she said, but there was despair in her eyes.

"Is there something to eat?" Brother Jacob asked, knowing the answer.

"A little flour," she said, placing her leg out in front of her, "and salt. Mix it with water and make dough balls. Cook them on the end of a stick. Take care they don't fall in the embers."

Pouring the last of the flour into his cup, Brother Jacob added salt, stirring the concoction into a paste, rolling it then in the palm of his hand.

"There's enough for two each," he said, holding the gray balls out for her to see.

As she poked the fire with her walking cane, a droplet of water fell from her chin, sizzling in the coals.

"Hold them just above the fire, and make certain they don't burn."

Pulling his tunic about him, he turned the stick as directed, and the dough balls swelled against the heat, smelling of burned flour.

The sun dropped low, a fuming sphere in the evening shadows, but it was without heat, and soon the evening chill deepened.

Rising, Brother Jacob put the dough balls in a tin, adding wood to the fire and offering her one of the balls.

"No," she said.

"But you must eat."

"I'll eat when there's game."

"But we've seen nothing for days now."

"It's meat I need," she said.

He chewed on a dough ball. It tasted of nothing, salt maybe, and was filled with ash and grit.

"When we get to the crossing, someone will be there with fresh beef, and we'll fix you a nice hot soup. That would do, wouldn't it?"

"That would do nicely," she said.

"You're certain you don't want some?" he asked, holding out the pan.

"It's you and Shorty doing the work," she said.

Turning away, he ate the remainder of the dough balls.

When the last of the sun fell across the prairie, a mourning dove cooed its plaintive song. The solitude

of the prairie drew him in at times, tugging at his heart
with its siren call.

"I need help," she said.

"Sorry?"

Lifting herself up, she pointed her stick to the brush
outcrop to the east.

"I wouldn't ask if there were any other way," she
said, "but I need help to the bushes."

"Oh," he said, his face flushing.

"Over there, and I'll call you when I'm done."

Bending over, he hooked her arm over his shoulder,
the old pain rushing into his neck. Like children tied
in a three-legged race, they made their way to the
bushes, where he helped her into position. Moving
back to the camp, he waited, his eyes trained on the
red coals, blocking from his mind the sounds beyond
the ribbons of heat.

"Come," she said, rattling the bushes.

Eyes averted, he helped her back to camp.

"I'm sorry," she said.

"You mustn't worry. It is okay. How is your leg?" he
asked as he helped her sit back down.

Moments passed before she spoke.

"You might as well know," she said, pulling her skirt
to her knee.

From the firelight he could see a patch of skin the
size of a frying pan, dark and ominous around the
wound. Pressing against it with her fingers, she bled
the gas from under the decomposed flesh, and his
stomach lurched.

"Progressive gangrene," she said. "The leg is dying."

"Maybe it's just laudable pus. Maybe the wound is
healing itself."

"There's no blood reaching the wound," she said.
"When the flesh dies, it cuts off even more vessels and

so on until the leg consumes itself." Looking away, she fell silent for a moment. "Anyway, I've seen many die from it. It's not so bad."

"Is there nothing to be done?" he asked.

Lowering her skirt, she shook her head.

"Pray that my life has not been misspent, Brother Jacob."

That night they made their beds close to the fire, their fronts burning from the heat, their backs burning from the cold. Exhausted, Nurse Cromley fell into an uneasy sleep, mumbling broken bits of conversation with people long since gone from her life. Once, she laughed, a sound distant and foreign in this place.

Crossing himself, Brother Jacob prayed, not for her deliverance, because he no longer believed that possible, but for her quick and peaceful death. Strong people died hard, and her strength was without question. A coyote called from somewhere deep within the prairie as he dozed.

At some point in the morning hours, he sat upright, his heart pounding in his chest. Reaching for his rifle, he searched the darkness that surrounded the tiny camp like a black and suffocating tide.

"Who is it?" he asked, his words fading at the edge of the light.

Lifting herself on an elbow, Nurse Cromley peered into the darkness. "What?" she whispered.

"Something woke me," he said, "as certain as the voice of God."

"You were dreaming," she said. "Go back to sleep."

"I'm going to light the lantern."

"But it's freezing."

"I'll not sleep the night."

"Wait," she said. "I'll go with you."

"But your leg."

"And what can I do to hurt this leg?" she said, lifting

herself up with her walking stick, pulling the blanket about her shoulders. "I'll light the lantern. You keep an eye out, just in case."

With a stick from the fire, she lit the wick, waiting for the tiny flame to grow before dropping the chimney down and locking it into place.

"Okay," she said.

"Okay, what?" Brother Jacob asked.

"Let's find out what woke you."

Holding the lantern high, Brother Jacob balanced the carbine across his arm.

"Maybe it was a dream," he said.

"It's that way out here sometimes," she said.

The coyote lifted its voice again, emptying their hearts of courage.

"Oh, my God!" Nurse Cromley said.

Spinning about, Brother Jacob brought the carbine to his shoulder, his heart surging in his ears.

"What!"

"There."

"Where?" he asked.

Pointing to the sole of her shoe, she shook her head.

"In the future take me farther from camp when I'm in need of help."

"Oh," he said sheepishly, "indeed."

Inching their way through the darkness, they were nearly back to camp when a single refraction of light caused Nurse Cromley to clutch Brother Jacob's arm.

"Oh," she cried out.

The hair on Brother Jacob's neck crawled when he spotted the eyes in the lantern light.

"What is it?" she whispered.

"It's huge," he said. "See how far apart its eyes are."

"A cougar," she said. "They can get very brave when food is short."

"What shall I do?"

"Shoot it," she said.

"I'm not certain what it is."

"Shoot it anyway," she said.

"And if I miss?"

"Then there will be only a walking stick and a monk's tunic to be found."

Sometimes Nurse Cromley's bluntness left him breathless. Steadying the tremble in his hand, he sighted in, the shot careening through the night with a whine, but the eyes neither blinked nor stirred.

Grabbing his arm again, Nurse Cromley leaned in close, her hands as icy as his own heart.

"Shoot it again," she said, "before it charges."

He slid a cartridge into the breech and squeezed off another round. But the creature only stared back.

"It's ole Blue Tongue, isn't it," he said, "come back for vengeance."

"There's something wrong here," Nurse Cromley said, her voice dropping. Black soot strung into the air from the lantern as she hooked her walking stick under her arm and moved in closer. "I'll be," she said, "a skinned buffalo, bogged down and butchered where he stands. Look at those eyes, still clear, and black as coffee."

"God's provided after all," he said.

"Or someone with a knife and a good deal of courage," she said. "He's taken the best cuts of meat, but I'd guess he earned them. The coyotes took their share, too. Go get a pot, Brother Jacob. Now we're going to have our fill."

As dawn broke, fat clouds squatted on the orange horizon, and buffalo broth filled the morning air with a heartening aroma. Bellies full, Nurse Cromley and Brother Jacob spooned the last of the broth from the bottoms of their bowls.

"I told you there was hope," Brother Jacob said,

looking at the glory of the breaking dawn. "And there is no place one can know the true hand of God like in this grand and exalted cathedral."

"It's only because your belly is full," Nurse Cromley reasoned with a smile. "A few hours ago it was but the archfiend's nest, as I recall."

"Still," he rose, scratching at his beard, "there is food for a few more days now, and the strength we need to go on. We have Shorty to pack our goods, and winter is still at bay."

"Perhaps," she said, rising, pulling her leg under her. It was but a stump now, void of feeling. "I'll pack the meat, if you can call it that, mostly fat and gristle, but it's nourishing at least. You bring in Shorty. With luck, we can drag out a few more miles today, providing your neck and your faith hold out."

"My faith is intact, sister. My neck is another matter altogether."

As Brother Jacob made his way down the valley, clouds gathered in the north, and a chill wind swept in. Shorty's tracks twisted in a crooked line along the dry creek bed, his steps labored from the burden of his hobble.

Making the bend, Brother Jacob stopped short, his spirits falling at the sight before him. Shorty's legs protruded like sticks from his dead and bloated body, his flank torn where the coyotes had fed during the night. Without Shorty their chances of survival were diminished. Without him, supplies and food would have to be left behind.

When Nurse Cromley saw Brother Jacob, she knew something was wrong, the shuffle of his feet, the pitch of his shoulders, the silence that followed him into camp.

"Where's Shorty?" she asked.

Turning away, Brother Jacob watched the last of the

morning sun disappear behind the gray bank of clouds.

"Dead," he said, burying his hands into his pockets.

Her heart broke in that moment; tears filled her eyes, not for herself so much as for him, this tired old man who wanted nothing in the world but to be left alone to his prayers. Leaning against her walking stick, she started to speak, to tell him of her great sadness, to soothe his bitter disappointment somehow.

But her words failed when winter's first snow careened from the smoky sky, catching in the gray of his beard and the cuffs of his tunic.

Twenty-four

Wind swept down the broad plain of the Cimarron crossing at Deep Hole Creek, driving the sand and snow ahead in a stinging swirl. Chucking his hat down tight over his ears, Lance Corporal Inman dug at the riverbank with determination. Now and again he would stop, blow into his freezing hands, and begin again.

From the sidelines, Private Tanner watched, a blanket over his shoulders, crystals of snow clinging to his coal-black hair.

"It's crazy," Tanner said. "Besides, Sergeant Wilson ain't going to like it one bit, and what you going to do when the river comes up? You ain't no beaver," he said, grinning, " 'cause a beaver's got a tail for swimming and a brain for thinking, ain't he?"

Stopping, Inman leaned on his shovel, his breath coming in steamy clouds.

"I'm sick and tired of the wind blowing up my backside and listening to you snore, Tanner. We ain't going nowhere, are we, and Sergeant says make a permanent camp. Well, sleeping on the ground with snow stacking on my face ain't my idea of a permanent camp."

Putting the blanket over his head, Tanner clamped it tight under his chin.

"It ain't but a sandy bank, Inman. What's to keep it from coming down and burying you alive?"

Kicking his foot up on the growing pile of sand, Inman leaned forward, his arms propped on his knee.

"Ain't big on learning from your fellow man, are you, Tanner?" Picking up a cottonwood post, he planted it just in the doorway, wedging it against the roof, driving it tight with another post. "Seen how Captain Wallace shores them soddys, what with cottonwood posts. Guess I can do the same, and then I'm digging a hole in the top for a chimney and a nice cozy fire. When you boys got ice hanging off your balls, guess you'll come visiting."

"I ain't going in there." Tanner shook his head. "Even if I freeze stiff as a carp. Sergeant Wilson says a construction detachment will come soon enough to build the redoubt. Ain't that I don't trust your building, but that river sand your digging is likely to cave in just thinking on it."

"Not right for a man to sleep in the open like a buffalo in a snowdrift," Inman said. "Even them Cheyenne snug down in their teepees for a winter blow." Falling silent, he propped his foot on his shovel and rested his chin on the handle. "It's a wonder how they live such, Tanner, you know, surviving in a place like this, eating better, sleeping better, having more fun than on my best day."

Brushing the snow from his hair, Tanner looked up from under his blanket.

"Ain't having that much fun now, are they?" he said.

Pulling at his hat, Inman leaned in. "I'm telling you, Tanner, isn't a day goes by what I don't hear the screaming in my head. Not a night passes that I don't wake with my heart in my throat. It's a wrong thing we did. Every man here knows it, and knows only the half of it at that. I seen things happen I can't even talk about. I can't even tell you, my best friend."

Walking to the edge of the river, Tanner cracked the thin ice with the toe of his boot.

"Things I don't want to know, and things I don't think on. A soldier ain't got a choice, has he? It's his duty, like, and if he stopped to think on it every time he killed a Indian or buffalo, then what kind of soldier would he be?"

"I don't know," Inman said, his voice falling. "All I know is them screams rattle in my head day and night, till sometimes I think I'll go crazy."

"Can't," Tanner said.

"Why?"

"You all ready are crazy."

Loading his shovel with sand, Inman pitched it in the air and let it rain down on Tanner's head.

"And a buzzard puked you up on a rock." He laughed at his friend's antics.

Sitting back down, Tanner wrapped the blanket about himself and watched Inman dig.

"Wonder what's for supper?"

"Better not to know till faced with it directly," Inman said. "Thinking on it ahead of time makes it worse."

"I ain't eatin' no more wormy rabbit, nor boiled wheat, neither, for that matter," Tanner said, shuddering. "Sometimes I think I might die from want of a decent meal, a beefsteak seared in an iron pan, what with a raw onion and a slice of Cookey's bread."

"And a glass of lager," Inman said, "just off-cold with a foaming head."

"Maybe Jimson has some beefsteak hid, and he ain't telling no one."

"Wouldn't make no difference," Inman said. "By

the time Jimson got it cooked, it would taste like boiled wheat."

Rubbing his belly, Tanner leaned back, looking up into the falling flakes of snow.

"My mamma could cook a shoe tongue and make you beg for cold seconds."

Closing his eyes, Inman held his face to the sky.

"I remember my mamma's breakfasts," he said, "fork-tender sourdough jacks drenched in molasses, topped with dollops of thick, sweet cream; slabs of sugar-cured ham smelling of hickory and glory itself; couple three dippy eggs, side dish of taters shaved thin and fried crisp and speckled with black pepper, washed down with cold buttermilk and steaming black coffee. If a man lived through it, and many didn't, it was nigh time for supper."

"Ohhhh," Tanner groaned, holding his stomach. "I can't stand it, and what did we have for breakfast, boiled wheat with sugar water. The longer I chewed, the bigger it got. I still ain't sure who was eatin' who."

From up on the hill, Corporal Hall waved his hat.

"It's the corporal," Inman said, brushing the sand off the seat of his pants, "wanting us in. Time for rabbit hunting, I reckon, or confiscating busthead liquor."

"Or stacking firewood or digging privies," Tanner said.

"It's the corporal gets the pay," Inman said, "and the lance corporal gets the job."

By the time they reached the hill, Corporal Hall and the others gathered near Sergeant Wilson's tent. A saddled Cavalry horse danced at the end of Hall's arm. Just as Inman started to ask about the horse, Wilson and a strange soldier stepped from the tent.

The sun broke from behind a cloud lighting the snow that gathered on the sergeant's hat. Wilson's hard-set eyes panned the men, settling on Inman.

"This here's Corporal Cooper sent direct from General Sully out of Dodge. There's bad news he's bringing and thought best he tell it hisself. Go on ahead, Corporal."

A cold wind swept from the north, flurries of snow stirring across the camp. Studying the ground, Cooper gathered his thoughts.

"It's our own Sergeant Westhoff," he said, clearing his throat, "didn't come back. He was bringing news of the construction detachment ordered out of Fort Supply to start this here redoubt." Hitching up his pants, he looked around the camp. "Fact is, he never made it back to Dodge, so after a proper wait, the General sent me out looking. Yesterday I came upon a body, or what was left of it." Pausing, he looked at Wilson before turning back to the men. "It was him alright, missing a fair patch of scalp he was, too. Probably caught in the open by a hunting party. There weren't no tracks, having been washed out, by the looks of it." Pausing, he reined in his feelings and pulled a pistol from his belt. "It's a hard thing, you see, 'cause his wife's awaiting word back at Dodge, and all I got is this here side arm that belonged to him." Tucking the pistol back into his belt, he shrugged. "Beats me why they didn't take it. Never heard of an Indian leaving a side arm untouched."

"Maybe they was skittish," Wilson said. "Hunting parties ain't big on bad fighting odds. Maybe they figured there was a detachment waiting over the hill."

"Maybe," Cooper said. "Guess it don't matter much anymore. Dead is dead, ain't it?"

Slipping on his gloves, Sergeant Wilson took the reins from Corporal Hall.

"It's a shame," he said, handing the reins to Cooper. "But people been known to die, even in their prime. Least your man ain't hunkered down in no redoubt with the north wind blowing up his skirt day and night."

"No, sir," Cooper said, settling into his saddle, "he ain't worried 'bout no redoubt, north wind, either, for that matter."

Turning, Wilson caught the eye of each man there, securing in the brief glance what he was preparing to say.

"Turns out you boys in Dodge ain't the only one's with a run of bad luck."

"What do you mean, Sergeant?"

"Our own Lieutenant Roland got wiped off under a tree by his horse. Caught him just here," he pointed to his neck. "Poor feller didn't have a chance. Why, broke his neck clean as a whistle, didn't it, boys? Didn't even blink nor say goodbye, did he, boys?"

Pulling up his reins, Cooper hooked his toes into his stirrups, shaking his head at the news.

"Damnable way to go, ain't it?" he said.

"Sure is," Wilson said, "although I seen worse."

Moving close to Inman, Wilson looked up at Cooper. "Guess you'll be going back to Dodge with the bad news, then?"

"To Fort Supply first," he said, "with orders for the quartermaster, if I ain't froze or scalped like poor West-hoff."

"Find yourself east of the Cimarron, you're going the wrong way," Wilson said, "too far south and you'll be shaking hands with Black Kettle."

"Thanks," Cooper said, tipping his hat.

As he topped the hill, Cooper's figure faded against the graying sky. For the first time in ten minutes, Inman took a breath. The icy wind bore through his clothing, chilling his heart, freezing its beat deep within his chest.

"Could I see you in your tent?" he asked, turning to Wilson.

Pulling off his gloves, Sergeant Wilson stuck them under his belt, rubbing his hands one upon the other, washing away the evil they had wrought. Without a word, he ducked into his tent. Following, Inman brushed off the last of the sand that still clung to the knees of his britches.

"Keep your voice down," Wilson said without turning around. "This here is a tent."

"It's about Westhoff," Inman said.

"What about him?"

"What if they find out? What if they find out it was us kilt' our own man and took his scalp?"

"Ain't no one finding out, Inman, 'less you open your mouth."

"And all them Indians we kilt'," Inman said, "whilst they slept. What if they find out about that, or what if the Indians come to take revenge for what we did to them?"

Turning around, Wilson bore down on Inman, his immense face red and swollen.

"Listen, you," he said, his eyes narrowing into lethal slits, "dead men don't talk, not Westhoff, not Indians, not no one including you, do you understand?"

"Yes, sir."

"Only you and me knows about Westhoff, and it ain't likely that I'm going to talk. That leaves you, Inman. My best advice is for you to keep it shut, bury it so deep that no man can wring it out, drunk or sober. Now, get on out of here before the others get their curiosity up."

"Yes, sir," Inman said.

Hard flurries of snow stung his face as he stepped from the tent, dingy clouds swirling and churning in confusion. The sun peered with disinterest from beyond the clouds, a distant and dying organ, a faded and milky eye. The smell of cooked wheat churned his stomach, a sodden, wet smell, like boiling chalk. The thought of it all raged through him, and he kicked dirt spiraling into the air.

"Wasn't me ordered those Indians kilt', or me shot that courier out of his saddle," he said under his breath. "Wasn't me done those things and ain't me going down for it."

That night it snowed in earnest, flakes the size of hen eggs floating down, silent sheets of snow stacking one upon the other. Even with a crackling fire, the wind stung cold, a relentless torture against men and horses. The camp grew quiet as the gale heightened, and the men set to wishing and praying its frigid grasp might ease, but wishing and praying eased nothing, not the snow, not the wind, not the loneliness in their hearts. As the night fell, the snow came and stacked in frozen drifts against the thinness of their blankets.

A crystalline dawn woke them, shimmering drifts of snow rising and falling across the prairie. The men stomped their feet and rubbed their hands, their breaths rising undisturbed in the morning stillness.

Already the smell of boiled wheat slogged from Jimson's pot, moving through the camp like a poisoned fog.

Like mules at a feed trough, they chewed the glutinous mess, masticated flour gathering in the corners of their mouths, filling their stomach and teeth with indigestible bran.

Sucking at his hot water, Tanner wrinkled his nose in disgust and looked at Inman.

"I'm telling you I can't take it no more," he said. "Bad enough I got to sleep in the open like a mule, but I got to eat like a mule, too."

"You smell like a mule," Inman said, "and got the

same personality and general good looks. Guess you just as well eat like one."

Scraping the last of the boiled wheat into the fire, Tanner watched as it steamed in the coals, starchy bubbles rising and bursting from the heat.

From the other side of camp, Jimson watched.

"Ain't good enough for your delicate taste?" he asked, crossing his arms.

"Ain't good enough for slopping hogs," Tanner said, rising, dusting his hands.

"Maybe if you did a little less complaining and a little more hunting, there would be more meat around here."

"Maybe so and maybe not," Tanner said, looking at Inman for encouragement.

"Hey, Corporal Hall," Inman said, "how about me and Tanner do a little hunting today, 'fore we shit away our lives eating mule food?"

"Worth a try," Hall said, "what with fresh snow on the ground. Stay south of the river, and don't go getting into trouble."

"If we bring back a buffalo, we'll just eat it standing raw," Tanner said, "so's Jimson won't make boiled wheat out of it."

"You bring back a buffalo," Jimson said, "and I'll eat it raw myself. In the meantime, I guess you won't mind if I fix boiled wheat for supper, just in case."

"Come on, Tanner," Inman said, "let's get out of here 'fore he decides to serve up a helping of prairie grass."

As the sun rose, its cold orange light filled the morning. The horses circled the corral, steam rising from their wet backs. Taking a chew, Inman rolled the cud into its customary position and watched Tanner catch up their mounts. By the time they rode out of camp, the sun sparkled on the newly fallen snow, and the memory of the fearful night faded away.

By noon they'd seen not a single animal worth shooting. The snow was a blank page, inscribing the passage of the least bird or bug, but there was no sign nor track of buffalo or deer.

Stopping for a rest, they built a small fire, holding their hands over it for warmth. With considerable effort, Tanner pulled off his wet boots, wiggling his toes close to the fire.

"Guess there'd been a buffalo about, we'd shot it by now," he said.

"Guess so," Inman said, cutting himself a sizable chew and tucking it away.

"But there ain't," Tanner said.

"No," Inman said, spitting into the churning coals of the fire, "there ain't."

"I can smell boiled wheat drifting clean across the prairie," Tanner said.

"Ain't wheat," Inman said, "its your socks on fire."

"Oh, oh, shit," Tanner hollered, pinching out the flame on the end of his sock. "Guess you just let me burn up, wouldn't you?"

Sitting down on a stump, Inman put his elbows on his knees and his chin in his hands.

"Sure would like to have a bowl of my mamma's vegetable soup." He sighed.

"You ain't going to start that again, are you?" Tanner said. "It's hard enough without you going on about your mamma's cooking all the time."

Gathering up his chew, Inman fired a shot into the snow.

"Take fresh cow knuckles and put 'em in a pan," he said. "Cook 'em in the oven till the grease is bubbly brown in the bottom, add onion, carrots, potatoes, a turnip maybe, fresh tomatoes and corn right off the cob. Put a little salt and pepper in there and a dash or two of vinegar and let her simmer till the smell sets you to howling like a lovesick coyote. When you can't stand it no more, lay down a slice of sourdough in the bottom of the bowl and dip it over with steaming hot soup."

"Ohhhh," Tanner moaned, holding his scorched toes in his hand. "I can taste it now, and with bone marrow dipped on like a chunk of butter, and a whole glass of cold, sweet milk on the side."

"And then a nap," Inman said, "stretched out on a feather bed with a comforter pulled over your head."

"Sure beats sleeping in a snowbank and eatin' boiled wheat, don't it?" Tanner said.

"Sure does," Inman said, giving his cud a turn.

For a while they sat without talking, each studying the things in his mind. Pulling back his shoulder, Inman looked at Tanner.

"I've been thinking on this thing with the Indians," he said, "and with that courier found dead."

"What's done, is done," Tanner said, looking away.

"There's a thing in me won't let it go, Tanner. There's a thing in me needs to talk it out."

But Tanner didn't answer nor take it up on his own, and when the last curl of smoke twisted from the dying fire, he pulled on his boots, and they mounted their horses. Hooves crunched against the white silence as they moved northwest along the banks of the Cimarron. By late afternoon they'd not spotted a single track, and already the sun was setting, inclining rays as cold and empty as the prairie about them. In despair, Inman pulled up his horse, standing in his stirrups for a last look around.

"Guess we just as well turn back," he said. "There ain't no buffalo between here and California that I can tell."

"Crow and boiled wheat for supper," Tanner said, dejected.

"Look there," Inman pointed, "tracks going off." Dismounting, he took a close look. "Ain't but a coon," he said, following the tracks to where they disappeared into a hole beneath a dead cedar tree. "It's in there, tracks down, none out."

"It's meat, ain't it," Tanner said, "and better than boiled wheat. Reach in there and get it."

Rolling his eyes, Inman spat against the stump.

"Guess that ain't a lance corporal's job today, is it?"

"Well," Tanner said, laying down his carbine, "it ain't coming out with a whistle, is it."

Pulling at his chin, Inman studied the situation.

"Take your knife and cut a forked stick from them branches. We'll reach it down in there and twist up his fur. Guess he'll be coming out, whether he wants to or no."

By the time Tanner cut the stick and sharpened the prongs, the sun drifted below the horizon, and the last light of day waned against the gray sky.

"There," Tanner said, holding up the stick.

Getting down on all fours, Inman peered into the black hole.

"Can't see a blame thing," he said. "Just run it on down there and give a twist."

Doing as directed, Tanner eased the stick down the hole until it stopped. Looking up at Inman, he gave a wink, twisted the stick one sharp turn, and pulled for all he was worth.

A fierce growl issued from the hole, then a cloud of dust as the critter kicked and fought against the tenacious clutch of its enemy. The last rays of the sun flickered away just as it exited the hole, feet dug into the ground, teeth clamped about the stick, tail pitched above its back.

"It's a skunk!" Tanner yelled.

"Swing it around!" Inman said, backing away. "It can't spray stink when it's in a swing."

Holding it at arm's length, Tanner swung around in a hard and deliberate circle, stirring well the vile and evil mist spewing from under its tail. Throwing down the stick, he grabbed his eyes and set to gagging, a strange honking sound, not unlike southbound geese or mules complaining at the cinch. Saliva drooled from his lips as he tossed his head to and fro.

Bringing about his carbine, Inman shot the skunk just as it was disappearing down the hole again.

"Got him," he shouted.

But Tanner was not talking, and all attempts to console him failed. After an hour, he still had not moved, nor spoken, nor acknowledged the blinding reek coming from his person. Standing at last, he brushed the snow from his knees.

"Get the skunk," he said. "I'm ready to go back."

"You can't take no skunk back to camp," Inman said. "Jimson will kill us both."

"Get the skunk," Tanner said.

There was a lethal and unmistakable tone to his voice, so Inman tied the skunk on Tanner's saddle, wiping at his eyes with the sleeve of his shirt.

The moonlight lit the night as they rode back, the smell fuming over them with its lingering and foul reek. Just beyond camp, Inman stopped to wait. As Tanner approached, the stink of skunk puckered the glands under Inman's ears, causing his eyes to water.

"Hadn't you ought to throw away that skunk now," he said.

Sliding off his mount, Tanner untied the skunk and proceeded to skin it out.

"You can't take no skunk into camp, Tanner. Jimson will have your hide."

"It's my skunk, and I intend to have it," he said, climbing back on his mount, laying the skunk carcass across his lap.

All were asleep when they entered camp, the fire muttering under a bed of coals. Without a word Tanner rummaged through the cook box until he found Jimson's cook pot, dropping in the skunk, setting it on the fire.

One by one, the smell of skunk penetrated the soldiers' consciousness, and they rose from their beds like spirits from their graves. Dumbfounded, they watched on as Tanner chewed at a skunk leg, his lips shiny with grease. Even Jimson was speechless, hopping around the fire, stopping from time to time to kick a spray of snow into the coals with his bare foot.

When finished, Tanner wiped the grease from his mouth, sucked at a tooth with contentment, climbed under his blanket, and went to sleep.

There was a cold breakfast the next morning, hardtack and sourdough, seeing as how Jimson's cooking pot stank of skunk. No one was talking to Tanner, of course, and in the night someone had thrown his boots into a snowdrift on the edge of camp.

"What's that stink?" Sergeant Wilson asked, filling his cup at the fire.

"Skunk," Jimson said, "brought in by Tanner there and cooked in my pot. It's a wonder the fool didn't eat our horses or shoot us in our blankets."

"That right, Tanner? You cooked a skunk in Jimson's pot?"

"Yes, sir," Tanner said, looking at his feet. "I just couldn't stand the thought of eating boiled wheat no more."

Pushing back his hat, Wilson looked up at Tanner.

"It's a ignorant man what would eat a skunk, Tanner."

"Yes, sir."

"A man eat a skunk would do 'bout anything, wouldn't he?"

"Yes, sir," Tanner said.

"Like cook it in our pot, so to speak?"

"Sorry, sir, but it just took me over."

"I guess you'll be digging a new latrine, won't you, Tanner, and eatin' boiled wheat out of that skunk pot till it's time to take your pension?"

"Yes, sir," Tanner said, hanging his head.

"Get on with it, then, and don't let me see you looking up from your work or leaning on your shovel, or there will be worse than that waiting for you."

That afternoon Inman was at a loss without Tanner about. Picking up his shovel, he made his way along the bank of the Cimarron to his diggings. Even though the day was cold, the winds had abated, and the sun fell warm across his shoulders. Squeezing past the cottonwood post, he worked at the back of the hole, shaving away the sand with the blade of his shovel before scooping it out the door. With considerable care, he rounded out the ceiling as he went. The digging was easy but precarious. Without the bracing, the whole thing would come down in a smothering slide just like Tanner said.

It was in the late afternoon, just as the sun dropped below the bank, and the cold chill of evening bled through the door, that Inman stopped to rest. At first he thought it was a shadow, a limb sweeping in the cast of evening, but then there was the turn of a shoulder, chevrons in the fading light.

"Sergeant Wilson?" he asked, his voice reverberating in the confines of his dugout.

"Come to talk," he said, peering into the opening, "about what happened."

"Yes, sir," Inman said.

"You told anyone yet?"

"No, sir, I ain't, but sometimes I don't think I can stand it."

"Some folks can't live with hard decisions, needing to share out the burden with others."

"What we going to do?"

There was only the telling crack of the cottonwood brace as Wilson's heel drove hard against it, the suffocating crush of the ceiling, and the chilling quiver deep beneath the sand.

Twenty-five

Leaving poor Housman dead and buried atop the windswept hill was a hard thing. Even though Dr. McReynolds had buried plenty in his day, the responsibility of Housman's death struck hard and sent him spiraling into a depression. To make matters worse, they'd traveled miles north to find a shallow crossing, and the weather closed in to boot, snow falling, cold, wet flakes covering their shoulders and hats as they worked their way along the trail.

Even in the bitterness of the cold, Sarah rode uncomplaining next to Cookey, flashing a warm smile from under her head wrap when McReynolds happened by. But by noon the trail had disappeared under a white blanket, the glare of snow erasing the horizon and landmarks.

"Like being in a cow's belly, ain't it?" Wallace said, standing in his stirrups. "Can't tell up from down or front from backwards."

"Maybe we ought to stop," McReynolds said, brushing the snow from his hat.

"Maybe," Wallace said, "what with the wagons mucking down. There's a stand of cedar for fuel just over there, and no shortage of snow for drinking, I guess."

"Still, it's hard stopping like this in the middle of

the day," McReynolds said. How often Sergeant Number had advised him to keep moving no matter the cost. "The longer sitting on the trail, the more chance of mishap," he added.

"True enough," Wallace said, "but, then, the fastest way ain't always straight ahead, is it? Fightin' this snow ain't a winning deal, and if a man wound up lost, things could get bad pretty fast."

Turning in his saddle, McReynolds looked back on the train disappearing into the curtain of snow.

"Make camp then," he said, "and send a detail out for firewood. Corral the horses in that stand of trees. Maybe we could empty out a wagon or two."

"Right," Wallace said. "We can cut cedars to set the supplies on, keep 'em out of the wet, and use the wagon for hauling wood in." Pausing, he leaned forward on his saddle horn. "It ain't us I'm worried about altogether."

"What do you mean?"

"We got plenty of food, even in a fix, and then there's always the horses to eat, given no choice. But with the grazing covered over with snow, the horses could weaken fast in this weather."

"Maybe it will let up."

"Maybe," Wallace said, looking up into the flakes.

"Well, going or staying isn't going to keep it from snowing," McReynolds said with a shrug.

Dismounting, he worked his way back to the cook wagon.

"Fix up some hot soup, Cookey, and plenty of it. Might be a long night."

"Yes, sir," Cookey said.

Reaching for McReynolds's hand, Sarah slid from the seat.

"I'll help," she said, brushing against his chest, their eyes locking for that single moment. "I need to help."

Snow gathered in the rich folds of her hair, setting her eyes aglow. Avoiding Cookey's glance, McReynolds turned away.

"I'll get the men started on woodcutting," he said, "while there's light left."

But even as the men cut and hauled from the stand of trees, the snow thickened, plummeting from the heavens, subduing the world in a white whisper.

Soon a fire roared, the scent of burning cedar, a comfort and balm in the falling temperatures.

From a distance McReynolds watched Sarah work, moving from task to task with grace and efficiency, her delicate hands half frozen in the cold. What kind of a man would bring a woman here, such fragility pitted against the hardship of the prairie? But then he knew, didn't he, what kind of man.

By nightfall, pitched tents drooped under the heavy snows, their peaks protruding like frozen toadstools from beneath the drifts. Walking about the camp, McReynolds talked to the soldiers as they ate their supper, teasing, kidding, encouraging them wherever possible, because he saw the uncertainty in their eyes, because he knew how it was.

That night as they crawled into their tents, they wrapped themselves in blankets and curled against the penetrating cold. Above, snow spilled from the heavens, filling the black sky, cascading like a silent waterfall onto the small camp below.

When morning came, the world was lost in white, and the men stood about the fire, slapping their hands together and rubbing their ears. Even a hearty breakfast of sourdough biscuits, hominy, and sugar-cured ham failed to lighten their spirits. Something dark and foreboding had ridden into the camp, into their hearts and minds.

By midmorning the sky darkened, gray clouds drifting low overhead, and a gale blasted from the north, its icy howl chilling their souls and their hopes. Eddies of snow swirled through the camp, stinging their faces like windswept sand, and the horses churned in the corral with backs steaming.

Standing over his fire, Cookey poured McReynolds his coffee.

"You doing alright, Cookey?" McReynolds asked.

"Oh, yes, sir," he said, smiling. "Where would I rather be 'cept in a snowdrift cooking for bonehead privates what can't pitch their own tents or clean their own plates."

"Good coffee," McReynolds said, looking over at Sarah.

"Thank you, sir," Cookey said. "Did I ever tell you the secrets of good coffee making?"

"Believe you did, Cookey."

"And how are you doing, Major?" Sarah asked.

"We'll be okay," he said. "There's plenty to eat, fuel, and shelter, too, if you can call it that. If the storm doesn't last too long, there's little to worry about."

Pushing her hair from her face, she looked at him, straight into his soul, where the truth lay.

"And if it does?"

"Well," he said, pouring the coffee dregs into the snow, "it's the horses mostly. This kind of cold, they take a lot of feed. They burn lots of energy just keeping warm. With this snow cover, there's no forage. The right circumstances, and we could lose a lot of stock. Without horses, things get complicated pretty fast. And your husband," he added, his voice dropping, "will be alright, I should think. There's good shelter at the crossing and with no traveling to be done."

"It's the Cheyenne, ain't it, sir," Cookey said, "dancing and drumming and praying for snow. And just when everything's settling in for an evening at the fire, a silent arrow whistles through your ear." Shuddering, he turned about, scrutinizing the horizon. "Gives me chills just thinking on it. Course, if a man's got to go, guess it's as good as the next. Least it wouldn't be like poor Housman, looking up out of that water with no hope for another breath."

"That was an accident," Sarah said, "and nobody's fault. It could've happened to anyone."

"Yes, ma'am," Cookey said, "an accident, that's all."

As night fell, the snow began again, white flakes dipping like falling leaves. Building their fires high, they moved in close, their talk full of bravado, and the winds came, sweeping, moving drifts, storm-tossed waves in a white sea. One by one, the men made their way to their beds, searching for buried tents, and a silence fell in the camp.

Some time in the night the snow stopped, and stars filled the inky sky, temperatures dropping, the cold entering their tents like an unwelcome stranger. Beyond in the corral, the horses huddled, churning shifts from inside to out, each horse taking its bitter turn against the frozen perimeters of the herd.

Sitting up, McReynolds listened to the rustle of the horses, his face stinging against the cold. Opening the flap of the tent, he looked out, moonlight flooding the ivory night.

Several minutes passed before he saw her standing there, shawl pulled about her shoulders, hands tucked into her sleeves. Joining with the night, she held her face to the moon, as if to soothe the loneliness within her. Never was she more beautiful.

"Sarah," he whispered.

She did not answer, her eyes falling on his as she made her way back to her tent. At the door she turned once more before entering. It was a moment of truth, a moment beyond his control. Slipping on his clothes, he made his way across the camp, the squeak of his boots against the frozen snow, the snores of soldiers as they slept in the small warmth of their beds.

At her tent flap, he searched for the strength to turn about. Perhaps it was too many hardships, too many compromises, too many mistakes and regrets of life that gathered in that single moment, to weaken and destroy his resolve.

"Sarah?" he whispered again.

Gathering her gown, she opened the flap, and he went in.

"I shouldn't be here," he said. "I couldn't stop."

In the darkness of the tent, her breath fell against his face, her hand touching his.

"I've been thinking of you," she said, "the way you talk to the men, the way you encourage them and make them feel safe."

"If only they knew," he said.

"You must know that I do not love David, that the things he has done have destroyed what love there was."

"I have no right," he whispered, the smell of her warmth in the confines of the tent.

"Neither law nor man assigns my love," she said. "I'll not be bound by the rule of others in these matters."

"Don't you ever have any doubts?" he asked, slipping his hand about her waist, the curve and sweep of her hip, the warmth of her body in the cold.

"My life is little else but doubts," she said, taking his face between her hands, kissing him, a gentle kiss lingering on his lips. "I know that I have a brain, that I must reason with that brain, and make the best decisions that I can. Whatever happens after that, happens, and I don't intend to look back."

Burying his face in the warmth of her neck, he held her tight, moving her into the emptiness within him, into that place haunted by the passing spirits of others.

"I don't know," he whispered, "if I can give any longer. I don't know if there's anything left."

Leading him to her bed, she locked her delicate fingers in his.

"The power to love is never gone," she whispered, "but only moves more distant within us."

And in that moment he knew that she was his, that no matter the cost nor dishonor, this woman was his. No man nor memory would diminish what they felt for each other. Slipping his hands under her gown, he lifted it free, exploring her body, her warmth, her sleepy scent.

"I love you," she whispered, her breath plunging into his core.

"And I love you," he said, his words falling about him.

Moaning, she lay back, the dove's guttural song, so primitive, unmistakable, and he came to her, entering her life forever. In those dark hours, in the forced quiet of their passion, they bound their lives, and the snow fell, covering them in white.

Morning found McReynolds standing at the horse corral, Wallace at his side. Snow hung heavy in the trees, limbs drooping in resignation to the ceaseless snow. Pulling up his collar, he examined the half-frozen horses, heads lowered, backs humped, rears into the icy wind.

"What do we do now?" he asked Wallace.

"There's grain left," he said, pulling at his chin, "enough for traveling but not for staying. If this snow keeps up, well, guess you feed it now or later, don't make much difference."

"Maybe we could send some men ahead, get some help."

Wiping his nose against his sleeve, Wallace squinted up at McReynolds.

"It's belly-deep drifts as far as you can see, Major.

Ain't likely they could get through, and even if they do, ain't likely they could get back in time to help these fellers out much."

Walking around the corral, McReynolds examined the horses. Some of the older ones trembled against the cold, their noses running, their eyes slack with weakness.

"Maybe if we had someone in charge who knew what he was doing, maybe then."

Taking a chew from his plug, Wallace looked up through his eyebrows.

"Guess we ain't talking about a doctor with shiny boots here, are we?"

"Had more in mind, an overworked engineer," McReynolds said, "if he was willing."

Spitting into the snow, Wallace wiped at his mouth and studied the shivering horses.

"Never was much one for volunteering, Major. Course, if I was ordered, that would be different."

"Consider it an order, Captain, and take four or five men with you. Head north along the trail as best you can. See if you can't find some squatters willing to sell a little grain. If nothing else, head on up to the redoubt or even Dodge, if the going's good. Bring back some grain and fresh horses. If the snow eases, we'll start north on our own, so don't go too far afield."

"Oh, no, sir. Guess we won't be dallying along too much in this weather."

Burying his hands in his pockets, McReynolds thought for a moment before turning to Captain Wallace.

"About those howitzers?"

"The ones we don't have?" he said, lifting an eyebrow.

"If you do happen to get as far as Dodge, remind Sully that a redoubt doesn't have much of a defense without howitzers. It's a thin line we have if anything should go awry."

"Ain't my lips he's accustomed to," Wallace countered with a grin, "but I'll give it a try."

The men looked small and insignificant as they rode from camp that afternoon, a light skiff of snow falling from the gray sky. The horses plunged into the snow, lunging against the drifts like great rocking horses, the men waving their hats as they rounded the trees and disappeared from sight.

From the fire, McReynolds watched them until the last, his stomach knotted with anxiety. Making decisions with other men's lives at stake was a hard thing, but, then, wasn't that something he did every day, weighing action against consequences? Still, this was different, men riding into the unknown on his orders. There was no skirting the responsibility, no burying your mistakes as Wallace would say.

When he looked up, Sarah stood at the edge of camp.

"Good morning," she said.

"Morning," he said, the night rushing back in all its sweetness.

"They've gone for help?" she asked, dabbing at her face with the back of her sleeve.

"The horses are not faring well in this cold. With no forage, no break in the weather, we could lose a great many of them in a short period of time. I thought it best they go for help."

Stooping, she poured a cup of coffee, her thighs against the soft folds of her dress awakened the image of their thrust and power and consummate hunger.

"It was a hard decision," she prodded.

"Horses don't travel well in deep snow like this, lunging to stay atop the drifts and they can't of course. Soon enough they are exhausted and quit. There's little to do beyond that. But with luck perhaps the drifts are lighter farther north. Without wagons they could make good time, at least to the redoubt or maybe even Dodge, where there's fresh mounts and grain."

"Coffee?" she asked, holding out the cup.

"No, thanks."

"I know you feel we've betrayed people," she said, lowering her eyes, "but that's not so."

Before he could answer, Cookey strolled across the camp, his ears wrapped with a scarf and tied under his chin like a bonnet.

"Morning, sir," he said. "It's a frosty one, isn't it?"

"Cheyenne, likely." McReynolds winked at Sarah. "Drumming up storms and causing all kinds of mischief."

"Ain't it so," Cookey agreed, shaking his head. "Yeast won't rise, coffee won't brew, and there's probably a Cheyenne aiming down my ear this very minute."

"Keep the meals hearty, Cookey, and plenty of it. This kind of weather saps a man's energy."

"Yes, sir," he said, "and I've fine help, too, hard-working she is, and pretty as a spring blossom."

"Indeed," McReynolds said, catching her eye, falling into their depths.

That night the sky opened, flakes the size of a man's hand careening from the heavens. The men scraped snow from their tents to keep them from collapsing under the weight. Huddling close to the fire, they talked amongst themselves, their voices muffled and rounded in the night, and they wondered of Wallace, of the men riding somewhere along the trail, of the dangers they faced in the blinding snow. Even Cookey's stew and sourdough failed to lift their spirits, and soon they drifted off to their tents.

But it was McReynolds who did not sleep, lying in the cold of his tent, wondering of the things he'd done. On this bitter night men struggled for their lives because of him. On this night a man's wife waited beyond in her tent for the sound of his voice.

As darkness drew down, the camp fell silent, the occasional cough or yawn as the men moved into sleep. But there was no stilling McReynolds's mind, no peace nor slumber, only the anguish of winged and uncontrolled thought.

And he went to her as he knew he would, lost in her passion, driven by his needs, by her needs, left by the indifference and callousness of others.

Afterward, they talked of David, of his obsession, of his coldness and driving ambition, but even then McReynolds knew it was a small and ugly thing he did, justification for his own lack of honor. To demean David diminished his own guilt, made it right, or, at least, less wrong.

In each other's arms, they fell into an uneasy and guarded sleep, and when he woke, a north wind howled across the plains, snapping the tent in an icy and relentless gale. Snow clattered against the tent as it crystallized in the falling temperatures. That night as he made his way back, he knew that the men he'd sent out might well be lost.

Four days passed without a word, each morning breaking in a world of ice, frost sprouting from the trees like whiskers, fog hanging like a gray curtain in the valley.

On this day Cookey was at the fire preparing the morning coffee, Sarah working at the skillet. Anxious to see how the horses survived the night, McReynolds cut through the stand of trees, avoiding the others altogether as he made for the corral.

Even as he approached, the devastation of the bitter night was apparent, a half-dozen horses lying dead on their sides like great frozen mountains. The others stood in groups, heads down, a pathetic and desolate lot. Without sufficient fodder, their enormous capacity to generate heat had failed, each passing hour decreasing their resistance, compounding their vulnerability. Trembling, they watched him with dark and sad eyes, his heart breaking at his helplessness.

Flour covering her hands, Sarah studied McReynolds face as he warmed at the fire.

"How are they?" she asked, pouring his coffee.

"It's not good," he said, "seven gone, more soon, if we don't get feed for them."

"Is there nothing you can do?"

"I've sent a detail to butcher out the carcasses. We'll hang them in the trees just in case this snow never stops, and we need food. We've plenty of meat." He shook his head. "We may have to pull these wagons to the redoubt ourselves."

Taking a camp chair, she locked her fingers about her knees and stared into the fire.

"And what of the men? Do you think they'll come back?" she asked.

"Of course," he said, but the uncertainty was there in his voice, in his eyes.

"You are sorry," she said, "about us?"

Checking for Cookey's whereabouts, McReynolds turned.

"It isn't that. I want to be with you more than life itself, but it's a dishonorable thing I've done."

"I, too, am dishonorable."

"No," he said, "it's not you who's responsible."

Reaching over, she took his hand.

"Making you unhappy is not what I wanted. We can't change what's happened between us, but we can stop it from happening again."

That night he did not go to her tent but lay awake instead, shivering against the cold, listening to the coyotes quarreling among themselves at the prospect of weak and dying horses.

It was just before daylight, that time when the sounds of night are hushed with the demands of a new day, that he heard them. Sitting up, he listened, straining to hear, and then it came again, the unmistakable crunch of horse hooves in the frozen snow. Slipping on his icy clothes, he exited his tent, stopping, listening again.

"Hello?" he said.

From across the camp, Cookey stuck his head out of his tent. "Hello," he said, "you a Cheyenne?"

"It's me," McReynolds said, waving him down with his hand.

"Sorry, sir. What you hear?"

"Horses, I think. Listen."

And then there was no mistaking, horses coming through the trees, specters from the frozen prairie.

"It's Captain Wallace," Cookey called out, "come back on his own."

The sun broke on the distant horizon, a clear and cold dawn.

"Wallace," McReynolds said, his heart leaping at his return.

Lifting his head, Wallace looked down from his horse. Frost glistened in his beard, his eyes hollow with fatigue. Only two men followed behind, trail worn and half frozen.

"Ain't going to muck up your shiny boots out here in this snow, are you?" Wallace said, trying a smile.

Wrapping Wallace's trembling arm over his neck, McReynolds helped him down.

As they gathered about the fire, Cookey made hot coffee, gravy and biscuits, with smoldering mounds of fried fatback. Once they were fed and filled with coffee, McReynolds turned to Wallace.

"The others?"

"Lost," he said.

"How?"

"The snow was blinding, coming so thick we couldn't see our horses' ears. When it wasn't snowing, it was blowing, and that was even worse. Wasn't two hours before we was lost, belly deep in snowdrifts and worn to a frazzle. The only way forward was to get off and walk, leading our horses, but even that didn't work most of the time." Shaking his head, he brought back the images. "Left one horse standing in a snowdrift, wore out he was and frozen to the core. Guess I ought to have shot him but didn't have the heart."

"Did you see anyone, find any help?" McReynolds asked.

"Nary a soul," he said, "not man nor bird." Sipping at his coffee, he looked for the answer there in the fire. "There was one thing. About ten miles out, we came across some tracks, horse," he added, "shoed, Cavalry maybe or whiskey rancher, lost soon enough in the moving snow."

Standing, McReynolds walked to the edge of camp and looked out on the prairie. The sun edged over the horizon, glittering on the newly fallen snow, a touch of warmth in its light.

Turning to face Wallace, he said, "What happened to the others?"

"By the second day, the snow lightened, and we could make our way horseback again, but snow is one thing, cold another. Temperatures dropped, deadly cold it was, a piercing cold that numbed thinking to a dead stop." Wallace looked into his coffee cup. "One by one, they fell away, just sitting down in the snow and refusing to go another step. All the begging and pleading made no difference. I told Hanson to get up or I'd shoot him where he stood. 'Shoot you behind the goddamn ear,' I said, but he just looked at me with them eyes and sat down in the snow." Looking over at Sarah, he shrugged his shoulders. "That's where I left him, sitting in the snow just like that horse."

"It's not your fault," she said. "It's no one's fault."

"No," he repeated, "it ain't no one's fault." Rising, Wallace ran his fingers through his hair, looking at the stand of trees where the horses were corralled. "How many did we lose?" he asked.

"Too many," McReynolds said. "Even if we don't lose more, we'll have to leave some of the wagons behind, supplies, too, I guess. If the weather doesn't turn soon, we're in trouble, I'm afraid."

But it was in the evening, as the sun quivered low on the horizon, and the day's events pressed in that McReynolds felt the full brunt of his decision, of sending men to their deaths, of sending them there in vain. He had made the decision, and it was the wrong one. Now he must live with this forever.

The orange light of sunset fell across the drifts, casting their tips like toasted meringue. Sarah worked at the fire, bundled against the damp cold of evening. Even now in all his guilt, he wanted her still, needed her beyond reason. This, he knew, of those who mattered in his life, none would have made his choices, not Renfro, not Twobirds, not his old friend Number. They were his choices alone, as sad and dishonorable and unwise as they were.

At some point, he was aware of a presence, someone watching from the perimeter of the camp, a man on horseback watching them from a distance. A chill raced down his back and pooled in the pit of his stomach.

Reaching for his carbine, he stepped forward.

"Who are you?" he asked.

The horseman dropped his reins. Under his heavy coat was the telling blue of a Cavalry uniform, and McReynolds lowered his carbine.

"Cooper, sir," he said, "out of Dodge."

Behind the beard was the strain of the trail, an unmistakable weariness in the eyes.

"Climb down," McReynolds said. "Warm yourself at the fire."

With a slow and deliberate swing of his leg, Cooper dismounted, squatting at the fire, holding his hands to warm while Cookey poured hot coffee.

"It's a long ride from Dodge," he said, blowing on the coffee, "and a hard one at that." Sipping, he let the coffee linger on his tongue, closing his eyes. "Been riding in circles in this snowstorm. Thought for a while they wouldn't find me till first thaw."

Circling the fire, Wallace pulled up a camp chair and cut himself a chew.

"Must of been your tracks we saw out there," he said, picking the flecks of tobacco off the blade of his knife.

"Must of," Cooper said.

"What is it that you're doing out here?" McReynolds asked.

"General Sully sent out Sergeant Westhoff to contact a Lieutenant Roland, to confirm the construction of a redoubt at Deep Hole Creek and then on to Supply with orders for the quartermaster sergeant."

The sound of Roland's name caused Sarah to look up from her cooking.

"That's where we're headed," McReynolds said, "with the construction crew."

"Yes, sir, figured as much, seeing your building supplies and all." Looking into his cup, he thought a while before beginning again. "Westhoff never made it back, so I was dispatched to find him."

"And did you?" McReynolds asked.

Looking up, Cooper nodded. "Yes, sir, I did. Kilt',

he was, and a scalp lock taken. This here side arm was still in his belt."

"They didn't take his side arm?" McReynolds asked.

"Peculiar, ain't it?" he said, turning the revolver over.

Holding her dress back from the fire, Sarah dipped a steaming bowl of stew out of the pot and handed it to Cooper.

"And what about the others, the redoubt detachment?" she asked.

Taking a slurp at the stew, he looked up from under his hat.

"Oh, yes, ma'am," he said, wiping at his chin with the sleeve of his shirt. "I found them alright, digging in they were and complaining some. But ain't that natural?"

Casting a glance up at McReynolds, Sarah took a deep breath, and turned to the fire.

"Yes," she said, "natural enough, I suppose."

Finishing his stew, Cooper crossed his arms, warming his feet against the fire. The evening darkened about them as the day's heat bled away. Looking into the flames, Cooper spoke, his voice distant and cool, as if speaking to the lonely drifts of snow or the frozen hills that rolled away into the distance.

" 'Cept that Lieutenant Roland feller," he said, "wiped off his horse under a tree, he was. Broke his neck, they said. Didn't blink nor say goodbye, they said, neither one."

And the silence of the night shattered with guilt, with grief, with unspeakable joy.

Twenty-six

There was precious little food that could be taken along, but Nurse Cromley did her best, wrapping the cuts in thin layers one upon the other, stowing them in the blankets they would carry on their backs. The task came easily to her after years with the Osage. The lesson of packing too much was a hard and inevitable one, and one seldom forgotten. What was taken was carried without help, and a word never said. How often she'd abandoned some article or other, something she'd thought indispensable, dropping it at the side of the trail as the miles wore away her strength and resolve.

Pulling herself up, she hooked her walking stick under her arm, avoiding looking at her leg. It was there, she knew, a dead and ugly thing connected to her body. Snow clung in Brother Jacob's brows and melted on his cheeks like great wet tears as he loaded the last of the supplies.

"Are you ready?" she asked.

Leaning down, he hooked her arm over his shoulder, the old pain settling in like an unwelcome relative.

"Which way to the crossing?"

"South," she said, "that's all I know."

"South it is, then," he said.

It was a slow and deliberate journey they made,

trudging through the snow, a raggedy and miserable pair of vagabonds inching across the prairie. At noon they stopped to eat, shivering against the cold as they chewed on the strips of buffalo meat. Neither spoke as they ate, conserving their strength to stave off the cold and the gnawing reality of their circumstance.

By nightfall they'd won only a few miles, their muscles aching with fatigue and cold. Somewhere beyond the gray clouds, the sun dimmed and sank below the horizon. It was dark when they found the rock wall, an abrupt outcropping that jutted from the floor of the prairie. In its mass was a strength and comfort, a refuge for their fears.

As the shadow of night stretched across the plains, Brother Jacob carried wood from a nearby creek, and soon firelight danced up the face of the wall. Neither spoke of the day, its brutal toll apparent in their silence, but the warmth of the fire gave them courage, loosening the manacles of despair.

"Perhaps if I fried the meat on a stick," Nurse Cromley said, "it would taste less like saddle leather."

"And more like fried saddle leather," Brother Jacob said.

Propping her foot on a piece of firewood, Nurse Cromley turned the meat in the fire, grease sputtering in the coals. Even in the dim firelight, the tone of her leg was ominous. Neither spoke of it in the absence of solutions.

While Nurse Cromley prepared the meager meal, Brother Jacob said his prayers, his hands clasped in a desperate wish at the tip of his chin. When finished, he looked up at Nurse Cromley, his eyes wet with tears.

"It's Brother Alexander you're thinking of?" she asked.

"There was so little he wanted," he said, "and so

much he deserved. In the face of this cruelty my faith stands beyond reach. I despair in its inadequacy to account for what it has done. There is little but emptiness and bitterness left in me. Everything I thought true is deception, a cruel joke played on the most naive and vulnerable of us all."

"You mustn't lose your faith," she said. "Without it there is naught but nature, as certain in its cruelty as in its beauty."

Holding the stick out to him, she waited as he unthreaded the meat, dropping it from one hand to the other as it cooled. Leaning in on his elbows, he chewed with concentration as he looked into the fire. His hands were old, Mary thought, twisted and knurled from the years.

"There is too much of man in God," he said, a morsel of the meat clinging in his beard, "too much that stands between. How is one to ever know the truth? It is like standing in a room of mirrors with one's own image staring back from all directions."

"When I was a young girl, I was determined to go to the convent," she said, "but my father wouldn't let me. He saw something in me that I couldn't see, so I became a nurse. Sometimes we are unable to see God through our own eyes."

Wiping his hands on his tunic, he leaned back against the rock wall.

"It is like a tree that stands alone," he said, "bearing against the wind. In its isolation it must turn inward, strengthen from within. I think it must be that way, from within. I think God must be from within."

But Nurse Cromley didn't answer, her back to the fire, her eyes locked on the figure standing in the darkness at the edge of camp.

"Have you come to kill us?" she said. "There is little for your trouble."

Brother Jacob rose, his carbine beyond reach.

Moving closer, the figure stopped again.

"To share your fire," he said.

There was something telling in the voice, something familiar, her mind racing back through the years.

"What's ours, you're welcome to," she said, reaching for her crutch.

"Mind telling your friend there in the dress to leave that carbine be. I ain't shot a woman in a long time, even one with a beard."

"This is Brother Jacob," Mary said. "He's a monk as you can see. It's alright, Brother Jacob. I think he means us no harm."

"What's your business?" Brother Jacob asked.

"Staying alive," the man said, stepping into the light, "and taking pleasure where it's offered. Lately that ain't been too often, lame horse, no food, and then this here blinding snowstorm."

Nurse Cromley's crutch clattered to the ground as she caught herself, her hand over her mouth.

"Adam Renfro," she said. "Isn't that just like you, stepping out of a blizzard without so much as a warning."

Pushing back his hat, Adam scrutinized the face of the woman who stood before him.

"Mary Cromley," he said, reaching for her hand. "Come to save my life one more time."

"It's a poor lot you're depending on to save lives, Adam," she said, looking up into his face, the same face as she remembered, but tired now, older. "By morning there's likely to be nothing left of us." Turning she reached for Brother Jacob's hand. "This is Brother Jacob, my friend and savior. He's carried me halfway across the country without so much as a complaint."

Shaking his hand, Adam smiled.

"Had my hat knocked off more'n once for being out of step," he said, "but it's a brave man to wear a dress in this country."

Smiling, Brother Jacob looked down at his raggedy tunic.

"As Nurse Cromley's friend, you are welcome in my camp anytime," he said, "and you are right, of course. The tunic has been cause of considerable grief on occasion."

"We've much to talk about," Adam said, turning to Nurse Cromley, "but first I must bring in my horse, and I've something to show you."

"Horse," she said, "thank God. We are on foot, with no way to even carry our food." Reaching for her crutch, she balanced against it. "I'll fix you some meat while you are gone and boil some water. The meat is of poor quality, but filled with grease and energy to keep you warm."

Within half an hour, Adam returned, stepping from the darkness with Buck at his back and Creed at his side.

"This is my son, Creed," he said. "Creed, this is Nurse Mary Cromley. She's had cause to save my life on occasion."

"Hello," he said with an uncertain handshake.

"Hello, Creed," she said, pulling her leg under her.

"Twobirds," Adam said, pointing to Creed. "I was able to find her that spring."

"Yes," she said, smiling. "It would be Twobirds. I know your mother, Creed. In fact, I think you can say we are friends."

Looking up at his father, Creed shrugged.

"My mother's dead now," he said.

"Oh," she said, glancing at Adam. "I'm so sorry. She was a brave and wonderful woman. It's a hard thing to lose one's mother."

"She knew my mother," Creed said, looking up at Adam, "from before."

It was for Creed a moment secured to a world he'd never known, a reality beyond the stories of his father.

"And this is Brother Jacob," Nurse Cromley said to Creed, "my friend and human crutch. There is a strength within him matched only by your father."

And so that night they built the fire high, bringing Buck under the shelter of the wall. Soon Creed fell asleep, exhausted from the day's walk, followed by Brother Jacob, who soon snored under his blanket. From time to time Buck would blow and shake his head.

Even in their weariness, Adam and Nurse Cromley talked into the night, of Twobirds, of Dr. McReynolds, of Lieutenant Sheets's demise in the Cross Timbers so many years earlier. As the snow stacked on their shoulders, they talked of times past, of the winter they'd spent together in the Osage camp, of the fleeting years since. Their breaths lingering in the freezing cold, they talked on, in it a healing, a closing, and a tucking of their lives. Reaching for her hand, Adam held it in his own.

"About the leg?" he said.

Her eyes filling, Nurse Cromley turned away.

"The leg is lost," she said, pausing, "and so am I."

The words broke about him like shattered glass, releasing his own pain and grief and loneliness, and he struggled to compose himself against the bitter reality of her story.

From then, they did not speak, holding each other's hand as the storm deepened, and the night drew down like a black and final curtain.

Morning came with a blast of bitter and driving wind. Buck was too lame for Nurse Cromley to ride, but was able to carry their meager supplies. Once they were packed, it was decided that Adam would take the first turn helping Nurse Cromley, that he and Brother Jacob would spell each other off as the need arose. This left Creed to lead Buck and to carry the extra carbine.

"Soon enough your neck will plead for relief," Nurse Cromley said, putting her arm about Adam.

"Never been known to complain about snuggling with a pretty girl." Adam winked.

Both knew of the dreaded path ahead, of their dire circumstances, of the depleted supplies and worsening weather. Still, hour after hour they tramped through the deepening drifts, searching the horizon for signs of life and hope. Battling against the deepening snow, Nurse Cromley's strength was soon depleted, her fever mounting unopposed. Hope was dying, as certain as the blackened leg that swelled beneath her.

From behind, Creed struggled with Buck, pulling against his reins, urging him forward with encouraging words, with violent threats. Eyes wide, Buck resisted, his head thrown back against Creed's wrath, vaulting forward in panic at the engulfing drifts.

By the second day, both supplies and strength exhausted, the frequency of their rest periods increased. Each rest was more difficult to end, the cold whispering for a moment more.

That night Nurse Cromley boiled the remaining meat, while Adam and Brother Jacob hunted the canyon for rabbit with Brother Jacob's remaining shells. From under his blanket, Creed watched Nurse Cromley as she worked at the task.

"It smells good," he said, "even without salt or anything."

"Wish it were more," she said.

"We could eat Buck," he answered, grinning. "I'm tired of pulling him across the prairie."

Taking her seat, she looked at Creed, seeing Two-birds in his eyes.

"You are a lot like your mother," she said. "I remember her well, you know. She saved my life when I was bitten by a rattler. Although, sometimes I think she doubted the wisdom of that decision."

"I've never saved anybody's life," he said, "but I'm a good hunter and tracker."

"Yes," she said, "you would be."

"I killed a rabbit with a rock."

Studying his face, she handed him a cup of the broth. In his eyes was an intelligence, a curiosity, enigmatic like the pieces of an unfinished puzzle.

"I've been with the Osage many years," she said, "and have learned much about the wilderness. These are lessons you have learned, too, from your mother and father. They are lessons of life and will serve you well, no matter which people you are with."

Sipping at the broth, Creed thought on her words.

"But I have never been with my father's people nor know of his world. We are going to start a freight line and haul goods along the new trail."

"How exciting," she said, rubbing at her leg, "a freight line. Your father was always a great one with the mules. A freight line would be just the thing."

"And I am to help him, but then the bullwhacker said that soon the trains would come from the north, that they are great machines that run without tiring, that wagon freight is doomed as surely as the buffalo and the Indian. This is what he said, and that soon white people will fill the country and make it their own. But he was not to be trusted, and my father had to kill him."

In the distance a rifle report broke the silence of the evening. Their eyes met, each hoping that the shells were not wasted.

"They've gotten something," she said.

"My father seldom misses," Creed said, "and holds his shots until needed."

Sensing his unease, Nurse Cromley waited, filling his cup again, taking her place by the fire in silence. It was the Indian way, to wait, to let time answer the unknown.

"I am to live among them now," he continued, "to be a part of my father's world."

"It's not such a different world, Creed. There will be things to adjust to, but you will do that with ease, and soon you will have them doing your will. I've watched how you manage yourself, and I'm very impressed."

Flashing a quick smile, he shoved his hands into his pockets and walked to the edge of camp.

"I see them," he said, "and they are carrying game."

As Adam and Brother Jacob approached, Nurse Cromley could see the lightness of Brother Jacob's step and the rabbits bouncing over his shoulder.

That night they roasted the rabbits, turning them on a spit until golden brown, the aroma filling the night with promise. Never had food tasted so good, grease gleaming on their fingers and chins as they gorged themselves on the roasted flesh. Brother Jacob wrapped the largest rabbit in a blanket away from predators, laying aside all remaining bones of the others for boiling later on. One never knew, and they would make a palatable soup if it came to that.

Soon Brother Jacob slept, like a great hibernating bear beneath his blanket, and Creed nodded against Adam's shoulder.

"Go on to bed, boy," Adam said, fluffing Creed's hair, "before you fall into the fire."

Smiling, Creed climbed under his covers and was soon asleep.

Even the cold failed to dampen their spirits as they sat around the fire, their stomachs full for the first time in many days. In the distance a coyote bayed at the moon, its voice rising in a trembling lament.

"It's a bitter night that would discourage a coyote," Adam said.

Adjusting her leg, Nurse Cromley worked at her boot, loosening it from the swollen flesh.

"You must be very proud of that boy, Adam. He's strong and wise to be so young."

Nodding, Adam looked into the sky.

"I ain't never regretted his coming along. He's been a necessary link in my life. Don't know what I would've amounted to without him. If anything should happen to me . . ."

"What could happen to an ole mule skinner like yourself," she said.

"It's some hard things I've come across, Mary, in a Cheyenne winter camp."

There was something in his voice that alarmed her.

"What do you mean?"

Pushing back his hat, he studied her face. There in her eyes he could still see the beautiful young nurse so dedicated to her beliefs, the strength of her convictions washing away the lines of weariness and pain.

"First sign we came on was a cow, least I think it was, as ugly a creature as I ever saw, had a blue tongue long as my arm. Recent dead it was. Arrows shanked in its heart."

"Ole Blue Tongue." Mary looked up in surprise.

"You knew this beast?"

"Our milk cow," Mary said, "fair trade brought home by Brother Alexander."

"Liked to have been around to trade him some

mules," Adam said. "Seen bobcats made better milkers than that." Pulling the blanket over Creed's shoulders, he looked up at Mary. "That ole cow had put up one hell of a fight."

"What she lacked in milk, she made up for in gumption." Mary smiled.

"Those were Dog Soldier arrows, sacred ones at that." Pausing, Adam stared off into the night. "We found them Dog Soldiers," he finally said, "and their families, laying like plucked flowers among the fallen leaves of their winter camp. It was as hard a sight as I've ever seen—women, children, horses, all butchered in the morning dawn as they slept and dreamed their dreams. Sometimes I wake up with my heart pounding just thinking on it."

"But who?"

"Soldiers, I think, by the looks of it."

"They killed them all?"

"All, or nearly so." He shook his head. "Looked like one dragged off into the prairie. Ain't likely he made it, though."

"One thing I know," Mary said, "living with the Osage these years, this thing will not go unpunished as long as there's a single Dog Soldier left. They won't be particular about taking their vengeance."

"It was a stand of oak," he said. "Creed was there and will carry its memory the whole of his life. His mother's gone, his people, too, for that matter. It's the white world that's left for him, and now this."

Reaching out, she touched his arm, her dear and noble friend, to comfort him as best she could, and the fire flickered its protest against the blackness around them.

The next few days were but a whirl of snow and bitter cold, a blinding push against the maddening drifts. Game disappeared altogether as the cold deepened, driving even the most hearty animals into their shelters. To make matters worse, Nurse Cromley's strength failed, her fever soaring against unchecked infection.

Exhausted, they stopped early, digging for wood under the ice-encrusted drifts. Creed stayed with Nurse Cromley as Adam and Brother Jacob hunted for food, plying her with his natural humor to revive her spirits. But her pain was now too great, her situation too desperate.

When Adam and Brother Jacob returned empty-handed, a pall fell over the camp.

"We could eat the other rabbit," Brother Jacob said.

"No," Adam said. "We may need it more later."

So they cracked the rabbit bones, exposing the marrow, bleaching them white in boiling water. Pouring a cup of the broth, Adam offered it to Nurse Cromley.

"Give it to the boy," she said.

"But you are ill and need it more than any of us. Here, there is enough."

"All of us here know how it is," she said. "The living must not suffer because of the dying. I was once left behind to die. It should have been so. Now, there is not enough food."

"We are not leaving anyone behind," Adam said.

"Tomorrow you will go without me. You can make it to the crossing, and there will be help there."

"You would surely die here alone," Brother Jacob said.

"Together we will all die," she said. "I have done what was meant for me, and so I am content."

"But of those who leave you behind," Brother Jacob said, "how do we live with such a decision?"

"And so we all die," she said, "because of principle and self-righteousness? These things are of no consequence. We must do this for each other, or all is lost."

"There is time to talk of this tomorrow," Adam said. "Now we must rest."

The enormity of her suggestion followed them to their beds, its absurdity and its logic.

During the night, the winds came again, and the clouds churned heavy with snow. Once, Adam rose to stoke the fire and to check on Creed, flakes spitting in the coals like angry hisses. Crawling back under his blanket, he curled against the brutal cold, knowing in his heart that things had gone wrong, very wrong indeed. The Cimarron crossing at Deep Hole Creek might as well be a thousand miles away under their circumstances. Perhaps Mary was right. Perhaps there was no other choice. It didn't matter to him to die here. His life ended the day Twobirds was placed on the scaffold. He was but a ghost already, a shadow, a flame winking away. If not for Creed, he would've ended it himself that day. But there *was* Creed, in this place, and on his own. He could not let him die.

When a reluctant sunrise broke on the horizon, its heatless light quivered over the frozen landscape.

Nurse Cromley knelt next to Adam's bed and shook his shoulder.

"Adam," she said, "Adam, wake up."

"What is it?" he asked, rubbing the cold from his face.

"Brother Jacob is gone."

Together, Adam, Mary, and Creed stood at the top of the hill, bearing against the bitter morning. Below them, the lone tracks of Brother Jacob twisted across the white valley of snow and disappeared into the orange light of sunrise.

Twenty-seven

Brother Alexander's decision to leave was less noble than he would have liked, more selfish than self-sacrificing, and motivated by a compelling need to detach himself from the chaos of the world.

Even now as the bitter winds burned his face, and the maddening drifts gathered about his legs, there was within him a freedom and exaltation he'd never known in all his years at the monastery. There was within him a pure and clear view of God's world and of his place in it. Now in his waning years, he had at last found what he'd been searching for, dreamed of so often in the isolation of his cell. Now at last there was naught between him and God's eye but the spirit as pure and clear as a mountain stream, and it filled him with joy.

Turning, he squinted against the glare of the drifts, scanning the horizon. For a moment he could smell the smoke from Nurse Cromley's fire, the aroma of cooking rabbit. Wrapping his blanket about his shoulders, he lowered his head and moved into the swirling snow.

How long or how far he walked he could not be certain, but when he dropped, exhausted, onto his knees, there was but the endless plains about him, the ringing silence of distance and emptiness, the singular rise and fall of his own breath.

Throughout the day the temperatures had dropped,

the cold deepening in its pain and circumstance. Hands numbed and swollen, Brother Jacob searched for the few matches he'd taken, his heart leaping at their absence, before finding them lying deep in the seam of his tunic pocket.

Hand over his eyes, he searched the prairie for shelter, for wood for his fire. On the horizon a rock outcrop loomed against the gray dusk, a monolith sprouting from the belly of the earth. Was it the same where they had camped a few days before? Things changed on the prairie, seen from a new direction or light.

Rising, he blew into his frozen hands, and wiped at the ice crystals that gathered on his beard. It may be near or it may be miles away. Even on a clear day, distances were deceiving. But his options were few. A night in the open prairie without shelter or fire might cost him his life.

Hours passed as he walked, his eyes locked onto the ridge, his lifeline and landmark. As daylight faded, the winds stilled, and the sky swelled with stars, an unbounded spectacle as the glory of the universe opened above him. And there before him, rising into the heavens, a cathedral of rock, a monument and shrine to the glory of God, and he fell to his knees. Even in the darkness, he could see the dead coals of their old campfire. Water dripped from his nose and froze on the cuff of his tunic in the plummeting temperatures as he prayed, as he prayed like he'd never prayed in his life.

And so it would be, here, in this place, God and he would abide in daily intercourse, without man, without cares, without the petty concerns of the world.

An hour's climb up the southern slope of the outcrop brought him to a rift, a split in the rock, opening into the heart of the cliff. Facing south, it would provide protection from winter winds, and the sun would heat its face. In the summer the cliff would shade the opening from the relentless sun. A frozen stream crossed the valley no more than a mile away. Mesquite and cedar grew in abundance from between the fallen rocks to provide fuel for his fire. This would be His place, God's place.

Gathering wood, he tossed it into the cave before squeezing his big frame through the opening. Once inside, he crumbled the rotten wood into a small pile, cupping the match between his hands against the draft. Soon shadows danced up the walls as the fire grew, and the smoke rose out of the cave opening. Holding his hands against the flames, he blew on the fire, his breath clouding in the warming temperatures as the fire flickered into life.

Now for the first time, he examined his new dwelling, a sparse and stoic place, jagged rocks lodged in chaos, not smooth nor waterworn but jammed and crushed by the sudden shift of rock. Overhead, a slab lay caught against a network of stone, patient in its inevitable slide to the bottom.

It was a fine home, though, his home, and it was within arm's reach of God's Heaven. Here he would build a cathedral, a monument to the glory of God. Here he would build with his own hands, a living tribute, a temple for God's eyes alone. Picking up a sharp rock he scratched a cross above the opening and fell to his knees, his heart bursting with the certainty of his decision.

Only then did he see them, their tiny red eyes shining in the light of the fire. Like silent sentries they lined the rock above him, watching his every move from their lofty perch, rats the size of a man's hand, a dozen or more scampering from the darkness, leaning from the ledge as they scolded him with angry squeaks. Their razor teeth flashed in the light, no place for the likes of humans or monks.

Stoking his fire higher, Brother Jacob watched them from the corner of his eye. As if by signal they would retreat from the ledge, to gather among themselves, to plan a strategy for his demise, to charge forth again with new determination and rage at his presence.

It was on the third such foray that Brother Jacob fired a well-chosen rock, crushing one of the rats, its legs jerking, its mouth slack in death.

Unblinking eyes watched from above as he threaded the rat onto a stick. Examining his catch, he placed it on the fire to roast. Soon the smell of cooking meat filled the tiny cave, tinged with char as the blackened tail twisted in a crisp from the heat.

His stomach lurching, he took his first bite, pulling his lips back so as not to touch the flesh. It was not so bad, and he took another, more confident bite, allowing himself to taste the meat. There was a scurry on the ledge above, the twisting of nose whiskers, the conferring, the bobbing of heads like deacons in a church.

When finished eating, Brother Jacob belched and wiped his fingers on the front of his tunic. After stacking the tiny bones of his meal on a flat rock near the wall, he leaned back to enjoy his fire. Soon his lids grew heavy, head nodding, chin drooping against his chest.

It was during the night, after the fire had died, when a scalding pain shot through his leg, sitting him upright in the pitch black of the cave. Grabbing at his leg, he squeezed at the hateful thing attached to his calf, squeezing its life from between his fingers, its squeal dying away. In disgust he flung it from him, searching for his matches, rekindling his fire with trembling hands.

When at last the blaze grew bright, red eyes from the ledge watched on with interest. Stacking wood onto the flames, he examined the teeth wounds in his leg and swore never again to neglect his fire. It was the only thing they feared, his fire, and it was all that stood between him and the legions teeming in the bowels of the mountain.

When he awoke for the second time, the fire had dwindled once more, sputtering and fuming under dying coals. Adding more wood, he could see them in the shadows as they surrounded the body of his attacker, a chilling tug-of-war ensuing as they tore at its flesh. Heaving a large rock into their midst, he crushed a large female as she hesitated for a last unfortunate bite of her brother.

So this was to be his hermitage, his retreat, a hideous battlefield for brutish and vile creatures, an obscenity on the sanctity of his altar. Falling to his knees, he prayed, his hands lifted to the heavens. It was more than he could bear. What was he to do? What was it that God wanted of him?

As the morning sun struck through the opening above, his sanctuary filled with light, and the rats scurried into the dark recesses of the cave. There in the blue morning sky was the answer. As long as there was the light, he was safe, not only was he safe, but God had provided an endless source of food. There was only two things he must do: keep the fire going, and keep the trap baited.

As the days passed, his plan worked, worked without fail. Each night he placed a portion in the shadows where the cave narrowed, where it wound and twisted into the jumble of rocks. Stoking his fire high, he would doze while they waited in the darkness, for the dying of the fire, for the flesh of their luckless brothers. Each night he rose with rock in hand to wait as they scrambled from the shadows. With practice, his aim grew keen. But the rats were undaunted, their hunger driving them from the depths and into the crushing certainty of his rock.

Never did he allow his fire to go out. Much of his day was consumed in foraging for wood, in keeping the fire alive, in removing the ash to the back of the cave. It was the fire alone that stood between him and the dark desperation from below.

Sometimes he climbed high onto the outcrop, working his way through the craggy rocks to where the twisted cedar grew. There in the far reaches was the best wood, hot with pitch and resin. In the night, after prayers, he etched icons into the cave wall, tributes to God, to His temple, and then lay in wait for the rats to come, firing his stone with accuracy into their squirming masses.

On a still winter day, while hunting for wood in the upper extent of the outcrop, he found the knurled cedar, a spirit tree, turned and weathered in its exposure. Even on such a day as this, its trunk was warmed from the distant sun, radiant with God's being. The decision was instant, to carve from this tree a grand and wonderful crucifix, an image of the highest order and beauty. The crucifix that he wore about his neck would serve as a model. With exacting care he would make from the tree a thing of beauty, a work to bring tears to the eyes of God.

Two trips it took to drag the heavy tree the full distance from the top, another day to work it through the narrow opening of the rift. Once in, however, it rose to the ceiling of the cave with perfect measure. Within hours he'd shaped the cross piece, securing it with the belt of his tunic. In time, he would carve the figure of Jesus in relief, His soul and breath rendered from the red heart of the cedar.

That night he slept little in anticipation of his project, rising early the next morning to replenish his wood supply, to bait his trap, to get his primitive tools in order. By noon he was at work, fashioning the wood, wearing it smooth with stone tools. In the confines of the cave, the cedar's aroma filled him with happiness, this the crown jewel of his work.

By evening the weather turned; cold, blustery winds whistled through the jagged rocks above. Overhead, clouds raced through the sky, streaming by with purpose and intent. Stepping back, he admired his work. The head of Christ was emerging from the cedar, His figure buried still deep in the wood. Holding up the rosary, he followed the lines of the crucifix, each turn, each bone, and each angle properly positioned. How proud Brother Alexander would have been of the care he exercised in its execution.

Even now in the half light, he could hear the rats gathering beyond the shadows, gathering and waiting for the remains of their brethren.

It was a feeling first, a vague and uncertain knowledge of someone's presence that caused him to look up; there in the light of dusk, the terrifying outline of feathers against the sky, the slashes of war paint, the strung bows. Perhaps they were apparitions, the fleeting shadows of night, the twilight between dreams and reality to which he had become so accustomed.

"Who are you?" the words formed, but even as he spoke, a foot drove hard into his stomach, his breath rushing away, gall rising bitter as he crumbled onto the floor.

Above him stood a warrior, a ferocious scar severing the whole of his misshapen face. In his hand was a knife, and in his eyes was the unquenchable thirst of retribution.

The warrior's eyes narrowed in the darkness, his scar reflecting in the light of the fire.

"Little Dog," he said, as if the world knew, as if the world knew without explanation.

Catching his breath, Brother Jacob pulled himself against the wall.

"Welcome to my home," he said.

The words fell as thin and dying echoes in the confines of the cave as Little Dog thrust his lance into Brother Jacob's open mouth, prying apart his jaws, seizing his tongue and slicing it away with the downward thrust of his knife. Blood dribbled unchecked from between Brother Jacob's crushed teeth, his tongue quivering in the dirt next to the collection of rat bones on the flat rock.

Yanking the rosary from his neck, Little Dog tuned it in the light of the fire, studying its figure, lifting his eyes to the cedar cross.

Two warriors dropped through the rift opening, leggings frozen with snow, smears of war paint under their eyes. Pointing to the cedar tree, Little Dog snapped an order. Only the swish of their moccasins could be heard, the gamy smell of rats and death riding in from the rift. With rawhide strips they tied his arms, his feet, and hung him from the cedar tree before leaving.

In that moment Brother Jacob would have told them of his innocence, of his forgiveness, of his love, if the words could have come. But they could not come. They would not come now, not in a thousand years. The words were buried too deep under the grunts of anguish and sorrow, under the despair and hopelessness of them all.

The moonless night drew down cold over the prairie as Brother Jacob moaned in the silence of his cave, his terrible weight, his constraints, his tortured and swollen mouth.

Beyond in the depths, blackness mounted like a

deep and swelling tide. Straining forward from his station, he listened to Little Dog's horses as their pace quickened onto the prairie, to the sputtering flame as it flickered away, to the fervent squeaks of the rats as they leapt from their ledges and into the darkness.

Twenty-eight

Stunned by the death of her husband, Sarah retreated to her tent, and for the next several days kept to herself. Her meals were taken alone, and the men fell quiet in her presence. It was a time for grieving, the one thing soldiers understood best. It was of paramount importance. Grieving relinquished pain, honored death, made of it a significant and worthy event. If death were honorable, then so, too, were their lives. It was, after all, what they were about. Nothing came so hard in soldiering as the unabsolved grief of fallen comrades.

During the day Sarah rode at Cookey's side, a black shawl pulled about her shoulders. At night she retreated to her tent to eat alone in the darkness. It was the right thing to do, the men said, a woman grieving for the loss of her husband. As they passed her tent, their voices would lower to a whisper. Sometimes a man would drop his hat in respect or cross himself as he passed by her tent.

It was McReynolds who grew dark and detached, barking orders to the men, demanding immediate attention to the building of the fire, or the packing of the horses. It was McReynolds who cursed Private Owens for dropping a medical-supply box, and McReynolds who dumped Cookey's biscuits in the fire for being inedible rocks.

"It's the Cheyenne done it," Cookey said, red rising into his neck, "turned my flour to stone dust."

"It's your bloody incompetence," McReynolds shouted. "All you're asked to do day in and day out is provide edible food. It doesn't even have to be good food, just edible."

"Yes, sir," Cookey said, head down, "I'll fix a new batch right away."

"Never mind," McReynolds said, dumping away his coffee. "No one is any longer hungry."

Rising from his chair, Captain Wallace cut a chew and loaded his cheek.

"Wonder if I could talk to you a moment, Major?" he asked.

"About what?" McReynolds said, his face still flushed with anger.

"It's a private matter, sir, if you don't mind."

"There is no privacy in this outfit, Captain, but if you want to go to my tent, we could try."

Buttoning up his coat, Captain Wallace nodded.

"I reckon that's private enough."

Once in the tent, McReynolds lit a candle and set it on his camp table. Besides giving off passable light, it helped keep the chill at bay.

"Alright," he said, pulling out a camp chair, "what is it that's so all-fired important, Captain?"

"Don't know how important it is, Major. But the men are afraid to come in to the fire for fear of being eat alive."

Rubbing at his hands, McReynolds looked away.

"It's the trail, I suppose. Nothing's going right, the weather, the death of Housman."

Taking up a chair, Wallace hiked his foot across his knee, leaning forward like he did when studying a construction problem.

"Guess it could be that," he said.

"What do you mean?"

"Nothing, 'cept sometimes it's hard to see your own hand in things."

Standing, McReynolds paced the small area between the chair and the camp table.

"Well, you must mean something. You're in my tent, spitting tobacco juice and telling me my business."

Pushing back his chair, Wallace stood.

"Sorry 'bout fouling your tent, Major, and 'bout caring one way or the other."

As he started to leave, McReynolds reached for his arm.

"Wait," he said, "I didn't mean to be short. It's just that . . . it's just that things have been hard of late. I'm not sure why." Sitting down, he looked up at Wallace. "I've spent my whole life out here on these plains, dealing with saddle blisters, broken bones, and snakebites. I've made no money, done no research, advanced mankind not one iota. It's been a hard and lonely life, and worst of all, it's been a life replete with ingratitude. There's no one to leave behind, no one left who cares one way or the other." Reaching for his pipe, he filled it, packing the tobacco with his forefinger, striking a match on the bottom of his boot. With long puffs, he brought the pipe to life, smoke curling into the light that streamed through the tent opening. "At the risk of feeling sorry for myself, it just seems to me it's a bleak and fruitless journey all and all."

Rubbing at his beard, Wallace looked him in the eye. Light from the tent opening fell across his back and warmed a spot, like a warm hand laid there between his shoulder blades.

"Can I speak off the record, Major."

"The record never stopped you before, Captain."

"Well, off the record I'd say that you've fallen in love with that lieutenant's wife. Now, long as that lieutenant was alive, being the son of a bitch we all knew him to be, it seemed an acceptable thing to do. Now he's dead, and there ain't no one between you and your conscience. The only son of a bitch left standing is yourself, Major, and so you're looking for someone else to blame, like Cookey, or me, or your own life's journey."

Pushing back his chair, McReynolds rose, his eyes flashing.

"I ought to knock you down for that," he said, his fists clenched at his sides.

"I been knocked down before, Major, and by bigger men than yourself. Knocking me down or belittling Cookey won't change the facts none, will it?"

"Pulling back the tent flap, McReynolds let the cold air cool his face. Across the compound, Cookey worked at a new batch of biscuits, his breath rising into the cold. Beyond the smoke of the fire was Sarah's tent, snow swirling in eddies near the entrance. What Wallace was saying was true. There was only one son of a bitch left standing, and it was time he faced up to it. Tapping the ashes from his pipe into the palm of his hand, he dusted them off into the snow.

"I've not amounted to much, Captain, not what I intended to at least. My wife died under my hand, and I've spent my life hiding out on these plains, I suppose. I've not amounted to much, but I've always made certain that I hurt no one else, that is until now." Walking back to his chair, he propped his foot on it and looked down at Wallace. "I've lived my life as honest and straightforward as I could, taking from no man what was his, but this thing I've done is dishonorable, and I don't know how to fix it."

Leaning back in his chair, Wallace fired tobacco juice out the tent flap.

"Most of my fixing has to do with stables and such, Major, but this much I do know about living. It's mighty hard to be perfect, impossible I'd say. Being dishonorable ain't the privilege of a few, but a common and universal ailment. It's what you do about it that matters, seems to me." Standing, he pulled the collar of his coat up about his ears. "It's just knowing you're a son of a bitch, like everyone else, that matters, Major, just knowing it and forgiving it, is what matters." Stepping out into the cold, Wallace turned around. "Guess I'll be going, that is unless you still want to knock me down."

"No," McReynolds said, "takes someone bigger than me to knock down a man like you, Captain."

It was coming on dusk by the time Cookey finished his baking. As the men helped themselves to the stew and biscuits, he watched McReynolds from the corner of his eye, not speaking nor acknowledging his hurt, but just watching and keeping his distance.

When supper was over, Cookey made his way to the horse corral. It was his way, to get away from the rabble after supper, to have a moment of his own, and it was there that McReynolds found him.

"Cookey," McReynolds said.

Stiffening at McReynolds's presence, Cookey stood. "Yes, sir."

"Mind if we have a talk?"

"No, sir," he said.

The sun's rays fell cool and orange against Cookey's face. It was an older and more worn face than McReynolds had realized. It was easy to think of enlisted men as boys, even though many had spent long years in the hard service of their country.

"About those biscuits, Cookey."

"Yes, sir," he said, dropping his head, "I knowed it wasn't the Cheyenne all along. I forgot the baking powder. Horse turds they were, sir, less the aroma and rising qualities. I just forgot, I reckon. Can't think why."

"I admit to having had better biscuits, Cookey," McReynolds said, "but that's not why I'm here."

"Sir," he said.

"I'm here to apologize."

"Oh, no, sir," Cookey said, looking away. "I done my job bad, that's all, and it ain't necessary for no apology."

Squatting down, McReynolds picked up a stick, scratching circles in the snow at his feet.

"Look," he said, tossing the stick into the bushes, "my dumping your biscuits had nothing to do with you or with the biscuits."

"It didn't?"

"It had to do with me, some things I've been trying to work out for myself. You just happened to be in the way. Do you understand?"

"I think so, sir," Cookey said.

"It's just that admitting to being a son of a bitch doesn't come easy for some of us."

"Oh, no, you ain't that, sir. I've been in the Army a considerable part of my life and seen some outstanding sons of bitches, and you ain't nowhere close."

"I just discovered I belong to the human race, Cookey. It's a little frustrating, and I took it out on you. I'm sorry."

Embarrassed, Cookey ducked his head.

"Yes, sir," he said.

By the time McReynolds got back into camp, the men had settled into their tents, candlelight winking as they played cards or made entries in well-worn diaries. Someone laughed, a winning hand; the loser cursing, slapping down his cards in disgust. Overhead, stars popped into existence, and the winds receded into the clear black night.

After checking on the sentry, McReynolds walked by Wallace's tent, to talk more maybe, but there was no sign of life. Pouring himself a cup of coffee, he sat by the fire, watching Sarah's tent. They had not talked since the news of her husband's death. How do you talk about someone's death you've wished for?

Adding wood to the fire, he lit his pipe and listened to the sounds of the night. A coyote barked in the distance, a young female, sent forward by the pack to bait an unsuspecting victim into its trap, the same strategy employed by the Cheyenne, so effective in its simplicity.

A candle lit in her tent, her shadow moving within, standing first, then bending, then standing again, her arms above her head the way she did, combing her hair loose with her fingers. Smoke curled from the fire, filling the night with its pungent aroma, and the feelings within him stirred. Reaching for a stick from the edge of the fire, he lit his pipe again, the coal glowing red against his face as he drew against it. When he turned back, the candle had blinked away, and he knew she had gone to bed; knew she'd turned on her side, leg bent to ease her back; breasts spilled soft and firm within her gown; the musty smell of her hair, tinged with smoke from the fire; the warmth of her body against the cold blanket of her bed.

"Sarah?" he whispered into the darkness of her tent. But she did not answer, his heart sinking at the silence. "Sarah, we must talk."

"I know," she said.

Heart leaping, he moved inside, his breath roaring in his ears. Just then the moon rose on the horizon, casting its light through the loose webbing of the tent, and he could see her figure, lying there as he knew she would be.

"I didn't know what to say," he said, "how to say it." He could hear her moving, rising on an elbow, hair falling across the whiteness of her shoulder. "I've felt so guilty from the start and then for this to happen.

It was like I made it happen somehow. It was like I killed him with my thoughts."

"You can't kill people with your thoughts," she said. "Even children know better."

"Yes," he said, "but children don't have the same thoughts."

The coyote bayed, in the far distance now.

"I'm sorry he's dead," she said, "because it's not in me to wish death, but I'm not sorry he's gone from my life. His death brings a finality to my feelings, but it does not make me responsible." Reaching for his hand, she pulled him onto the bed, her fingers cool in his. The heat of her body pulsed there against the cold blanket, the smell of her hair, the tinge of smoke from the fire. "You know how it is with me," she said, "and nothing has changed. When alive, he was gone from my heart no less than now. Nothing except his death has changed, and that was with the gods."

With his finger he traced the lines of her face, the brows, like charcoal strokes swept across a white canvas, the flutter of her lids against the tips of his fingers, the fullness and heat of her mouth. With his lips he traced them again, etching them in an indelible image in his heart and in his mind. In the distance the men laughed again, clapping their hands as if in celebration of the moment.

"Captain Wallace says that I've just got to admit to being a son of a bitch like everyone else," he said, "but there's something more, something I've never told anyone."

Waiting, she held his hand. This much she'd learned about life: There was always more that had not been told.

"Go on," she said.

"Many years ago when I was an assistant surgeon, I came to admire and befriend a young corporal by the name of Renfro. Even though we were quite different, I found him to be a fine and generous soul for whom I had the greatest respect. When a young Kiowa girl by the name of Twobirds fell in love with him, it seemed a just and right thing. But then Renfro died in the alabaster cave, at least that's what we thought, and I fell in love with her." Taking a deep breath, he rubbed at his face. "It was like my love and respect for both of them came together in one."

Taking her hands, he turned them over, looking into the past.

"Renfro was not dead," he continued, "and came back many months later."

"And then you lost them both?"

"Yes," he said, "both. So many years ago now, but the pain is still there."

"And you're afraid it will happen again?"

"I've got to be certain, Sarah."

"When we get to the redoubt, then you'll know?"

"It's just that I can't go through that again, not now."

Putting her hands on his face, she pulled him to her, kissing him with a gentle sweep of her mouth.

"Until you're certain then," she said.

The weather warmed the next couple of days to the relief of them all, but their euphoria was short-lived as the trail melted away into red grease, miring the wagons, clinging like blood clots to the bottoms of their boots. The wind, still chilled from the snow, stung their faces and sent their hats sailing across the prairie.

Sarah abandoned her black shawl, rolled up her sleeves, and went back to work with Cookey. Her demeanor with McReynolds was cordial but distant, giving him the room she knew he needed. In turn

McReynolds relaxed, the men sensing the change, kidding and laughing among themselves even as the trail taxed their resolve.

With a full reserve of horses, the going would have been tough. With the diminished numbers, the wagons ground to a stop with every impediment, the horses lunging against their collars, their necks white with sweat and salt. Again and again they were unharnessed and doubled to another team in order to make a hill or cross a gully. So exhausted were the men by night, that it was all they could do to eat their suppers before falling into their beds. With red-stained feet they tossed and turned under their blankets, awaiting the break of yet another day.

The trail split, one leading northwest across a flat expanse of sand and sage, the other turning northeast into a succession of red gullies. Squatting, McReynolds tried to determine the traffic that may have passed. Turning to Captain Wallace, he shrugged his shoulders.

"I can't tell," he said. "It could be either one. The snow has wiped out the tracks, and either one could cut back to the north over the next hill."

Cutting a chew, Wallace nibbled it off the blade of his knife and squinted against the sun.

"Begging your pardon, Doctor, given the obvious circumstance of your age and the advantage of medical school, I'm sure you've figured that a man could ride down one of these trails and take a look."

Pushing back his hat, McReynolds smiled.

"You know, Wallace, for a man who's spent his life digging privies for the Army, you come up with some pretty good ideas."

Grinning, Wallace shot a stream of tobacco juice into the red mud.

"Seeing as how I already volunteered once on this

outfit, maybe it's time the commander took on the responsibility hisself."

"Maybe so," McReynolds said, standing. "There's a few hours of sunlight left. Make camp here. The men and horses could use the rest. I'll ride out a few miles and see which of these is the Supply Trail."

"Yes, sir. Good idea, sir, if I do say so. I'd take a man with me, though; case I got into trouble or got lost or needed my boots shined off."

"Right," McReynolds said. "I'll be back by dark."

As he mounted his horse, McReynolds saw Cookey unpacking the chow wagon.

"Cookey," he said, "get a mount. You're riding out with me."

"Sir?" Cookey said, looking up from his work.

"Get a mount. We're riding out to see which of these trails leads to Dodge. I need a man to come along, lest we get into trouble."

"Yes, sir." Cookey grinned. "And a carbine, too, case we kick up a Cheyenne been ruining my biscuits."

"And a carbine." McReynolds smiled. "Make do, Cookey. We've only a couple of hours before dark."

"Yes, sir," he said, setting his cap down tight on his head.

Within minutes Cookey appeared, carbine at his side and a roan mare in tow.

"Which of these trails you figure leads to Dodge?" McReynolds asked.

Leaning back in his saddle, Cookey gave each considerable thought.

"This one, sir, into the canyons. I figure that other one leads to grass or water maybe."

"This one it is then," McReynolds said, kicking his mount into a walk.

Riding in silence, they worked their way into the red canyons, streaked with layers of gypsum and void of even the tenacious mesquite. So poor was the soil that even in the best of years, life failed to take a hold, but the trail was clear and well-worn.

It was McReynolds who broke the silence.

"Where you from, Cookey?"

"Kentucky, sir, mostly I guess."

"What brings a man like you to the Army? No harder job I can think of than trail cook."

"Fifteen years now, sir. Fifteen years of cooking and cleaning and moving to the next. It ain't a life for everyone, but for me it's all I ever was or wanted to be. Every morning when I wake up, I know for certain I got food to eat and a place to sleep. I got clothes for my back and friends to cuss. It's as certain as sunrise and a comfort to my soul. There's no place in the world I'd rather be."

Reining up, McReynolds studied the trail where it worked its way out of the canyon and back onto the rim.

"Looks like you were right about the trail, Cookey. Let's ride up onto the plateau to make certain."

"Yes, sir," he said, shifting his carbine. "Maybe there's Cheyenne waiting, drumming up mischief and the like."

"Well," McReynolds bantered, "the Cheyenne have all gone south to their winter camps, Cookey, which is a good thing for us. Without howitzers, a redoubt wouldn't stand a chance against a full-scale attack."

Kicking his horse, he started up the trail that wound onto the mesa.

"How is it you come to pick the Army, Cookey? Weren't there other things you could've done?"

"Oh, yes, sir. Could've made shine, raised hogs, cut wood, or hunted coon for pelts. Could've eat lard and biscuits off can lids every day of my life. Could've lived in a one-room cabin, slept on a straw tick, and gone barefoot in the snow. Could've had a passel of kids, with loaded diapers, crying at the tail of their mamma's flour-sack dress. That's what I could've done and could've had, sir, like those before me done and will do forever as far as I can tell."

As they broke the top of the mesa, the evening sun fell warm against their faces, the wind waning against the call of darkness. Pulling up, McReynolds studied the horizon, his horse snorting, shaking his head against the restraints of the bridle.

"There's a break, Cookey, and a stand of bois d'arc. Let's take a look and then head back. I feel certain this must be the main trail."

As they rode, the stillness of the evening drew down about them, an unsettling quiet, like a thick and inviolable fog. Pulling up, McReynolds climbed down from his mount, dropping to one knee.

"It's a Cheyenne, ain't it?" Cookey said, studying the horizon.

"No," McReynolds said, "a buffalo cow, dead a good long while, I'd say. Choked on that hedge apple. Funny thing, she's been split open by the looks of it and her stomach paunch removed."

"Coyotes or buzzards," Cookey said.

"Not unless they're carrying knives, Cookey. She was cut open clean, right through the sternum. Let's ride a little farther. See what this is all about."

"Yes, sir, if you say so. It's going down dark soon enough, though."

"We got a clear trail back, Cookey, and there's moon enough to see."

It was dusk when they rode upon it, a piece of cloth clinging to the weeds. Dismounting, McReynolds pulled it loose, studying it in the fading light.

"It's a bandage of some sort," he said, "blood-stained, I'd guess."

"And this." Cookey held up an empty whiskey bottle. "And over there," he said, pointing to a horse blanket nearly covered with sand.

McReynolds knew the instant he saw it what it was, the blond hair, matted and dull, the blue uniform, the shriveled corpse half buried in the dirt. There was no mistaking death in its timeless and silent pose.

"It's a soldier, Cookey, dead for days it appears."

Stepping back, Cookey crossed his arms to ward off the evil that lay there in the dirt.

"That courier, isn't it," he inquired, "that Sergeant Westhoff from Dodge?"

Shrugging his shoulders, McReynolds scraped at the dirt with his knife.

"Not Sergeant Westhoff," he said. "It's an officer's uniform. Look there, a leg wound and a scalp lock taken, too. Ribs broken from something." But it was the name tag sewed into the lapel of the coat that set him back on his heels, his knife dropping at his side. "It's Lieutenant Roland," he said, "Sarah's husband."

"Why didn't they bury him at the redoubt?" Cookey asked. "Just left him out here on the trail no better than a downed horse."

"Someone had their reasons. I'm just an Army surgeon, Cookey, but I can tell you this much, Lieutenant Roland didn't die of a broken neck."

By the time they'd reburied the body, making certain it was covered well from predators, night had fallen. Cookey and McReynolds mounted up, working their way back down into the canyons.

The ride back was a quiet one. The moon tracking its timeless path above as they rode single file along the trail. Neither spoke, their thoughts still back at the grave.

Not until they could see the campfire in the night, did McReynolds speak.

"I've something to ask of you," he said, pulling up.

"Sir?"

"It's a hard thing not to speak of what we've found, Cookey, but that's what I want from you. We've got to know what happened out there. We can do that a lot better if no one knows that we know."

"But what about Sarah?" Cookey asked, looking toward the camp. "It's her husband laying back there in that grave. She ought to know. It ain't right for her not to know."

"I agree. It's a hard thing I'm asking, but she's also got a right to know why he was killed and by whom. That's her right most of all, so I'm asking you not to say anything until we have the answers. I wouldn't ask this if it weren't important, Cookey. Do I have your promise?"

Moonlight reflected from the carbine that lay across Cookey's lap as he thought over the words. Pushing back his hat, he looked at McReynolds.

"I got no reason to believe this ain't an honorable thing to do, Major. You've got my word."

And so they rode into camp, their pact of silence sealed. After reporting to Wallace about the trail, McReynolds washed his hands, scrubbing them clean with the bar of lye soap that Cookey now kept on hand, washing them again until they stung in the night air, before making his way to Sarah's tent.

It was there that he slipped into her bed, smothering her mouth with his own. He moved into her arms, her breasts warm and exquisite against his chest, pounding with the beat of her heart, his heart; and she came to him as he knew she would, innocent and turbulent.

Lying in each other's arms, she turned to him, her breath against his ear, her finger resting on his mouth.

"You're certain?" she asked.

And the moon slid across the sky above them, casting its ivory light on the shallow grave at the side of the trail.

"Yes," he said, "I'm certain."

Twenty-nine

Even though the weather had improved, Nurse Cromley's condition worsened. Frequent stops were necessary for her to recoup, to lay her head in her arms, to gather her courage for one more try, but soon even the rests failed to revive her waning strength. Nodding against Adam's shoulder, she would mutter names from her past and turn her face up to him with an unaccountable smile.

Brother Jacob's rabbit lasted through the second day, and then there was nothing, leaving them to face a cold and hungry camp. Wood, too, was scarce, a few mesquite twisting like wire from the frozen ground, requiring more effort to dig than they were worth. Had it not been for the scattered buffalo chips, and Creed's relentless search for them, no fire would have been possible. It was Creed who squealed with delight at each one discovered, who stacked them like treasure next to the fire, who returned again and again to the frozen prairie for more while Adam attended to Mary.

"Take the saddlebags off Buck," Adam said when Creed returned with arms stacked, "and rub him down with a handful of sage. Without grass or grain, he needs all the attention we can spare."

"It's *me* pulled *him* halfway across the country," Creed said, stripping a handful of sage.

"Well, you get the next back rub," Adam said. "Now go on before dark sets in."

As he prepared Mary's bed, he glanced up from time to time to check on Creed. For a young boy, he was a good hand with horses, firm but patient, careful not to surprise or move too fast.

Stirring, Mary moaned as she pulled herself onto an elbow, her eyes clearing for a moment.

Pouring a cup of hot water, Adam handed it to her.

"Careful not to burn yourself. It's hot, but that's about all I can say for it."

Brushing her hair back from her face, he smiled at her.

"It's a tough go, Mary, but we're going to make it."

"You always did ride too far out," she said, "so far ahead that no one could keep up. I can't keep up anymore, Adam. There's a weariness in me like a powerful flood, and I can't keep my head above the water."

"It's alright, Mary," he said. "I'll swim you across and set you high and dry on the other side."

Reaching for his hand, she held it tight, fever burning in her touch. In her eyes sparked the intelligence, the determination, and the forbearance that had kept her alive against all odds. But a darkness was there, too, the pallor or her skin, the dullness of her hair, like a cotton dress too long in the sun.

"You can't swim for me, Adam. I have to swim for myself, but the waves are too high, the current too strong." Checking to see that Creed was still with Buck, she turned back the blanket. And the sight swept over him, the smell of slough and hopelessness. Turning her hip, she exposed her swollen and corrupted thigh, the sallow, dying flesh. Holding her hand tight, he looked into the fire for whatever help the gods might send. "There is no need to talk foolishness anymore," she said, lying back down. "We've sent one man to an uncertain death. Tomorrow you and Creed will go without me. Whether I make it to the Cimarron crossing or not no longer matters. This I know."

The dispirited and beaten sun descended below the horizon, surrendering the day to the inevitability of night. Adam did not tell her of the decision he'd already made in the lonely night hours, to leave her behind, to save Creed, to save even the silver that would protect him in the white man's world. When he turned to tell her these things, to rid himself of the burden, she slept, her eyes sunken and drawn against the pain.

When Creed returned, Adam prepared him a cup of hot water.

"She's sleeping," he said.

The chill of night reached in from the darkness as they huddled close to the fire, and Adam's heart broke at the lack of food to give his son.

"How far do you think it is?" Creed asked, looking up through the steam of his cup.

"It's hard to say. We're moving too slow, and in this weather."

"Maybe tomorrow," Creed said, "and there's always the chance of a rabbit. Even a turtle would be good, I think."

Reaching for a blanket, Adam wrapped it about his legs to ward off the chill.

"Creed, there's something I must say, something Mary and I have talked over."

Setting down his cup, Creed folded his arms, giving Adam his full attention, the way Twobirds used to, with intense dark eyes locked onto him.

"What is it?" he asked.

"She doesn't want to go on, Creed. It's not possible for her to go on."

"No," he said, "it's only a day or two. We'll make a travois, and Buck can pull her there. Tomorrow we will hunt first and snare a rabbit. With food she will do better, and the weather has lightened, I think."

"Gangrene has taken the leg. To move her will only add to her pain. We can come back for her as soon as we have supplies, fresh mounts."

"But we can't ride away and leave her, without food, without even wood for a fire."

Standing, Adam pulled the blanket about his shoulders and looked out into the blackness of the night.

"Perhaps you are right, Creed. Who knows what tomorrow will bring. You get some rest. I'll wake you when it's light."

When Adam woke the first time, he could hear the gentle breathing of Creed beneath his blanket. Mary lay on her side, the moon breaking, casting ephemeral shadows over the prairie. When he awoke the second time, the fire smoldered beneath the ashes, and the moon lay prostrate on the western horizon. Her back to the dying fire, Mary moaned beneath the twisted blanket.

Touching her shoulder, he whispered, "Mary?"

But she did not answer, so fragile and sick with fever, her body trembling against the night chill. Spreading his blanket over her, he lay down beside her, pulling her close for warmth. How gaunt and spare she was, her flaring hips, her lank breasts so cool against his arms. He slept then, holding her thus, his heart burdened with her failing life, with the callous and uncaring world.

Dawn broke on a frost-covered morning. But even as the sun rose warm on his face, Adam knew that Mary was dead, had flown from his arms in the night. Rising, he bid her farewell and saddled Buck before waking Creed.

"She died in the night," Adam said. "It's what we all hope for when it comes, dying among friends. It was Mary's way to spare us the pain of decision, I reckon."

Pulling on his boots, Creed turned away.

"I'll go find chips," he said, "to make the fire hot."

The morning was spent preparing the scaffold. It's what Creed wanted.

Searching the shallow canyons for saplings, they drove them deep into the frozen ground, tying them together with strips of cloth. Afterward, they wrapped Mary in her blanket and lifted her onto the scaffold. With Buck in tow, Adam waited while Creed placed Twobirds's beaded satchel under the blanket, and they left her there to face forever the rising suns.

Throughout the morning, they made their way across the open prairie, cutting southward to the Cimarron, a broad expanse of dried sage clinging and clawing at their legs, its pungent aroma stirring into the wind with each step. Following behind, Buck's great head bobbed, his flanks sunken and gaunt from lack of nourishment. At midday Creed spotted rabbit tracks in the sand, but they were old, dew having crusted and rounded away their edges.

Rising from their knees, neither spoke of their disappointment, nor of Mary, nor of the scaffolds that burned forever in their memories. As they walked through the endless sage, their hearts ached with emptiness.

When they stood at the bank of the river, Buck pushed at Creed's back with his nose, urging him forward to water.

"Is it the Cimarron?" Creed asked, turning to Adam.

"Appears so," Adam said, pushing back his hat, "but I ain't certain about the direction of the crossing. Upstream, I'd guess."

"Maybe we could follow the bed," Creed said, catching up Buck's reins, "that way we wouldn't have to fight the sage. It's a clear stretch as far as you can see."

"Clear enough," Adam said, "if it's solid. There's quick spots here and there on the Cimarron, no clay or bottom, just water bubbling up through sand, like stepping into a bowl of corn mush a hundred feet deep."

Tucking his hands into his pockets, Creed looked up at him.

"It's the sage," he said, "wore Buck out."

"Well, we can give him a watering," Adam said. "It's not so salty this far north. Let me go first, then follow my tracks out until we find out what we're dealing with here.

After working his way down the bank, Adam stepped out onto the riverbed, shifting his weight from one foot to the other to test the firmness of the sand.

"Bring him down," he called, waving his hat.

With natural caution Buck edged onto the riverbed, his nose touching the uncertain ground before him. With a flip of his lip, he tested the water, letting it dribble back over the bridle bit. Satisfied that everything was alright, he sucked in immense draughts, shaking his head from time to time with contentment.

"It's solid walking," Creed said, rubbing Buck's neck. "Maybe we could take the outside, along the bank and away from the mainstream. We could make much better time in the open, even with the bends in the river."

Studying the situation, Adam shook his head.

"Maybe so. It's easier treading, that's certain, and Buck's not faring well in the sagebrush, but there's the quicksand to worry about, and it's harder to get the lay of the land." Seeing the disappointment on Creed's face, Adam shrugged. "We'll try it for a ways. If it turns up boggy, we'll go back to the sage."

"Come on, Buck," Creed said, "let's get a move on."

With renewed energy and freedom from the brush, they made good time, moving into the westward swing of the river. Revitalized from his drink, Buck nibbled at the brim of Creed's hat, pulling it from his head and onto the ground.

As evening fell, sunset lit the Cimarron with color, and the wind fell quiet for its evening rest.

"We'll camp here," Adam said, pointing to a backwash. "There's plenty of driftwood for a fire and a windbreak, too. If it don't come a-flood, it'll make a good camp. Tie Buck to that stump and drag that wood in while I get us some water going."

"Sure would like something besides hot water," Creed said, digging at the pile of wood.

No sooner had he spoken, when a jack popped

out of the woodpile, his ears flopped, his eyes bulging, his body frozen against detection.

"Rabbit! Rabbit!" Creed yelled, grabbing up a stick.

Just as Adam turned, the rabbit bolted, springing into the air as if shot, angling across the sand with sudden and unpredictable shifts in direction. Close behind was Creed, his stick held high, his black hair askew. It was Adam who circled wide, altering the rabbit's path, driving him ever nearer the river's edge. Back and forth it went, first toward Creed and then back to Adam, each time its course closer to the water. In a final round, it swung once more toward the river, its body pitched as it bore against the sand, skidding out of control, spinning into the waiting arms of Creed, who dispatched it with his stick. Grinning, Creed held the jack up by its ears and danced in a circle.

"Good job!" Adam clapped his hands, and they laughed.

With his bowie, Creed sharpened a spit while Adam topped off the fire. Together they cleaned the rabbit, peeling away its hide, opening its carcass, rinsing it clean in the waters of the Cimarron. By the time the sun set, the aroma of fried rabbit filled the air, and they rubbed their hands in anticipation. Ravenous, they pulled the rabbit apart, eating it to the last, picking and sucking the bones clean.

Afterward, they drank sage tea and listened to a coyote sound a cold trail somewhere downriver. With stomachs full, their thoughts turned to those left behind, the moment diminished by their absence.

Finishing his tea, Adam checked the bags of silver, placing them next to his blanket. On the other side of the fire, Creed lay on his back, studying the stars.

"I want to talk to you about the silver," Adam said.

Sitting up, Creed wrapped his arms around his knees.

"The silver doesn't matter so much to me, Father. I would rather have another rabbit, twice as big as this one, bigger even."

"You must come to understand its use, Creed. In the white man's world, it counts for all. With this silver you can become educated, learn to read, have great knowledge and power. It's what your mother wanted for you. It's what I want for you. I've gone through life following easy dreams, but times have changed. Men like me can't survive out there anymore. This silver can make of you more than I could ever be, but you must promise to use it with purpose, to fill your head with knowledge and wisdom. When we get to the crossing, we cannot speak about the silver this way, so I want you to promise me that you will do these things. Men have given their lives for this silver, and its use is in your trust. Do you understand what I am saying to you?"

"Yes," he said. "I will do as you ask."

This was what his father wanted, to say this thing, and so he did, but in his mind it was an odd thing, the useless silver, its burdensome weight and green smell. Maybe later he would understand, when they arrived at the white people's camp. There, he would watch and see how it was done. For now, it was enough to say this thing.

That night they both slept hard, with stomachs full, with a sweet and balmy breeze sweeping in from the southwest, with the blessed end of suffering.

Even as dawn broke, the winds warmed, ice and snow shrinking away under its gentle and warm breath. While saddling Buck, Adam hummed a distant tune, confident now that they would arrive at the Cimarron crossing soon. Creed, too, sensed the change, skipping stones across the glimmering water; the boy still was there, yet under the bravado of manhood.

By noon they'd traveled many miles; Adam led the way, followed by Creed, with Buck at the end of his arm. With lightened steps they pushed onto the crossing, their thoughts on the future now and the things that might be.

Perhaps it was the sound first, a deep snort, full of alarm, the kind of alarm grounded in sudden and certain fear.

"Father," Creed cried.

When Adam turned, he could see what had happened. Buck's legs were sinking beneath him. In that brief moment, he knew that it was too late, that solid ground was not within reach, that a boy and man, nor a dozen men, could ever pull a grown horse from such a bog. Dropping to his stomach, he reached for the saddlebags, the tips of his fingers just reaching the tie.

"Hold my belt, Creed."

Pushing out farther still, his face touching the quaking sand, he loosened the saddlebag ties, tossing them onto solid ground.

Terrified, Buck leapt again and again against the grip of the quicksand, each leap burying him farther into its suffocating hold. Eyes rolling white, he pitched his head, squealing against the certainty of his trap. Grabbing the reins, Creed hung on, pulling with all that was within him, pleading for Buck to move.

"Let him go," Adam yelled.

"Come on, Buck," Creed cried.

"It's too late," Adam said, grabbing him about the waist.

"No!" Creed shook his head. "Not Buck, not now."

But even as he spoke, the sand pooled across Buck's back, his breath shortening against its awful weight.

"You go on," Adam said. "I'll be along."

"We don't even have bullets to shoot him," he cried.

"Go on, like I said."

"But if we pulled together—"

"Get on around the bend. I'll be along."

Walking away, Creed tuned for a last look before rounding the bend.

Adam rubbed Buck's head, the round slope of his nose.

"Whoa, boy," he said, "easy, ole Buck."

Reaching into his boot, he pulled his knife, opening the jugular with a quick flick of the blade. Buck bolted at the fleeting pain, his blood spilling into the waters of the Cimarron.

By the time Adam caught up, Creed's jaw was set, the bags of silver over his shoulders.

"Here," Adam said, taking the bags, "it's done now."

And so they walked in silence, their hearts broken at yet another loss. At noon they rested, the sun rising warm above them.

"It isn't fair," Creed said, speaking for the first time.

"That's a fact," Adam said, leaning against a tree. "It's a pain and hurt that no man should bear, but we all do. You can wail against the injustice all you want, boy, but it won't make no difference. In the

end, you either go on living or you die. That's your
options, Creed, so you just as well spare everyone
your grief. No one can change it or make it what it's
not. It's injustice and soul-sickening hard, but that's
how it is."

Looking back down the river, Creed nodded his
head.

By the time the sun hung low in the west, they
stood high on a sweeping cliff carved by the churning floodwaters of the Cimarron. Overhead, buzzards
circled in the blue sky, banking and falling against
the southwesterly breeze. Below them, soldiers stirred
about their camp, the raw blue of their uniforms distinct against the muted cast of the prairie.

"It's the Cimarron crossing," Adam said, squinting
against the falling light. "Anything you want to know
'fore we go down?"

For a long while, Creed stood silent, watching the
birds as they dipped and soared over his memories,
over the spirits of those he'd loved.

Tucking his bowie tight against his belly, he
shrugged his shoulders.

"Let's get on," he said, "while there's still light to
see."

Thirty

In a relentless drive, Little Dog's band pushed toward the Cimarron crossing. By evening of the second day, they stood on the high plateau overlooking the Dodge-Supply trail. Below them a thin line wound across the prairie, seeking its own level like the great Cimarron itself. From their vantage in the eroded rocks of the capstone, the trail was little more than the muddied ruts of endless wagons, passing evidence of the white man's obsession for dragging useless objects across the prairie.

Mounting up, Little Dog looked down the trail.

"No wagons for many days," he said, "no large guns from the north. Without the guns, the camp can be taken."

Circling the ruts, Crooked Leg pulled up his horse.

"The white man can fight from behind his walls with the howitzer guns, but without them, he will not stand against the Dog Soldiers."

As they made their way back up the rugged trail, Little Dog's blood stirred within him. Soon his pain would stop, his vengeance appeased. Soon the fire burning within, the smoldering embers of his broken life, would turn cold and die. Beyond the vengeance, life mattered not, did not exist for him. Beyond that moment, there was but emptiness and desolation, the inexorable unwinding of time.

"Tonight we will camp in the rocks and prepare ourselves for battle," he said. "The crossing is not far now, and our spirits must be pure. There will be great danger, but the honor also will be great."

Following behind, Crooked Leg did not answer, his mind drawn into the battle to come, caught now in the vengeance of his brother.

That night a warm wind swept the great prairie, and the bitterness of winter vanished with its arrival. It was the way here, the clash and struggle of seasons exploding into the chilled blue sky.

As evening fell, they built their fire high, the crackling of flame under the moonless night. With crossed legs they sat on the damp earth, firelight in the blackness of their hair. The pipe was passed, executed with precision and accuracy of rule. When the drum commenced, they fell silent, women and children melding into the shadows beyond the fire.

The beat of the drum moved within them, laden with courage, with resolve and determination. They smeared earth under their eyes, slashes of ash across their bodies, each mark an accession into the world of battle, into the world of warriors—bold, fierce, and immutable.

It was Little Dog who rose to his feet, the yellow light of the fire illuminating the scar across his face. The drum fell silent as he raised his hands.

"I tell this story," he said, "of Little Dog and Crooked Leg. While hunting, they heard a terrible sound, like the cries of a thousand coyote wailing from the horizon." Moving closer to the fire, he looked into the eyes of the men. "Is this not true, Crooked Leg?" he asked, turning.

Nodding, Crooked Leg held his bow in the air, his head down as he stared into the fire.

"This is true, what Little Dog says. I heard it with my own ears, like a thousand coyote wailing."

"The dogs came in from the hunt," Little Dog continued, "circling our feet, whining in fear at what they heard. We could not drive them away or make them hunt. The spirit Maiyun flew about overhead, and the sun darkened as our shadows fled from us."

"This is true," Crooked Leg said, "and we feared that the *mistai* would steal away our spirits and the spirits of our children."

"When it charged from the woods, it was a most terrible sight," Little Dog said, "its serpent tongue, the color of turquoise, dragging between its legs, smoke bellowing from its nose, eyes glowing like burning embers. The dogs fell on their backs and wet themselves at the sight before us."

Walking about the fire, Little Dog waited, letting the power of his story work its way. From behind him, the children and women mumbled of the hideous beast, looking over their shoulders into the shadows.

"Even as it charged," Little Dog said, "I dropped to my knee to string the sacred arrows of my father. No ordinary hunting arrow would kill such a beast. This I knew."

Moving to Little Dog's side, Crooked Leg spoke, "Little Dog's bravery will be spoken of for many years to come," he said. "Even the rutting buffalo bull would flee under the charge of the blue-tongue beast."

Pulling his arrows from his quiver, Little Dog held them above his head. "These arrows I sank into the heart of the Blue Tongue, with only the feathers left sticking from its chest, these sacred arrows shanked into its heart, but it did not stop. It could not be killed, nor wounded, even with the sacred arrows."

"Never have I known an animal to live with a shanked arrow in its heart," a warrior said.

Spinning about, Little Dog's eyes locked onto the eyes of the warrior.

"This was a beast from the underworld," he said.

"What did you do?" the warrior asked. "Have you then killed the blue-tongue beast from the underworld?"

"We fled to the trees," Little Dog said, "and the beast went into the woods, but each time we tried to climb down, it charged, smoke blowing from its nose, the tree trembling from the blow of its ugly head."

"This is true," Crooked Leg said, holding his bow to his chest. "Leaves and twigs rained on our heads as it charged time and again. Three days we lived in the tree, waiting for the beast to leave, but it was always just beyond sight, waiting to charge."

"But on the third day at sunrise, it came and stood at the base of our tree." Lifting his hands in the air, Little Dog turned, the firelight glistening on the brutal wound across his face, a badge of courage and experience for the others to see. Turning to the men, his eyes narrowed. "It then spoke to me with a voice like spring thunder."

Moving back from the fire, Crooked Leg looked up through his brows at Little Dog.

"It said," Little Dog continued, "that it had come from the underworld to tell of the last days of the Cheyenne, that the Cheyenne were women, going to the white man for food and for protection, that the Cheyenne were no longer warriors, that their bones would bleach in the sun like the buffalo before them. And when this was then said, the blue-tongue beast walked into the woods, the sacred arrows still shanked in its heart."

Clenching his fists, Little Dog crossed his arms across his chest.

"The next morning our people were butchered and left to rot on the prairie, just as the Blue Tongue said. Now it is time for the Cheyenne to be warriors and men once more. It was the fear in their hearts that released the blue-tongue beast from the underworld. Now we must rise and destroy our enemy, so the blue-tongue beast can return in peace to its place of darkness. Soon the Cheyenne will call themselves warriors and men once more."

The drums thundered as they rose to their feet, the women joining in the dance, followed by the children, who were uncertain now of what might lurk in the darkness. And into the night their dark and bent shadows loomed and moved among the rocks above the trail, dancing to the drum, to the certainty of their destiny.

At midnight Little Dog held his arms to the sky, sweat glistening from his body, his thirst for reprisal pitched with the fury of the drum.

"It is Little Dog who will lead you," he cried, "Little Dog who stands without fear to face the enemy."

The hardened bodies of the warriors spun, gyrating like painted tops about the roaring fire, the lockstep shuffle of their women, circling the camp, moving to the throb and call of the drum.

"It is Little Dog who has spoken to the great blue beast," Crooked Leg said, "who leads the Cheyenne into the battle of men. It is Little Dog who has no fear, feels no pain, cannot die."

"Bring the buffalo skull," Little Dog said, "and the rope. Little Dog's courage is of the great blue beast, and no man can stand before it."

Dropping away from the dance, Crooked Leg brought forth a buffalo skull, dried and weathered horns, vacant and staring eyes, and threaded a rope through its empty sockets. Taking out his knife, he opened the skin of Little Dog's back, blood oozing from the shocked and gaping wounds.

Standing before Little Dog, he spoke. "It is the courage of Little Dog that we will follow into battle."

And Little Dog stared into the fire, the throb of the drum rising into the night, as Crooked Leg thrust his finger into the wounds, winding his finger under the warm and trembling muscle, threading through the rawhide rope, tying it off in a wet and bloodied knot.

Fixing his eyes on the glowing embers of the fire, Little Dog did not cry out at the pain howling through him, nor at the lurching nausea, nor at the blinding lights flashing before his eyes.

The warriors rose to the crescendo of the beating drum, faces gleaming from the heat and triumph of the moment, forming rows, the corridor of peril and terror.

Hands stiff at his sides, Little Dog drove its terrible length, the buffalo skull skittering and scattering embers into the black night. And again, he ran, embracing its fire, its heat, its blinding and healing pain, but the buffalo followed him still, its hold still strong and unforgiving in his bloodied back.

Again, the warriors chanted from the corridor. "Like the blue-tongue beast, like the beast of darkness, like the blue-tongue beast who knows no fear, who cannot die."

Legs trembling, Little Dog struck down the corridor once more, the twisting, bucking skull wearing away his will to go on.

Moving from behind the fire, Crooked Leg stepped into the corridor, saw Little Dog's hesitation, saw the ruptured and damaged sinew stretching from his back, the tortured eyes, the agony he faced. Reaching down, he swept a child into his arms, waiting for Little Dog to pass once again, waiting for the moment to drop the child onto the tracking skull.

There was a snap, like the cracking of a whip, as the child dropped onto the skull, the sinew tearing loose its awful hold, Little Dog collapsing to his knees, blood dripping into the sand between his arms.

From behind, warriors burst into dance; pivoting, whirling dervishes celebrating this rarest bravery. And so through the night they celebrated the boundless courage of their warriors, the strength of their gods, and the blue-tongue beast now manifest in Little Dog's power.

When at last they fell exhausted about the dying fire, Crooked Leg rose and helped Little Dog onto his feet, moving him to his bed. There, he cleansed the site, rubbing bear grease into the wounds, laying him among the robes.

"It is a wise choice we have made for our leader," Crooked Leg said, "a man who speaks with the blue beast itself."

A slight smile turned at the corner of Little Dog's mouth as he eased into sleep.

"You were just too high in the limbs of the trees, my friend, to hear the conversation between the gods."

When morning came, the women took bear grease to where Little Dog lay, massaging away the stiffness so that he might rise from his bed. Afterward, they prepared food, giving the warriors half again their portion, moving back then from the fire as they ate.

War paint still on their bodies, the warriors sat in silence. All was prepared for the battle ahead. Their destinies had been set, their oaths taken. The women, too, were hushed and silent, staying a distance from the men. It would not be good to speak now or weaken the warriors in any fashion. Their journey ended here among the rocks. They would not go farther, but wait for the return of the warriors and word of their fate.

After they ate, the warriors painted their horses and renewed the arrows one last time. Mounting up, they paraded about the camp, their eyes fierce, their jaws clenched and determined. With chilling yelps, they struck out down the hill to the Dodge-Supply trail.

Pulling up his mount, Little Dog studied the wagon tracks once more, turning first to the south, and then to the north.

"We go north," he said at last.

"But Little Dog," Crooked Leg said, "the Cimarron crossing lies south."

"Perhaps the howitzers come still from the north," Little Dog said, "and we would find them at our backs. It is a chance we cannot take."

And so they turned north away from the crossing, riding hard through the morning hours, stopping to water their horses from a seep under a fallen tree. At noon the band fanned out onto a plateau, the smell of sage drifting on a damp and warming breeze. To their left the plateau sheered away, a cliff carved and worn from the distant river at its bottom. Buzzards circled high over the rift, sweeping skyward in the rising currents of warming air.

Crooked Leg spotted them first, a small band of soldiers, a half-dozen men on horseback, working their way along the canyon's edge. Behind them, two teams of mules labored against the immense weight of caissons.

Dismounting, the warriors dropped to their stomachs, creeping forward through the grass. From behind the protection of a rise, they watched as the detachment inched its way southward.

"It is as you thought," Crooked Leg said to Little Dog. "They go to the crossing with the howitzers."

Turning his head skyward, Little Dog held his hand over his brow to check the time of day. Blood seeped through his buckskin shirt, where the buffalo skull had been tied, and in his eyes was the cold and indomitable longing for vengeance.

"We will move to the canyon's edge behind those rocks," he said, "where it turns to the west. Soon they will face the sun, and we will take them."

With muscles throbbing, Little Dog strung his bow, bringing it about in the direction of the first soldier, who now rounded the bend. As leader, Little Dog was afforded first shot, the others waiting in the rocks for his signal. The torn muscles of his back trembled against the tension of his bow, and the courage of his deeds swelled anew within him.

The arrow's flight was pure and straight, as he knew it would be, piercing the soft breast of the soldier's mare. With a surprised grunt, she dropped to her knees, the soldier spilling over her head, his arms outstretched in alarm.

Following suit, the other warriors leapt from the rocks, the whine of arrows, the distressed wail of soldiers clutching their mortal wounds, pitching from their mounts under death's terrible summons. Soon none was left standing. From behind, the mule drivers struggled to control their teams, the mules kicking and pitching at the smell of blood and death ahead. And when they could hold them no longer, the drivers leapt from their seats to run up the hill. But from behind, the warriors yelped and shrieked, their horses closing in with murderous and thundering hooves.

Surrounded, the mule skinners fell to their knees in terror, spittle drooling from their lips, trembling and begging for mercy. One, whose beard was thin and mottled and whose brows sprang like gray wire from above his eyes, raised his hands over his head, the audacity of flesh and bone against the terrible and irrevocable power of the Cheyenne.

Dismounting, Little Dog grabbed the mule skinner's beard, yanking him onto his feet.

"Little Dog," he said, pointing to the bloodstain on his buckskin shirt that now spread like a bloody claw. "Dog Solider," he said, bringing his elbow about in a shattering swing.

Stunned, the mule skinner fell onto his back, his nose smeared across his face, a bloody mass. Whirling about, Little Dog caught the other mule skinner with a crushing blow of his foot, tearing his ear from its roots, a dangling and useless flap bleeding into the collar of his shirt.

"Tie them to their guns," Little Dog said, "for it is the right of the warrior to die with his weapons."

Hands bound behind them, the mule skinners were lashed with a length of rawhide to the howitzers, and sat down with their backs only feet from the yawning canyon rim.

In a futile plead for his life, the bearded mule skinner muttered something unintelligible through bloated lips, but even as he spoke, the caisson was rolled to the edge and pushed over. There was a snap of the line, and a moment's silence before he disappeared over the side.

Less willing, the other mule skinner cursed the Dog Soldiers as children of Hell, as villainous and cowardly savages, as the evil squat from Satan's bowels. With ear swinging by a thread at his jaw, he spewed his hatred and damnation upon them, and when the snap came, his fingers clawed the earth, his shirt dragging over his head, exposing the hair on his back and the red band of his underwear. Even as he dropped from sight over the edge, his hatred rose from the canyon below, fading into its depths.

Circling back, Little Dog and his warriors counted coup, took scalps, horses, and weapons from the fallen enemy. Riding hard, they moved south once more, toward the crossing, past the camp where their women and children now waited, but they did not stop.

With Little Dog at the lead, with the gods on their side, and with the howitzers crushed at the bottom of the canyon, nothing would stop them now.

Thirty-one

The depletion of the teams complicated life in more than one way for McReynolds. Forward speed of the train was reduced to a painstaking crawl; even hills of modest ascent proved too much to pull for the overworked animals. The remaining horses, valiant as they were, blowed and strained, their great necks bent against the weight of the wagons. Detours were inevitable, adding hours to an already tedious journey. Had it not been for the break in the weather, things would have been intolerable indeed.

They passed Lieutenant Roland's grave without notice, and by noon of the second day stood at the breach of vast red canyons, a yawning expanse of gullies and tortuous crevasses that twisted and turned in aimless confusion. Vegetation was nonexistent, little but naked clay baked and cracked from the outlandish heat of summers. On the rare occasion it rained, soil turned into a red and impenetrable grease, so void of nutrients that even the tenacious sage withered and died. In the heat of summer, dust devils spun about like howling and angry gods, giving all who entered the canyons pause.

"I don't know," McReynolds said, turning to Wallace. "Once we go in, there's no turning these wagons about."

Picking up a handful of the red dirt, Wallace sifted it through his fingers.

"It's weeks to skirt it," he said, "and then I don't know if it would be any better. At most it's a couple days' ride through these canyons, a three-day walk if it comes to that. The crossing is just hours beyond, once we're through. If worse comes to worse, we can always send someone ahead for fresh horses."

"I don't know," McReynolds said again, walking away, turning back.

"Course," Wallace said, "there's a chance you might get your boots all dusty with this here red dirt, if that's what's worrying you, but then there's the rest of us could wipe 'em clean with our shirttails or throw down our coats so's you could tread on 'em if the going gets tough."

Pushing back his hat, McReynolds looked at him.

"You know, Captain, I could have you up for insubordination, lashed maybe, or rations cut."

"Could," Wallace joked, "but then who'd volunteer when the snow flies, or corral longhorns for the Cheyenne to massacre?"

Mounting his horse, McReynolds took one last glance at the towering cliffs.

"True enough, Captain. I'm taking your advice."

As they moved out, the sun fell warm across their shoulders. A mild breeze swept in from the Mexican desert, and for the first time in many days, the chill faded from their bones.

Three hours in, the trail took a curve to the right before twisting up the side of a fearful hill. Rocks clung to the sheer walls above, waiting for the slightest nudge to plunge them into a terrifying crush to the canyon floor. Gathering at the base of the hill, the men stood about, studying the ascent, the impossible grade.

Dusting his hat against his leg, Wallace turned to McReynolds.

"It's a fair climb with a full team, and impossible with what we got left. We'll have to double up, and even then, I ain't too certain."

Climbing down from his wagon, Cookey looked up the spiraling path.

"It's the Cheyenne, ain't it, waiting in them rocks with bows drawn and damnation in their eyes."

"It's a hill, Cookey," Wallace said, "and a blamed high one. If there's a Cheyenne waiting behind one of those rocks, he's dead tired or asleep from the climb."

"This is a job for an engineer, Captain," McReynolds said. "Unhook your team, Cookey, and bring it forward. We'll double them up, and then bring the teams down for the next and so on. It's going to take a while, but there is no other way that I can see."

Taking out a chew, Wallace cut off a thin slice, tucking it into his cheek.

"Glad to be volunteering again, Major," he said. "Let's start with the chuck wagon since it's lighter and less likely to shy horses. That turn up there goes off into nothing but blue sky. The least mistake's going to be a screaming thrill clean to the bottom."

Shooting a stream of tobacco into the red dirt, Wallace looked at Cookey from under the brim of his hat.

"Need a volunteer to operate the brake," he said, "someone who ain't assigned to bringing up the drag or to digging privies the rest of his career."

"Yes, sir," Cookey said, scratching at the salt-and-pepper whiskers that had sprouted on his chin. "I was fixing to step up to my duty, sir, in case you needed me to operate the brake or take a Cheyenne arrow."

"That's good," Wallace chuckled. "An enlisted man with a sense of duty is a rare and charitable thing, and you are to be commended for stepping forward."

"Yes, sir," he said. "All along I been wanting my chance to ride up a mountainside of mad Cheyenne and falling rock. Told the boys this morning that maybe today I'd step forward and take my turn for duty. It ain't something a ordinary man understands, sir, the call to duty and all."

"Well, Cookey," Wallace chimed back with a shake of his head, "maybe we could get started before either me or the team dies of old age."

By the time the chuck wagon was readied and the team doubled, the sun hung low in the western sky. Unaccustomed to doubling, the team jumped harness just as they were prepared to begin, sidling off, reins dragging in the dirt. With considerable cussing and hat throwing, Wallace managed to reharness the team, hooking them in tandem to the chuck wagon.

At last he and Cookey climbed onto the seat, screwing down their hats for the ride ahead. From the side, Sarah and the men looked on. With brow furrowed, McReynolds rode in a circle about the wagon, checking to see that everything was in place.

"Well," he said to Wallace, "what do you think?"

"Think we'll ride her into the clouds, and be back for supper." Wallace grinned. "One thing about it," he said, gathering up the reins, "either way I won't have to eat Cookey's biscuits tonight."

With a snap of the reins, the team lurched, uncertain, gathering to purpose as they moved up the trail against the pull of the grade. With muscles trembling, they lunged ahead, the wheels of the wagon scattering rock down the precipitous incline. Through the din, Wallace's whoops and hollers rose, driving them ever upward and onward.

With jaws clenched, Cookey rode the brake, taking up slack anywhere the trail dipped or the wagon rode too close to the brink. As they rounded the bend, both stood as if preparing to fly, the water bucket bouncing from its mooring, dropping in a free-fall into the ravine. From time to time, Cookey stole a glance into the rocks overhead, looking for Cheyenne, waiting for the silent arrow soaring in against the sun.

And then they were gone from sight, a cloud of dust drifting down the canyon like a silent morning fog.

"They okay?" Sarah asked, pushing the hair back from her face.

"Sure," McReynolds said. "I think so. I don't know," he added. "Guess we'll find out soon enough." Walking to the bottom of the trail, he looked up the grade, at the hairpin curve disappearing into the rocks. "We'll make camp here," he said. "It's too late for another team up today, and no way of knowing when they'll get back."

Stepping to his side, Sarah brushed his arm; a tingle fired through him at her touch, the smell of her sachet, the shine of her eyes in the light.

By the time camp was pitched, dusk fell across the canyons, shadows washing in like a dark tide. The fire was banked on the lee side of an embankment, the smell of smoke and fried fatback filling their camp.

With Cookey and the chuck wagon gone, Sarah assumed the responsibilities as best she could, working at the biscuits, stirring fatback into the pot of black-eyed peas. From across the way, McReynolds watched her work, the cut of her waist, the turn of her ankle, the wisp of hair that curled at her neck. There was a grace in her movements, a consolation in her soft and resonant hum, a feel of home in the camp. The anxiety of the trail lessened in her presence, for him, for all who took solace from her beauty and company.

As darkness fell, the evening cooled, a fog rolling into the canyons, hushing their voices with its cover. Twice, McReynolds walked to the trail head, straining to see beyond the blanket of fog, listening for the sound of hooves, the jingle of harness, the telling voice of Wallace. Each time there was but the mocking rejoinder of his own calls against the night mist.

From her place by the fire, Sarah watched his return, knew his distress.

"They'll come soon," she said.

"Yes," he said, pouring a cup of coffee. "It's early yet. We've no way of knowing how far it is to the top, and then there's the unhitching and the securing of supplies once they are there."

No sooner had he spoken, when the voices came from the mist, the rattle of harness as the horses shook their heads in anticipation of rest.

"Yo," Wallace called out. "Anybody here?"

Standing, McReynolds tossed the remainder of his coffee into the fire.

"Over here," he called, "with dinner waiting."

Stepping from the mist, Wallace held taut the reins of the lead horse. Not far behind, Cookey led the second team, his hat pulled down on his head, squashing his ears out at peculiar angles.

"Ain't leftover biscuits, is it?" Wallace grinned. "I've had all the punishment I can stand for one day."

"We set those aside for the howitzers," McReynolds said, in case we run out of cannonballs. You get that wagon to the top?"

"Course," Wallace said, handing the reins over to Private Holland. "See they're taken care of, Private. They've earned their keep this day."

Pulling up a camp chair, Cookey collapsed into it, his arms folded across his chest.

"Well," McReynolds said, waiting.

"Well," Wallace said, sitting down beside Cookey, "it's a treacherous track up that mountain, alright. There are times the trail disappears from sight, wheel hubs dragging against the canyon wall to keep from pitching over the side. It's steep, too. One horse less, and we'd still be up there, I suppose."

"It's the Cheyenne, mostly," Cookey said, "up in the hills, watching and waiting and chucking down rocks when you least expect. I think I saw one hiding behind a mesquite, big as a plow horse he was, with feathers flowing down his back and scalps dangling off his waistband."

"Well, I didn't see no Cheyenne," Wallace said, pouring himself a cup of coffee, "and I couldn't hear nothing over Cookey's screams every time we took a bend. Mostly, it's just a narrow and rough haul, no place for skittish horses or doctors with shiny boots."

"Don't you worry about the doctors, Captain. They've dealt with the backsides of Cavalry soldiers, as fearful a sight as known to man."

Sipping at his coffee, Wallace looked up at him.

"Well, you got a point there, Major. That's a troubling image, sure enough."

And so they talked into the evening as Sarah served their supper. To have them back eased McReynolds, lifted his spirits, the mischievous banter of friends filling the quiet of the evening.

As the fire faded, Captain Wallace and Cookey drifted away to bed, exhausted from the trials of the day. Throughout the evening, the mist had thickened, surrounding them in its cocoon, muffling their voices, falling cool against their faces. As Sarah finished the cleaning, McReynolds watched her, moisture gathering in the folds of her hair, shimmering like pearls in the glow of the fire.

"Well," he said, "they're home safe."

Pushing her hair from her face, she sat down and folded her knees into her arms.

"Tomorrow we must do it again," she said. "We must all go up."

"Yes, but then Captain Wallace knows what to expect, doesn't he, has his strategy down. It shouldn't be a problem."

"I've been thinking," she said, "you know, about David, about his death. It's so odd, him dying that way. It's not the way David would have died, being wiped off his horse with a tree branch."

"Let's walk," he said.

Slipping her fingers into his hand, she followed him into the cool mist and down the trail. At the base of the mountain, he put his arm about her waist.

"Let's go up," she said, "for just a ways."

"Alright, for a ways."

The grade steepened, and he held tight her hand as they worked their way toward the bend. Within a few minutes, they'd reached the place where Cookey's water bucket had sailed into space.

"Here," she said, standing at the precipice. "Let's stop here."

Pitching a rock over the side, McReynolds listened in vain for the sound.

"What did you mean," he said, "about your husband dying the way he did?"

Finding a place to sit, Sarah leaned back against the canyon wall, thinking before she spoke.

"David was a lot of things," she finally said, "but he was not stupid. Being wiped off by a limb is not something he would allow to happen. It's too common, and he would never have permitted it."

Moving to her side, his shoulder touched hers, the warmth of her body, the glisten of her eyes in the mist, the smell of her, like rain in the heat of summer. With his finger, he traced the delicate line of her face, the sweep of her brow, the full and inviting curve of her mouth. For a moment she held her breath, savoring his touch.

"We don't always choose how we die, Sarah."

Taking his hands, she held them to her face.

"He was an excellent horseman. I've never known for him to be thrown."

"Sarah," he said, pulling her to him, "let's not talk about it."

Lifting her face, she kissed him.

His passion mounting, he fumbled at the tie of her dress, but she stopped him, deepening his appetite, the momentary touch of her hand.

"I need you," he said, but she resisted, her hand against his chest.

"It's in the needing," she whispered, her fingers working at a button on his shirt, her touch, her heart-stopping touch, nails trailing across his chest, breath hot against his skin. It was in the needing, she said, and so it was, rushing hot through his veins.

Releasing his hand, she threw back her head, laughing, fulsome and spilling with pleasure, the pocket of her throat, the flutter of her heart against his lips, a moment more in the needing.

Removing her blouse, she let it fall, cupping her breasts in the night mist. He touched them, their fullness and weight, the cool firmness of her nipples, but still, she waited, because it was in the waiting. When there was no more, her will surrendering against the driving tide of passion, she came to him with abandon and with a hunger born of the fast.

Afterward, they dressed, and he gathered her into his arms, to warm her against the night. Beyond the mist a coyote yipped, short barks spawned by the cold smell of prey. She leaned against him, her head on his shoulder.

Several minutes passed before he spoke.

"Remember what you said earlier, Sarah?"

"About David?"

"Yes," he said. "There's something I need to tell you, something I should have told you before."

"What is it?" she said, sitting up.

"You were right, I'm afraid."

Her hand tightened against his.

"What do you mean?"

"He didn't die from an accident, at least that's what I think."

"But how would you know this?"

"Cookey and I found his body, back where the trail branched. I didn't want to tell you, or anyone for that matter, not until I knew what was going on. But then after what you said, it just wasn't right for me not to tell you. I'm sorry, Sarah. I wouldn't deceive you for anything."

"But who? Why?"

"He was left behind, by the others apparently, but there were signs of Indians, too. It doesn't make sense."

"And no one else knows?"

"Just Cookey," he said, "and I've sworn him to silence until I can find out the truth."

Rising, she walked to the edge of the trail, staring into the mist that swirled in the darkness below.

"We came by his grave then," she said.

"I'm sorry, Sarah. It was a cruel thing, but I was afraid, afraid of more than I was willing to admit, I think."

Turning, she walked back, kneeling at his side, whispering as if someone might hear.

"But it was the soldiers who said he was killed in an accident. Why would they lie about a thing like that?"

"Yes," he said. "It was the soldiers who lied, or the courier, or both. Until I find out why, it must be kept a secret, do you see?"

As they made their way back to camp, they walked in silence. When they parted, she took his hand.

"I love you," she whispered.

The triumph of words, more ascending and powerful than the needing itself, the pledge of love, and through the night, the words lifted and fell with the sweetness of dreams. Even as he rose to greet the challenges of morning, they remained with him, like the lingering fragrance of her sachet, and the touch of her hand under the darkness of night.

With most of the cooking utensils and supplies at the top of the mountain, breakfast was a reheat of supper: black-eyed peas, biscuits, and black coffee.

"Morning, sir," Cookey said, ladling out a helping for McReynolds.

"Cookey," McReynolds said, "you ready for another go up the mountain?"

"Oh, yes, sir," he said, "volunteering's a way of life for me. Anytime there's a man's work to be done, or danger to be had, I'll be stepping forward to do my share."

"You're a fine example of soldiering, alright," McReynolds said, "every commander's dream."

Sitting down on a camp stool, McReynolds ate his peas, thinking about the day ahead.

"I want you to drive a wagon yourself today, Cookey. You've been up once already and know where the rough spots are. Have one of the carpenters run the brake for you. The others will follow on horseback. Captain Wallace and I will bring up the rear with the lumber wagon. It's the heaviest and slowest."

"Yes, sir," he said, "and this time I'm having my carbine ready, case one of them Cheyenne chucks a rock or cuts loose my water bucket again."

"Good idea, Cookey, but make sure it isn't one of our own you're shooting at."

"Oh, no, sir," he replied, grinning. "I seen plenty of Cheyenne in my time, dancing up war and trouble. I won't be shooting no soldiers, sir."

By ten o'clock the teams were doubled, and the men and Sarah were saddled and ready to go. Captain Wallace inspected the harness one last time before climbing onto the seat next to McReynolds.

"Well, Major," he said, "you ready?"

Checking the brake handle, McReynolds nodded.

"Have to ride out of here sometime," he said.

"Keep that brake snug, and when I holler, bear down hard. If we get in a slide, the brake brings her around. We'll ride her to the top and be home 'fore dark. Make the General happy, won't we, bringing in his favorite Dr. Smooch." Wallace grinned.

"You just get us to the top, Captain, and leave the smooching to me."

With a wave of McReynolds's hat, Cookey popped his reins and headed up the trail, dust boiling behind as he made the first turn. Even as he disappeared around the corner, his whoops echoed through the canyon.

When the last of the soldiers disappeared, Wallace looked at McReynolds.

"Here we go," he said, bringing his reins down in a crack, dust rising from the backs of the startled horses.

Foot braced against the bed, McReynolds slipped the brake, keeping enough tension to bring it down fast if he needed. The horses lunged against the incline, against the terrible weight and burden of the wagon. Ahead the trail narrowed, doubling back in a terrifying curve, sheer rock on one side, a fathomless drop on the other.

"Oh, my God," McReynolds said, rising from his seat.

"Now," Wallace yelled. "Brake her now."

Teeth clenched, McReynolds leaned into the brake, the squeal of metal against metal drowning away his own involuntary yell. The wagon straightened, moving into the wall, sparks firing from the wheel hub as it bit into the rock. The thunder of hooves roared as the horses struggled against the grade. Chancing a glance over his shoulder, he looked over the edge and into the thin blue depths below.

"Again!" Wallace yelled, leaning into the pull. "Bear it down, Doc, 'fore we go over the side!"

Hauling on the lever, McReynolds gave it all he had, locking it down, the wagon correcting against the dead slide of the wheel.

It was the sound first, a sickening and telling crack as the wagon tongue gave way at the drawbar, the horses pulling away, unencumbered now by their burden. When the wheels hooked the wall, McReynolds pitched forward against the footrest, still clinging to the brake lever even as the wagon rose into the air. Dust boiled about, and for a single terrifying moment he waited for the whistle of free-fall that would end his life in the brutal rocks below. The only sound was the eerie creak of the wagon as it settled against the embankment.

Hands still clutched on the brake lever, he called out, "Wallace, are you alright?"

But there was no answer, the smell of dust and wheel grease filling the air.

"Wallace," he called again, his arms trembling as he held to the brake, fearing to release it for even a second.

"Down here," Wallace said from somewhere under the wagon. "Hurt bad, I think. Caught up in the wheel. My hand's gone."

By looking through a crack in the floor planking,

McReynolds could see Wallace, his shirt twisted in a ball between the hub and wheel pin, a pool of blood gathering in the dirt beneath his arm. His body hung suspended over the side of the rift, secured by nothing more than the twist of the shirt and the grace of God.

"Don't move, Captain, I'm coming down."

Bringing himself into the upright position, McReynolds placed his feet against the wagon floor, sweat dripping from his nose as he eased loose the brake in small and measured increments, listening, waiting, releasing again, arms burning with fatigue against the tension.

With a sudden lurch, the wagon sent dirt and rock tumbling into the abyss, a heart-stopping screech as the bed scoured along the rock wall.

"Stop!" Wallace yelled. "It's unwinding the hold!"

Pulling back, McReynolds put his weight into it, his arms numbed with fatigue.

"You alright?" he called out.

"Bleeding out," he said, "and my strength's going fast."

"Any chance you can pull yourself up, Captain? Letting go of the brake isn't much of an option at the moment."

"It's the one hand I got," he said.

Then there was only the sound of Wallace, struggling against the pain and the fear.

"Captain," McReynolds called again.

"I been thinking," Wallace said, "that I'd like to apologize for accusing you of smooching the General."

Bearing down on the brake, McReynolds clenched his jaw, sweat beading across his forehead.

"And for making light of my boots," he said. "It's the rare moment I can command such respect."

From below, Wallace took slow and deliberate breaths, pooling his strength before he spoke.

"There was never any doubting the respect, Doc. You remember that when it comes."

There was no moment when that time came, no moment when McReynolds stopped pulling. Even as the tremble spread like poison through his body, even as his hands blackened and saliva drooled from his lips, even as his voice rose in unconscious cries of agony, there was no moment when he stopped pulling.

There was only the moment after, when the wagon rolled from its mooring, pitching in a quiet arc into the rift, when he leapt away to save his own life, when there was only the severed hand and the looming silence of his ole friend's absence.

By the time McReynolds reached the top of the trail, the horses were yet to be caught, the splintered wagon tongue still dragging between them like his own shattered life.

Sarah sobbed as he told his story, and the men listened with grief and disbelief, but it was McReynolds who stood at the trail head long after they were gone, staring at his bleeding and treacherous hands with tear-filled eyes.

The sun stood at high noon when the train stopped and waited for McReynolds to climb up the high bank of the Cimarron. Below him, the meander of the river twisted in the light. From the soldiers' camp on the opposite side, the whinny of horses announced their arrival, the smell of camp smoke, the sound of laughter riding in on the wind.

Standing on the bank, McReynolds studied the redoubt site below. It was a place of little consequence, a muddy and ugly backwash in a distant and alien land. Already its price in blood was far too high.

Turning, he signaled to the others, but it was with trepidation and regret that he rode in that day to the Cimarron crossing at Deep Hole Creek.

Thirty-two

Gathering about, the soldiers watched as the wagons crossed the shallow river. Exiting from his tent, Sergeant Wilson put on his hat and buttoned his uniform. The smell of boiling wheat rose from the pot over the camp and settled in the valley.

Dismounting, McReynolds walked forward.

"Sir," Sergeant Wilson said, popping a salute. "Glad you are here. We've been anxious about your arrival." Taking the reins of McReynolds's horse, he handed them to Private Tanner. "Rub him down, and see to setting up the major's tent. You forgotten how to salute, soldier?"

"Sorry, sir." Tanner saluted.

"It's been a time since we had an officer about, sir. The men are a little rusty with their manners," Wilson said.

"We've a woman with us, Sergeant," McReynolds said, pointing to Sarah, who sat next to Cookey on the wagon. "Sarah Roland. She'll be needing some assistance with her tent."

"Lieutenant Roland's wife?"

"It's okay, Sergeant. We came across the courier on his way to Supply. She knows about her husband."

"Crying shame," he said. "Still, it's dying for your country that matters."

"Accident, I understand, something about his horse?"

"Wiped off under a limb, he was. Just closed his eyes and went to sleep. Man couldn't ask for better dying when he comes to it."

Taking off his hat, McReynolds looked into the sun, letting the heat warm his face.

"And we all come to it, Sergeant, so they say. Had our own share of bad luck. We've lost Captain Wallace and Housman, not to mention wagons and a fair number of horses. It's going to be a sight harder to build and defend this redoubt now."

"Sorry to hear about the captain, sir. He was a good soldier."

"Yes, he was a good soldier. Well," he said, turning away, "have the howitzers come from Fort Dodge?"

"No, sir. Snow's been heavy for moving howitzers, I'd say. Quiet as death around here mostly, just a mule skinner and his half-breed kid camping down by the river. He bought some boiling wheat with a silver coin. Seems harmless enough, so I let them stay a spell. Then there was that Cooper feller looking for his sergeant. Claims the sergeant was kilt' and scalped, but there ain't been no signs of depredations this far north. Might have stumbled onto a hunting party, I figure."

Folding his arms, he looked over McReynolds's shoulder at the wagons behind him.

"See you brought Cookey, sir. Want me to put these men to unloading? Maybe there'd be time for bread making."

"The sooner the better, Sergeant; meanwhile, I'm

going to meet with the carpenters and go over the redoubt plans."

"You are welcome to my tent, sir, while the boys get yours set up."

"I'll do that, Sergeant."

The tent was immaculate, exuding military rigor, boots and gear laid out, lantern cleaned and polished, bed smooth and tight. Pulling up a camp chair, McReynolds rolled out the plans, laying his pistol on one end to hold them down.

When the carpenters arrived, they waited at the tent door, uneasy about their summons.

"Sit down, men," McReynolds said. "I've asked you here to discuss the redoubt plans. We all know that it's not going to be easy with Captain Wallace gone. I'm going to have to depend on you to get this thing done. I'll help any way I can, but I'm not an engineer nor even a carpenter. You men talk things over as we go and then come to me. Give me the best advice you got, and then I'll make the decision. I know more than any of you how badly we need Captain Wallace, but we don't have him. We have to do the best we can. Do I have your support?"

"Yes, sir." The corporal nodded. "Best we can, sir."

"Good. Now, tell me where you think we should start on this thing."

"We ain't never built a redoubt, sir," the corporal said, "but there's the parapet there, that has to be built up first, and then the wall and gun platforms. You can see right here, sir, where they go, one offset on each side for the best coverage. I'd start with the parapet, dig out this river sand and pack her high as she'll go. It needs to be close to the river, but not so close we get drowned first rain."

"And then there's timbers to be cut," the private

added, "cut, hauled in, and squared out. It don't take no carpenter to cut timbers, sir. If it was me, I'd send the share of these soldiers to cut and trim timbers. The others I'd put to digging sand. We could have a fair stronghold within a few days."

"That's right," the corporal said. "Once we're able to defend ourselves, then we can start worrying about sleeping quarters and such. First things first, I'd say."

Lighting his pipe, McReynolds studied the plans.

"Looks good to me, men," he said. "Captain Wallace has taught you well."

"Yes, sir." The private smiled.

McReynolds recognized him then as the soldier who'd taken off the end of Wallace's thumb with the hammer.

"Get some rest," McReynolds said, "because we're starting this thing in earnest come daylight. The sooner we get protection up, the better off we'll be, and I want to mount those howitzers soon as they arrive. Any questions?"

Standing, they prepared to leave, when the corporal turned.

"There is one thing, sir, now that it's brought up."

"What's that?"

"Me and the others been talking. Come the right time, we'd like to give Captain Wallace a send-off, sir. It's a deserving man who lays in the canyon back there, and only right he gets what a soldier's got coming."

Filling his pipe, McReynolds struck a match on the bottom of his boot. With slow puffs, he drew down the flame, the smell of tobacco moving through the tent.

"It's a fair thing you ask," he said. "Come sunup, we start with a proper farewell to our own Captain

Wallace, and then we'll go to work. It would be an unhappy Wallace who kept a man from his work too long."

Afterward, McReynolds made his way down to where Cookey and Sarah were preparing the evening meal. Hands covered with flour, Sarah worked at the loaves, a strand of hair falling across her eyes. Several of the soldiers watched from their tents, the aroma and prospect of fresh bread causing them to gather in anticipation.

"What we having, Cookey?" McReynolds asked, pulling up a camp chair.

"Onion sandwiches made with sourdough bread and smeared with the last of the butter, pinto beans seasoned with smoked hocks, onions, black pepper, a dash of vinegar, and a dollop of molasses. Course, there's my secret ingredient."

"And what could that be, I wonder?" McReynolds said.

"Mustard seed," he said, "tossed in to plump in the cooking, bursts of flavor and heat, lovely as a redhead's kiss, begging your pardon, Miss Sarah."

Turning, Sarah smiled, pushing the hair from her face with the back of her hand.

"Something tells me we can't go wrong with this meal," she said. "Private Tanner says they've been eating boiled wheat and sugar water for days."

"Cookey," McReynolds mentioned, rising, "Sergeant Wilson says there's an ole mule skinner and his son camped down on the bank of the river. Send a man and invite them for supper. Sounds like a meal no one should miss."

"Yes, sir," he said, "couldn't stop them in any case, when they get a whiff of these here beans."

By the time the sun eased behind the high bank

of the Cimarron, McReynolds had made his rounds of the camp, taking time to remove a splinter lodged under Private Holland's nail. Working his way up the bank, he could hear the laughter of the soldiers as they gathered about the fire. Sarah stood at the pot of beans, ladling helpings into their waiting bowls. The men looked into her face as they passed, for the flash of her eyes, for the tug on their hearts with the turn of her smile.

The fire flickered against the gray dusk of evening as they ate, the gentle breeze dropping away with the passing of day.

How long the man and his son had been there in the shadows, McReynolds couldn't be certain, the lone figure hunkering over his bowl, the boy at his side. Something swept through McReynolds at the sight of him, something familiar but distant, the tilt of his shoulder, the turn of his chin, the way he cocked his hat to the side. After eating, McReynolds decided to talk with him, but when he looked up, he was gone.

"Was that the mule skinner?" he asked, turning to Cookey.

"Yes, sir," he said, "a strange sort, ain't he? Keeps to hisself, the men said, him and the kid."

Finishing his coffee, McReynolds rolled the redoubt plans out under the light of the campfire for one last look. Soon the men drifted away to bed or to card games or to the telling of endless stories under the dim light of lanterns.

"Good night, Major," Sarah said. "You mustn't fret too much over the plans, you know. We've good carpenters, haven't we?"

"It's the supply list, and the tools lost in the canyon," he said. "It's going to require some improvising, and without the captain . . ."

"Well, you mustn't worry. Things will work out."

"Yes," he said, "of course they will. Good night, Sarah."

When McReynolds woke, the dying fire sputtered, smoke twisting into the stillness. The redoubt plans had curled under the dampness of evening, and a cricket chirped from somewhere down on the river. Rolling up the plans, he slipped them under the seat of a wagon and started for his tent.

Perhaps it was the distant saw of the cricket, or the ivory light of the moon falling on the water, or the quiet manner of the mule skinner that turned him from his plans. Whatever it was, he cut left down the path and made his way in the darkness to the banks of the Cimarron.

Even from a distance, he could see the fire. A breeze swept down the river valley, knurled tree limbs swaying and stretching against the light of the moon.

From the firelight he could see their meager belongings, a few worn blankets, a parfleche bound and tucked under a saddle. On the far side, the boy slept, his long black hair shining in the flicker of the fire. In that moment McReynolds doubted the wisdom of his decision to come, a stranger's camp in the middle of the night.

"You have business here," the voice said from the darkness, "best state it fast and clear."

A chill raced down McReynolds's spine as he spun about.

"I'm the redoubt commander," he said, searching the darkness for the voice. "I didn't get a chance to talk with you at supper."

Only then did he see the glint of the carbine, the looming shadow behind it.

"It's an uncommon hour to call," he said, "and likely to get a man shot."

"Yes," McReynolds said. "My apologies."

Stepping into the light, Renfro lay down his carbine.

"Well, long as you're here, just as well sit."

"Thanks," McReynolds said, "but I wouldn't want to wake the boy."

"It's the way of the young to sleep through most anything," he said, " 'cept supper. We appreciate the invite. Boiled wheat and glue have a sight in common."

Pushing back his hat, Renfro sat down at the fire, folding his long legs under him Indian style. Following suit, McReynolds warmed his hands against the flame.

"Sorry for breaking in," McReynolds said, reaching out his hand to shake. "It's just at supper I thought for a moment I knew you."

Taking his hand, Renfro cocked his head, studying McReynolds's face.

"Adam's the name," he said. "My boy and I are headed to the Santa Fe Trail to pick up a few mules for freightin'."

Whether it was the name, or the voice, or the dark and penetrating eyes, the pieces fell together in that moment for McReynolds.

"Adam Renfro?" he said.

Stiffening, Renfro's hand dropped to his carbine, and his eyes bore down on McReynolds.

"Who might you be," he asked, "to know such a name?"

"Joseph McReynolds," he said. "Dr. Joseph McReynolds."

Hands dropping to his side, disbelief swept Adam's face.

"It's a unlikely thing," he said, "you and me here after all these years. I reckon you was going to turn me over for desertion, it would've happened 'fore now." Leaning toward the fire, elbows planted on his knees, he took in McReynolds's face. "Time's been good to you, Major. Wasn't for that splash of gray, I'd knowed you anywhere."

The years fell away in that moment as McReynolds gripped his ole friend's hand once more. Here was a man who'd earned his place, who'd commanded the respect of all who knew him.

"Fact is, we both have gotten older, Corporal."

"Yes, sir," he said, leaning back on his elbow, "it's the way of things, and no might in the world to stop it as far as I can tell."

"And the boy?"

"Twobirds's boy, he is, and a fine one, too." Pushing back his hat, he stared into the fire as he thought. "She's gone, you see, kilt' by the cholera and her own kindness. Kilt' me, too, hadn't been for the boy there."

For a moment McReynolds's heart stilled, and he looked up at the moon slipping high above.

"I'm sorry," he said, "for you and the boy, and for myself, too, I guess."

Standing, Adam stoked the fire, adding pieces of driftwood retrieved from the muddy bank of the Cimarron.

"There's more darkness than light in our meeting, Major." Pausing, he took a deep breath before beginning. "The boy and I come across Nurse Cromley.

All those years gone by, and there she was afore me, just like you here tonight. But a broke leg got her throwed away, and there she was with an ole monk, both half starved and worse for the wear. He left in the night, to save on food, I reckon, but gangrene had taken her leg. It was too late. There was naught left but her spirit and smile. We left her on a scaffold. It was a hard thing, but that's the way of it."

Stunned by the news, McReynolds gathered himself up. Renfro waited.

"It's as if my past closed out this night," McReynolds said. "They were alive in my memory. The knowing ends it now, steals it all away."

"My voice will be linked with this sorrow," Renfro said, "and that I regret. But the eyes of the woman, the one in camp, watched you tonight. There is still much you have to live for, I'd guess."

"I've filled my years with medicine, with the Army, with the demands of the day," McReynolds said, "not knowing the great emptiness within me. When Sarah came into my life, it was as if I awakened from a great and deep sleep."

As the moon arched across the sky, they talked of the past, of the perilous expedition they'd survived under Lieutenant Sheets so many years earlier, of the lives they'd carved for themselves, of their dreams and hopes for the future. They talked of Housman, and of Captain Wallace, and of Sergeant Number, shot and killed by another's hand. They talked of the years spent, of freight lines, and of Creed's future, now that his mother was gone.

And as the night deepened, Adam told McReynolds of the swollen corpses of the Dog Soldier Clan among the grove of trees, the shod horse tracks, the bloodied and trampled grass.

"If one of those Dog Soldiers survived, he could be on his way here with reinforcements," Adam said. "I don't have to tell you the driving need of a man so injured."

"Sarah's husband," McReynolds relayed, tamping tobacco into his pipe, "Lieutenant Roland, was in charge of this expedition." With a stick from the fire, he touched off the tobacco and looked up at Adam. "He's dead now, a fall from his horse, least that's what I was told." Rubbing the smoke from his eyes, he thought back on the events of the last few days. "I came across Roland's body where the Supply trail branches off, just south of the red canyons. One thing's certain, he didn't die of a horse fall. Someone is lying, and I don't know why."

"Maybe these men had themselves a raiding party of their own," Adam said, "and things got out of hand. It's the kind of thing that can happen with young soldiers left on their own."

"Only Cookey and Sarah know about all this at this point," McReynolds said. "I want to keep it that way until I can get to the bottom of things."

"If these boys been up to no good, there's little chance of depending on them in a pinch. There's not a man in the lot, far as I can tell. Given the lack of howitzers, we could be in for a fine ole time."

"Sully's sending howitzers," McReynolds said, "down from Dodge, but they should have been here by now. Sergeant Wilson thinks it's the bad weather, maybe."

"Maybe," Adam said, "maybe not. I'd be for building that parapet and digging in soon as possible, just in case."

Standing, McReynolds donned his hat and reached for Adam's hand.

"It's a full circle we come, isn't it, Corporal? I'm glad I know about Twobirds and Nurse Cromley, and I'm glad it's your voice I'll hear with their memory. You and the boy want to join us in the camp? It would be safer there."

"Thank you anyway, sir, but guess we're doing okay. We're accustomed to running alone."

Making his way back up the trail, McReynolds stopped to knock the tobacco from his pipe. Below, he could still see the glow of Renfro's fire. From beyond the river, a coyote lifted its quivering voice into the soundless prairie.

There was within McReynolds a deep and terrible loneliness, the ragged edges of his life having been trimmed away. But it was the throb and pain of a wound, he knew, that must come before the healing.

Thirty-three

Dawn broke with the crack of rifles as the soldiers fired off their salute in honor of Captain Wallace. The bugle's call rose into the morning brightness, and the men snapped to attention as the riderless horse was paraded about the grounds. The flag was hoisted high, a moment's silence filling them with the glory and distinction of death.

When all was done, McReynolds put the carpenters in charge of the parapet; six men to assist in the digging, while Sergeant Wilson and another six cut timbers at the river's edge. By the time McReynolds got around to checking on their progress, it was coming on noon. Even though the carpenters were themselves skilled, their ability to organize and lead was unfortunate; men wandering about unassigned, sitting, smoking, telling stories while others worked.

No sooner had McReynolds reorganized the crews, when Sergeant Wilson's wagons clambered up the trail, fresh-cut timbers teetering from the beds.

"Where do you want them, Major?" he asked.

Turning up his hands, McReynolds shook his head. "You'll have to ask the carpenters, Sergeant."

"It's a engineer, we need," Wilson said. "Them carpenters don't know a redoubt from a barn raising."

Overhearing the conversation, Renfro made his way down to the wagons, Creed following at his side.

"It's considerable trouble they're having with the sand giving way, Major," he said. "Could use those timbers to shore up the sides, given they're too spindly to stop a bullet or arrow, either one."

Turning on his heel, Sergeant Wilson bore down on Renfro.

"This here's Army business, mule skinner, and you need to stay out of it."

Stepping between them, McReynolds held up his hand.

"Take it easy, Sergeant. Maybe it's an idea we should consider. Bigger timbers would make a better wall, and there's enough light left."

"Mule skinners and kids got no business in the work area, Major. It's a danger and breach of the rules."

"It's alright, Sergeant. I've invited him and the boy into camp."

With a hard stare, Wilson popped the reins and pulled away.

"Didn't set out to cause you trouble, Major," Adam said, pushing back his hat.

"Who's your pal?" McReynolds asked.

"This my boy, Creed," he said.

"Hello, Creed." McReynolds shook his hand. "Welcome to Deep Hole Creek."

"Thank you," Creed said, his dark eyes shining in the sun.

"You and your father will be eating with us while you're here, won't you? It's plenty of food we have and a mighty good cook."

"Boiled wheat sticks in my teeth," he said.

"If we eat, we help," Adam said. "That's the way it has to be."

Smiling, McReynolds put his hand on Creed's shoulder. There was the dance of youth in the boy's eyes that lightened his own spirit.

"I can use all the help I can get," he said. "After dinner, maybe you and Creed could keep an eye on the digging. My carpenters aren't used to keeping things organized, I'm afraid."

"It's a deal," Adam said, "and fair pay in Cookey's bread."

That afternoon the sun warmed them, and the chill of winter faded from their minds and bodies. Throughout the valley, the men's voices rose and fell as they worked at their jobs. The aroma of baking bread wafted from the camp, and the winds fell silent in repose.

Just as the shadows stretched across the valley, Sergeant Wilson and his crew arrived with the second cutting of timbers, unloading them in the gray of dusk, the snap of Wilson's orders punctuating the evening. Horses snorted against their burdens and against the men who cursed them from daylight to dawn.

After supper, the men stayed about the fire longer than usual, their work invested now, their claim made on Deep Hole Creek. The anxiety of the trail faded with the reality of the redoubt, because beyond in the darkness, a sandbank grew, a barrier against the evils and fears of the prairie. It was in itself no more than a pile of sand, to be reinforced with bags of sand later, but soon unconquerable guns would man its walls. This brought them comfort.

From his vantage McReynolds watched as Sarah worked. The opportunity to be alone with her vanished with their arrival at Deep Hole Creek, and he missed her.

Making the rounds, McReynolds searched out Renfro, finding him on the bank of the Cimarron watching the waters in their silent journey to the sea.

" 'Lo," McReynolds said.

"Major," Renfro replied, standing.

"Where's the boy?"

"Tired out from all the excitement, so he turned in. Thought I'd enjoy a bit of the evening 'fore I followed suit."

Taking out his pipe, McReynolds loaded it, packing the tobacco with the end of his finger.

"I'm in need of advice, Renfro. Those redoubt plans overlooked the placement of the guard stations. It seems a fair oversight to me and thought maybe you'd take a go at the plans."

"My book learning ain't what it should be, Major."

"It's experience I need," he said, lighting his pipe. "I've enough book learning to get us all killed."

"Lead the way then, Major."

Once inside the tent, McReynolds unrolled the plans, turning the lantern higher in order to see.

"It's here I'm thinking," he said, "where you could see both directions of the river."

"Yes, sir, that's good," Adam said, "if you are expecting an attack from the Navy, but that stand of trees would be the best cover for Indians. It's surprise they want, and surprise that counts every time. With guards posted here, you'd have a chance at early warning at least."

Before McReynolds could answer, there was a noise at the door of the tent.

"Who is it?" McReynolds asked.

"It's Private Tanner, sir," he said, sticking his head through the opening.

"What is it, Tanner?"

"Sorry, sir, didn't know you had company. I was wondering if we could talk?"

"It's not a good time, Private, as you can see. There's

the chain of command, as you well know. Take your problem up with Sergeant Wilson."

"Yes, sir," he said, looking over his shoulder, "it's what I know, but it's the one thing I can't do. It's a private talk I need, sir."

"What is it then?" McReynolds asked.

"It's a *private* talk, sir, that I need."

"Whatever you have to say can be said in front of us all. It won't leave this tent, if that's what you're worried about."

"Yes, sir," he said, scratching at his head. "It's just that Sergeant Wilson ain't one to take light a break in command."

"Nor I, Tanner. I'm assuming that what you have to say warrants such a breach."

"Yes, sir," he said, "I think it does. It's about Lance Corporal Inman, sir."

"Inman?"

"Yes, sir. He was kilt', sir, when his dugout collapsed. I helped dig him out, and I ain't slept a wink since. It was the look on his face, I reckon, and the sand in his eyes, like he didn't even have time to blink."

Knocking the tobacco from his pipe, McReynolds blew on the stem to open it up as he thought on Tanner's story.

"Why hasn't this been reported to me? A death in the command is to be reported directly and immediately to the commander."

"That's just it, sir. No one's talking, for fear of the same."

For a brief moment, Adam and McReynolds looked at each other through the dim light of the lantern.

"It's about what happened in that grove of trees, isn't it?" Adam asked. "About them Dog Soldiers all kilt' in their beds whilst they slept?"

Pain swept Tanner's face.

"Lieutenant Roland ordered us in, took us in at daybreak," he said. "We was just doing what he ordered, doing our duty."

Adam moved into the light of the lantern.

"You kilt' them all to the last?"

"It was our duty, Lieutenant Roland said so, as long as there was a Indian standing anywhere, our own kind was at risk for being kilt' or worse, so he took us in at daybreak, just as the sun broke enough to see."

Walking to the tent flap, Adam opened it to let the night air wash over him, the unfolding story rising within him like a sickness.

"It was Inman," Tanner continued, "heard the screaming in his head at night. It was Inman waking up with sweats and couldn't let it go."

"What are you trying to say?" McReynolds asked.

"I watched Inman build that dugout, every step of the way. Modeled it after Captain Wallace, he did, with bracing and everything. It was the bracing that was broke, kicked in to bring the roof down. That's what I think, lashing or no."

Holding the empty pipe between his teeth, McReynolds studied Tanner's face.

"Now, I'm going to ask you something," he said, "and I want the straight truth. Nobody's giving lashings, you hear, and nobody's going to let Sergeant Wilson give lashings, either."

"Yes, sir," he said.

"Was Lieutenant Roland swept off his horse and killed that day?"

Dropping his head, Tanner folded his hands in his lap. A breeze swept through camp, the lantern light brightening for a moment, the beads of sweat glistening on Tanner's forehead.

"No, sir, he wasn't."

Turning, Renfro looked at McReynolds.

"How was he kilt'?" he asked.

"A Dog Soldier," Tanner said, "come up out of the dead ashes over his kilt' baby and opened up the lieutenant's leg with his knife. It was a mean cut, meant to kill, bone deep from knee to pocket, just as the lieutenant shot away his face, but the deed was done, wasn't it."

"You certain that Dog Soldier was kilt'?" Renfro asked.

"Ain't likely a man would survive such a wound or want to, by the looks of him. After that, we took the lieutenant back to camp, but he was bleeding bad and cussing everyone and saying how he needed something for the pain, saying how God left him to die amongst ignorant misfits and savages, saying if he lived he'd see the lot of us hanged. Course, he was bleeding to death, that was plain to see, so the sergeant sewed him up, stitched him like a sack of flour." With the sleeve of his shirt, Tanner wiped at his forehead. "It went on and on," he said, "with the lieutenant screaming and hollering and begging for him to stop the whole time."

"Wasn't there anything to be given, Tanner, not even some whiskey?" McReynolds asked.

"Oh, no, sir. Whiskey ain't allowed."

Sitting back down, Renfro folded his arms over his chest and looked at Tanner.

"What about the whiskey you boys take off the trail?"

"You tell it straight, Tanner," McReynolds said, "just like it happened."

"There was that whiskey about, and a fair bit drunk that day. It was then that Sergeant Wilson came up with his plan."

"Plan?" McReynolds asked.

"Yes, sir. He said that if they ever found out we kilt' all those Indians without orders, we'd be in a heap of trouble, lose our stripes most likely, if not our hides, and that it just weren't right for us to take the blame for what the lieutenant brought down. If the lieutenant doesn't make it, he says, then we'll just go on our way like nothing ever happened. Indians always killing each other back and forth, he said, and nobody to know the difference."

"And you let Roland suffer the whole time without so much as a drop of that whiskey?"

"I took him a bottle when the sergeant and Inman went off to hunt deer. Drunk as a lord, he got, cussing and crying and saying how he'd been abandoned to die among the heathen."

"Was he bleeding, Tanner?"

"No, sir, not as far as I could tell."

Remembering his empty pipe, McReynolds filled and lit it.

"Rare that a man dies of a leg wound if the bleeding's stopped," he said.

Walking to the tent flap, Tanner looked out. Satisfied they were alone, he turned about, lowering his voice.

"That's just it, sir, Lieutenant Roland froze to death that night, stiff as a beaver he was, and his blanket twenty feet away in the bushes, like someone uncovered him in the night to perish in the cold. Sergeant Wilson said it was the act of God and none of our business one way or the other. If Lieutenant Roland's time had come, it wasn't up to us to say otherwise, and if anybody asked, he was swiped off his horse and died without a word."

Drawing on his pipe, McReynolds let the enormity of Tanner's words sink in.

"Someone killed him then, one of our own?"

"That's what I'm thinking, sir, the same killed poor Inman, and Westhoff, too, far as I know."

"Who?" McReynolds asked.

There was silence as Tanner thought, the rise and fall of his breath in the tent.

"Sergeant Wilson," he said, "and he'll do the same to me the minute he finds out I was here."

Knocking the coal from his pipe, McReynolds ground it out with the heel of his boot.

"I want you to go on back to your tent, Private, and don't tell another soul about this, do you understand?"

"Ain't likely I'd cut my own throat more often than is required, sir."

"Good night, Private. It was the right thing you did in coming."

"Yes, sir," he said, looking over at Renfro.

After Tanner left, McReynolds sat in his chair for a considerable time trying to fathom the story he'd just been told.

Rolling up the redoubt plans, Renfro handed them to McReynolds.

"Strikes me that boy smells of skunk, Major. Suppose he's telling the truth?"

"It's my opinion that he is," he said.

"I best be getting back to the boy."

"Yes," McReynolds said, dropping his pipe into his pocket, "it's a dark night for a boy alone."

A breeze swirled through camp, lifting the tent flap, shadows swaying up the tent walls from the lantern.

"What you going to do, Major?" Adam asked, his eyes darkening under the brim of his hat. "It's a wrong against humanity's been done and crying out to be righted."

"I'm going to bed," he said. "It's a terrible thing that has been told here tonight, and it's shaken my thinking. If it's a conspiracy they've done, justice will follow, and those who are guilty will be punished.

That's my promise to all those who might have suffered at their hands."

Opening the tent flap, Adam turned.

"I know you to be a man of your word, and I ain't doubting you will do as you say. We've had our go at things, best we could, and what comes, comes, as I see it. But there's the boy out there, and I hope it ain't run out for him 'fore it even gets started. That's what I hope, Major, if hoping ever mattered."

Thirty-four

The beam of morning light shot through the tent flap and into McReynolds's eyes, sitting him up straight in his bed. Running his fingers through his hair, he threw his legs over the side of his bunk. The reality of Tanner's story seeped into his consciousness like a bad dream, and his stomach tightened at the day that lay ahead.

By the time he was dressed and made his way down to breakfast, the morning had warmed, a low thin fog still hanging over the waters of the Cimarron. As he approached camp, the aroma of coffee and fresh baked bread welcomed him. Soon enough he would have to initiate military protocol, reveille, formations, the endless inspections that maintained control in an untamed land. For now, the men rose at random, drifting in half asleep to their breakfast.

From across the way, Sergeant Wilson finished his beans while sitting on a wagon seat, and a pang of dread shot through McReynolds. After a sleepless night, he'd decided what to do, what he always decided under compelling uncertainty, face it straight on and to hell with it. After breakfast, he would call Sergeant Wilson to his tent, confront him, make a decision, and hang him from a blackjack if it came to that.

At the camp table, Renfro and Creed waited as Sarah served them generous helpings of refried pintos over slabs of bread. Behind her, Cookey worked at a vat of yeast, his hat askew, whistling a disjointed tune. Waves of blackbirds swept the horizon, settling in the stand of trees across the river, their chatter filling the morning like a thousand distant bells.

"Morning, sir," Cookey said. "It's a fine morning, ain't it?"

"It is," McReynolds said, "as morning's go." Holding out his plate, he waited as Sarah served up his breakfast, waited to catch her eye, waited for that shared moment. "It's to be a full day, Cookey, with men working hard. Stir up a hearty meal."

"Yes, sir," he said, "ham hocks and cabbage, it is, boiled taters, onions, plum butter, sourdough bread, and pickles for the scurvy, if they ain't tinted or stole by the Cheyenne."

Blackbirds rose skyward, banking against the sun, spiraling into the distant blue of the sky. Silence fell upon the prairie, a still and suffocating quiet, causing McReynolds to set down his plate. Turning, he looked at Renfro, at Creed who'd just risen from his seat, at Sarah, poised with ladle in hand. It was a paralyzing and terrible revelation.

The arrow struck with a thud, an unforgiving thud, like an axe in a tree, or a cleaver in a side of meat. Dropping to his knees, Cookey clutched the shaft of the arrow buried deep in his bowels. A scream of pain and humiliation rose from him as he fell across the vat of yeast.

By the time McReynolds hit the ground, the sky darkened with arrows, and the war cry of the Cheyenne turned his blood to ice as they mounted their attack. From all about, there were the groans of dying and terrified soldiers as the arrows rained down.

By rolling over and through the spilled yeast, McReynolds was able to reach Renfro, Sarah, and the boy, who all had managed to take cover behind the overturned camp table. From time to time, Renfro rose, firing his carbine with deliberate aim into the onslaught. At his side, Creed readied shells and handed them to his father. Clutching her knees, Sarah trembled, her face white with fear.

Taking a moment from his firing, Renfro turned to McReynolds.

"You're in fair danger coming here covered in sourdough, Major. I ain't had my breakfast yet."

"Not likely to, by the looks of it," McReynolds said.

"That's a lance drove in the ground," Renfro said. "They came to stay."

"I don't have a weapon," McReynolds said.

"There's a lot of boys dying around here, Major. Just as well you do what you can."

But without his medical bag, there was little to be done, tying off wounds, comforting the frightened and dying soldiers as best he could. A few had managed to get to the sand wall. Others lay in the open, or behind clumps of sage, defenseless against the assault.

The attacks turned sporadic, a few warriors at a time charging from unexpected directions, or a single warrior yelling out of the trees at full bore, driven by the bravery of comrades and the prospect of honor, terrifying in his randomness and ferocity.

Sarah held Cookey's head in her lap, talking to him, pushing his hair back from his face. But Cookey did not answer, indifferent to the terror and starkness about him, dead from the Cheyenne arrow that grew from his belly.

When the attack stopped, it did so without warning, an eerie silence mounting through the valley, as frightening in its way as the calamity and destruction of the battle itself.

Leaning against the table, Renfro lay his carbine

across his lap, and shook his head at what he saw. The loss was staggering, bodies strewn through the grass, steam still rising from half-eaten breakfasts.

"Is it over?" McReynolds asked.

"It ain't never over," Renfro said, "until it's done."

With water from the cooking pot, McReynolds washed the blood from his hands.

"Who kills us?" he asked.

"That's a sacred arrow there in Cookey's belly," Renfro said, "Dog Soldier, the one who got away be my guess. He's a man with little to lose."

"How much time do we have?"

"Five minutes, tomorrow, I don't know, but it's coming, that's sure. It's revenge they intend to have."

Lifting himself up, McReynolds surveyed the area between the camp and the trees. Bodies of warriors and horses lay twisted where they fell. Daybreak shimmered on the slow-moving waters of the river.

"I've got to get to the tent for my medical bag and instruments," he said. "There's little I can do without them."

"I'll go," Creed said. "I'm fast on my feet."

"That you are," Renfro said, "but seems a job for me. Here," he handed Creed his carbine, "give me that bowie, case I get interrupted."

"I'll go," McReynolds said.

"This is mule skinner's work," he said, slipping the bowie under his belt. "Don't require a heap of thinking, does it?"

"Everything's in my tent," McReynolds said, "all you can carry."

"Don't you boys go anywhere till I get back," he said, ruffling Creed's hair.

"You can count on it," McReynolds said.

Mindful of the bank of trees, Renfro worked his way toward the tent, moving low but fast, slipping from sage to sage. Death and misery lay everywhere about him, calmed forever under the rising sun. At the bank overlooking the river, that place where he favored his evenings, he spotted Sergeant Wilson saddling a horse.

Moving up from behind, he spoke. "Early for a ride, ain't it?"

Spinning about, Wilson took him in.

"Mind your own business, mule skinner."

Stepping in, Renfro lay his hand on the bowie.

"It's a sad day you brought down, Sergeant. Maybe you should see it out."

Pulling his carbine out of the saddle holster, Wilson laid it in the cradle of his arm.

"Ain't you the one," he said, "stinking of the trail, you and that half-breed kid."

Whether Wilson moved, whether his finger tightened against the trigger of the carbine, or whether it was no more than a fleeting thought, mattered little against the lightning thrust of Renfro's bowie.

"It's little enough pay," he said, looking into Sergeant Wilson's paling eyes, "for the misery you've dealt this day."

By the time Renfro returned with the medical bag and instruments, Sarah and McReynolds were busy working among the fallen. The beat of a drum rose from across the river, speaking of covenants not kept, of broken promises and avenging hearts.

"Yours," Renfro said, handing McReynolds the black bag.

Digging through its contents, McReynolds took out the arrow extractor, an ominous contraption of metal and cable designed to snare the intractable arrow, to force it backward through tendon and tissue and unspeakable pain.

"It's all we've got," McReynolds said, holding it up.

With that he set about to save those he could, and

through the day the rendering cries of soldiers echoed across the valley.

While McReynolds and Sarah attended the wounded, Renfro reinforced the barricades with what he could find and organized those few who could still work. After that, the dead were buried, shallow graves in the sand, their hats placed to mark their end. It was a sad and awful task borne in silence. When all was done, he placed the men around the perimeter with orders to fight to the last and to pray for victory.

Darkness fell as cold and black as the hope in their hearts, the endless pulse of the drum, the dread awaiting in the trees beyond. The fire was built small, and small comfort it was, to warm what food could be found, to be taken in tins to the outposts where there it was eaten by men, alone and frightened, denied the companionship of fire and friends. When the drum at last fell silent, they were thankful for this, at least.

When all was done that could be done, Renfro took up his place behind the table. After a final check of the men, McReynolds joined him there, too exhausted to eat. Curled in a blanket, Sarah slept next to the fire, her bloodied apron still tied about her waist. Creed lay next to her, asleep on his arm, hair falling across his forehead.

"What's our chances?" McReynolds asked as he rubbed the weariness from his eyes.

Looking to make certain Creed was asleep before he spoke, Renfro shook his head.

"They took a heavy toll when they hit us by surprise, so many in the open, others with no weapons to defend themselves. It's a small and hopeless lot we have left, Major. There's no holding them when they come again."

"If only the howitzers had been sent," McReynolds said.

"Time for honest talk, Major, and things that need to be said, should be said."

"Maybe they won't attack again." McReynolds dug for his pipe but found it missing. Taking off his hat, he looked into the black sky above for the answer. "Maybe they figure they've taken enough losses and will just go away."

Pulling his knee into his arm, Renfro watched Creed as he slept next to the fire.

"You might remember the day, you, me, and Twobirds stood in the Cross Timbers and watched Lieutenant Sheets die in the grip of that black bear," he said.

"Like it was yesterday," McReynolds said.

"And you might remember that I was still in the Army that day and that I left with Twobirds on my arm."

Fishing in his other pocket, McReynolds found his pipe and knocked it against his boot.

"I remember," he said.

"And all these years you never told anyone I was still alive nor sought to come between us, even though you were in love with Twobirds yourself at the time."

Filling his pipe, McReynolds tamped the tobacco with his finger.

"That was many years ago," he said, "and we both thought you were dead. Twobirds would never have been unfaithful to you, nor I for that matter."

Lifting himself up, Renfro checked the river.

"Black as black," he said. "Couldn't see a Cheyenne if he was standing on your foot." Sitting back down, he leaned back against the table, falling silent in thought. "That's a fact, Major, about Twobirds, about you, too, for that matter, and in all those years no one ever gave me reason to believe otherwise. That's why I can say what I'm about to say."

"If there's something on your mind, you best get on with it 'fore those Cheyenne arrive," McReynolds said, touching off his pipe with a match, "because once they attack, I am going to be too busy for conversation."

"Living on our own was hard," Renfro said, "afraid of the whites, afraid of the Indians, too, I reckon, but soon enough she told me."

"Told you what?" McReynolds asked, nursing his pipe back to life.

"That she was with child."

"Guess you couldn't have been too surprised. Even mule skinners ought to know where babies come from."

"And I know how long it takes for a woman to know such things," he said.

"What are you getting at?" McReynolds asked, searching Renfro's face in the darkness.

"Thing is," he said, "from the beginning I've loved that boy like my own, more than my own in some ways." Reaching over, he brushed Creed's hair back from his face. "But he's yours by blood, and you've the right to know."

Standing, McReynolds looked at Creed and then at Renfro.

"Before you say anything," Renfro continued, "I need to get this done, while there's time. Back there at camp is the Spanish silver that was left in that cave. I took it, you see, hid it away in fear that Lieutenant Sheets would be back. Now it's under that walnut tree where me and the boy is camped.

"That silver never meant anything to me, Major, never crossing my mind to go back to that cave until Twobirds died. I took it for the boy, for him to make his way."

As McReynolds looked into Creed's face, he searched for the words to say to Adam, to express his sorrow, his happiness, his astonishment that this child before him was his own.

But the words were not there, nor could they have been heard above the requital beat of the drum that rose once more beyond the waters of Deep Hole Creek.

Thirty-five

The sun eased over the horizon, a fuming and bloody orb, as Little Dog held the arrow out for the others to see. The scar cast an angry slash across his face, resolve burning in his eyes under the orange light of dawn. Holding the horses, Crooked Leg watched, his hand swollen from a soldier's desperate bite. The other warriors listened, their horses dancing in anticipation.

"This is my father's sacred arrow," Little Dog said. "I take it into battle, and with it I will stand until the last, until my enemy is no more." Circling, he showed them the bloody tracks across his back. "The blue beast has spoken, and Little Dog has shown his bravery. When this is finished, my people will rest and will know that it has been done. This I promise on my father's sacred arrows: No Dog Soldier will retreat beyond the lance until there is no enemy left standing."

"We have given our oaths," Crooked Leg said, "and we will follow."

Raising their bows above their heads, the warriors danced, their voices joined in solidarity.

"First we take the soldiers behind the wall of sand," Little Dog said, pointing to the half-finished parapet. "They are the strongest and best armed. Once they have fallen, the others are few and will be easily killed."

"We will follow you into battle," Crooked Leg said, "and will not dishonor the oath. It is the way of the Cheyenne to face his enemy and kill him."

Stepping to his side, Little Dog lifted Crooked Leg's hand.

"This is my brother who has followed me many times into battle. More than once I have placed my life in his hands. There is none more courageous, more skilled with the bow than Crooked Leg."

Again, the warriors danced, their war whoops rising into the still dawn, and the drum spoke its singular message to those who waited.

Swinging onto his war-horse, Little Dog dug his heels into his side and rode hard into the river. The war cries of the warriors were close behind, their courage as one, an impenetrable shield against the enemy.

Death came soon, the shock of bullets against flesh, the rising fear as they rode into the blaze of carbines. Bodies pitched from terrified horses, blood swirling into the slow waters of Deep Hole, the need to hide, to run, to postpone life a single moment more. But this day they rode on, the gods with them, the intrepid Little Dog at point. Undaunted, he filled them with courage, his yelp rising above the fray, his horse charging into the face of the enemy. As they mounted the wall of sand, the cries of soldiers rode through the valley, the silent arrow spurning pity and hope in its course.

When it was done, Little Dog dismounted, taking a scalp from the quivering body of the last soldier and holding it up for the others to see. Beneath his feet, the sands ran slick with the blood of his enemy, the gasps of the dying like whispers about him. He waited for his pain to stop, for his soul to fill with the sweetness of vengeance, for life to shine once more through the darkness.

From behind, Crooked Leg touched his shoulder, pointing to the upturned table at the edge of the camp. Stringing an arrow, Little Dog dropped low, moving with stealth, with the certainty of a practiced and deadly hunter. At his side, Crooked Leg was trained on the parameters, watching where Little Dog could not. It was their way, moving, thinking as one.

Whether it was ignorance, or fear, or unyielding courage, a man rose from behind the table to face them, his hat pushed back on his head, his jaw clenched. In his eyes was the audacity and grit of a wounded buffalo. As he leapt the table, he unsheathed a large knife from his belt, and his cry shattered the stillness.

When Crooked Leg let loose his arrow, the man was half the distance between them. As it drove into his chest, he did not falter nor turn from his course. It was Little Dog's arrow, shanking deep in its mark, that brought the man to his knees, that took the life from his eyes.

Slipping another arrow from his quiver, Little Dog brought about his bow, kicking aside the camp table with his foot. Before him, a woman sobbed, her hair tangled, her head covered with her arms. At her side an officer lay moaning, his shirt bloodied, his carbine empty, his bag of medicine spilled in the dirt at his side. Behind them, a young boy stood, his fearless eyes shining with tears, a rock poised in his hand.

It had come then, the moment Little Dog had waited for, the finish, the retribution. But in the face of the boy, he saw his own people, his child, his Owl Talker, rocking on her knees under a quiet spring morning. A cry of despair fell unheard on the ears of his enemy as he took the sacred arrow from his quiver and handed it to Crooked Leg.

"I can no longer go on," he said, "nor bear the shame."

With a draw of his bow, Crooked Leg placed the arrow deep and certain into his ole friend's heart, waiting that brief and liberating moment before turning to the boy.

"I leave this brave warrior here as he died in battle," he said, speaking in Cheyenne, "as a warrior killed in this place."

Lowering his rock, the boy nodded, wiping at his eyes with the back of his hand.

Leading Little Dog's horse, Crooked Leg rode into the river. Behind him, the warriors yelped in victory, in the uncertain knowledge that for today they reigned supreme. Hanging from their belts, the scalps of their enemies reddened their leggings, their horses churning the lifeless waters of Deep Hole Creek as they rode away.

Lying side by side through an unrelenting and dark night, McReynolds, Sarah, and Creed waited in fear of the Cheyenne returning, the thundering horses, the terrifying war cries, the awful beat of the drum. But the night passed in uneasy silence, a warm dawn casting its orange light on the carnage about them.

On the bank of the river, they laid Adam on a scaffold, Creed placing the bowie at his father's side.

"It ain't never the knife that makes the man," he whispered, reaching for the strength that had been nourished within him.

A horse nickered at the edge of the trees, and they caught it up. Soon other horses followed. When there were enough for a team, they hitched them to a wagon, loading sufficient food and supplies to get them to Dodge.

Before they left, they stopped at the walnut drift log and dug the bags of silver from the sand. The wound in McReynolds's shoulder throbbed as he lifted the last into the wagon bed and climbed onto the seat next to Creed.

"Are you ready?" he asked.

Nodding, Creed clasped the seat, to secure himself, to forge what he held inside, to defy the truth of the moment.

With a snap of the reins, they pulled into the waters and past the Dog Soldier lance still driven in the sand. A scalp lock tied to its end turned in the morning breeze. Behind them, the half-finished redoubt rose like an ill-fated pyramid in the morning light.

As the sun rode into the sky, the wagon creaked northward like a tired and ancient turtle. Soon, Creed fell asleep, Sarah moving him onto her shoulder against the bounce of the wagon.

A great monolith appeared on the distant horizon, its reach striking into the heart of the prairie. With each passing mile, it mounted larger until McReynolds pulled up to savor its towering grandeur.

From high in its rift, Brother Jacob looked down, a thousand scars under the cuffs of his ragged tunic where the rats had chewed away his rawhide bindings. Forming his hands around his mouth, he called out his name for a final time.

But the words fell mute among the jagged rocks as the wagon moved away down the shadowed trail.

The Wingman Series
By Mack Maloney

William W. Johnstone
The *Mountain Man* Series